When the black, hairy thing fell out of the envelope and landed on her outstretched hand, Mariah screamed and leaped back, dropping both the envelope and the creature. Nothing happened after a few seconds, and she slipped around the walls to the broom closet, her eyes never leaving the manila envelope. Pulling out the broom, she raised it to waist level, bringing it down hard, over and over. Then, cautiously, she used the handle to slide the envelope off the remains of what lay underneath. She expected a sticky mess, but the paper slid easily away from the black, hairy whorl.

It wasn't a tarantula. It wasn't a spider at all. It was hair—a few curls of familiar black hair flecked with gray. It was David's hair, she was certain. She picked up the envelope to examine it more carefully. Inside were several stiff sheets of paper, which she withdrew. They were 8½-by-11-inch photographs of a man and a woman, naked, on a bed, in various positions of lovemaking. It was her husband, David, and Elsa.

Mariah fought down nausea, pushing away the pain and anger. Why had she been sent the envelope? Why now? It was a game of terror they were playing with her, teasing, threatening. But *who?* And what did they want her to do? Or not do, she suddenly thought. What are the rules here? How do I know how to play along if I don't know the rules or the object of the game?

After receiving her master's degree in international affairs, **Taylor Smith** spent twelve years as a Canadian diplomatic, intelligence and Privy Council officer. As a diplomatic officer specializing in human rights issues, she covered United Nations affairs and Eastern Europe before the fragmentation of the Soviet Union.

As a Privy Council officer, she provided the Canadian prime minister and cabinet with advice on Canada's relations with its intelligence allies, including the CIA and Britain's MI6.

Taylor is originally from Winnipeg, Canada, but has lived, worked and travelled extensively in Europe and Africa. Currently, she lives in southern California with her husband and two daughters, and writes full-time.

It is no accident that Taylor Smith's first novel for Mira Books should delve into the complex world of political intrigue and espionage.

"Guilt by Silence is the perfect techno-thriller with the added bonus of having a woman's touch to soften the edges."

—*Affaire de Coeur*

GUILT BY SILENCE

TAYLOR SMITH

MIRA BOOKS

*First published in Great Britain in hardback 1995
This paperback edition 1996
by Mira Books*

© M.G. Smith 1995

ISBN 1 55166 048 2

58-9602

*Printed in Great Britain by
BPC Paperbacks Ltd*

This book is dedicated with love
to Richard, who endures and encourages,
and to Kate and Anna, to whom the future belongs.

"Secret guilt by silence is betrayed."
—John Dryden, *All For Love*

Acknowledgments

Although this work of fiction is meant to entertain, its writing was made a good deal easier by the many people who read part or all of the manuscript to verify the scientific facts it contains, and/or who answered my endless questions on their particular areas of expertise. It goes without saying that I owe to them the accuracy of the facts contained herein, while any errors that might stubbornly remain are no one's fault but my own.

I would particularly like to thank: Jaye Orr, for checking my medical facts; Harv Pulford, for the computer stuff; Larry Butler of the Los Angeles Fire Department, for so much useful information on collision fires; Dan Young of the Orange County Fire Department, for the inspiration of gasoline explosions and tungsten pins; Marsha MacWillie, crime scene analyst with the Garden Grove Police Department, who let me hang around and watch her do what she does so well; J. L. Ragle, former Deputy Coroner of Orange County, and the host of forensic experts he brought to his seminars; Peter Ernest of the CIA Office of Public Relations, who kindly answered my questions on CIA career paths and the Agency's priorities in a post-Cold War world; my writing friends, including Margaret Gerard, Roy Langsdon and Marjorie Lensebrink *et al.* at the UCI advanced fiction workshop, who read and advised; Elaine Shean, who proofread the manuscript and provided moral support and occasional baby-sitting services to get me through this; Pat Teal, agent and morale booster; and finally, my friend "C"—my inside source in the nuclear regulatory field, who verified the nuclear facts but asked, only half-jokingly, if I couldn't *please* make the regulators' lives easier by adding a footnote saying, "But really, folks, this could never happen here." Well, I hope it couldn't. With people of C's dedication in the field, we could yet luck out.

1

Mariah circled the block three times. There were plenty of open spaces in the parking lot, but she wasn't ready to face him yet. Shouldn't this get easier at some point? she wondered. She should have begun adjusting by now. So why couldn't she accept that this was the way things had to be?

Just once more around, she promised herself, passing the entrance. One more time, and then she would do it again—go in and pretend. Pretend that nothing had really changed—that they were still a family. That they could cope. Pretend that his being in here was just a minor inconvenience. Pretend that it didn't matter that he would never hold her in his arms or make love to her again. Pretend that Lindsay didn't miss his stupid jokes or his hockey lessons or the giggling conspiracies the two of them used to mount whenever Mariah tried to reprimand them about junk food and the rules about bedtime.

David was in there waiting, she knew—he had nothing to do but wait for her and Lindsay.

It was ten months since the accident in Vienna; six since she had brought him back home to Virginia. In the first weeks they were back, friends and family had come to visit wearing carefully crafted, upbeat smiles that never wavered. But their eyes, when they saw him, were shocked and frightened, even though Mariah had tried to prepare them for the devastating changes the acci-

dent had wrought. They would pat his arm bravely at
first, but then Mariah would see them subtly with-
draw, their fingers recoiling from his atrophied muscles and the bone-thinness of the flesh under his shirt.
After that, they almost never touched him again, except perhaps for a quick squeeze of his gnarled hand as
they left.

They would ramble on one-sidedly to him about
things David probably wouldn't have cared about even
if he could have responded—and they knew it. But what
else did you say to a genius whose mind—or what was
left of it—was revealed only through an occasional
flicker in his dark eyes?

The visitors would glance anxiously at Mariah, wondering whether he knew who they were and what they
were talking about, but even she had no way of knowing for sure what registered with him and what didn't.
Sometimes he seemed to be taking in everything, his
eyes reflecting something like amusement or interest, or
narrowing, as if he were pondering some problem. But
other times, he seemed lost in an inner world that she
couldn't reach. The eyes would fix momentarily on a
face, then drift away, distracted by a curtain blowing at
a window or a speck of dust dancing in a sunbeam.

These days, very few people came to see him anymore.

Finally pulling into a parking space, Mariah tilted the
rearview mirror and gave her sandy hair a poke or two
to fluff it up a little. The cut was soft but short—practical, hair for a woman with no time to fuss. She wore
almost no makeup, except for a little mascara to darken
her fair lashes. She ran her fingers absently under her
eyes to erase the end-of-day smudges that turned her
gray eyes smoky. Then she paused. The eyes watching
her from the mirror were critical, asking her for the
thousandth time if she couldn't have arranged things
differently. She had posed the same question every day

since it became clear that David wasn't going to recover from his injuries.

A runaway truck had plowed head-on into his car as he waited to pull into the driveway of the American International School in Vienna, climbing over the hood and crushing the passenger compartment. Everyone said it was a miracle that Mariah's husband and daughter hadn't been killed outright, but it was a qualified miracle at best: David's skull had been fractured like an eggshell; Lindsay had come frighteningly close to losing her left leg.

But despite the reproachful gaze of the eyes staring back from the mirror, Mariah knew that she had had no choice. She couldn't give him at home the extensive care he needed, especially with their daughter's recovery to worry about, too, and a demanding job that provided the income and insurance to cover staggering medical bills—a State Department job, she always told people, the lie second nature by now.

She sighed and turned the mirror away. Grabbing a paper bag off the front seat and slinging her purse over her shoulder, she climbed out of the car.

Across the parking lot, another pair of eyes—a mismatched pair, one green, one ice blue—watched her lock the Volvo's doors and start toward the building's entrance.

Rollie Burton gnawed thoughtfully on the inside of his cheek while in his hand, a six-inch blade appeared and disappeared in a steady rhythm. The knife was one he had picked up years ago in Hong Kong—a beauty, with superior balance and a blade of fine Sheffield steel. Its intricately carved ivory handle depicted a Manchu dynasty garden of roses and ivy. There were rust-colored stains in the handle's deep crevices, as if the roses themselves had bled as they were carved.

He flicked the catch on the ivory handle and the blade snapped open again, glinting under the parking-lot lights. Pushing the point against his gloved left hand, he retracted it, only to snap it open on the next heartbeat. Snap, retract. Snap, retract. Over and over.

He had her picture in the leather case on the seat beside him, as well as the down payment on the job—ten thousand dollars in small, used bills. There was also a loaded Sig-Sauer automatic and an extra clip of ammunition. But he preferred the blade—silent and swift, especially in his skilled hands.

She was prettier in person than in her picture, he thought. The overhead lights in the parking lot emphasized high cheekbones and a full mouth. He would have guessed her to be in her early thirties, but the voice on the phone had said she was thirty-nine. She was small but she moved fluidly, with a grace usually reserved for cats and dancers. Although it was impossible to make out her shape under the flowing trench coat she wore, he knew that a body had to be in superb condition to move that well. He wondered idly who would want to waste her—not that he cared, as long as he was paid for his work.

When the phone call had come the previous day, the voice had said they wanted it to look like a random act—one of the dozens of muggings that happen every day in the greater Washington area. The voice had had an eerie quality: flat, tinny. Burton was used to job offers from odd quarters, but there was something really creepy about that voice. Still, it wasn't as if it had asked him to do anything unusual. Things were a little slow these days, but in his prime, Burton had handled dozens of wet jobs, most of them in tricky foreign environments. This one looked to be a piece of cake.

When he'd agreed to take on the job, the caller had directed him to a Dumpster behind Bloomingdale's at Tyson's Corner. There he had found the case of cash and the photo, as well as information on his target's regular movements. Sure enough, Burton had picked her up just where he'd been informed she could usually be found each Wednesday evening—at the Montgomery Convalescent Care Home in McLean, Virginia.

There was no fixed deadline—just do it soon, the voice had said. The sooner the better, Burton thought, glancing around the quiet parking lot. He had expected to track her for a few days before making his move, but twenty-five years in the business had taught him that you don't pass up a prime opportunity when it's handed to you on a silver platter. No point in dragging these things out.

He had his hand on the door handle, ready to slip out of the car. She was almost halfway across the parking lot, but Burton knew he could be on her in a few quick strides. He was still wiry and fast when he shifted into high gear.

Waiting for precisely the right time to move, he considered his options. With a bigger target, he'd aim for the space between the second and third ribs—a neat slash to the heart, then out. If there was a struggle, an upward slice in the gut was effective but messy, and the target took longer to die. In this case, however, the best bet was the throat. Rollie Burton was a bantamweight, but she was smaller. It would be easy enough to grab her by the hair for the split second it would take to do the job. Cut and run, he decided, stepping out of the car and silently closing the door. He'd have to remember to take her purse, for appearance' sake.

It was only a little past five, but a cold night had already set in, the lonely smell of an early-winter rain in the air. Burton moved through the shadows of the old oak trees that dotted the lot, their dark, skeletal branches trembling overhead. He was coming up just behind her, the fingers of his left hand flexing in anticipation of the grab, the right thumb poised over the hair-trigger catch on the knife.

Suddenly, there was a bustle at the main entrance fifty yards away. He held back, crouching deeper into the shadows as the front door opened and three people came out—an elderly woman and two men who might have been her sons. The men huddled around her, supporting her by the elbows, murmuring as she cried softly.

Cursing under his breath, Burton pocketed the knife as his target walked from the parking lot along a short walkway to the entrance. She stepped out of the path of the family coming down the staircase, watched them for a moment, then ran up the front steps of the nursing home. Burton turned and headed back to his car, regretful but philosophical. No matter—he might still have a chance to get her on the way out. Besides, if this was too easy, he might feel he hadn't earned his fee. That'd be a shame, he thought, snorting lightly. Guilt had never been his strong suit.

2

As she passed through the front doors, Mariah noticed that she was holding her breath. Sooner or later, though, you have to breathe. She made it past the receptionist and almost as far as the east-wing nursing station before drawing her first breath, hoping the delay would help—but it was futile, of course. Little sensors in her nose had been at work even as she nodded to the woman at the front desk, an early-warning system for the incoming olfactory assault. And when she finally inhaled, her stomach plunged as always at the smell of medicine and antiseptic, starched linen, and flesh slowly dying.

The young nurse at the station smiled brightly as she saw Mariah approach. "Hi, Mrs. Tardiff," she said.

The nurses knew her well by now—knew she normally used Bolt, her own surname, not David's, but she had told them she had no objection to being called Mrs. Tardiff, if they preferred. Most, especially the older nurses, seemed more comfortable with that, likely suspicious of her disregard for the proper order of things. David would have been more insistent than Mariah herself on her right to use her own name, but he was in no position to argue with anyone—on points of principle or anything else.

"He's been looking forward to seeing you," the nurse said. "The orderly rolled him into the hallway an hour ago."

Mariah nodded and forced a smile. This nurse had a sweet disposition and meant no reproach, she knew, but she gave herself a mental lashing anyway. "Traffic," she said. "It's awful tonight." The nurse smiled sympathetically.

Mariah turned the corner and headed down the hall. His was the last room on the right and she could see his wheelchair outside the door, past all the other lonely souls—ancients, most of them, waiting and watching with futile hope in their eyes each time a visitor entered the corridor. Mariah smiled at some of the old-timers as she walked by, pausing briefly to squeeze the hand of the old lady who always called her Thelma and asked about the boys.

"They're fine, Mrs. Lake, just fine," she answered, as she always did, now that she had given up trying to explain that she wasn't Thelma—wondering, as she always did, who the real Thelma was and whether the boys were really fine

She turned once more toward David. She could see him clearly now, watching her every step—those deep brown eyes with irises so dark that the pupils were invisible. Large, innocent eyes that looked right into your soul. Who could resist them? Certainly she had never been able to.

She had met him in the mid-seventies, the year before the Central Intelligence Agency had recruited her. She was a graduate student at the University of California at Berkeley, a political science major specializing in the Soviet-American arms race. When her liberal arts background left her bogged down in the complexities of nuclear weapons, her thesis adviser sent her to the head of the physics department. He, in turn, introduced her to David Tardiff, one of the department's youngest and brightest doctoral candidates.

But if physics brought Mariah and David together in the first place, biology took over pretty quickly thereafter. Mariah was taken by surprise. Her mother's life had been ruined by Mariah's father, a poet and novelist still lionized in literary circles, long after his death. He was no hero to Mariah. How could he be, after abandoning his young child and pregnant wife to pursue his own self-absorbed whims?

Buffeted by a cascade of losses that began with her father's betrayal, Mariah had grown up determined to chart an independent course for her life—one that certainly didn't include falling under the sway of some boy wonder from New Hampshire. David Tardiff was on the short side, barely five-eight. Compared to the strapping, blond, too-cool-for-words beach boys she had grown up with in southern California, Mariah found him a bit on the homely side, his nose a little too large, his mop of black curls a little too unruly. And he was cocky, she told herself—funny and bright, but awfully sure of himself.

Still, as she had listened to him wax enthusiastic about physics and hockey—his other driving passion— her long-standing defenses against emotional involvement crumbled. Within three months, they were living together in a tiny Berkeley apartment, making plans for the future. But then things changed—that was the *first* time she lost David.

The University of California runs a top-secret nuclear weapons research facility at Los Alamos, New Mexico, on behalf of the federal government, and Berkeley's physics department supplies many of the lab's research staff. It came as no real surprise, then, when six months after they moved in together, David was offered a job at the Los Alamos weapons lab.

Mariah followed him into the desert to work in earnest on her graduate thesis. But if New Mexico provided a good working environment for the thesis, it was no place to nurture their relationship. The split finally came the day Mariah watched a military truck towing a canvas-draped missile through the center of town. She confronted David late that night when he came in from the lab.

"David, this isn't the place for us."

He was nuzzling her neck and missed the point. "How about the dining-room table?" he asked, wrapping his arms around her more tightly. "Don't you just love all this space? So many options!"

Mariah poked him in the ribs with her elbow, laughing in spite of herself. "That's not what I'm talking about, you pervert!" Her smile faded. "I mean Los Alamos."

He held her at arm's length, his twinkling dark eyes betraying the clever comeback he was formulating—but her own expression must have squelched the urge. "What's wrong with it? You've got teaching prospects here. And it's a clean, safe place to make babies and raise a family," he added, pulling her close again.

"Safe? It's a nuclear bomb factory! Don't you ever think about what it is you *do* over at that lab?"

"We do science—good science, with equipment that any university researcher would kill to get his hands on."

"Yeah, well, *kill* is definitely the operative word here. You guys design nuclear weapons, David!"

"We unlock the secrets of the atom," he corrected her, wagging his finger. "Come on, Mariah, lighten up! The lab does some nonmilitary work, too, you know that. And this work is exciting. The atom holds the key to unlimited energy—not to mention incredible bio-medical and industrial advances. Weapons are the least interesting part of it."

"That's just a cop-out. If there's one thing this lab stands for, it's the creation of the bomb."

"You can't blame scientists if the government perverts our work," he said, a stubborn frown forming on his forehead. "We can't be responsible for the ethics of the whole nation. The weapons work could be stopped, if people had the guts to say 'no more.'"

"Oh, dammit, David," Mariah said sadly. "I'm not stupid—or naïve. I know we won't get rid of nuclear weapons tomorrow, now that the genie's out of the bottle. But we design a new bomb, and then the Russians build one bigger than ours, and then we make ours even more deadly, and on and on and on. I just can't watch you waste your talents by helping these guys develop the ultimate doomsday machine. Because that's the real reason you're all here, and you know it."

They'd had the same argument a dozen times since David had accepted the Los Alamos job. The silence between them as they pulled away from each other that night had simply concluded the debate once and for all with a permanent agreement to disagree. In the end, she had left David and New Mexico and taken a job as an analyst at CIA headquarters in Virginia—telling herself that whatever she might do to help restrain the Soviet nuclear threat could also make the work of David and his Los Alamos colleagues superfluous.

For two years, their only contact was a diminishing trickle of letters and phone calls. Then one day, out of the blue, David had shown up on her doorstep, gaunt and distraught after an accident in the lab had claimed the life of one of his colleagues—a young technician who had died a gruesome, lingering death after accidental exposure to radioactive materials. David had become thoroughly disillusioned with weapons work and said he wanted only to build a career in teaching and to marry her.

They were never separated again. Lindsay was born nine months later and their lives had seemed charmed—until a careering truck in Vienna had brought it all crashing down.

* * *

As he watched her approach along the long hallway, David's mouth lifted lopsidedly, the paralyzed left side drooping while the right struggled upward. Mariah smiled back at this man that she had loved for so long—still loved, she reminded herself. Still loved but missed horribly even as she sat beside him during the few short hours that she managed to snatch with him each week.

"Hi," she said warmly, putting a hand around his neck and touching her forehead to his. She closed her eyes briefly, trying not to notice that faint aroma of decay that clung to his atrophied body, despite all the toiletries she brought in for him.

"How are you, lover?" She kissed his forehead and ran her fingers through his hair, giving the curls an encouraging nudge toward the frothy chaos that had once been their preferred arrangement. "Sorry I'm a little late. Traffic."

He blinked. She dropped in his lap the paper sack she had brought in from the car, then moved behind the chair. "Let's go sit. I'm beat." She wheeled him into his room, where she kicked off her shoes and shrugged out of her trench coat, tossing it on the bed and pushing up the sleeves of her suit jacket. Then she moved him over to the computer table in the corner.

"Headstick?" she asked. One brown eye closed, opened, then closed—the signal for no. He seemed alert and Mariah berated herself again for having made him wait.

She put aside the headband with the attached stick that he used to tap the keyboard when his faltering right hand became exhausted. The left hand was useless, drawn into itself and held tightly against his chest by the constricted arm, perpetually reverted to a fetal position except when he was deeply asleep and his muscles finally relaxed.

Mariah removed the paper bag from his lap and pulled a rolling table over his thin legs. She lifted his right hand, bringing it to rest on the computer keyboard. His bony index finger reached out shakily and landed on a key. Mariah looked at the screen and saw the letter L—Lindsay.

"She's at the swimming pool," she said. "I'm picking her up on the way home." Mariah leaned back against the windowsill and smiled at him. "She's doing great in the water. The coach says she may even make the team next year. She's such a fighter, David."

His eyes regarded her intently.

"And the doctor says it's doing wonders for her leg," she went on. "It's definitely growing and he thinks there's a chance it might eventually catch up to the other one." Mariah reached into the paper bag she had brought. "Lindsay couldn't come, but she did bake cookies for you—chocolate chip!"

Slow, lopsided grin.

"She does this to irritate me, you know, just because I'm allergic to chocolate. I hope it gives you both zits!"

David watched her pull out one of the cookies. She put it in his hand and wrapped his fingers around it. The tendons on the back of his hand stretched taut like puppet strings as he lifted the cookie to his mouth with agonizing slowness. Mariah took some shirts out of the bag and walked over to the small wardrobe next to the bed. David's eyes followed her every step as his jaw slowly worked on the cookie.

"I washed your flannel shirts for you. It's getting frosty out there." He didn't go out much, of course, except when she and Lindsay took him for walks on the weekend or, once a month or so, home overnight. But it was a recognition that he was alive and the seasons were still turning.

Mariah came back and pulled up a chair next to him, wiping a line of chocolate drool that ran down from the corner of his mouth, then stroking his arm absently as she spoke to him. She talked about Lindsay and her new school, their evenings, office gossip, inconsequential stories of people, some of them old friends, some people he didn't know. It didn't matter, as long as she could make him feel that he was still part of their world.

As she rambled on, David's eyes watched her and smiled. It was the only part of him that was recognizable anymore, Mariah thought. The orderlies always managed to do something peculiar with his curly black hair. Not their fault, really—they hadn't spent years watching him step from the shower and give his head a distracted shake until each curl found its own equilibrium, had they? Now, the way they combed it, the curls were straightened and flattened, parted at the side, giving him a strangely organized air that he had never possessed when he was in charge of his own grooming. And he was getting grayer. In the ten months since the accident, he seemed to have aged a decade or more beyond his forty-one years. His frame, slight to begin with, had withered to a wispy frailty.

Only the eyes held the essence of the man David had once been. They were also the only part of him capable anymore of reflecting a familiar emotion. The emotions she saw there these days were fleeting and elemental—pleasure at her coming, sadness at her leaving, frustration during his rare attempts to communicate.

Once though, in Vienna, when he had fully emerged from the coma into which he had been plunged for several weeks after the accident, Mariah had seen in those eyes the terror of realization.

For several days previous, there had been times when he seemed to recognize her. In those moments of brief lucidity, he had struggled to reach out to her, but his body had become permanently contorted, twisted into an unnatural stiffness by the misfiring synapses in his brain. The effort exhausted him and he would lapse again into catatonia. One morning, however, Mariah had stepped off the hospital elevator to the sound of unearthly shrieks coming from the direction of his room. Her heart pounding, she had raced down the corridor, the heartrending cries growing louder as she approached his door.

It was what she had most dreaded—the one thing she had prayed would never come. Multiple skull fractures from the accident had left irreversible brain damage. She had seen the X-rays and CAT scans herself, had had the damage explained in detail, and she knew that his life was over, even if his heart still beat and his lungs still drew breath. The only thing the Viennese doctors hadn't been able to tell Mariah with any degree of certainty was what portion of his cognitive abilities would be left when—and if—he ever regained consciousness. She had found herself, incredibly, beginning to pray that he would die rather than understand what he had become.

But when she stepped into the room that morning, she knew that her worst fear had come true. David was screaming in inarticulate anguish, having awakened to discover that his body had become a tomb—and that he was buried alive.

Mariah shuddered now at the memory of his cries, guttural and incoherent, and of the terror in his eyes as he searched hers for a sign of hope that this was only a passing nightmare. She had sat next to him for hours, rubbing his back and stroking his hair and holding his twisted body until his screams had subsided to choking sobs and then faded altogether.

In that time, she had watched a light in those newly conscious eyes flicker and die. She never knew whether the calm that finally settled on him was madness or some kind of divinely inspired state of grace. It didn't matter, she thought, as long as it gave him peace.

It gave her none, however. Most of what was left of her husband—Dr. David Tardiff, nuclear physicist and ex-boy wonder, harmonica player and Wayne Gretsky wannabe, love of her life and father of her only child—had died that day. All that remained now was this sad shell of a man—that, and a hard angry fist in the pit of her being that was perpetually raised in defiance of the God or the fates that had allowed such a thing to happen.

Mariah glanced at her watch. "I have to go soon, David. Lins will be almost done with her practice."

His head lolled on the headrest as he turned his eyes to her, their expression sad, wistful as always. But he held her gaze fixedly and then his right hand reached out to hers, resting on the arm of his chair. He grappled for her wrist. Her hand followed his as he moved it shakily into his lap.

"Oh, David," she said softly. She rested her head against his shoulder for a moment, then lifted it. "Just a minute," she whispered. She rose and went to the door, closing it firmly, regretting the absence of a lock. The room was a private one, but institutional privacy is a contradiction in terms.

The first time this had happened was one Saturday when she and Lindsay had taken him home to their condo overnight. It had been late in the evening. Lindsay had gone up to bed after helping her get David settled on the sofa bed in the living room and Mariah had been lying beside him, outside the covers, reading to him while soft music played in the background. She wasn't sure whether or not he followed the words, but her voice and the music seemed to relax him, and he'd looked almost like a gaunt version of his old self, lying there under the quilt.

Suddenly, Mariah had glanced up and seen him watching her with an expression of acute longing in his eyes and she had known what he was thinking about. It had taken her breath away. No one had ever mentioned it during his long hospital stays, even though she had discussed with the doctors every other conceivable aspect of the prognosis for his physical and mental recovery. But she had understood all at once that whatever else was to be denied him for the rest of his life, some basic needs had not disappeared.

That night, she had done what she had to do to give him the comfort that only a wife or lover can offer—she had made love to him as gently and delicately as she knew how. And although he was unable to reciprocate, she had comforted herself with the memory of the hundreds of times he had held her and loved her. Then she had crawled under the covers beside him, rocking him and crying silent tears, feeling in her arms the familiar and yet awkwardly unfamiliar outlines of his body.

Now, sitting close beside him in his nursing-home room, she gave him comfort again and then held him for a while before she had to go. His eyes were closed when she left him.

Mariah stood at the top of the steps outside the front door, inhaling deeply to clear her lungs of institutional air, forcing her mind to make the transition back to life beyond David's world. She closed her eyes briefly, then opened them again and started down the steps.

Preoccupied, she failed to notice the figure waiting under a tree next to the sidewalk. It was only when he said her name that she glanced up, startled out of her reverie. She narrowed her eyes to make him out in the shadows, then recoiled in surprise.

"Paul? Paul Chaney—what on earth are you doing here?" she asked, moving quickly from astonishment to instinctive wariness.

He came forward and they met at the bottom step. "Waiting for you." He bent down and they exchanged busses on both cheeks, the European-style that transplanted Americans adopt awkwardly at first, then maintain as a lifelong habit as they come to appreciate the comfort of the ritual.

He pulled back and she studied him under the lamplight. He was tall, his lankiness emphasized by the soft, brown leather bomber jacket he habitually wore and was wearing now, the collar turned up. He had a full head of blond hair, graying at the temples, just-so blue eyes and a photogenic face that could be earnest, penetrating or morally indignant as required in front of the television cameras. On air he dominated the screen, his presence imposing. Off camera, he also had what Mariah thought of as his helpless-but-comic puppy-dog shtick that he cultivated especially for the attractive and—preferably—rich and well-connected women that he seemed to attract like a magnet, all of whom seemed intent on nurturing him.

Based in Vienna, Chaney was senior foreign correspondent for CBN, the Cable Broadcast News network. In the three years she and David had known him there, Mariah had watched—appalled, amazed and ultimately amused—the succession of women he had trailed on his arm who had tried to sink their hooks into him. He had been too slippery for all of them, although an aggressive blonde who called herself Princess Elsa von Schleimann had looked for a while as if she might actually reel him in.

"What are you up to?" Mariah said. "I didn't know you were back in the States."

"Just got in yesterday. I'm working on a story."

"What happened to the princess?" Mariah, anxious to mask her unease, hoped the question came across as mischievous.

Chaney seemed startled, then frowned. "Found herself a real prince, I guess." They shuffled awkwardly, the old tension rising between them like a sudden fog. Finally, Chaney broke the silence. "How have you been, Mariah?"

She glanced away into the trees, her lips pressed tight. Then she sighed and turned back to him. "All right. My daughter's doing better. She's settled into a new school now, here in McLean, and she's making a good recovery."

"I'm glad." Chaney glanced up at the front door of the nursing home and then back at Mariah. "And David? Is there any hope?"

Mariah shook her head slowly, watching the sidewalk as she crushed a dried leaf under the toe of her shoe. "If anything, he's losing ground. He's been having seizures—from the scar tissue on his brain. For a while, he'd been able to type a few words on the computer, but now he seems to have lost even that." She looked up as a sudden thought occurred to her. "Are you going in to see him, Paul? He'd like that—someone from the old days, from the team."

Chaney smiled. He had been an honorary member of the Vienna Diplomats, the haphazard team of amateur foreign hockey players that played pickup games whenever they could find an opponent and get ice time on one of Vienna's rinks.

"I already have. That's how I knew you were coming—a nurse told me." He moved closer, so close, she could smell the leather of his jacket. "Can we talk, Mariah?"

How was it that Paul Chaney always managed to do this to her? Mariah wondered. Make her feel vulnerable and uneasy. On alert, her defenses aroused—against what, she was never quite sure. Something.

She shook her head and mustered up an apologetic grimace. "Sorry, I can't. I have to pick up Lindsay." She glanced at her watch, half turning away already. "I'm late. She's waiting for me. It's been nice seeing you, Paul, and I'm grateful to you for visiting David, but—"

Chaney moved to block her path and put his hands on her shoulders. "Mariah, please. This is important. I need to talk to you about what really happened in Vienna. About the people who did this to David—and to your daughter."

"What are you talking about? Nobody did this! It was an accident!"

"I don't think it was. I think it was deliberate. I'm not sure about some of the details, but I'm trying to find out."

"Oh, no," she said, shaking herself free of his grip. "I know you. You're trying to come up with some sensationalist news item—Chaney's exposé of the week. Well, forget it. There's no story here. What happened to David and Lindsay was nothing but a horrible, ugly traffic accident."

"Give me a break, will you? David was my friend. I wouldn't say something like this if I didn't believe it was true."

"Give *me* a break, Paul! Do you believe you're the only person that this thought might have occurred to? I was working in the embassy. Don't you think I insisted that every effort be made to find out *exactly* what happened? We had people breathing down the necks of the Vienna Police every step of the way during that investigation. But it *was* an accident—so drop it, please! We've been through enough."

She started down the path to the parking lot. Chaney never actually raised his voice, but it seemed to ring through the night. "It wasn't, Mariah. And I think you know it."

Mariah stopped. She turned her head slowly to look at him over her shoulder, fixing him coldly in her gaze. "Stay away from me, Chaney—and from my family. I'm warning you."

* * *

Across the lot, Rollie Burton watched from his vehicle, his eyes narrowed. The woman drove off, tires squealing as she pulled out. Only then did the man walk over to another car—a white Buick with an Avis Rent-A-Car sticker—and disappear in the opposite direction.

Burton pocketed the ivory-handled blade. He hesitated a moment, drumming his fingers against the steering wheel. He knew who that guy was—couldn't remember his name, but was sure he'd seen him on TV. The news, that was it. She obviously knew him, too, although she hadn't looked thrilled to see him. Maybe there was more to this job than he'd thought. For sure, he wasn't happy about doing his work under the nose of some media hack. He was going to have to tread carefully.

Burton flipped the key in the ignition and put the car in gear, turning his grungy Toyota right as he headed out of the parking lot, following in the direction she had taken.

3

Mariah spotted her daughter as soon as she pulled up in front of the school. Lindsay was sitting at the top of the wide staircase at the main entrance, her mass of hair a burning bush under the overhead lights. She was deep in conversation with another young girl, and the two of them were feigning indifference to the group of boys nearby. The boys, falling over themselves in their rush to impress the girls, were performing death-defying skateboard tricks up and down the staircase. Their only reward was, alas, two pairs of pretty thirteen-year-old eyes rolled heavenward each time one of them tripped over his own gangly legs. In spite of the dread that clung to her like soot, Mariah grinned. Some things never change.

When Lindsay spotted the Volvo, she stood and waved goodbye to her friend, then started carefully down the stairs. Her arms were laden with books, and her pace stopped and started as the damaged left leg followed the stronger right, one step at a time. Mariah gripped the wheel, suppressing the urge to jump out of the car and run to take the books and offer a supporting arm. But Lindsay had thrown away her crutches a few weeks earlier and reacted angrily on those rare occasions when Mariah forgot her determination not to hover and fret. The ache in her mothering heart was less easily suppressed, however.

She leaned over and opened the passenger door. Lindsay dropped heavily into the seat, weighted down by her books. Mariah took them from her and placed them on the back seat while the girl lifted her left leg with her hands and settled it into a comfortable position before pulling in the right and shutting the door. Mariah watched her buckle up, then passed her fingers gently over Lindsay's damp red curls, pushing the perpetually unruly mass back over her shoulders. The color was a throwback to ancient Bolt and Tardiff ancestors, it seemed, but the curls were pure David.

"Hi, kiddo. Sorry I'm late. I got held up at the home."

Lindsay's head snapped toward her mother, her expression shifting instantly from adolescent lightheartedness to all-too-adult anxiety. "Is Daddy all right?"

Mariah was putting the car in gear, but she stopped, hesitated, then patted her daughter's arm. "He's fine, Lins. He loved your cookies." Lindsay settled back into her seat, a smile replacing the fear in her eyes. "I was running late, that's all."

Lindsay shrugged. "It's okay," she said. "Our practice went a little over. I just got out." Mariah pulled the Volvo into the road, turning right. "Mom? Where are we going?"

"Home, of course."

"Why are we going this way?"

Mariah glanced around, noticing where she was and realizing with a start that she had made a wrong turn. "Oh, for—"

"Hello-o! Earth to Mom—come in, Mom. Are you with us?"

"All right, all right. Sorry. I'll pull a U-turn at the next light."

Lindsay shook her head and then promptly launched into a long and detailed report on recent developments in the ongoing drama of thirteen-year-old social politics. Today, it seemed, two girls had decided to ostracize a third for some perceived infraction of teenage standards of decorum.

Like anyone who read all the parenting books, Mariah knew that teenagers lived in a parallel universe of strange customs and even stranger preoccupations. Still, she hadn't quite been prepared when Lindsay suddenly turned into one of those hormone-tossed creatures.

After observing her daughter's friends, though, Mariah had concluded that Lindsay was different, old beyond her years, more given to sober reflection. Mariah put it down to the accident and its awful consequences. Most youngsters were certain that they were invulnerable. Lindsay had learned early—too early—what a fragile illusion that was. Under the circumstances, it was probably a good sign that Lindsay could get caught up in the same trivial issues as her friends.

"Isn't that mean, Mom?"

Mariah had only been half listening, waiting for a break in the on-coming traffic so she could turn around, thrown off by meeting Chaney again.

"What? Oh—for sure," Mariah said, snapping back into focus. She glanced at Lindsay. "So what did you do about it?"

"I told Megan I thought she wasn't being fair and that I didn't care what she said, Jenna was still my friend. Boy! It makes me so mad!" Lindsay folded her arms across her chest, eyes flashing.

Mariah smiled. "Good for you, kiddo. You're a loyal friend. Don't let the mob mentality rule."

"Yeah!" Lindsay said, her lower lip jutting out as she nodded. "Some people think they know it all—like the rest of us should just sit back and let them rule the world!"

Dieter Pflanz knew something about what it took to rule the world—or at least, manage good chunks of it.

And he knew how easily that control could be lost if you didn't pay attention to details.

He glanced at his watch, calculating the time back East. Ignoring the sleek designer telephone on his desk, Pflanz reached into a cabinet behind him and pulled out a sliding shelf on which sat a bulkier unit. He turned a key next to the number pad and punched in a series of digits. Spinning his chair to face a big plate-glass window, he leaned back and propped his feet on the sill. A digital click in his ear traced the signal of the long-distance call. Crooking the telephone receiver against his shoulder, Pflanz picked up an India rubber ball from his desk, powerful fingers compressing the dense sphere as he watched the scene below him.

The California sun was still well above the western horizon. From his eighteenth-story aerie in McCord Tower, at the heart of Newport Center, Pflanz could see the late-afternoon surfers heading toward the beach— the diehards braving the cold December surf in wet suits. He shook his head as he watched all the cars with surfboard-laden roof racks wending their way along the Coast Highway. Despite the fact that he'd been based here for a decade now, he had never gotten used to the southern California life-style. "Laid-back" was not in Dieter Pflanz's vocabulary. The daily sight of beaches packed with strapping young surfers and volleyball players only filled him with contempt. It was symptomatic of a society gone soft.

The telephone at the other end of the line began to ring as the connection was completed. Halfway through the third ring, it was picked up. "Hello?"

"It's me. Going to scramble."

"Roger."

Pflanz punched a button under the telephone keypad. After a brief delay, a light began to flash on the unit. At the other end of the line, he knew, a similar light would be flashing. A long beep following a series of short ones confirmed that the scrambler was operational. From here on in, anyone trying to monitor the call would hear nothing but a piercing whine. Only the synchronized software of the two machines was capable of decoding the electronic gobbledygook passing across the connection.

"Okay," Pflanz said. "We're set."

"I've been expecting your call. How's it going?"

"We're coming in tomorrow. There's one stop en route—a charity thing. We arrive in D.C. in the evening. McCord sees the President on Friday."

"I heard. He's up to speed."

"Good."

"What about New Mexico?"

"It's on for tonight."

"Tonight? Jesus, Dieter! So soon?"

"We have no choice. Everything's in place. Either we do it tonight or we miss the window of opportunity."

"Are you sure about this? If anything goes wrong, this could blow up in our faces."

Pflanz squeezed the rubber ball tighter. "Nothing's going to go wrong, George. Not," he added pointedly, "like that mess in Vienna."

There was a long sigh on the other end of the line. "Hell, don't talk to me about that. We're still cleaning up."

"What about the woman?" Pflanz asked. "She's back in operation now?"

"She's nothing to worry about."

"She hasn't made the connection?"

"No. She's off the file and preoccupied with her family. Trust me—Mariah Bolt poses no threat to us."

"She'd better not," Pflanz growled. "Alright, look— I'll call you when I get in tomorrow."

"No. Call me tonight, when you hear from New Mexico."

"It'll be late."

"You've got my home number. Call. I'll be up till I hear."

"Roger."

Pflanz cradled the receiver and closed the cabinet housing the secure phone. Then he leaned back and watched the sun sinking lower toward the Pacific.

A big man, with a hawk's beak for a nose and hands like bulldozer shovels, Pflanz still looked at forty-nine as if he belonged in jungle fatigues instead of the corporate uniform that he mostly wore these days. Despite the suit, though, no one would mistake him for anything but a security man—the ever-watchful, hooded eyes missed nothing. His massive shoulders hunched forward, giving him the appearance of a bird of prey poised for takeoff.

He had spent a quarter of a century mounting complex security operations, first as a CIA covert operative, then as chief of security for McCord Industries. McCord's head office was in Newport Beach, California, with subsidiaries in eleven American cities and fourteen other branches worldwide. It was a multifaceted business with diverse interests ranging from electronics to construction engineering, with dozens of difficult foreign projects that sometimes demanded special arrangements to ensure the safety of the employees. And the extracurricular activities of the company's president and CEO, Angus McCord, added yet another dimension to Pflanz's security duties.

You have to pay attention to detail, he told himself again—even the tiniest. That's the key to success. You can't leave anything to chance because it's the little things, the loose ends, that are sure to foul you up. Despite the assurances on the other end of the line a moment earlier, he'd been convinced all along that the Vienna episode had left too many loose ends—loose ends that he himself had already begun to tidy up.

* * *

Rollie Burton's battered green Toyota was parked across the road and down the street a little way from Mariah's condo in McLean, but the town house was still dark. He had lost her in heavy rush-hour traffic outside the nursing home, but from the look of things, he had beaten her here. When he finally spotted the Volvo coming up the street, the sight of two figures in the front seat gave him a jolt. He peered closely as the car passed under a streetlight. Oh, shit, he thought—she's got a kid. The voice had conveniently neglected to mention that.

The garage door began to rise as the Volvo approached the driveway. Burton slumped in his seat, tugging a baseball cap low over his eyes, watching the car pull into the garage. The brake lights flashed and then went dark as she killed the engine. Inside the lit garage he could see an interior door leading into the town house. When the automatic door began to drop, Burton glanced at the sweep hand on his watch: It took about five seconds to close.

The garage was on the side of the house facing the street, he noted, taking careful stock of the landscape. There was a cedar hedge running along one side of the driveway, with open lawn extending down to a cross street on the other. No prying neighbors. He nodded in satisfaction—good cover and a quick escape route.

The front door was around the corner of the town house, facing a footpath. It was part of a network of well-treed walkways and ravines that ran throughout the parklike condominium complex, radiating like a spiderweb from a recreation center at the hub. The trees were mostly evergreens, pine and spruce, casting deep shadows. Good possibilities there, too, he thought. Maybe she was a jogger. Burton loved joggers.

Then he pursed his lips, weighing the problem of her daughter. Nobody was paying him for the kid, and he had no intention of getting caught. But if he ever was—God forbid—he knew what happened to prison inmates who offed kids. On the other hand, he could wait forever to catch her alone at home.

First the reporter, now this—I don't need this kind of grief, he thought, exasperated. Why can't things ever be as simple as they seem?

Gathering up her briefcase, Mariah again resisted the temptation to carry in Lindsay's books, walking ahead into the house as her daughter reached into the back of the car for her things. By the time Lindsay came into the kitchen, Mariah had already opened the freezer and was examining the neat piles of plastic storage containers, their contents labeled and dated, part of the determined effort she had been making in recent months to try to get the chaos of her life under control. She withdrew a chicken cacciatore left over from one of the double-size recipes she prepared on weekends, put it into the microwave and shrugged out of her coat. She fixed Lindsay with a frown as the girl stood poised to drape her own jacket over a kitchen chair. Lindsay sighed deeply, rolling her eyes. Mariah pursed her lips, then held out her hand for the jacket that Lindsay handed over with a winning smile.

The rewinding hum of the answering machine greeted Mariah when she returned from the hall closet. Lindsay was hunched over the kitchen counter, pen poised as the machine began to play back messages. Typically, they all seemed to be for her. It was a mystery how, after a full day spent together, so much urgent business could accumulate among a bunch of thirteen-year-olds in the two short hours since junior high had been dismissed. Mariah set a pot of water to boil for the pasta as a string of disembodied adolescent voices crackled across the kitchen. Just as she began chopping vegetables for the salad, the machine beeped again and Mariah froze at the sound of a deep, professionally modulated voice.

"Mariah? It's Paul Chaney. I'm staying at the Dupont Plaza. I'm only in town for a few days, but we really do need to talk. Call me, please." He gave a room and phone number before ringing off.

Lindsay was madly writing down the numbers as the message ended and the machine rewound itself. "Mom! That's the TV guy who used to play hockey with Daddy in Vienna, isn't it?"

Mariah glanced at the girl and nodded, then turned back to chopping vegetables. It was the last message on the machine—he must have headed straight for a phone as soon as she left him at the nursing home. The knife came down hard as she slashed at a piece of celery. "Time to wash up for dinner," she said.

"Are you going to call him, Mom?"

"I doubt it. Can you set the table, please?"

"Why not?"

"The table, Lindsay!"

"Okay, okay! I'm setting!"

Lindsay limped over to the cupboard and began taking out dishes. Mariah watched her daughter's slim shoulders as she reached for plates. Coppery curls tumbled down the back of the girl's gray sweatshirt. During the ten months Lindsay had been recuperating—first in a wheelchair, then, until recently, in a leg brace and hunched over crutches—she had grown phenomenally. Now that she was upright again, it came as a shock to Mariah that this child—her baby—had already surpassed her own five foot two and might even overshoot David's five-eight.

She's no baby anymore, Mariah thought—not after everything she's been through—and she doesn't deserve this dismissive exercise of parental authority. She closed her eyes briefly and took a deep breath. "I've got a ton of work at the office, honey. I just don't think I've got time for Mr. Chaney this week, that's all."

"It sounds kind of important," Lindsay said, setting out plates and cutlery. "I mean, he seemed really anxious for you to call."

"I hardly know the guy, Lindsay. And to be perfectly honest, I never thought much of him when we were in Vienna, even if he was your dad's buddy. Anyhow, he's probably just calling to be polite. Reporters," she added scornfully, "they make everything sound like a national crisis. I'll call if I get a minute, maybe."

Lindsay shrugged and Mariah changed the subject as they moved to the table.

The evening, as always, passed in a weary blur of homework and piano practice, housework and laundry. It was nine-thirty when Mariah went into Lindsay's room to encourage her to pack it in for the night. The lights were on but Lindsay was in bed under the covers, her eyes closed. In one hand she held David's old harmonica. Mariah stood for a moment watching her, swallowing the lump she felt rising in her throat.

The radio was vibrating with an insistent beat, the bass turned up to the max. Mariah reached over to lower the volume and then moved around the room, picking up discarded clothes with a sigh and depositing them in the laundry hamper before turning back to the bed. Posters of rock stars and TV idols stared down at her, strangely juxtaposed with others of puppies and kittens. Old stuffed toys took up so much of the bed that Mariah always wondered how Lindsay managed to turn over at night. Despite regular urging that she cull the herd, however, Lindsay insisted that every one of the fuzzy creatures was indispensable.

Bending over the bed, Mariah tried to remove the harmonica without disturbing her, but Lindsay's eyes opened, glistening, as soon as Mariah touched her hand. She sat down on the edge of the bed, reaching out to stroke her daughter's cheek. "Is your leg bothering you?" Lindsay nodded miserably. "I'll get you some Tylenol and the heating pad," Mariah said, rising.

"Mom?"

Mariah had been moving toward the bathroom, but she stopped and looked at the girl.

"I miss Daddy so much," Lindsay whispered, tears washing over her dark eyes.

Mariah sat back down and wrapped her daughter in her arms, rocking her gently and stroking her hair. As the child sobbed, her own chest and throat ached with the effort of holding back tears. "I know, Lins," she whispered. "So do I."

Lindsay buried her face in her mother's shoulder. As her crying subsided, she caught her breath in great, shuddering sighs. Her voice, when it came, was muffled against Mariah's body. "I have such awful thoughts sometimes. I know I should be thankful we weren't killed. But when I think about Daddy—how he is now, in that place," she said, pulling back and looking down guiltily, "I feel so angry. Sometimes I even hate him—and then I hate myself for feeling like that."

Mariah stroked Lindsay's hair. "It's normal to feel angry, honey. What happened in Vienna isn't fair. It's horrible and not fair—to you, to me and especially to Daddy. Can you imagine how much he wants to be here with us?" Lindsay nodded. "But sometimes life *isn't* fair, sweetie—you just found that out sooner than most kids. It won't always feel this bad, I promise. Just give it some time. And you know what?" she added, lifting her daughter's chin. "I couldn't have handled what happened to you and Daddy if you hadn't been such a terrific kid. I'm proud of you, Lins—and I'm so glad you're my daughter."

Lindsay's lip quivered even as she smiled, and she threw her arms around her mother's shoulders. They held on to each other for a little while. Then Mariah tucked her securely under the covers. "You'd better get some sleep if you're going to go back tomorrow to battle Megan the tyrant. Let me get your tablets and heating pad."

When Mariah turned out the lights a few minutes later, her daughter was snuggled under the blankets, hugging a bald teddy bear and looking calmer. Mariah kissed her, then stepped out of the room and closed the door behind her.

Moving into the living room, she settled wearily onto the sofa and opened her briefcase, pulling out a stack of magazines and press clippings. The best part of highly classified work was that it wasn't supposed to be brought home, however hectic things might be at the office. While Mariah could use her evenings to catch up on press speculations on her most recent area of study—the interwoven networks of international terrorism—the top-secret reports to which she had access at the Central Intelligence Agency weren't something to be left lying around on coffee tables. Spot checks of briefcases at the agency's exits ensured that overzealous employees didn't attempt to carry out the crown jewels.

She started to read a few press clippings, but found it impossible to focus on the printed words. The feeling was rising in her again—the gut-wrenching anxiety that she tried to block out by concentrating on Lindsay and the daily effort to rebuild some normalcy in their lives. Why did he have to show up today, after all this time? What kind of game was Paul Chaney playing now? Why would he say it wasn't an accident when she knew for a fact that it was?

She had told Chaney only part of the truth, of course. He had no idea of her CIA connections nor that the Company, and not just the embassy, had gone over

David and Lindsay's accident with a fine-tooth comb to rule out any possibility of foul play. And although Mariah had been too busy running between hospital rooms to take part herself, someone she trusted absolutely had seen to it that no stone was left unturned in the Company's investigation of the disaster. No, Mariah thought, the bottom line is that Chaney doesn't know what he's talking about.

She leaned back and massaged her temples, then glanced at her watch. Propping her feet on the coffee table, she grabbed the television remote and flicked on the ten o'clock news. As the screen began to glow, two figures came into view—the "CBN Nightly News" anchors. They fit the standard TV-news format. The man, Bob Michaels, was in his mid-forties, telegenic, conservatively dressed, sober. Beverly Chin, by comparison, was younger, more brightly dressed and seated on the right side of the screen, where the eye is naturally drawn. She smiled a great deal, although her face became serious when she read from the TelePrompTer. Her Chinese features and the good looks of the African-American weatherman brought a politically correct racial balance to the news team.

The newscast opened with the latest on the aftermath of a terrorist triple-header that had occurred three days earlier. Forty-seven deaths and scores of injuries had resulted when bombs had exploded simultaneously in London's Trafalgar Square, Paris's Eiffel Tower and at the Statue of Liberty in New York. The horrifying brilliance of the attacks—their stunning coordination and the pointed symbolism of the three targets, all objects of intense national pride—was such that dozens of groups had jumped in to claim responsibility and threaten further action if their demands were not met. A coordinated intelligence effort had narrowed the field of probable attackers to one fundamentalist religious group and two "liberation fronts."

Mariah watched the item closely. Now that the Soviet Union was defunct, she had been assigned a new focus of analysis. She was in the middle of drafting a paper on the arms market for interconnected terrorist groups and she thought she might have uncovered a new supplier with possible links to Libya. There was no evidence of a connection to this ghastly terrorist triple play—not yet, anyway—but she was determined to keep at it, knowing that a coordinated assault like this had to have had strong and experienced backing.

The news report, however, told her nothing she didn't already know. When it ended, the screen shifted back to the grave features of anchorman Bob Michaels.

"The Cold War may be over, but there seems no end to troubles in the former Soviet Union. There was rioting again today in the streets of Moscow, as another cold Russian winter sets in and food shortages loom large. Correspondent Paul Chaney reports that some cash-strapped Russians may become desperate enough to try to sell the country's nuclear arsenal."

Mariah's heart began to pound furiously. She leaned forward in her seat as the tall, lean figure of Paul Chaney appeared on the screen, standing in front of the State Department building. He was wearing a sport coat and tie instead of the habitual bomber jacket—his concession to the camera. It looked as if the report had been videotaped earlier in the day.

"Since the end of the Cold War, the Russian and American governments have agreed to drastic cuts in nuclear arsenals. Thousands of weapons researchers have seen their funding disappear as the former superpowers cut weapons programs to cash in the promised 'Peace Dividend,' freeing up military funds for domestic purposes.

"But there are those who would be willing to pay a high price for these cast-off weapons—and for the experts to operate them. In Vienna, the International

Atomic Energy Agency—the IAEA—has been fighting for more power to inspect nuclear weapons sites to ensure that these arsenals are destroyed as promised. The IAEA has also proposed a registry of nuclear scientists to make certain that these specialists don't auction off their skills to the highest bidder.

"I asked an official here at the State Department why our government has not been more supportive of the IAEA's efforts."

The scene shifted to an office, where a white-haired man in a pin-striped suit sat, hands folded, behind a desk. A line on the screen identified him as William Hoskmeyer of the State Department's Nuclear Affairs Division. Mariah knew him well—he was a pompous idiot.

Hoskmeyer: *"I think you have to see it as a question of equity. If we insist that the Russians allow snap inspections by outsiders of their nuclear facilities, then they have every right to insist that we do the same. Frankly, Mr. Chaney, we're not prepared to do that—to give foreigners unrestricted access to American security installations."*

Chaney: *"So how do we know that Russian weapons and expertise won't end up in the pockets of madmen and terrorists in exchange for much-needed dollars?"*

Hoskmeyer: *"Because we're dealing with honorable men now. This government in Moscow is as committed as we are to nuclear nonproliferation. We're confident that the agreements on force reduction that we've struck with the Russians will be fully respected—both the letter and the spirit. And we're monitoring closely, of course."*

The scene shifted back to Chaney in front of the State Department building. *"Despite Washington's apparent lack of concern, there is evidence that unstable governments and terrorist groups are scrambling to acquire* nuclear weapons—and that whistle-blowers in the IAEA are being silenced. Some of these potential customers can pay top dollar for smuggled nuclear weapons and the specialists to handle them. If they succeed, we may find ourselves looking back fondly on the Cold War—when only Moscow and Washington appeared likely to blow up the planet.

"Paul Chaney—CBN—Washington."

The news continued, but Mariah wasn't listening to the television anymore. She snapped off the set, staring numbly at the disappearing glow.

David had been working in Vienna for the International Atomic Energy Agency and had been in the forefront of IAEA officials seeking greater powers to stop the spread of nuclear weapons—and Paul Chaney knew it.

But what Chaney couldn't know was that it was Mariah herself—not David—who had blown the whistle on a suspected nuclear weapons ring. And that if David and Lindsay's accident in Vienna had been an attempt to silence a whistle-blower, it should have been Mariah—not David—who was the target.

"But it wasn't," Mariah whispered. "Dammit, Chaney. I would have been the first to know."

No one could have guessed that the five men at the corner table were doomed.

They were sitting in the Trinity Bar (*"Live Country Music Every Nite!"*) just on the outskirts of Taos, New Mexico. Around them, the usual Wednesday-night crowd of ranch hands and laborers, most in jeans and Stetsons, moved through the smoky haze to the rhythm of a steel guitar. At the front of the bar, a singer in a fringed shirt stood under a spotlight, his throaty twang straining to be heard as he begged Ruby not to take her love to town.

Admittedly, the three Russians were a little conspicuous. In the crowd of sweat-soaked Stetsons and dust-lined faces, their crisp Levi's marked them as dudes. And the new white cowboy hats looked incongruous above round Slavic faces. The two Americans with them seemed drab by comparison: rumpled corduroy pants, casual shirts and down ski jackets. The younger one—thirtyish maybe—wore wire-rimmed glasses patched at the nosepiece with adhesive tape. The other man was in his fifties, white-haired, with a weary countenance.

Five matching black leather briefcases on the floor under the table provided the clue to the brotherhood that united the men. Each case bore a gold-lettered inscription stenciled in the corner: Los Alamos National Laboratory. Their obituaries would note how the five former enemies perished together just at the moment they had joined forces to put their scientific genius to work for the benefit of mankind.

A tired-looking waitress, eyes ringed with black mascara, bleached hair teased and sprayed to defy the law of gravity, balanced a tray on her hip as she deposited another round of drinks on the table and cleared the remains of the last round. Five pairs of eyes were fixed on the low neckline of her ruffled white blouse each time she bent over to put down or pick up a glass or bottle. "That's five Coors and four vodkas straight up, right, boys?" she said, straining to be heard over the music.

"But Russian vodka, yes?" Blue almond eyes sparkled in a flushed round face, watching the topside of her breasts roll with her up-and-down movements.

The waitress raised her eyes heavenward and nodded without breaking the rhythm of her work. "Yeah, yeah—Smirnoff—good Russian vodka." The two Americans at the table exchanged amused glances. "That's twenty-four-fifty, fellas."

Larry Kingman dropped a twenty and a ten on her tray. Once again, as he had on the last two rounds, he waved away the change she had begun to count out.

"Well, thanks! Thanks a lot," the waitress said, taking a real good look at him now and smiling warmly. For an old guy, she thought, he was kind of cute. "You just holler if you need anything else, okay?"

Kingman smiled and nodded. The woman lingered a moment, then wandered reluctantly over to a table where some good ol' boys were calling loudly for refills. Kingman raised one of the shot glasses of vodka and held it out over the center of the table, looking at each of the other four faces in turn. "To the future, gentlemen," he said. "To science."

The Russians lifted the three remaining shot glasses. *"Na zhdoroviye,"* they said in unison, tossing back the clear liquor, then slapping the glasses down on the stained wooden tabletop and reaching for the beer chasers.

Kingman directed an inquiring eyebrow at the younger American seated next to him. Scott Bowker was frowning, but he grasped one of the beer glasses, touching it briefly to his lips. Kingman shook his white head as he watched the younger man. "What's up?"

Bowker glanced at the Russians, then around the room. "We shouldn't be drinking like this."

Kingman leaned back in his chair and smiled indulgently. "Relax, Scotty. We'll let you be designated driver, okay?" Bowker's frown deepened even further. "Re-lax," Kingman repeated. "Everything is under control. Now, enjoy."

One of the Russians, at Bowker's left, grinned and put an arm around his shoulders, squeezing good-naturedly. "Larry is right. Enjoy! We are allies now— comrades in a common struggle. The Cold War is finished and we, my serious friend, have all won. Now," he added, "we work on the same side." The Russian raised his glass and nodded above the brim before taking another swallow of beer. The others echoed his nod. Scott Bowker looked pointedly at his watch, then at Kingman.

"Yup," Kingman acknowledged. "It's getting late. We should be going, boys. Tomorrow's a big day."

The five men drained their glasses, then stood and gathered up their briefcases. Kingman shifted uncomfortably, stretching out knees that were stiff and swollen after three days of playing guide for the Russian visitors. He trailed the others to the door, offering a nod and a warm smile as he limped past the blond waitress.

"'Bye now," she said, giving him a wistful wave. "You come again, okay?"

They walked out of the beer-and-smoke fog of the tavern and into the cold night air of the New Mexico desert. The parking lot was full: pickups and old beaters, a few motorcycles, gaudy yellow license plates proclaiming New Mexico—Land of Enchantment. Kingman tossed a set of keys to Bowker as the men approached a minivan. Bowker unlocked the doors and the Russians slipped into the back seats. Kingman shut the sliding rear door and climbed into the front passenger seat.

They pulled out of the parking lot and turned south on NM 68, the main highway linking Taos and Los Alamos. The men fell silent, contemplating the landscape eerily lit by a cloud-draped moon over the Sangre de Cristo—the Blood of Christ—Mountains. A powdery snow had been falling while they were inside and it muffled the sound of the tires on the road. The Pueblo Indians believe that the spirits of the dead linger on the mesas of New Mexico, guarding the land. In this spectral glow and eerie silence, it was easy enough to believe that ghosts were hovering nearby. Watching and waiting.

The highway curved along the banks of the Rio Grande, hugging the line of the rushing river. It was past midnight and the road was virtually deserted. As the van sped along toward Española and the Los Alamos turnoff, a single pair of lights could be seen approaching from far off, flashing between the hills.

Kingman rolled down his window, the wispy white strings of his breath escaping into the night. He inhaled deeply, drinking in the cold, fresh air—infinitely preferable to the hops- and nicotine-soaked atmosphere of the Trinity Bar. Then he rolled the window up again and glanced back at the men in the rear of the van. The two Russians on the rear-most bench were heavy-eyed, their heads lolling with the motion of the vehicle, on the edge of dropping off to sleep. But Yuri Sokolov, sitting on the center bank of seats, had his gaze fixed on the road ahead, his thoughts impenetrable but obviously stone-cold sober, despite his consumption at the Trinity Bar.

At fifty-two, Sokolov was acknowledged in the arcane world of nuclear physics as the most brilliant mind in the field. Until recently, of course, his reputation in the West had been based entirely on the discoveries of meticulous spycraft, since he had never before stepped outside the Soviet weapons community, nor knowingly circulated a paper in the West.

Sokolov glanced briefly at Kingman, then focused again on the road ahead, watching the snow spinning through the van's headlights—remembering Moscow nights, perhaps. They were intellectual brothers, Kingman reflected, forced to live their lives as enemies until suddenly, one day, someone had decided to change the rules. Now they had a common purpose—always had, maybe. The vagaries of politics irritated him. There was neither method nor reason to human behavior, and politicians were more irrational than most. Only science was constant, sane.

The single set of headlights rolling north on NM 68 toward the van belonged to a tanker truck making a night run to Taos. Diamond-shaped plaques on the tanker noted the contents as gasoline—hazardous material, highly flammable. The rig was hauling over eight thousand gallons of unleaded fuel and doing sixty on the open road.

When the two vehicles collided, the explosion could be heard all the way to Taos. The fireball rose eighty feet into the air, lighting up the night sky, although the only immediate witnesses to the event were jackrabbits and owls. The heat generated by the fire was enough to twist steel into Silly Putty and incinerate anything else unfortunate enough to be caught in the vicinity. Within a matter of seconds, even the asphalt road was ablaze.

Another car traveling south on NM 68 came upon the accident six minutes after the collision. After realizing that nothing could have survived the inferno, the driver turned back toward Taos to telephone for help from the Trinity Bar. When the emergency vehicles arrived, there was nothing they could do but try to keep the blaze from spreading to the surrounding juniper and piñon trees. It took three hours for the fire to burn itself out. Fire fighters doused the site with foam to guard against another flare-up, but this only served to seal the tomb.

The next day, curiosity seekers from both sides of the closed highway swarmed over the hills for a look, but nothing was left at the scene except surreal metal sculpture, smoldering ash and the stench of burnt rubber.

A piece of evidence that had miraculously survived the impact of the crash and resulting blaze—the van's rear license plate—allowed state police to trace the ownership and determine that it had been signed out to Dr. Lawrence Kingman, deputy director of the Los Alamos National Laboratory, who had been squiring around some scientists visiting New Mexico under the Russia/U.S. Nuclear Cooperation Pact. Someone at

Los Alamos remembered that Kingman and a few others attending a dinner at the Hilltop House Hotel earlier that evening had headed down the mesa for drinks afterward.

The police spoke to a waitress at the Trinity Bar who clearly remembered the group and was able to confirm that there had been three Russians and two Americans. The Russkies had been obvious, she'd said, rolling her eyes at the memory of the new cowboy getups they had worn. The table had ordered several drinks over a couple of hours, although they hadn't been staggering or anything when they left. She was really sad to hear about the accident—the older American had seemed like a good guy.

The federal government took a close interest in the follow-up investigation and insisted that the van and the remains of its occupants be returned. The coroner explained that anything they scraped off the melted highway would consist primarily of American automotive technology and very little by way of identifiable human remains. Investigators were sifting through the rubble, but the blaze appeared to have made as effective a funeral pyre as any crematorium could boast, if a little less tidy.

All the same, the federal men were insistent, and around northern New Mexico everyone knew that you didn't argue with the feds. They had played a mysterious role in the area ever since World War II, when Manhattan Project scientists working at Los Alamos had conducted a top-secret test—code-named Trinity—of the world's first atomic bomb. The Trinity test had led directly to the bombing of Hiroshima and Nagasaki and the end of the war with Japan.

If the feds wanted a bulldozed pile of ashes and twisted steel, the coroner decided, they were welcome to it.

4

His secretary hadn't arrived yet when Mariah entered her chief's office the next morning to go over the report on the new terrorist arms connection. Frank Tucker was there, though, standing at the window and talking on the phone. She hesitated in the doorway, but he spotted her and waved her in, raising a finger to indicate he would be done in a minute.

Perching herself on the edge of his desk, Mariah examined the dusty framed photos of his kids and grandson while she waited. A photo collection can be revealing, she thought. She picked up the picture of Carol, Frank's daughter, standing in a wedding dress beside her husband, Michael. They had been married four years earlier, just a few weeks before Mariah and David had left for Vienna. Examining the picture, Mariah smiled as she remembered Frank's uncharacteristic beam when he had walked his daughter down the aisle. His only regret, he'd said, was that his wife hadn't been there to see their daughter happily married.

Next to the wedding picture was a shot of baby Alex, Carol's son—"the ankle biter," Frank called him, his pride obvious behind his good-natured grumbling. He had been born eight months earlier, but the only photo Frank seemed to have was the infant's hospital picture, little Alex's face red and squashed like that of every newborn babe since the beginning of time—Lindsay included, Mariah thought, touching the photo with a soft smile. She returned the baby's picture to its place on Frank's desk and picked up the remaining frame.

And then there was Stephen, Carol's twin. The high school graduation photo was at least ten years old. Joanne Tucker's leukemia had been diagnosed when the twins were two, and they were fifteen when Frank's wife finally lost her battle with the disease. Carol had become the family's mother substitute during the long crisis, but Stephen had reacted with anger and defiance, most of it directed against Frank. It hadn't been an easy time for either of them. Maybe it would have happened, anyway, Mariah thought, a normal conflict between a strong-willed father and an equally stubborn son. In the end, after a period of sullen rebellion and minor scrapes with school authorities, Stephen had finally managed to pull his act together. Now, at twenty-eight, he was a computer specialist deep in the bowels of the CIA. But despite the fact that he had followed his father into the Company, the two were still as different—and incompatible—as night and day.

Frank hung up the phone and turned to Mariah. "Okay, what have you got for me?"

"The latest take on that new arms link," she said, slipping off the edge of the desk and into a chair across from him. "You know, I still don't know why we're doing this, Frank."

"Doing what?"

"Chasing crazy Irishmen and Libyans and Iranians and God knows who else. How did we get into the terrorist game? You and I are supposed to be Soviet experts."

"Times have changed. The Soviet Union is kaput."

"Yes, but their nukes aren't. Why didn't they make you head of the new nonproliferation unit? You were the logical choice—and that's where I wanted to be, too."

"Call it career development. Guess they decided we should widen our focus a bit. Anyway," he said, more briskly, "let's get on with this report. That was the seventh floor on the phone just now. The director wants to read it over the weekend, so we're going to have to hustle and get this baby delivered."

"It's under control."

Frank nodded. He was the one who had recruited her into the Agency and had been something of a mentor for much of the past sixteen years. Mariah knew he had total confidence in her.

Tucker had approached her on the recommendation of one of her professors when she was doing her graduate degree at Berkeley. She had met with him one afternoon in an off-campus office—a huge man, completely bald except for bushy black eyebrows that seemed to be compensating for the deficit of hair on the rest of his head. Years later—over a late-night glass of Frank's secret stock of Glenlivet that they had broken out to celebrate the closing of a difficult file—Mariah had given in and asked him whether he shaved his head for the pristine bowling-ball effect. He did.

She could have a bright future with the CIA, Frank had said. They were looking for people like her with a strong understanding of the Soviet Union and its military capabilities. She had been astonished, then a little appalled, when she realized that this intimidating man from CIA headquarters at Langley was serious about offering her a job. It was the mid-seventies. The Vietnam War had just ended and "peace, love and good vibes" was still the operative theme on American campuses. The CIA, to put it mildly, was not in good odor—especially at Berkeley.

All the same, Mariah had spent several years studying the Soviet threat and she had no illusions about Moscow's ambitions, either. It was just naïve, she was convinced, to think you could face down that kind of threat without decent intelligence work. She had never seen herself in the spook business, but Tucker's offer had been intriguing, his arguments persuasive as he talked about the importance of solid intelligence analysis to help a government avoid the snake pits out there.

But Mariah and David had become seriously involved by then and he had already been offered the job at the Los Alamos National Laboratory, so she turned Tucker down and followed David to New Mexico. But then, six months later, she left New Mexico and said yes to a career as a CIA analyst, after all—even if it also meant the end of her relationship with David. That didn't seem to be going anywhere, anyway.

Mariah had gone through the basic Company training program and had then been sent to work as an analyst in the Soviet section headed by Frank Tucker, undaunted by his reputation as a chief who ate analysts for breakfast. To be sure, working with Tucker was challenging. The fierce glare of the beetle dark eyes under those black eyebrows had terrified a legion of analysts.

And no secretary had stayed with Tucker for more than a few weeks until Personnel had finally had the wit to park Patricia Bonelli outside his door, a New Jersey native with a truck driver's vocabulary who could give as good as she got when Frank Tucker got too far out of line. Someone had once told Mariah that Patty and Frank had a legendary, rip-roaring battle the first day she came on stream. But when Frank realized that Personnel had sent him the female equivalent of Genghis Khan as a secretary, he broke down and roared with laughter—much to the amazement of the trembling staff in the section, who had expected a bloodbath.

His secretary had been with him for almost twenty years now. When Mariah had appeared on the scene, Patty had recognized a kindred spirit and had explained the fundamentals of dealing with Frank Tucker.

They boiled down to this, she said: never cringe, never apologize, and never—but *never*—screw up. Easier said than done, maybe, but it suited Mariah to a T. She had worked with Tucker, off and on, for most of her career since.

"Are you okay, Mariah? You look dead on your feet."

She glanced up sharply. Frank Tucker could never be accused of being the most sensitive man in the world. If he thought she was looking tired, she must look godawful, Mariah realized.

"I'm fine. I didn't sleep very well last night." She hesitated, debating whether or not to raise the subject of Chaney. But they had been over this ground many times during the investigation of the accident. Mariah knew what Frank's reaction to Chaney's claims would be and she knew who she trusted. It wasn't Paul Chaney. Leave it, she decided—don't keep picking at this scab. Let it heal. "Where were we?"

"You were telling me about the Libyan connection."

"Right. Tripoli station has an asset who says Libya may be shipping arms through the island of Madeira."

"Have the birds picked up anything?"

Mariah nodded. "I was down with the satellite recon boys yesterday. There was a shipment out of Tripoli three weeks ago on a state-owned Libyan vessel. The birds picked up markings on the crates that said they contained tomatoes, but the Libyans don't usually export vegetables to Madeira. And there was an awful lot of security watching over those so-called tomatoes."

"What happened to the crates when they arrived in Madeira?"

"The photo resolution isn't quite as clear as on the pictures from Tripoli, but the Libyan ship off-loaded some crates onto a smaller ship. They look to be the same ones. That ship subsequently set sail for Le Havre, France.''

"That's a long, roundabout trip for tomatoes," Tucker said, tapping a pen against his big knee. "From Le Havre, of course, it's just a short hop to Paris or across the channel to the U.K. These guys could conceivably have supplied both the Trafalgar and the Eiffel bombers."

"Yup," Mariah agreed. "Except the crates weren't on board when the ship docked at Le Havre. French Customs inspected the hold after a quiet suggestion from our station in Paris, but they found no tomatoes—nor anything else resembling the crates loaded in Madeira."

"Were there other ports of call before Le Havre?"

Mariah shook her head. "We don't think so, but there are several thousand miles of open sea between the two points and the ship wasn't under constant satellite surveillance. NSA was monitoring the boat's communications, but they didn't hear anything unusual."

"They could have had a prearranged silent rendezvous with yet another vessel and done a quick transfer on the high seas," Frank suggested. Mariah nodded in agreement. His pen took up a staccato beat on his knee. "So who owns the ship out of Madeira?"

"It's a Liberian-registered vessel belonging to Niarchos Transport."

"The Greek outfit?"

"Ah, well—here's where it gets interesting," Mariah said. "Niarchos was bought out last year by a company called Triton Transport, which is in turn owned by another company called Ramsay Investments."

Frank shook his head. "Bloody big business! Such a spiderweb of interlocking connections. Who can figure these people out?"

"I think the idea is that we're not *supposed* to figure it out too easily," Mariah said dryly. "But you know of course that Ramsay Investments is Angus Ramsay McCord of McCord Industries.''

Tucker leaned back in his chair and whistled softly. ''Great! They're going to love this upstairs—the President's buddy, a terrorist gunrunner!'' He rolled his eyes and then fixed Mariah soberly. ''Not likely, kid. Give me something I can sell.''

''Are you saying you want me to suppress the evidence, Frank?'' Mariah asked, her expression incredulous.

''No, but neither do I want us leaping to conclusions on the basis of a possible shipment of so-called tomatoes on a vessel with a tenuous link to the richest man in America—a guy with a philanthropic reputation just this side of God's.'' Mariah rolled her eyes. ''I know, I know,'' Tucker said. ''I don't buy that crap, either. But unless you want to spend the rest of your career counting goatherders in Ulan Bator, you'll be very careful about linking McCord to terrorists—unless, that is, we come up with a hell of a lot more evidence than this. If it's out there,'' he added, ''I personally will be more than happy to act on it. But in the meantime, tread carefully, Mariah.''

The McCord Industries Learjet taxied to a halt in front of the Fargo, North Dakota, terminal and the pilot cut the engines. Dieter Pflanz checked out the terrain, scowling at the sight of the waiting crowd. He turned to his boss, sitting across from him in one of the deep upholstered armchairs that were arranged in clublike groupings throughout the cabin.

Gus McCord's face fell as he glanced out the window and spotted the long black limousine at the head of a caravan of vehicles lined up on the tarmac. ''Aw, for crying out loud,'' he moaned, turning back to the four other passengers on the private aircraft. ''Jerry, I told you to tell them to keep it simple. This is embarrassing."

A young man sitting across the cabin unbuckled his seat belt and then stood and looked over McCord's shoulder at the retinue waiting on the runway. "I know, Gus." Jerry Siddon grimaced apologetically as he ran a hand back though his hair. "I tried."

"Yeah, well, try a little harder next time," McCord grumbled. "People are gonna think I'm putting on airs."

"Come on, dear," Nancy McCord said, patting his arm with a smile as she rose from her seat. "They all know you wouldn't do that. People here are proud of you, that's all, and grateful for everything you've done for your hometown. Let them spoil you a little."

Her husband seemed unconvinced as he stood up, brushed his pants and buttoned his navy blue suit jacket—bought off the rack, despite the fact that Angus Ramsay McCord was a billionaire several times over. The shirt he was wearing, like every shirt he owned, was white. The tie was typical, too—conservatively striped in muted colors. At sixty-one, he was still wiry, the suit jacket covering only the tiniest paunch. He weighed one hundred thirty-eight pounds, wringing wet, and stood only five foot six (five-eight in his elevator shoes), although the aggressively erect cut of his steel gray hair added almost another inch to his height. Under lashless lids, he had small, light brown eyes that never seemed to blink. In conversation, these eyes, like tiny copper nails, could fix people with an intensity that left them feeling impaled.

The uniformed young man who served as steward on McCord's personal aircraft came forward from the closet in the aft section carrying a black, Russian sable coat. Nancy McCord glanced at the soft, rich fur and then out the window, where sleety gusts of snow were swirling across the black asphalt, whipsawing the legs of the people in the welcoming party. She shook her head regretfully. "No, Miguel, the blue woolen one, please."

Miguel exchanged coats and Gus McCord took the cloth coat from him, holding it up for his wife. "That's my girl," he said, hiking it over her shoulders while her arms slipped down the sleeves. She turned to smile at him, her clear blue eyes enveloping him in the love that had been his anchor for the past forty years.

She'd been just nineteen years old, and Gus only twenty-one, when they had married. Cynics said Angus McCord had courted Nancy Patterson to win the favor of her father, a California businessman who had made a fortune during World War II selling equipment and spare parts to the Long Beach naval shipyard. McCord had just completed his military service as midshipman on a navy destroyer when his captain had introduced him to the industrialist. There was no doubt that having Robert Patterson as a father-in-law had helped launch McCord on the way to his first million, but Gus and Nancy had been a love match from the start. Four kids and five grandchildren later, they still were.

The steward brought out the coats of the four men on the aircraft and then hurried to open the door. An icy blast of air rushed in as Gus McCord shrugged into the tan, three-quarter-length down parka that his wife held up for him.

Pflanz pulled on his own parka, suppressing a grin at the obvious discomfort of McCord's executive assistant. Jerry Siddon shuddered as he turned up the collar of his overcoat. A Los Angeles native, Siddon was less than ecstatic, Pflanz knew, when he had to accompany the boss on these hometown swings in wintertime. But the new neonatal unit of McCord General Hospital was opening today in Fargo. It had been planned as the most advanced facility for the care of premature babies in the northern United States and had been financed almost entirely by the McCord family. The neonatal unit, in addition to the cancer wing and the heart institute, would help cement the reputation of McCord General as one of the country's preeminent health-care facilities, putting Gus McCord's hometown firmly on the medical map.

Dieter Pflanz headed for the open door of the aircraft. At Pflanz's insistence, and after a foiled kidnap attempt several years back, McCord almost always traveled with two bodyguards now. But the one place Gus refused to have the burly guards present was in his hometown, and so the bodyguards had flown ahead to McCord's next stop in Washington, D.C. Pflanz was not in the habit of doing guard duty, but he often came along for the ride to discuss business with McCord, and the imposing presence of the former covert operative would give pause to even the most determined adversary. He patted his chest, feeling the comfortable bulge of the Smith and Wesson semiautomatic holstered under his suit jacket. He expected no trouble, but it always paid to be prepared.

Jerry Siddon nodded to the other passenger in the aircraft, and McCord Industries' private photographer followed close behind the security chief. The photographer, Pflanz was certain, would get plenty of shots of McCord's arrival and the opening ceremonies at the hospital. Gus McCord was being actively courted by both major parties as a possible presidential contender when the current administration's mandate ran out. While he professed impatience with Washington, both bureaucrats and the squabblers in Congress, McCord had never firmly shut the door on a political career, dangling teasing hints from time to time that would send the parties' politicos into a mad frenzy of courtship. It had been Jerry Siddon's idea to keep a personal photographic record of McCord's civic contributions.

The security chief and the photographer were the first to step out the door of the plane. Pflanz slipped on dark glasses, despite the gray overcast, while the photographer took readings on his light meter, adjusted the aperture setting on his camera and snapped a few quick shots of the waiting dignitaries.

As Pflanz descended the steps, his eyes swept over the scene, taking in the roof of a gray terminal building nearly invisible against the big, prairie winter sky. His gaze dropped to the faces pressed against the glass of the terminal's observation lounge. Satisfied that there was no obvious danger lurking in those quarters, he took up a position near the bottom of the aircraft steps and turned his attention to the crowd on the tarmac—a dozen or so people, those in front smiling bravely while the lesser lights in the rear ranks stamped their feet against the bitter cold and blew on their hands.

The knot of dignitaries near the limo included a man Pflanz recognized as Fred Hansen, the mayor of Fargo, his wife and two hospital administrators who had visited the McCord head office in California several times. The other men and women in business dress appeared to be local bigwigs. A couple of more casually dressed men detached themselves from the crowd—press, Pflanz decided, watching them warily nevertheless. The one carrying a canvas sack focused his camera on the door of the Lear. A cameraman from the city TV station also stood peering through the lens of a video camera perched on his shoulder.

McCord's own photographer had taken up position next to the local press when Gus and Nancy emerged from the aircraft. They waved from the top step and then descended, hand in hand, like the President and First Lady that Pflanz suspected they might someday be. Jerry Siddon followed a discreet few steps.

The mayor and his wife moved forward to meet the McCords, the rest of the ground party streaming after.

Gus McCord dropped his wife's hand and took the mayor's outstretched one, slapping the politician's shoulder with his other hand.

"There you are, Fred, you old son of a gun," McCord said heartily. He cocked his thumb toward the limo. "You expecting the queen of England?"

The mayor chuckled. "No, Gus, we laid it on special for you. It's a loaner from Vigan-Carlson."

McCord threw back his head and roared. Vigan-Carlson was a local funeral parlor. "I'm not dead yet— no thanks to you," he said, rubbing a prominent bump on the bridge of his nose.

The break had happened forty-five years earlier during a high school baseball game. It was the bottom of the ninth. Fred Hansen had flung the bat after a base hit and it had caught McCord, playing catcher, square in the face. Masks and other protective equipment were unheard of in the poor farm community just outside Fargo where the two men had grown up. They'd been lucky to have a ball and bat.

"Yeah, you always were a hardheaded old cuss," Hansen said, grinning. He nodded in the direction of Dieter Pflanz. "You bring that guy along to make sure I don't take another crack at it?"

"Nah! He carries Nance's suitcases. She always was a lousy packer!" McCord grinned affectionately at his wife, who slapped his arm and then stepped forward to greet the mayor and his wife.

"Isn't he awful? How are you, Fred?" She kissed his cheek before turning to embrace his wife. "And Stella. How good to see you. What a beautiful coat!"

Stella Hansen's lined face, heavily caked with makeup, lit up as she stepped back from Nancy's hug and stroked the dun-colored fox fur she was wearing. "Gorgeous, isn't it? It's an early Christmas present from Fred. He wanted me to have it for the opening."

"You look lovely, and so cozy."

"But Gus has given you a fur coat, surely," Stella said, checking out Nancy's cloth number.

"Nothing like yours," Nancy said truthfully.

Stella Hansen smiled triumphantly at her husband, then turned to McCord. "Well, Gus, now you know what Nancy wants for Christmas. Aren't you just awful not to have thought of it before?"

"You got me there, Stel," McCord said, shrugging sheepishly. "But what do you want—I'm just a farm boy. This fancy stuff is beyond me, I swear."

Stella's eyes danced over him and her face folded into the layers of her most winning smile. A flake of black mascara separated from her lashes, settling on the soft pink down of her cheek. Gus McCord had been friends with Stella's older brother when they were kids. Gus had asked her out to a school dance once but, to her everlasting regret, she had turned down the scrawny little guy in favor of the captain of the football team. Then John Lindquist—he of the boozy breath and groping hands—had gone off and gotten himself killed in Korea after his senior year, leaving Stella obliged to spend six months discreetly visiting an aunt in Minneapolis.

Watching Gus McCord now as he moved down the line of the welcoming committee, shaking hands and slapping backs, Stella marveled again at her inability back then to recognize his potential. But who could have known the hyper little guy had had it in him, for crying out loud? Of course, Gus had been smart, marrying a rich girl. Stella watched Nancy McCord as she followed close to Gus, smiling warmly at the people he introduced. It was a good thing her old man had had money, Stella thought, because Nancy had always been kind of a plain thing—always wore her hair simple, just a blunt cut curled behind her ears. She'd gone gray real early on, too, and then white, although it looked kind of nice now, Stella had to admit, kind of striking, especially with those bright blue eyes. And she was still trim—she must go to one of those fat farms that the magazines said rich people like Liz Taylor hid out in when they'd blimped out.

Stella smoothed her fox fur, grateful for the way it camouflaged her own ample body. Still, when she was younger, she'd had a body to kill for—that's what John Lindquist had always said, and Fred had thought so, as well. He'd panted after her all through high school and had just about choked when she'd returned from Minneapolis and said she'd think about marrying him, after all. And now Fred was mayor and Stella got to ride in the back of an open convertible in the Fourth of July parade, and she got to meet some big shots, and she had a fur coat that even Nancy McCord envied. So things had turned out all right, really, even if she and Fred didn't fly all over the world in their own private plane.

They climbed into the limousine, Gus wedged between Stella and Nancy, while Fred took up one of the jump seats facing them. Jerry Siddon slipped into the other jump seat after arranging for the photographer to ride with the TV camera crew, which was racing ahead to set up at the hospital before McCord arrived. The limo dipped when Dieter Pflanz climbed into the front passenger seat. The driver gave him a nervous smile, to which Pflanz replied with a curt nod.

During the ten-minute ride to the hospital, Fred Hansen went over the schedule one more time. "You'll have about thirty minutes to tour the new unit before the official opening," he told McCord. "Then we'll have some speechifying and ribbon-cutting and such. Then it's off to the hotel for lunch. Should be all done by around two, then we'll get you back to the airport. Jerry here tells me you're flying out today to Washington?"

Stella Hansen's eyes grew wide. "Are you going to be seeing the President? What's he really like?"

McCord shrugged. "Pretty much like most folks, Stel. Puts his pants on one leg at a time."

She shook her head, obviously skeptical. "I can't imagine what you must think of poor little Fargo, Gus, after all the places you've been and people you've met."

"There's nothing poor about a place with air as clean and people as fine as this city's," McCord said soberly. "Don't ever think different, Stel."

Glancing back, Pflanz saw Stella Hansen looking as if she would melt. He and Jerry Siddon exchanged fleeting looks of amusement as they listened to McCord charming the mayor and his wife. Siddon, Pflanz reckoned, would be calculating once again the number of months to the presidential primaries. He had listened to the eager young aide explain *ad nauseam* why Gus *had* to run. McCord had everything going for him, Siddon said—money, charisma (despite less-than-classic looks), a charming wife, nice kids and photogenic grandchildren, a Horatio Alger personal history and an outstanding record of community service. He couldn't possibly lose.

And if Gus McCord went to the White House, Pflanz knew, Jerry Siddon intended to be there as his right hand. Siddon was thirty years old, and had been working for McCord Industries for five years after graduating from Stanford near the top of his business class. But it was his extracurricular activities on behalf of American Families of Missing Vietnam Veterans that had brought a teenage Jerry Siddon to Gus McCord's attention. Siddon's father had disappeared in a bombing raid over Hanoi in 1970. Jerry had been the youngest member of a delegation from the AFMVV that had approached McCord in the early eighties to help finance and organize a search for men rumored to be still alive in Vietnam. With the tacit support of the CIA, a mission had gone ahead under the direction of Dieter

Pflanz and a team of quietly hired mercenaries. But the evidence the contingent obtained had been inconclusive.

As a result of that first meeting, however, Siddon had caught McCord's eye and his sympathy. The billionaire had subsequently underwritten Siddon's college studies and guaranteed him a job upon graduation. Siddon repaid the debt with hard work and unstinting devotion to the interests of Gus McCord. Today, those interests included reaping good PR value from the opening of the latest in a string of McCord charitable facilities.

To Pflanz, however, these hometown good deeds were just so much chaff, incidental to the real mission.

"What's bugging you, Mariah?" Frank Tucker asked, studying her closely.

She had risen from her chair to leave his office, but when she got to the door, she hesitated, her hand resting on the knob, a frown creasing her forehead. Then she turned back to face him. "Did you see the news last night, Frank? CBN?"

Frank exhaled a long sigh and he shook his head regretfully. "Damn. I was hoping you had missed it."

"Oh, I saw it—and Paul Chaney. And not just on the tube."

"What do you mean?"

"He was waiting for me when I left David last night," Mariah said. She moved away from the door and ran her hand along the line of books on Frank's credenza, straightening the edges—an instinctive reaction against chaos. "And he left a message on my answering machine." She stopped cold and looked toward the ceiling, her jaw clenched. "Oh, dammit, Frank! Lindsay took the message off the machine. If she ever—"

"Whoa! Slow down. You're not making any sense. Sit down and tell me what happened."

She drummed her fingers on the edge of the credenza, then turned and leaned against it, crossing her arms tightly across her chest, looking down at the toes of her shoes. "Paul Chaney showed up at the nursing home yesterday," she said finally. "He had seen David earlier and was waiting for me. Said he needed to talk about what really happened in Vienna—something about the people who did this to David and Lindsay. He called my house, too. And then I saw that thing on the news."

"You knew him in Vienna, didn't you?"

Mariah nodded. "David knew him better than I did. They played hockey together, but we all used to get together after the games. And he hung out on the cocktail circuit, of course, trolling for news leads—and women," Mariah added wryly. "He and David got to be good friends and Paul used to drop by our place a lot, but I never felt very comfortable with him. He's one of those guys who figures he's God's gift to womankind."

Tucker watched her closely, and then a grin formed at the edge of his lips. "Make a pass at you, did he?"

Mariah grimaced and nodded.

"Had he been in touch since you got back to the States?"

Mariah shook her head. "He came to the hospital in Vienna a couple of times, but I hadn't seen him in months before he showed up yesterday."

"Does Chaney know you're CIA?"

"No, I'm sure he doesn't. David wouldn't have told him—he was absolutely discreet. During the entire three years we were in Vienna, there was never the slightest hint that my cover was blown, with Chaney or anyone else. As far as anyone knew, I was simply an embassy administrator. Chaney always seemed more interested in David's work at the IAEA. He often turned to David to demystify some of the complexities of nuclear issues, and he knew that David was working to beef up the agency's policing role."

"So what do you think Chaney's on to now?"

Mariah glanced at him sharply. "That's what I was hoping *you'd* tell *me*," she said. She came forward and stood in front of his desk, leaning closer, hands planted in the middle of his papers. "Frank, you told me—you *swore*—that the truck hit our car by accident. You knew I wasn't in any position, between David's and Lindsay's injuries, to pay close attention to the investigation. But you promised me that every angle would be looked into."

"And it was." Frank brought his hammy fists together and stared at them intently for a moment before looking back up at her, his voice low. "Dammit, Mariah—don't you think I was blown away by what happened? I felt responsible. I recruited you, helped you get that assignment in Vienna. I felt bloody awful when things ended up the way they did."

Mariah's shoulders slumped as she watched his gruff old face transformed by guilt. She reached out and squeezed his hand. "It wasn't your fault, no matter what. But now, with Chaney, I'm wondering again...." She sank down onto a chair and stared at the floor. "It was just a fluke that I wasn't in the car. David should never have been there. He normally jogged to work, but at the last minute that morning we changed plans. Lindsay had a science project that she needed help carrying in and I had an early meeting with an asset, so David drove her to school. If they hadn't dropped me off first, neither of them would have been there when the brakes failed on that truck."

Frank nodded. Mariah knew she had told him this before, but the awful irony of it never left her. David's life had been destroyed in her place because she'd been too busy that morning to drive their daughter to school. Now, what if it wasn't an accident, after all?

"I've been thinking—was I the target?" she asked quietly, her eyes fixed on his. "Was it the CHAUCER operation? Was someone trying to kill *me* and made a mistake?"

Tucker's eyes held hers for a second and then his glance shifted away. Mariah flinched. They had known each other too well and for too long.

"Frank!" she said, alarmed. "Tell me, for God's sake!"

"I'm not sure."

Her focus moved from Tucker's face to an invisible point somewhere between them, but she saw nothing. Beyond the office door, the clatter of voices, the tramp of feet and the hum of office machinery faded, replaced by a cottony stillness. Then a wave came out of nowhere, washing over her, and she felt herself drowning. She fumbled for the arms of the chair and gripped them tightly.

She never saw Frank jump up out of his chair and move around the desk, nor did she feel his hand on her shoulder. It was only when he planted himself squarely in front of her and bent down to peer into her eyes that she began to rise again to the surface. Her gaze flitted from side to side, coming finally to rest on Frank's face when he had called her name for the third time, his voice urgent.

"Mariah! Are you all right?"

"All right?"

She was breathing, she knew—her shoulders rose and fell heavily with the effort of her lungs to grasp oxygen. But all right? No, she definitely was *not* all right.

"Who was it?" she asked, her voice husky. She clenched her fists, pulling in hard on the reins of self-control. Tucker's face came into focus and she held his eyes, her voice firm now. "Who did this to my family, Frank?"

He sat back on the desk and studied her for a long time. Then he walked around behind it. He stood, banging his knuckles on the green baize desk pad. "Leave it alone, Mariah. You can't change what happened, and you need to concentrate your energies on Lindsay and David. Let somebody else worry about the other stuff."

Mariah leaped from her chair and leaned across the desk between them. "Don't patronize me, Frank!"

His head snapped up. "I'm not patronizing, goddammit!"

"Then what kind of answer is that?"

"It's the only answer I can give you."

"It's not good enough!"

"It's the only answer you're gonna get, Mariah. This is a closely held file and you have no 'need to know.'"

He might just as well have slapped her face. She recoiled and stared at him, dumbfounded. His sharp frown held her momentarily, then his eyes shifted away and skimmed across the ceiling before coming to rest on her face again. "Look, I honestly don't know for certain whether what happened in Vienna was an accident or not. I thought it was at first, but now I'm not sure. If it wasn't, then your family got caught in the middle of some bloody dangerous business and you don't want to know about it, believe me."

"Oh, yes, I do," Mariah said firmly. "If someone did this deliberately, I definitely *do* want to know about it." His expression remained glumly resistant. "Frank! Dammit! Let me in! If I can do something—anything—to make sense of what happened and help bring down whoever did this, at least I won't feel so helpless. Give me a break, please?"

Tucker shook his head. "I can't, Mariah. Even if I wanted to—which I don't—it's not my decision. Operations is handling the file and access is severely limited. Besides which—I'm dead serious here—you've got

Lindsay to think about. You put yourself in the line of fire and she could end up an orphan. Is that what you want?''

"As opposed to what, Frank? As opposed to the life of a fatherless cripple that I've already managed to give her?''

"Don't do this. Don't punish yourself for something you weren't responsible for.''

"If not me, who? Tell me who, Frank—I'd love to punish someone else. I'd like to rip them limb from limb. I'd like to blow their goddamn heads off!''

Tucker dropped into his chair. "And that's exactly why you're no good for this case. You're personally involved. You've got no distance or objectivity, and that's a recipe for getting yourself killed. Now, I don't want to talk about this anymore. Go do your job and let me do mine.''

Mariah watched him as he opened a file in front of him and pointedly ignored her. She stood still, glaring at him, fists clenched. Then she wheeled around and headed for the door, throwing it open with such energy that it bounced back against the wall with a bang.

Pat Bonelli had finally arrived for work and was sitting at her desk when Mariah stormed out of Frank's office. She jumped as the door crashed. "Mariah! You scared the shit out of me!'' She stopped cold as she caught sight of Mariah's face. "Are you all right?''

It was the second time she'd been asked that question, Mariah thought. What did people think? Of course she wasn't all right!

Pat arched her neck to look in on Frank, almost as if she expected to see blood on the walls. "What happened?''

"Nothing,'' Mariah muttered as she stormed into her own office next door.

5

Even Dieter Pflanz had to smile when he thought back
on it later.

There was Angus McCord, billionaire industrialist—
one of the world's wealthiest and most powerful—
wearing a green surgical gown over his suit and a gauze
mask over his face. A cotton cap rested heavily on his
not-insignificant ears, forcing them to flap even more
than usual. He looked like a diminutive cross between
Marcus Welby, M.D., and Dumbo the elephant. Only
the tiny, wizened baby girl whose hand McCord held
through the porthole of an isolette, and the simultaneously proud and anxious expression on the faces of her
similarly gowned parents, revealed the serious nature of
the business at hand.

The Newborn Intensive Care Unit was a large room,
full of high-tech equipment and bustling staff. It had
been functioning for several weeks now, even though
the neonatal clinic of McCord General Hospital was not
yet officially open.

The isolette stood near the unit's big plate-glass window. To Pflanz, standing with dignitaries in the hall
outside, the preemie looked like a baby bird, lying on
her back, arms and legs splayed. Her skin hung loose
and wrinkled, and her spindly rib cage was protrud-
ing—she had been born too soon to have built up any
healthy baby fat. Repeated sticking for blood samples
had left bruises all over the little body. When McCord

arrived at the NICU, the baby was wearing patches over her eyes to protect her retinas from the bili lights set up over the isolette to treat her jaundice. The lights were turned off for now and the patches removed for the benefit of the visitors, but a tangled network of plastic tubes extruded from her minute nose and arms, and several wires were taped to her chest.

Cameras outside the glass enclosure whirred and snapped as McCord gently stroked the frail baby, listening as the neonatal specialist beside him described the prognosis for the three-pound, eight-ounce preemie—iffy, but looking better with each passing day that she managed to cling to life. McCord looked up at the baby's parents, his eyes smiling over the mask, and then back down at the tiny fighter in the isolette.

"You show 'em, little one," he whispered.

A few minutes later, he emerged from the NICU, soberly stripping off the hospital garb as he made his way toward the lounge that marked the entry to the McCord Neonatal Unit. His entourage fell in step behind, photographers and television camera retreating before his advance. When he reached the red ribbon strung across the lounge, McCord stopped and the hospital's chief of staff, Dr. Emory, pulled up alongside him. A hush fell over the assembled group of doctors, nurses, local politicians, community activists and media representatives.

"Ladies and gentlemen," Emory began, "this day has been a long time coming. It was almost seven years ago that the city of Fargo first expressed a desire to build an advanced neonatal care unit to serve this region. For the people of this community, it wasn't enough to say that this is a small city—that we couldn't afford the 'luxuries' of big cities like Boston and San Francisco. Our children deserve nothing less than the best. And so, the people of Fargo set out to acquire the finest neonatal facility that love and dedication—and yes, money—could build. And they did it with the generous support of North Dakota's most famous offspring—Mr. Angus Ramsay McCord. This fine hospital already stands as a testament to this native son's boundless commitment to our community."

A murmur went through the crowd in the lobby and heads nodded.

"And now, ladies and gentlemen, it is my very great pleasure to extend a warm welcome and our deepest appreciation to Mr. and Mrs. Angus McCord, and to call upon them to open this fine new addition to McCord General Hospital."

A round of applause accompanied Gus McCord to the front of the room. His face became flushed as he looked around and waited for the clapping to die down, but it went on and on. He grinned sheepishly and rubbed the bump on his nose, then looked over at his wife and shrugged. Turning back, he raised his hands and made a dampening wave.

"Thank you. Thank you all," he called above the noise. But the group showed no sign of letting up. Gus passed his hand over his brush cut as the applause rolled on. Then he seemed to have an inspirational flash.

"Shh!" he whispered loudly, his finger to his lips. "You'll wake the babies!"

The audience laughed, but the noise finally died down. There was a long silence as they waited expectantly for him to say something, but he seemed to be lost in thought, examining his shoes and shuffling awkwardly. One or two nervous throat-clearing sounds rose up from the room. His voice, when he spoke at last, was soft.

"I have a confession to make," he said, eyes still on his toes. "It's not an easy thing to say, for an old coot like me. But I'm here to tell you that I've fallen in love again."

A few chuckles sprinkled the room.

"The lady in question," McCord went on, stronger now, looking up at the crowd, "has the face of an angel and a form so exquisite it takes your breath away. Of course, there are those who will say she's too young for me, that these May-December romances never work out. But I don't care. Because when I look in her eyes, I know that she is the culmination of everything that is good and beautiful in this world. Her name is Jessica Boehm, ladies and gentlemen. She is five days old and she weighs just three and a half pounds. But she's a spunky little lady, and I am the luckiest man in the world for having met her."

McCord reached out a hand to the mother of the baby he had been caressing in the isolette. "And this is Mary Boehm, the mother of that wonderful young lady down the hall." Mrs. Boehm, tears streaming down her smiling cheeks, held on tightly to Gus's hand as the audience applauded warmly.

McCord's other arm reached out to embrace his wife, who had been standing off to his left. "And this beautiful lady, for those of you who don't already know her, is my wife, Nancy. We have been married for forty years. She is my courage, my inspiration and my best friend. She is also the mother of our four sons and the grandmother of five beautiful grandchildren. We have a good life. But like the parents of little Jessica, we have known the fear and pain of a baby's illness."

He and Nancy exchanged glances and squeezed hands.

"I believe," McCord went on, "that the sheer force of Nancy's mother-love saw our sick children through their darkest hours. But sometimes, when a baby is born too soon, or with special problems, even a mother's love needs a little help. This clinic is dedicated in ensuring that even the littlest ones like Jessica will survive and grow and thrive."

There was a round of applause.

"I would ask my wife, Nancy, and Mary Boehm—two of the finest and most determined mothers I know," McCord said, "to jointly do the honors of cutting the ribbon to open the McCord Neonatal Clinic."

Mary Boehm's surprise showed through her tears, but she quickly wiped them away as Gus stepped back. Nancy McCord moved beside her, offering a smile and a hug, and then handed Mrs. Boehm a pair of large surgical shears and held up the ribbon. Mary Boehm's hand was trembling as she reached out and snipped the wide red sash. It fell to a cheer and a hearty round of applause.

Dieter Pflanz looked around the room and noted that several full-grown men were conspicuously swallowing lumps in their throats. There wasn't a dry eye in the place. For a fleeting second, he felt the instinctive bristle rise up his spine as the crowd rushed forward to surround McCord, but then he relaxed again. It was obvious that there was nothing but goodwill toward Gus McCord in that room.

Watching the milling crowd, scanning those who were approaching McCord from all sides, Pflanz paid little attention to Jerry Siddon, who had moved next to him.

"That was a neat trick, wasn't it?" Siddon said.

Pflanz glanced down at him. "A neat trick?"

Siddon waved his hand toward McCord. "That performance," he said, grinning. "And turning the ceremony over to the baby's mother. Focusing the attention on himself by seeming to turn it on someone else. Very neatly done."

Pflanz arched one eyebrow. "You're very cynical today, young Siddon."

"Not cynical, just overawed at the man's skill." He glanced up at Pflanz, who was watching him closely. "You know what I mean. This guy's tough as nails. You know it, and so do I. That's how he made his fortune and his name. But look at him now."

They both turned back to McCord, who was guffawing with a group of old cronies, his hands buried deep in his pants pockets.

"He looks like he just drove in from the farm in the family pickup," Siddon continued. "Yet this is the same man who, in a few hours, will be standing toe-to-toe with the sharks and vultures in Washington. The man who may have done more than any other American to throw the Reds out of the Kremlin. I tell you, Dieter, this is the one. This is the guy we've got to put in the White House. He's the one who can make things happen."

The corners of Pflanz's mouth angled up ever so slightly. He doesn't need to be elected, Jerry boy, he thought. Things are happening already.

When Frank's secretary tapped on her door a few minutes after she had stormed out of his office, Mariah was standing at the window, staring down on Langley Woods situated beyond the high fence surrounding the Agency's headquarters.

"Mariah?" Pat hesitated, her hand on the door. Finally, she stepped in and shut it behind her. "What happened? Frank's in there bellowing on the phone and you look like you've seen a ghost. What's going on around here?"

Mariah glanced at Pat and then stared back across the trees, denuded now of their leaves. It was a bleak landscape this time of year.

Tucker's secretary was one of her closest friends, as was Frank himself. But Patty Bonelli and Frank were also an item—undeclared, discreet. It was a relationship that only Mariah and a few others in the office knew about. Mariah wasn't altogether certain when Pat and Frank's relationship outside the office had begun—for the first few years after his wife died, Frank had been too preoccupied with finishing the job of raising his kids to have time for anything else—but it had been going on for some time now. They seemed to be comfortable with it just as it was, neither one showing any sign of needing or wanting a more public commitment.

There was no way of knowing whether Pat was aware of the covert operation Frank had alluded to. As a senior secretary, she was privy to many of the compartmented cases that Frank and Mariah had worked on in the past, providing clerical support. But Frank had said that Operations was leading on this, and they always kept knowledge of their files to a minimum. If they had allowed Tucker in, it could only be because they had required his expertise. It was doubtful Pat knew anything, even if she were prepared to defy Frank and tell Mariah. On the other hand, Mariah thought, if Chaney had stumbled onto something, then it wasn't as closely held a secret as Frank thought.

"Do you know if Frank has been working on any major cases with the Ops people over the past ten months?"

"He and George Neville have been working on a file," Pat said. Neville was the CIA deputy director for operations—DDO. "I'm not cleared for it, though. I thought you were."

"Why did you think that?"

"Because Neville was in Frank's office the other day. Frank asked me to bring them coffee and when I opened the door, I heard Neville mention your name."

"What was he saying?"

Pat shook her head. "He clammed up when I walked in. What's this about, Mariah?"

"That's what I'd like to know. I think it's got something to do with the accident in Vienna."

"What do you mean?"

"Apparently, it was no accident."

"What?"

Mariah sighed and settled down on the edge of her desk. "Look, Patty, I don't know what's going on, but I shouldn't be saying anything. You know Frank—he'd throw a fit if he knew I'd told you this much, so do me a favor and don't mention it, okay?"

"I won't say anything. But what do you plan to do?"

Mariah turned back to the window. "I don't know. But I have to find out what really happened."

With Frank or without him, she thought.

When Pat left her office, Mariah stood at the window a few minutes longer, struggling against the pain and black fury that were threatening to short-circuit her brain. Forcing herself to turn away from the window, she caught sight of the computer terminal next to her desk. She sat down and flicked it on, her mind racing as the monitor raised its greenish glow.

After a short delay, the screen prompted her to enter her password, the first line of defense against unauthorized access to the Agency's data banks. All employees had a personal access code, known only to themselves and the computer. Security procedures required that the password be changed every month.

Mariah punched in her current personal code—"SIGMUND," the name of her neighbor's cat. After the mess she had found in her tiny garden, the feline had been on her mind the last time she had changed her password. The cursor moved across the screen as she entered the cat's name, but only Xs appeared—another security measure.

After a brief delay, the monitor flashed a message: "PASSWORD VALID. FILE SEARCH MODE. ENTER FILE NAME."

She returned her gaze to the keyboard and punched in "CHAUCER."

There was another short delay. Her stomach flipped when she saw the reply: "RESTRICTED FILE. ACCESS DENIED. ENTER NEW FILE NAME."

"Access denied, my foot!" she muttered. "That's my file!"

She punched in her password again: "CHAUCER."

"RESTRICTED FILE. ACCESS DENIED. ENTER NEW FILE NAME."

Her heart was pounding as she leaned back in her chair and stared at the stubborn message. Then she hunched forward again. "All right," she said under her breath, "let's try another approach."

She punched in a new file request: "MARIAH BOLT. PERSONAL LOG. VIENNA STATION."

The cursor flashed for a moment as the Cray computer down in the Agency's basement searched its data banks. Then a long list of document titles began scrolling down the screen—three years' worth of contact reports and intelligence assessments that she had filed while she was posted to the CIA station in Vienna. As her eye scanned the rolling list, Mariah's mind wandered back.

It was never a given that she would get an overseas assignment.

Despite its monolithic appearance, the CIA is a bureaucracy like any other, with internal divisions and rivalries. The most pronounced is between its operations (DDO) and analysis (DDI) directorates. Operations officers do the overseas clandestine work, while back at Langley, analysts sift through masses of intelligence garnered from various sources—like tea-leaf readers, they try to predict the future. These two sides of the house view each other with mutual suspicion bordering on contempt. The trained covert operators regard the analysts as ineffectual pencil pushers, shuffling papers and conducting endless intellectual debates while the world burns around them. To the analysts, the clandestine ops people are cowboys, too often launching risky and ill-conceived operations that end up backfiring and smearing the Agency's reputation. Limited interplay between these two directorates only feeds the skepticism and distrust between them.

Mariah had made her career among the analysts. Frank had recruited her because of her specialized knowledge of the Soviet arsenal, and for ten years she had helped track political and military developments in the Soviet Union. She had worked on various desks, sifting through intercepted communications for hints of what the Soviets were planning next, poring over the satellite photographs of secret installations, interpreting whatever gossip could be gleaned on who was up and who was out in the Moscow hierarchy. On a couple of occasions, under State Department cover, she had attended Soviet-American conferences posing as an administrative aide, meeting the faces behind the names in the intelligence reports and trying to figure out if there were moderates on the other side who would work for an end to the craziness.

During this time, David had been building a name for himself as a brilliant theoretician as well as a thoughtful writer on the need to contain the atomic beast that the scientists at Los Alamos had unleashed in 1945. When the Soviet Union had first begun to show signs of disintegration, he and Mariah had both worried about the danger of its nuclear arsenal slipping away in the confusion. David had developed a friendship with Hans Blix, the Swedish director general of the International Atomic Energy Agency, the U.N.'s nuclear watchdog. When Blix asked David to come to Vienna to help with the job of beefing up the IAEA, he was eager to accept.

Mariah had talked it over with Frank and he, in turn, had gone to DDO, George Neville. In the end, they had agreed to transfer Mariah to the operations side of the Agency and post her to the Vienna station under cover of the embassy's administrative section. For the period of the Vienna assignment, Mariah—somewhat to her chagrin—had joined the cowboys.

The list of titles on the screen ended with a reference to the last contact report she had filed in Vienna. It was a brief account of her secret meeting with the Hungarian diplomat she had raced off to see instead of driving Lindsay to school that terrible morning.

She fumed at the sight of his code name on the screen—"RELIANCE"—someone's idea of a joke, it seemed. The man was an alcoholic and a completely unreliable asset. He had been run by the Company for years, far beyond his capacity to provide anything useful by way of information on the crumbling Soviet empire in Eastern Europe. For this bum, I sent my family into a trap, Mariah thought bitterly.

But what she was looking for as she scanned the names of reports was "CHAUCER"—the code name of the Russian physicist who had confided her suspicion that Soviet nuclear weapons were being traded for hard currency. Mariah had met her through David's office, had recruited her, had been her handler right up to the day the woman disappeared.

Tatyana Baranova was serving in the multinational IAEA when Mariah first encountered her at an agency farewell party for a departing British inspector. Lindsay was there, too, Mariah suddenly remembered with a smile. In fact, truth be told, it was Lindsay who had opened the door to the CHAUCER operation.

She had picked Lindsay up from the American School, and the two of them had run up to David's IAEA office in the Vienna International Centre on the Wagramerstrasse. There they had found an office party in full swing.

Someone had placed a glass of wine in Mariah's hand and a soft drink in Lindsay's, and the two of them were sitting perched on a desk in a corner, laughing at David playing his harmonica and the impromptu chorus serenading the retiring British inspector with an off-key and tragicomic rendition of the Beatles' "Yesterday." When the song ended, half of the chorus was on bended knee, arms wrapped around the legs of the laughing Brit, imploring him to stay. Lindsay giggled at the silliness as the inspector turned several shades of red, struggling in vain to detach himself from the grip of the clowns at his feet.

"What a beautiful child!"

Mariah turned away from the antics across the room and found herself facing a woman who was watching Lindsay, bewitched, it seemed, by the copper curls and laughing dark eyes. She had apparently sidled up next to them at some point during the song. She looked to be in her early thirties, a few years younger than Mariah herself, short and on the pudgy side—the typical result of a starchy East European diet. She had a round, pleasant face and wide-set, pale blue eyes under overpermed blond hair. Her smile, as she glanced over Lindsay's head at Mariah, was the hesitant gesture of the shy and lonely. The eyes dropped quickly, back to the child.

Lindsay looked up, a flicker of self-consciousness crossing her features before the giggles overtook her again. "That's my dad," she said, pointing at the group across the room. "He's so crazy!"

The woman smiled once more, her eyebrows rising as she followed Lindsay's finger. "Which one? Mr. Hewlett, who is leaving us?"

"No, the one with the harmonica. He's a really good player. He taught himself. He can play anything, but he likes the blues best," she confided.

"Oh, I see. So you are Dr. Tardiff's little girl. What is your name, sweetheart?"

"Lindsay Bolt-Tardiff," Lindsay said, holding out her hand, very grown-up. "And I'm eleven—well, almost." They shook hands.

"Please excuse me," the woman said, her expression appropriately serious. "I meant to say 'Dr. Tardiff's fine young lady.' I am very pleased to meet you, Lindsay Bolt-Tardiff. I am Tatyana Baranova—you must call me Tanya."

"Hi," Lindsay said. She glanced back at Mariah. "This is my mom."

"Mrs. Tardiff. How do you do? You have a beautiful daughter."

"Thank you," Mariah said, smiling as she took the woman's hand. "Call me Mariah. Do you work with the IAEA, Tanya?"

"Yes, but I have only been here a few weeks. I do not know many of my colleagues yet."

"How are you finding Vienna?"

"It is very beautiful. Very expensive," she added, rolling her eyes. "There are so many things in the shops—my goodness, I can hardly believe it—but not many bargains."

"That's for sure."

"In Moscow, the shops have nothing. Here, it is the opposite, but expensive! How simple people live, I cannot imagine."

"There's a lot to see and do that doesn't cost a fortune, once you find your way around."

"I've seen the *Lippizaner* stallions three times!" Lindsay proclaimed proudly. "They dance!"

Tanya smiled warmly at her. "Just like your eyes, lovely one. Tell me, where did you get your beautiful hair? Your papa's is black and your mama is fair, but you—so beautiful, this hair!" She ran her fingers lightly across Lindsay's curls.

"I don't know. Daddy says I'm a throwaway."

"Throw*back*, Lins," Mariah said, laughing. She looked up at Tanya. "My grandfather had red hair. I've never met a redhead in David's family, but he says there were a few somewhere on the family tree, so I guess he must be carrying the gene, too."

"Why would Daddy carry his jeans? And what's that got to do with hair, silly?"

"Not jeans—*genes*. G-E-N-E-S," Mariah explained, spelling out the word. "The kind you inherit from your mother and father that determine if you'll be big or small—have brown eyes or blue. Red hair is uncommon because the gene is recessive. It hides, unless both parents pass it on."

"I knew that," Lindsay said, sniffing. "I was just testing to see whether or not you did." She turned to Tanya. "I have hockey genes, too."

"Hockey genes?"

Lindsay nodded. "From my dad and *not* my mom 'cause she comes from California and she hasn't got any winter-sport genes in her at all. My dad's teaching me to play hockey."

"You don't say!" Tanya exclaimed. "Well then, Lindsay Bolt-Tardiff, we have something in common, because when I was a little girl, believe it or not, I used to play on a girls' hockey team at my school in Russia. We had a small league, but we were very good—at least, *we* thought so. I played goalie."

"My dad plays center. I don't play any position here because they don't let girls on the teams. It's not fair! I have to just skate around with my dad and we pass the puck. But I've got a killer slap shot," she added. "I bet I could get it past you!"

"I am certain you could," Tanya said, laughing. "I have not played in many years. Now, I just like to watch."

"You could come and watch Daddy's team play on Saturday. Mom? Couldn't Tanya come with us?"

"Yes, of course. We'd love to have you join us. David's team is just a bunch of guys from some of the foreign missions. Your embassy has a house team, too—David and his friends often play against them. But they're playing a team from a local factory on Saturday morning. It's not professional caliber or anything, but it's fun. Why don't you come and watch with us?"

"Oh, you are very kind, but I don't think—"

"We could pick you up," Lindsay offered helpfully, checking with her mother. Mariah nodded.

As she watched Tanya searching for a response, Mariah saw in her eyes that sudden fear—the fear born of dire warnings from KGB officers about what lies in wait for those who consort with capitalist enemies. And as Tanya's eyes fell, Mariah saw regret, and then a flash of something else. Anger? Defiance?

"I would love to, really. But I do not think I can make it on Saturday. Thank you for asking." Tanya looked at Mariah, hesitating, and then she turned and smiled at Lindsay. "I should be going now. I very much enjoyed meeting you, Lindsay," she said, giving her a kiss on the cheek. "And you, Mrs. Tardiff."

Mariah had unobtrusively scribbled something on a piece of paper. When Baranova held out her hand, Mariah pressed the slip in and left it there when she withdrew her own. "I wrote down the name of the arena," she said quietly. "It's near the Alte Donau U-Bahn station, in case you find yourself free on Saturday, after all. The game starts at nine. It was good to meet you, Tanya."

The Russian woman held her gaze for a moment, and then turned and walked away.

* * *

In the end, Mariah recalled, Tanya had shown up that Saturday, somehow managing to shake the KGB watchers that kept tabs on all Soviet diplomats. And that was the beginning of it.

The hockey game was the only time, apart from the IAEA office party, that Mariah and Tatyana Baranova had ever met on open ground. But as the list of references on the computer indicated, they had met eight times again over the next fourteen months.

Then Tanya had disappeared and CHAUCER appeared to be wound up. Not long after that, David and Lindsay's car was wiped out in front of the American School.

Mariah highlighted the first reference to CHAUCER on the screen, hoping against hope to find a back door into the file through her personal log. But when she hit the Enter key, the same stern message appeared: "RESTRICTED FILE. ACCESS DENIED."

6

Rollie Burton stood in the shadow of a clump of blue spruce trees, invisible from the footpath, his mismatched blue-green eyes watching her through windows that ran the length of the swimming pool. His right hand nervously fingered the bumps and crevices of the carved ivory knife handle, anticipating the moment when he would put the blade to use.

A few minutes earlier, he had been sitting outside her house again, debating whether a break-and-enter job fell within the terms of his agreement with the voice on the phone and if so, how he would pull it off. Suddenly, she had surprised him by walking out her front door and heading off alone down the footpath. He couldn't believe his luck.

He had slipped out of the car and started after her, being careful to keep to the shadows. He hadn't had enough time to catch up and take her quietly before she arrived at the recreation center, but he was positioned now for a quick grab when she emerged. He hoped it would be soon. He was freezing.

He watched through the window as she stood at the edge of the pool, wrapping her toes over the tile lip. She crouched, arms pulled back, chin tucked, eyes riveted on the lane ahead of her. There was a brief pause when she seemed to hesitate. Then her arms snapped forward and her legs launched her through the air. The triangular point of her fingers poked an entry hole in the water through which the rest of her body neatly slipped, hardly rippling the surface. He watched as her legs kicked powerfully and her arms settled into the rhythm of the first lap. And as he did, Burton experienced a flicker of uncertainty. Most dames panicked when you jumped them, freezing like a deer caught in headlights. But she was strong—that much was obvious—and she might turn out to be a fighter.

He dismissed the worry with a snort. Hell, he'd taken down trained guerrilla fighters twice his own size. Ain't no dame nowhere ol' Rollie can't handle, he thought. And he loved the look in their eyes when they first saw the knife.

As Mariah dived into the pool, the shock of the cold water cleared her mind of all but the most elemental instincts for a few blissful seconds. But then her thoughts eddied back, rushing to fill the void, as her body acclimatized to the temperature.

The Mariah Bolt who had stormed out of Frank Tucker's office that morning was not the same woman who had walked in. For the past ten months, she had been running on automatic pilot, suppressing rage and pain in order to cope with David's and Lindsay's needs.

She had brought them home by military air ambulance, had seen David settled in—first in a neurological unit for further testing and diagnosis, then into a nursing home in McLean, Virginia, when his condition stabilized and the doctors had run out of hope.

She had also lined up doctors and physical therapists for Lindsay. That was the easy part of dealing with her daughter's injuries—the hard part was helping Lindsay cope with the emotional trauma of the accident. Conscious and in horrible pain from her crushed leg, Lindsay had watched her beloved father nearly die in the forty agonizingly long minutes that it took rescue personnel to arrive and pry them out of the wreckage.

While Lindsay seemed to have coped well with the tragedy, only Mariah knew the ache and fear she held inside, the tears too rarely shed.

And then there had been the practical matters of day-to-day living to get under control once they were back in the States—painful visits with lawyers and a judge to have David declared mentally incompetent and their joint assets signed over to her. There were financial arrangements to be made to ensure that he would have the care he needed for the rest of his life—a life whose term was uncertain, given the scarred remains of his brain and body and the likelihood of further complications.

Mariah had had to buy a car and a condominium alone, and move herself and Lindsay in, making sure that there was wheelchair access so that they could occasionally bring David home. She had arranged Lindsay's school and music lessons and physical therapy schedule, and had then gone back to work at a new job at CIA headquarters at Langley. Ever since, the weeks had blended into one another, a blur of racing between home and hospitals, office and school.

Now, suddenly, a new and overwhelming purpose was forming in her life—to find out why her family had been attacked and who was responsible. And then, to make the bastards pay.

Overhead, the private Learjet circled as the pilot awaited clearance to land at backed-up Dulles Airport.

Dieter Pflanz watched as Gus McCord rose and went to his wife, who was stretched out on the sofa that ran along one side of the back of the cabin. After ensuring that her seat belt was fastened, he pulled the blanket higher over her shoulders. Then his gaze settled on her face. Her eyes were closed and she appeared to be sleeping soundly. McCord had wanted her to stay home, but Nancy was a trooper and was as excited as Gus himself about the opening of the clinic. She had insisted that she wanted to be there with him.

The angina was getting worse, Pflanz knew. She'd suffered from it for about eight years now, but the last six months she'd apparently had pains almost every day. She tried to hide it from Gus but he always seemed to know when an attack was coming on. She'd slip away quietly and he'd follow to make sure she had her nitroglycerin, but she always insisted that she was fine and he shouldn't worry.

McCord gently lifted a stray lock of hair from her eyes and watched her for a while longer, studying the slow rise and fall of her shoulders as she breathed. Then he returned to the front of the cabin where Pflanz was waiting for him. Jerry Siddon was sitting on the far side, playing backgammon with the photographer.

Pflanz handed Gus a fax that had just rolled from the machine. McCord settled into a chair and buckled his seat belt, then pulled his reading glasses out of the inside breast pocket of his jacket. The bridge piece connecting the half-moon lenses settled above the bump on his nose and his copper eyes scanned the message.

It was from the Albuquerque office of McCord Industries. The company had had offices in New Mexico for years. Millions of dollars' worth of defense contracts poured into the state annually, and McCord Industries had always received its share, providing electronics and specialized equipment to the military research and production facilities in Albuquerque and Los Alamos. Defense work entailed special security problems, and the Albuquerque office held a strong contingent of Pflanz's people. One of his handpicked specialists had had a particularly active schedule this week. McCord seemed pleased to see, as he read the brief message, that all had gone according to plan.

"Shipment delivered. Customer fully satisfied," the fax said.

McCord nodded and looked up over the half moons at Pflanz. "Good work. I'll tell you now, Dieter, I had doubts about the timing—visions of a slipup. Should have known you'd pull it off, though."

Pflanz extended his arms, his massive hands gripping the edge of the table. "It's all a matter of paying attention to detail, Gus. You know that. That, and keeping the loose ends tidied up."

"What about the local officials in New Mexico? Are you sure they won't create any difficulties?"

"They won't. We had federal people move in soon after it happened and remove all the evidence. By now, the locals know better than to mess with the feds."

"Family?"

"Kingman was divorced years ago—no kids. His ex is still in Los Alamos. She's an M.D. and she's got a life of her own now. Bowker, the other American, was single. Parents dead. Had a brother in Idaho, but they weren't close. Looks like he bought the accidental-death story, no problem. Funeral's set for Saturday."

McCord's eyebrows shot up. "Not much to bury, I wouldn't think."

"Not much. They said it was one hell of a fire. They're shipping an urn of ashes to the brother, I gather."

"I'm glad his parents weren't alive. I can't imagine how I'd handle it if I got word that something like that had happened to one of my kids." McCord handed over the fax and leaned back in the chair, removing his glasses and rubbing his eyes.

The security chief watched him. It never ceased to amaze him that a man could have a taste for this kind of operation—which McCord obviously did—and still be so sentimental. To his credit, though, McCord had never let sentimentality get in the way of the tough decisions. He'd always said you couldn't fight a war without casualties.

* * *

Her arms sliced the water like a propeller through parachute silk as Mariah hurtled down the length of the pool. As she sailed over the black T mark near the end, her body instinctively pulled into a tuck, rolled, and pushed off again, returning along the roped-off lane in the direction from which she'd come. She churned on, counting out the laps, trying unsuccessfully to get ahead of her racing thoughts.

When the computer had refused to yield to her demands for access to the CHAUCER file, she had tried another approach—logging on to the Company's biographical data files. This tactic had proven to be only marginally more productive, but there was enough there for her to realize that she had seriously misjudged somewhere along the line.

The file on Tatyana Baranova had given her nothing she didn't already know, since most of the information was intelligence Mariah herself had fed into the system. Baranova had been thirty-one when they first met. Born in Moscow, parents both members of the Soviet elite—her mother an engineer, her father, like Tanya herself, a physicist.

Baranova was married to a medical researcher living in Moscow, although Tanya had confided to Mariah that they were estranged—unbeknownst to the KGB, which would never have agreed to her IAEA assignment had they known. Leaving a spouse behind was supposed to give Moscow leverage over citizens working abroad. When Tanya was first assigned to Vienna, however, the entire Soviet state apparatus was in the early stages of unraveling, and the system, fortunately, had not worked the way it was supposed to. No living children—she had miscarried a couple of times and had lost one infant after birth. Her attraction to Lindsay, Mariah had soon discovered, owed much to Tanya's quiet mourning for her own dead baby daughter.

But when Mariah had tried to delve further into the files to find out what might have happened to Tanya—she who'd risked so much by approaching an American—she had run into a brick wall. "CROSS-REFERENCE: OPERATION CHAUCER," the computer had told her. Yeah, right, she'd thought bitterly, and I know exactly what you'll tell me when I try.

Drumming her fingers on the side of the keyboard, she had debated which way to go next. And then, without really thinking, she had found her fingers entering "CHANEY, PAUL" on the keys. After all, he was the one who had reopened this wound when he had appeared at the nursing home. A short while later, a new file came up on the screen. In the corner was a photo of Chaney—it looked like a publicity still some archivist must have clipped from the media. Underneath, the basic biographic info:

CHANEY, Paul Jackson. *DOB:* 4/2/49, New York, N.Y. *Citizenship:* U.S. *Current address:* Lannerstrasse 28, Vienna, Austria. *Occupation:* Senior Foreign Correspondent, CBN Television Network, 700 Avenue of the Americas, New York, N.Y. *Marital Status:* Divorced (Phyllis Chaney Fordham, née Martin; New Haven, Connecticut). *Children:* Jackson John Chaney Fordham (male), born 6/17/83.

Mariah nodded grimly as she read the reference to Chaney's son—he was just a couple of years younger than Lindsay. David had mentioned once that Paul had a child he rarely saw. It had done little to endear Chaney to her; it reminded her too much of her own father. By his surname, Mariah guessed that the boy had been adopted by his mother's second husband. Maybe Chaney's son had been luckier than she'd been, Mariah thought. At least he had *some* kind of father.

She skimmed through the summary of Chaney's travels as a foreign correspondent. If she didn't know better, she'd say he had a death wish. Over the years, he had covered the Soviet Union, Afghanistan, the Middle East, Northern Ireland and South Africa, winning several journalism awards along the way, including one for his coverage of the Gulf War. She'd seen his work, of course, and as much as she hated to, Mariah had to admit he was good. She scanned the rest of the file, but there was little there of interest—mostly references to interviews he had conducted with various political leaders.

But suddenly, the name Elsa von Schleimann leaped off the screen. Someone else in the Vienna station—not Mariah, that much was certain—had alerted Langley to Chaney's links to the self-proclaimed "Princess." Every other Austrian, it seemed, claimed to be a descendant of the deposed Hapsburgs, but that alone wouldn't make Elsa worthy of mention in Chaney's CIA file. Nor were any other of his numerous lady friends mentioned. So why did someone think it important to note his association with her?

She made a new request: "VON SCHLEIMANN, ELSA."

"CROSS-REFERENCE: MÜLLER, KATARINA," the computer replied.

Mariah did as she was told, then waited until the new file flashed up, with Elsa's picture in the corner of the screen.

MÜLLER, Katarina (N.M.I.). *A.K.A.* Von Schleimann, Elsa; Golmer, Lisa; Brandt, Anna Katarina. *DOB:* 11/9/55, Leipzig, German Democratic Republic. *Citizenship:* German (East). *Current Address:* Unknown. *Occupation:* Unknown. Former officer (Lieutenant rank), East

German Ministry of State Security. *Marital Status:* Unknown. *Children:* Unknown.

There were half a dozen cross-references to other classified files—operations where Müller had figured among the adversaries. One of these, Mariah knew even before she read it at the bottom of the screen, was CHAUCER.

She sat back in her chair, clapped a hand across her mouth and closed her eyes, fighting down the nausea rising in her gut. Elsa—or Katarina Müller or whatever the hell her name was—was a former East German spy. But the East German regime had fallen and the Germanys had been reunited while David and Mariah were in Vienna. And when that happened, Mariah knew, Katarina Müller—like dozens of former intelligence operatives from the old Soviet bloc—would have become a dangerous loose cannon, free-lancing for whoever would pay the price for her deadly skills.

And suddenly, with absolute clarity, Mariah recalled the special attention that Elsa had always paid to David whenever Chaney had brought her into their company. At the time, Mariah had dismissed it as flirtation, obnoxious but unthreatening, even though she had noted that other men didn't seem to merit the same advances. But *everything* people like Katarina Müller did had a clear objective. David had been targeted. Mariah didn't know why, but she knew it as surely as she had known in Vienna that something had suddenly gone horribly wrong with the CHAUCER operation.

Foam churned behind her as she made her way up and down the pool, lap after lap. Tuck and roll at the wall, balls of the feet finding the hard, smooth tile and pushing away strongly, launching her, missilelike, back down the lane. Forty, fifty, sixty laps—in her ears only the sound of rushing water and her own breathing, until at last the exertion brought blessed forgetfulness of everything but straining muscles, heaving lungs and pounding heart.

Finally, she touched the wall and stopped, taking a few deep breaths and then letting herself sink to the bottom of the pool. Looking up, she saw the ceiling lamps dance through the shimmering filter of the water. An old man swimming laps in the next lane paddled by, his flesh rippling loosely on his gaunt frame. Across the pool, a few headless bodies were fluttering and she watched the slow-motion dance of their legs in the silence.

Exhaling a long, bubbling sigh, Mariah pushed herself reluctantly to the surface. She paused momentarily to stretch out trembling calf and arm muscles, then lifted herself from the pool with one smooth motion. In the locker room, she pulled out her gym bag and headed for the shower. She had chosen her condo largely because of its recreation facilities. The center had, in addition to the pool, a free-weight room, rowing machines, some Nautilus equipment and a couple of Universal sets. Mariah had decided that Lindsay's physical therapy would move ahead faster with access to a center like this, and it would make her own life easier, too—life was complicated enough these days without having to join some distant health club that she'd never find time to get to.

She stepped out of the shower and dried off, slipping into a sweat suit and pulling David's old hockey jacket on top of that. Lindsay was in the condo doing her homework. Mariah had sat with her daughter while she ate, but had put her own dinner in the oven until after her swim. Now she was starving.

The old man from the next lane in the pool was coming out of the men's locker room when Mariah passed through the lobby of the building toward the front door.

They exchanged nods as he held the door open for her. "Thanks," she said, smiling at his bright eyes under meticulously combed white hair. She could almost feel the pores in her skin closing tightly as she stepped into the cold night air, the old man following her. "Did you have a good swim?" she asked him.

"Sure did, thanks. I try never to miss my daily swim. Been doing it for years now—twenty laps, rain or shine."

"Good for you! I only manage three or four times a week, but I'm with you—best all-round sport there is. Easy on the joints and great for the heart and lungs."

They walked together along the path. "You look to me like a real competitive swimmer," the old man said. "I've seen you in there before. You ever swim in the Olympics?"

"I wish. I used to race in high school and college. I had my share of wins but I never made the Olympic trials. Too small to make the really competitive times. I finally had to concede that I'm built for endurance, not speed."

"Well, now, don't you underestimate endurance. Look at me—eighty-two years old and still tickin'!" The old man pounded his pigeon chest for emphasis.

"Eighty-two! You're kidding."

His eyes sparkled under the lampposts. "Nope. So you just keep on keepin' on there, young lady."

"I sure will—you're my inspiration. And my name's Mariah, by the way," she added, holding out her hand. "Mariah Bolt."

He took it in his and shook, his grip wince-inducing despite—or perhaps because of—his boniness. "Laughlin, John Laughlin. You call me John."

"Nice to meet you, John. This is my turnoff. See you again at the pool?"

"You bet," the old man said, beaming broadly. "You head right home now, Mariah. I'll watch you. You never know what kind of nasty characters are lurking about.'' He stood guard at the junction in the path.

She smiled and waved at him, feeling like a six-year-old again. ''Thanks, John. 'Night.'' She turned and headed toward her own house. Somewhere nearby, a car engine revved noisily and she started. Mariah glanced back, her hand raised for one last wave to the old man, but he was already gone. She frowned, then shrugged and headed for home—unaware that the old man had rolled quietly down a hill. As his body settled in the bushes at the bottom of the ravine, John Laughlin's thin limbs twitched a few times and then were still.

Mariah moved briskly along the path, lost in thought, her breath smoky in the cold night air. Suddenly, a twig cracked in the bushes behind her. And then she heard something else—another snap of some kind, but with a metallic quality this time.

She glanced around, then launched into a jog. As she ran, her hand slipped into the pocket of David's jacket to find her keys. Winding her hand around the key ring, she lifted it out, poking one key through each pair of fingers. Her senses on full alert, she held her hand ready. The clenched fist had become a barbed weapon that she was fully capable of using to good effect if the need arose. She strained her ears over the padded footfalls of her sneakers but heard only the hum of nighttime traffic beyond the trees and a siren wailing somewhere off in the distance.

She had almost reached her town house when she heard the rapid steps behind her, making no attempt now to conceal themselves. She raced around the last corner, taking the short walkway to her house in three quick strides. Bounding up the steps, she fumbled to extract the key—it was a choice between standing there minimally armed or getting the hell inside. She chose the wiser path of retreat.

The footsteps were closing in fast now, clearly audible on the other side of the trees. Cursing her shaking fingers, she struggled to get the uncooperative key into the lock. Finally, it entered the hole and flicked over. She pushed her way through the door, slamming it behind her and jamming the dead bolt home.

Only then did she take the time to look through the peephole. A figure in a baseball cap and dark windbreaker appeared at the bottom of her short walkway, his face obscured in the shadows, his form distorted by the curvature of the tiny glass viewport. Did he hesitate, she wondered, or was it her imagination? He continued toward the road, disappearing again into the trees.

Mariah took a deep breath, then rested her forehead against the door, debating whether or not to call the police. But what would she say? That someone was walking down the same path as she at seven-thirty in the evening and maybe chased her—or maybe didn't—and seemed to slow at her walk—or maybe didn't? Really.

"Mom?" Mariah jumped at the sound of Lindsay's voice just behind her. "What are you doing?"

Mariah pulled herself together and turned to face Lindsay's puzzled expression. "Nothing. It's okay. I was just jogging and I'm out of breath, that's all."

"Jogging?" Lindsay said, incredulous. "You hate jogging!"

Mariah started to say something, but then froze at the sight over Lindsay's head of a man stepping into the hall from the living room.

"Hello, Mariah," Paul Chaney said.

7

Mariah looked from Paul Chaney to her daughter and then back to Chaney. "What are you doing here?"

"Mom!" Lindsay was obviously appalled by her mother's manners. "He came about a half hour ago. I told him you'd be back soon and said he could wait."

Mariah shifted her irate glance to her daughter. "Lindsay, what have I told you about answering the door when I'm not home?"

"I looked through the peephole first," she protested. "You said never to open the door to a stranger. I didn't."

"Mariah, I'm sorry," Chaney said, stepping forward. "It wasn't her fault. I should have called first—but my last message didn't seem to get through."

"I got the message," Mariah said, putting down her gym bag and slipping David's jacket over a hook inside the front closet. "I've been busy." She turned to confront him, seriously tempted to throw him out the door, ignoring the fact that he had at least ten inches on her.

"Mom, I've been interviewing Mr. Chaney for the school newspaper," Lindsay said, her faced flushed.

Chaney smiled. "Call me Paul, Lindsay."

"Call him Mr. Chaney, Lindsay!"

"He said he'd take me down to the TV station and show me around the newsroom," Lindsay went on, her enthusiasm rendering her oblivious to the tension crackling between the two adults.

"Well, that's nice of him to offer, but Mr. Chaney's a very busy man and I'm sure you've got enough for your article already." Lindsay began to protest but Mariah cut her off with a warning finger. "Have you finished your homework?"

"No, but—"

"No buts. Upstairs, my girl. And say goodbye to Mr. Chaney before you go."

"Mom!" Lindsay cried, her voice shifting up an octave and her expression mightily aggrieved.

"Sorry, Lindsay," Chaney said, offering his hand. "Your mom's the boss. Maybe another time, okay?"

Lindsay shook his hand, all the while glaring at her mother. She hesitated a moment and then limped off toward the stairs, hobbling up one step at a time. Mariah watched her go and then shut her eyes, sighing deeply.

"Mariah—"

She turned to Chaney and gave him a withering look. He shuffled uncomfortably while she debated her options. Finally, she came to a decision. "Come into the kitchen," she said. He trailed in after her and took the chair she indicated. "I'm starving and I'm in a really bad mood, Chaney, I warn you."

"No kidding."

Mariah went to the refrigerator. "I need a beer. Do you want one?" At his nod, she took out two bottles, then leaned against the counter, twisting the caps angrily. "Some jerk just followed me down the path and scared the bejeezus out of me."

"Are you all right?"

Mariah waved off the incident with a disgusted grimace and passed over one of the bottles. Declining the glass she offered, Chaney took a long swig and then examined the label, giving her time to catch her breath.

Mariah drank from her own bottle and then studied him, savoring the tart bubbles on her tongue. His face was made for his chosen medium, the nose and mouth regular and inoffensive, the teeth right out of an orthodontic textbook. The gray hair at his temples, encroaching on the blond, lent an air of maturity to a smooth face that might otherwise have seemed boyish—especially given the stubborn cowlick that tumbled over his forehead, tonight as always. He was dressed in the L. L. Bean staples that he wore by preference—clothing that was sturdy and ready to chase down a story anywhere on the globe at a moment's notice. The leather aviator jacket would doubtless be hanging in the hall. His blue oxford cloth shirt, its collar open above a navy pullover, was a perfect match for his eyes. Chocolate-colored pleated pants draped his long, sprawling legs beautifully.

The beer in his hand was incongruous, Mariah decided. This was a picture of a man in a Dewar's ad—a modern-day adventurer, always ready to push the limits and defy the odds, unshackled by humdrum conventions. Nice work, if you can get it.

She pushed her wet hair out of her eyes, suddenly conscious of the discount-outlet sweats she had pulled on after her shower at the pool. The hell with it—she was damned if she needed to impress Paul Chaney.

"Have you eaten?" she asked reluctantly. She wanted to hear what he had to say for himself, but first she urgently needed to get some food into her body.

"Actually, no. I came straight over here as soon as I finished work."

"Why are you in Washington?"

"I'm following up a couple of stories. I'm also here to negotiate my next assignment with the network."

"You're leaving Vienna?"

"Maybe."

Mariah nodded toward the oven. "Well, supper is just leftovers, but there's plenty, so you might as well have some."

"As I recall, 'Leftovers Mariah' would put most restaurants to shame. And whatever it is, it smells great. My mouth has been watering ever since I walked in the door."

"It's moussaka." She picked up a large knife and reached for a cutting board. She planted them in front of him, then passed him half a baguette and a breadbasket. "Cut," she ordered.

"Yes, ma'am." Chaney lifted the blade and examined it briefly. "For a second there, I thought you were going to run this through me. I guess I deserve it, the way I've been sneaking up on you."

"Don't talk, Chaney—just cut." Mariah pulled the salad she'd made earlier out of the fridge and mixed up a vinaigrette, pursing her lips as she picked and chose from the array of spices in the cupboard. She poured the dressing over the salad and placed the bowl before him, removing the cutting board and knife that he had just finished using.

"Toss," she ordered, handing him salad servers. He saluted, deep lines forming at the corners of his mouth from the effort to suppress a grin. He started throwing the vegetables around, tossing a few on the table as he went. Mariah, glancing over her shoulder, rolled her eyes heavenward. Gathering up plates, napkins and cutlery, she set these on the table as Chaney cleaned up the bits of vegetable debris scattered about. The moussaka placed between them, Mariah sat down and they began to eat in silence.

As they ate, Mariah avoided his eyes, but she was conscious of his gaze drifting to her again and again, watching her every move. At this point, she was too stressed and exhausted to care. But in Vienna, his constant attention used to unnerve her. Chaney was David's friend and David had seemed oblivious to it, so she'd told herself at first that it was just her imagination. She'd carried on as if she didn't notice how he sat up straighter whenever she came into the room, how he glanced at her constantly, how he turned away abruptly whenever David touched her. If anything, it got worse over time. Even when the overbearing Elsa had become a regular on the scene, Chaney seemed to seek Mariah out, to try to engage her in conversation, to follow and offer to help whenever she left the room in search of food or drink. It was as if he couldn't believe that there existed a woman not susceptible to his charms. Mariah wasn't unaware of them, but she knew the pain that follows in the wake of handsome charmers like Paul Chaney. Charmers like her own runaway father.

And then, not long before David's accident, it had become glaringly obvious that she wasn't imagining dishonorable intentions where none existed. Chaney had tried to seduce her one night—on the terrace of the ambassador's residence, no less. Mariah had gone to a reception alone, upset that David was working late again and unable to make it. She had stepped out onto the balcony for some fresh air and Chaney had followed her. For the first time in a while, Elsa hadn't been with him that night. They'd chatted, but it had seemed meaningless to her—pleasantries, nothing more.

After it happened, she had asked herself whether somehow, unconsciously, she had telegraphed the wrong message. Was her unhappiness that night so conspicuous? Did she hesitate for a split second too long when he pulled her into his arms? Was it her fault that he'd thought he could get away with kissing her like that?

But she knew now that it wasn't. Elsa had pursued David; Paul had pursued her. They were a team. It seemed almost too farfetched to believe, but she was certain now that there had been a game going on in Vienna whose rules she had never understood. The question was, what was the objective? And would things have turned out differently if she had reciprocated that night instead of pushing him away, as she had done?

"Did your mother teach you to cook like this?" Chaney closed his eyes, savoring the lamb sauce.

"My mother never cooked anything that didn't come out of a can." He opened his eyes and looked at her, a crease marring the smooth line of his forehead. "She didn't have the time or the energy," Mariah explained. "She worked two jobs to feed and clothe my kid sister and me. My father walked out on her before my sister, Katie, was born. I was seven."

"I'm sorry, I didn't know."

"Why would you?" she asked sharply. Chaney's eyes dropped to his plate and he shifted awkwardly in his seat. "Anyway, it's no big deal," Mariah went on, a little appalled at how much she wanted to see him squirm, to hurt him—win one for all the little gippers. "A guy who'd do a thing like that, we were obviously better off without."

He put down his utensils and sat back in his chair, tracing the curve of the plate with his finger. When he looked up, his eyes were cold. "Is that it?"

"Is that what?"

"Is that why you've always disapproved of me?" He met her critical gaze head-on. "It's not like you ever did such a terrific job of hiding it, you know, Mariah. And no matter how hard I tried with you, there was always a barrier there I couldn't get over."

She was a little taken aback. She averted her gaze and pushed the food around on her plate. "I don't think it really matters what I think."

"Maybe not. But for what it's worth, I didn't walk out on my wife and child. They walked out on me—or at least, she did. My son was only six months old at the time. I came home one day from an assignment in Beirut to find an empty house and a notice from her lawyer that she had filed for divorce. Call me dense, but I never even saw it coming.''

"I don't want to know this, Paul."

"I know—but I want to tell you. She and the baby were living with a man she knew before I came along. Apparently, they'd gotten together again even before Jack was born. She married him the day after our divorce became final. Phyllis wasn't a particularly good wife to me,'' Chaney continued, "and I suppose I wasn't the husband she expected, either. But she *is* a good mother. And the one thing we agreed on was that we loved Jack and we wanted what was best for him. She convinced me that it would be less confusing for him if I just stayed out of his life as much as possible.'' Chaney's hand clenched into a fist on the table and he leaned forward. "But there hasn't been a day in the last ten years, Mariah, when I haven't agonized over it, wondering if I've done the right thing.''

As much as she wanted to believe it was an act, and despite hating the game he had played in Vienna, Mariah knew as she watched him that the pain in his eyes was real. She nodded slowly. "Okay. It was a cheap shot. I'm sorry.''

They turned back to their food in silence. Mariah handed him the serving dish. "Why don't you finish the rest of this?''

He glanced at it but shook his head. "No, thanks. It was great, but I seem to have lost my appetite. Is your blood sugar at a level where we can talk now?''

She hesitated, then held up a finger. "In a minute. I need to look in on Lindsay.''

She left the table and went upstairs to her daughter's room. Lindsay was sprawled on the bed, surrounded by books, her chin resting thoughtfully on one fist while the other hand held a textbook propped against a pillow. Mariah glanced at the study desk against the wall—

completely unusable. It was overflowing with CDs, loose papers and God knew what else. Even the computer had disappeared under a pile of discarded clothes. She clenched her teeth and said nothing. This was Lindsay's territory, she reminded herself, mentally reciting some child-rearing wisdom she'd picked up somewhere. If she wanted her room to look like the Wreck of the Hesperus, that was fine, the theory went, as long as no major health department ordinances were infracted.

"Hi," Mariah said.

Lindsay glanced up, startled, then sullen. "Hi."

"How's the homework coming?"

"Done. I'm reading ahead."

Mariah sat down on the edge of the bed, reaching out to massage her daughter's back. "Sorry I was such a grouch before. You know me when I haven't eaten."

"You treat me like a little kid! It's not fair!"

"I know, honey. I just forget sometimes how grown-up you've become. And seeing someone in the house like that gave me a fright, that's all. I really am sorry."

"Is Mr. Chaney still downstairs?"

"Yes. I shared the rest of the moussaka with him to try to make up for my bad manners."

Lindsay shifted onto her side and picked a piece of lint off her bedspread, rolling it between her fingers. "How come you don't like him, Mom?"

"It's hard to explain. He just rubs me the wrong way." Mariah studied her hands for a moment. "And maybe when I see him now, I think of your dad and how the two of them used to fly down the rink, passing the puck between them, showing off like a couple of overgrown kids. And maybe it just pisses me off that Paul Chaney can still have that and Daddy can't."

Lindsay nodded, then reached out to slap her mother's arm, smiling now. "Mom! There's that language again!"

Mariah winced. "I know, I know. I've been hanging around your Uncle Frank and Patty too long—they've corrupted my vocabulary. Are you about ready to pack it in?"

"I thought I'd have a bath."

Mariah nodded. She knew Lindsay's damaged leg ached most of the time, although she rarely complained about it. A hot soak in the tub had become an almost nightly ritual to help her fall asleep.

"I'll fill the tub for you. Bubbles?"

"Sure."

When Mariah went back downstairs a few minutes later, the sound of light splashing and music from Lindsay's waterproof radio were drifting out from under the bathroom door. She stepped into the kitchen and stopped dead, looking around in shock. The place was spotless, and Chaney was just loading the last of the dishes into the dishwasher.

"I'm impressed," she said.

He lifted the door to close the machine. "It was the least I could do. I'm not much of a cook's assistant, but I can usually manage cleanup detail." He glanced toward the ceiling, which was vibrating dully with the beat of Lindsay's music. "Everything okay in Teenville?"

"It is now. She wasn't too pleased with me. I embarrassed her."

"The capital crime of parents everywhere."

"I guess. Do you want another beer? Some coffee?"

"Coffee would be great." He moved out of her way and leaned against the counter while she set up the coffeemaker. "She's a super kid, Mariah."

"I know." She bit her upper lip as she spooned the coffee into the filter, cursing the tears that had sprung to her eyes. Turning her back to Chaney, she busied herself with the cups.

"I was sincere when I offered to show her around the studios downtown," he went on. "I'd really like to—she seemed so keen. Maybe she's another Barbara Walters in the making. Won't you let her go? You could come, too, for that matter."

Mariah shrugged, unsure of her voice. "We'll see," she said at last, furious at the dusky sound that came out. She jumped when she felt Chaney's hand on her shoulder, and spun around. "Don't! Don't touch me!"

He retreated to his corner, palms raised. "I didn't mean anything—just a friendly gesture, that's all." He watched her face for a moment, then dropped his eyes, shaking his head. "I'm sorry." He looked up at her. "Mariah, I'm sorry about what I did on the ambassador's terrace that night. It was stupid and arrogant and—"

"—and disloyal."

"And disloyal," he agreed. "I didn't mean to insult you. I just misread the signals."

"Signals? What signals? You'd better get that radar checked, buddy, because I didn't send you any signals!"

"No, you didn't. And I'm an ass. So could we just forget it ever happened? Please?"

Mariah glared at him. Why on earth didn't she just throw him and his telegenic mug out the door? Because I need to find out what he wants, she reminded herself, and what he knows.

"All right," she grumbled. "Make yourself useful— get the milk out."

A few minutes later, she led him into the living room, coffee cups in hand. He settled on the sofa and Mariah took up an armchair across from him, on the far side of the coffee table. Chaney sipped his coffee and glanced around the room. "This is nice," he said. "I like it better than your place in Vienna."

Mariah and David's embassy-owned apartment in Vienna had been spacious but furnished in typical government-issue style—bland, middle-class Americana.

Mariah's condo held fourteen years' worth of married memorabilia. It had an eclectic decor that mixed a couple of decent Persian carpets with art deco lamps, a leather sofa, some overstuffed wing chairs and a few antique cherrywood tables that she and David had collected during their prowls around the back roads of Virginia. Several original paintings and numbered lithographs adorned the walls. The overall effect was comfortable and warm.

"You didn't come here to talk interior decorating, Chaney. Let's hear what you have to say that's so all-fired important. And keep your voice down," she added, glancing at the still-vibrating ceiling.

He nodded soberly and leaned forward on the couch, his elbows resting on his knees. "I don't know if David told you this," Chaney said, "but he and I often used to discuss nuclear arms. He taught me a lot about the different weapons systems in the Soviet and American arsenals. And I know he was involved in our weapons program a few years back."

"Not for long. He was only in Los Alamos for about three years."

"But he knew his stuff."

"Obviously."

"Anyway, over the past few months, I've spent a lot of time looking into what happened to the Soviet weapons establishment after the country broke up. Their nuclear scientists are at loose ends, many of them stuck out in remote security zones, programs cut, no food or consumer goods coming in. As for the bombs, there were more than twenty thousand warheads floating around when the place fell apart."

Mariah nodded. "Most of them stayed in Russian hands. The other republics had a few thousand, but they're being turned over to Moscow, for the most part. Most are slated to be destroyed."

"Theoretically. But are all the weapons accounted for?"

Mariah made a T-shape with her hands. "Time out. I'm here to listen, not answer questions or act as some background source for your news stories."

"Understood. I'm just setting the scene here. I wasn't sure how much you knew about this weapons game."

Mariah rolled her eyes in exasperation. "I'm not just David's little woman, Paul, I work for the State Department." The old lie slid easily off her tongue. "I do know a thing or two about this stuff, you know."

Chaney regarded her closely. "You never told me exactly what you do, Mariah. David said you were an administrator of some sort."

Mariah hesitated. Chaney suddenly looked as if he wasn't buying it and she wasn't up for probing inquiries into her line of work.

"I *am* an administrator—facilities management—but I've been hanging around diplomats for fifteen years. I also helped set up conference sites for the arms negotiations with the Soviets. And," she reminded him, "I married a nuclear physicist. We had some unusual dinner-table conversations."

"All right," Chaney said. "Then you know that the biggest headache in those conferences was the problem of verification—how to keep track of who had what. Neither Moscow nor Washington would let the IAEA in on the act. They figured they could do the job with their own spies and satellite recon systems."

I know all about it, Chaney, Mariah thought. And I know those systems aren't foolproof.

"But they're not foolproof," Chaney said, reading her mind. "We know that weapons-grade fuels and components have been smuggled out in the past. But what about the finished product?"

She nodded impatiently. "I saw your report on the news last night. So you figure some nut like Ghaddafi is snapping up these weapons from the poverty-stricken Russians to build his own little arsenal. I hate to break this to you, Clark Kent, but that's not exactly a hot news flash. Despite what that idiot Hoskmeyer told you, a lot of people are scared to death that this stuff will leak out to every madman and terrorist with a bankroll.'' She put down her coffee cup. ''What's this got to do with David and Lindsay's accident?''

''Did David ever tell you he was approached to do— well, let's call it private consulting work?''

''What?''

''Was someone trying to hire him to help build a private arsenal?''

''No, of course not—and he would *never* do such a thing!''

''Didn't you notice anything strange about his behavior in the period leading up to the accident?''

''What are you getting at, Chaney? What makes you think David was approached?''

''I don't *think*—I know. I know when. I know by whom. I'm just not certain for what purpose.''

''Who approached him?''

''That's not important right now,'' he said.

She turned away and waved her hand dismissively. Chaney let out a sharp sigh of exasperation.

''Listen, Mariah, will you just *trust* me on this for now? You may not think much of me personally, but the fact is, I've got some pretty good contacts and I'm not playing games here. Someone destroyed a guy who—whether you believe it or not—I considered a close friend. So don't wave me off, okay?''

His expression was angry and the color had risen in his face. But what's wrong with this picture? Mariah asked herself. She knew exactly what was wrong with it. If David was approached to do something illegal, then Mariah knew who had done it. But she couldn't tell Chaney that without tipping him off to the fact that she had read the CIA file on Katarina Müller—also known as Elsa von Schleimann. And who brought Elsa and David together, Chaney? You did, you bastard!

"So you think he refused and someone tried to kill him, is that it?"

Chaney shrugged. "Something like that."

"Well, you're wrong, and I'll tell you why," Mariah said, leaning back in her chair. "If that truck was waiting to plow into our car, then it could only have been waiting for me—or Lindsay, if your conspiracy theory also extends to her. But it *wasn't* waiting for David because he wasn't supposed to be there that morning. He drove Lindsay only because there was a last-minute switch in plans."

"It might have been you, I suppose," Chaney said, his eyes narrowing. "Maybe it was a way to coerce his cooperation."

"Come on, Paul—think! That doesn't make sense. Why would David cooperate if they murdered his wife and child?"

"You're right. Then it had to be David they were after. I don't know how they knew he'd be there—maybe your apartment was bugged and they switched their plans when he switched his. But it was no accident," he insisted, meeting her skeptical look.

"Give me some facts, Chaney, or take a hike, because I have no patience for this vague garbage!"

He glanced away momentarily and then sighed. "I did some checking. Apparently, the driver of the truck that hit your car was a Turk who was in Austria on a guest worker's visa, a guy named Mohammed Kamal."

"So?"

"Well, there's one problem—the real Mohammed Kamal was back home in Ankara dying of AIDS when the accident happened. I visited him a couple of months ago, just two days before he died. He told me that he had sold his Austrian working papers to some Libyan three months before the accident in order to get enough money to go home to Turkey to die.''

Mariah's eyes were locked onto Chaney's face, but her mind was reeling. "What about the driver arrested by the Austrian police?" she asked, her voice flat.

"He was charged with reckless driving and auto theft. Unfortunately, he had a heart attack in jail a few days later and died. Whoever he was," Chaney added, "he couldn't have been much over twenty years old." The implication was obvious. "The guy never intended to be caught, I'm sure. He jumped out just before the impact and tried to take off on foot, but he was tackled and held for the police by some burly Viennese citizen."

"The truck was stolen?"

"It belonged to a courier outfit named Intertransport. Except that they had reported it stolen from their dispatch depot in Salzburg three days earlier."

Mariah stood and walked over to a wall unit holding the television, as well as books and baubles and pewter-framed photographs. She fingered a photo of David and Lindsay that they had given her for her birthday the year before. David was seated and Lindsay was standing behind him, her arms draped around his shoulders. She was leaning down, her cheek next to his, her red curls contrasting beautifully with his black ones. He was holding the hands she held clasped across his chest, and they were both beaming at the camera with the same expression of conspiratorial delight that Mariah had seen on their faces a thousand times. No father and daughter had ever been better buddies than these two.

She closed her eyes and took a deep breath, then turned to confront Chaney. "Look, you said yourself that there are hundreds of blue-sky guys floating around at loose ends these days."

"Hundreds of what?"

"Blue-sky guys. That's what the technicians at Los Alamos used to call the physicists. You know—head in the clouds? Always thinking about their latest arcane theorems, hopeless on the practical matters that we lesser mortals worry about. Blue-sky guys."

The corners of Chaney's mouth turned up.

"So why David?" Mariah asked. "Why would anyone approach David for a clandestine nuclear weapons operation? He hadn't done hands-on weapons work since he left Los Alamos fourteen years ago. Why would they imagine that he would cooperate with them?"

"That's what I was hoping you could tell me."

But Mariah just sat down and shook her head. "This doesn't make any sense, Paul. David was an excellent theoretician, but he was also a physicist with a conscience. Besides which, no one recruits an out-of-date weapons designer for an operation like this. If you were planning to buy yourself some ready-made nuclear weapons, you'd hire people with current skills to handle them—mostly engineers and technicians, in fact, not physicists."

Chaney leaned back on the sofa, frowning as he examined his sprawling legs. Then he nodded slowly. "Watchdog."

"What?"

He looked up. "Watchdog—David's role with the IAEA. That's the other possibility. He wasn't being recruited for the operation—he found out about it. And he was going to blow the whistle, so they silenced him."

Mariah felt a chill and shivered, reaching up to fluff her still-damp hair. Then she rested her palm against her forehead, where a dull ache was rising. "This is pure speculation on your part, Paul, and I'm tired. What do you want from me?"

"Was David working for the CIA in Vienna, Mariah?" She stared at him, feeling the blood drain from her face. "He was, wasn't he? He *had* to be, to have found out about an operation like that. It couldn't have been through the IAEA. They couldn't get near the Russian nuclear establishment. Even in countries where they are allowed to inspect, their efforts are pretty pathetic—you know that. They haven't got the budget or the personnel to do the job right. They have to ask permission to go anywhere, give advance warning—by which time, anything that they aren't supposed to see is well hidden. If the Russians are smuggling out nukes for cash, then the CIA would be the one to catch them at it.''

Mariah rose from her chair. "I think you should go, Paul. This conversation is getting to be ridiculous." She started to gather up the coffee cups.

"Aren't you going to answer my question?"

"All right, here's your answer—no. David was not working for the CIA—not in Vienna, not ever."

"Would you have known if he was?"

"Yes, Paul, I would have known. Even if he had tried to keep something like that from me, he couldn't have. I met him at Berkeley when he was twenty-five years old, and there was nothing about David Tardiff I didn't know. He was warm and funny and brilliant and he didn't have a devious bone in his body. He'd have made a lousy spook."

She went to the kitchen, dumped the cups on the counter, then got Chaney's jacket from the hall closet. He was behind her when she turned around.

"Mariah, you must have felt it—something was very wrong in Vienna. You know I'm not making this up." She handed him the jacket. He took it but stood there, not moving to put it on. "You know it, don't you?" he insisted.

"Yes! I know—all right?" Her eyes, when she looked up at him, were burning. "I know he was nervous about something, not acting like himself. After the accident, I put it out of my mind. I had too many other things to worry about. But I know something else, too, Paul—

you were there, right in the middle of whatever was going on. So don't come in here like the Lone Ranger, trying to ease your conscience! David lost everything and my little girl was damaged for life. Where were you when things started to go wrong? Playing stupid, dangerous games!''

"Mariah, please—"

She was already holding the front door open. "You and I have nothing more to say to each other. Leave me alone, Chaney."

Rollie Burton, in his battered green Toyota, was fighting fatigue and the cold and the urge to doze. He reached under the seat for the thermos of coffee he had stashed there. He was unscrewing the lid when a man stepped out the front door of Mariah's house. When he finally noticed him coming down the steps, Burton barely had time to sink into his seat, pulling his baseball cap lower over his eyes.

He had seen the man's shadow at the kitchen window after the Bolt woman had escaped his knife a couple of hours earlier. She had taken off like a shot, and Burton just hadn't been able to catch up after dumping the old man's body. Damn that old geezer, he thought, I would have had her and been long gone by now.

This job and that woman were beginning to get on his nerves. Women *always* got on his nerves. You start out thinking they're okay, but they always mess you up in the end. He was going to have to show her what happens when you cross Rollie Burton—show her like he showed the others.

Burton squinted at the tall figure heading toward the road. It looked like the same guy she'd met at the nursing home—the reporter. As Chaney climbed into his car, Burton recognized the white Buick with the Avis Rent-A-Car sticker and had his suspicions confirmed. He should have set a higher price, he decided, watch-

ing the car pull into the road. If the voice called again
for a progress report, he might just try to renegotiate the
deal. Nobody should have to work with reporters
standing by to stir up trouble.

The downstairs lights in the town house snapped off,
one after the other. She's packing it in early, he thought,
glancing at his watch—barely ten o'clock. A few minutes later, a light came on in an upstairs window and she
appeared, portable phone in hand. He saw her punch in
a number, then stand with the phone to her ear, absently running her free hand through her hair as she
looked out over the street. Rollie slipped down a little
farther in his seat, but he was parked in shadow and
there was no reason to think she could see him from that
distance.

Her body shifted suddenly and her lips began to
move. The call was a short one. She lowered the an-
tenna when it was done and then stood for a moment,
tapping the phone against her chin.

Burton's eyes were blazing as he watched her draw the
curtains. You should have let me take you today, lady,
he thought angrily. It would have been quick and pain-
less. You think you outsmarted ol' Rollie, but you'll pay
in the end.

With a vicious twist, he put the lid back on the thermos bottle and started the car's engine.

8

Mariah watched Stephen Tucker's finger on the Formica table as he widened the circle of condensation that had collected under his plastic cup of Coke. The nail, she noted, was bitten to the quick, as always. Poor Stephen—twenty-eight years old now and still the same intense bundle of nerves she had first met when he was twelve.

Time to get over it, Stevie, she thought. Growing up under Frank's stern gaze couldn't have been easy, but you should have learned to see through it by now. Why did so many people—Frank's son included—find it so difficult to recognize the basically gentle man that lay under that gruff, intimidating exterior?

Following Chaney's departure the previous evening, she had left a message on Stephen's answering machine, asking him to meet her for breakfast in a fast-food place not far from Langley. He had been waiting for her when she pulled into the parking lot at eight-thirty. He seemed both mystified by this unexpected invitation and awkward in her presence—but then, there weren't many people with whom Stephen Tucker had ever felt really comfortable. David, in fact, was one of the few who came to mind.

She had made one or two preliminary attempts at conversation, but Stephen had covered his shyness by turning his attention to the menu over the head of the gum-cracking cashier. Mariah had no difficulty limiting herself to coffee. Spoiled by the cafés of Vienna, she found she could no longer handle the greasy fare that people downed in places like this. Stephen was a case in point. The tray on the table between them was heaped with the wrappings from his order of eggs, sausages, hash browns and biscuit. Hard to believe that his father was a gourmet cook—but then, Stephen's eating habits, like so much else in his life, had always been more about rebellion against Frank than anything else.

Watching him tracing circles in the water ring, Mariah was astonished by how much Stephen had grown to resemble Frank. He had the same coarse hair along the back of his hands, the same bushy dark eyebrows and almost-black eyes. Stephen had also inherited his father's premature baldness, although he was still raking the last few wisps of hair across his head in a vain attempt to hide his pate. And he had the same large frame. But where Frank's bulk came from a powerfully strong body gone a little rotund with the years and his own fine cooking, Stephen was just a fat young boy who had become a very large, fat man. All the planes of his body were curved, pushing against the constraints of buttons and belt, no muscle definition to be seen anywhere.

But despite a physical resemblance to Frank, Stephen was painfully shy and withdrawn, possessing none of his father's blustering strength. In many ways, Mariah thought, he still looked like the lonely, confused boy who had spent most of his childhood watching his mother slip away from him until, at the age of fifteen, he had lost her forever.

In the first couple of years after Joanne Tucker's death, when Frank and Stephen's stormy relationship had degenerated to its lowest point, Mariah and David had often taken Stevie in to give him and his father a break from each other. He would stay with them for a few days, playing with Lindsay, who was just a toddler at the time, and devouring David's extensive science-fiction library. Mariah did it to take the pressure off Frank, knowing how rough things had been for her old friend when Joanne was dying. David, coming from a big, warm family—he had five brothers and sisters of his own—always had time for one more youngster, and he and Stevie had become fast friends. Mariah secretly doubted that Stephen would have pulled out of the tailspin into which he had fallen after his mother's death if it hadn't been for David's stabilizing influence.

She lay her hand now over Stephen's bitten fingers. He withdrew them quickly, then blushed and shrugged.

"We haven't talked in so long," she said apologetically. "It's pretty stupid, really, working in the same building. But you guys are so buried down there among the mainframes."

"We've got weird shifts, handling stuff coming in from different time zones," Stephen said. "Most of the computer ops people never meet anyone from DDI or DDO."

"When we left for Vienna, you had just joined up. I've been meaning to get together with you ever since we got back—see how you're getting on—but I've been so preoccupied with David and Lindsay." He nodded again. "So how are things going, kiddo?"

"Okay. Fine."

"How do you like the Company now that you're seeing it from the inside?"

"It's all right. Just a job, really, when you do the kind of work I do, except the equipment's better than most places."

"Frank tells me you've designed and sold some computer games on the side."

Stephen grimaced. "I'm surprised he'd mention it. He thinks writing games is a pretty stupid way for a grown man to spend his time."

"Well, you know your father—he's not into high technology. It's all Patty can do to get him to turn on his terminal in the morning."

"My father," Stephen said, "is a computer Neanderthal. My sister and I bought him a PC for Christmas a couple of years ago—figured he could index his recipes, if nothing else. I also thought he might understand what I'm doing if he tried a few games I've written, but the machine just sits in his den and collects dust."

Mariah shifted in her seat. It probably wasn't a good time to tell him that Frank had given her his copies of Stephen's games for Lindsay to use. "I know," she said. "But in his own way, Frank is proud of you. He said you've done really well with your games. I think he takes perverse pride in the fact that you make more money than he does."

"A lot more." There was wicked delight in Stephen's sudden smile. It was kind of nice to see.

"I'll bet. Not bad for a hobby. Your father showed me an *OMNI* article on computer games that rated *Wizard's Wand* as one of the best on the market."

Stephen looked up in surprise. "He saw that?"

It was Mariah's turn to look surprised. "Didn't you know?" When Stephen shook his head, she rolled her eyes. "You two! Someone should bang your pointy little heads together."

"Bald little heads, don't you mean?" He ran his hand over his pate.

"Whatever. Anyway, for my part, I hate your guts, Stephen Tucker," she said, smiling. "Lindsay has *Wizard's Wand* and it's addictive. When she gets into it, a bomb could go off beside her and she'd never notice. I'm not surprised it's done well."

He began poking holes in his disposable cup with a plastic fork. "How's she doing?" he asked quietly, his eyes riveted on the cup rapidly disintegrating in his hand.

"All right, I guess. It's been rough, of course, and I worry about her. But she seems to be pulling through."

Stephen finally stopped fidgeting and looked up at her, with those dark eyes so like Frank's. "But not David," he said.

Mariah shook her head sadly and dropped her gaze. One day, a couple of months after they returned to the States, she had run into Stephen just as she was arriving at the nursing home. She'd had no idea he would be there. He had already been up to David's room and when he saw her, Stevie had been able to muster only a few choked words. But then, seeing David for the first time had that effect on most of their friends.

He lowered his head now and Mariah noticed, when he spoke, that his voice was hoarse. "It shouldn't have happened to him. He didn't deserve this."

Mariah pressed her lips together tightly, fighting tears as she squeezed his hand, breathing deeply to maintain control. "Stevie," she whispered, "I need your help."

"Help?" His eyes were bright when they leaped to her face.

"There are things I need to know. About some stuff that was going down in Vienna when David and I were there."

"Stuff?"

Mariah sighed. "An operation I was involved in."

"So why do you need me?" He wasn't stupid—he knew exactly where she was heading. And she was appalled at herself for even suggesting that he break into compartmented files on her behalf, but she was desperate.

"Because I've been shut out. I can't get access to the files. And I need to see what's in there—what happened when I wasn't looking."

He leaned back in his chair. "What's this all about?"

"I'm not sure. Maybe nothing. I won't know until I get a look at those files. But I promise you, Stevie, I'm not planning anything illegal. I'm not selling out to the enemy or anything."

"Just stealing classified files."

"Picky, picky!" She waved her hand, the effort at levity failing miserably. Watching Stephen watching her from under his lowered lashes, she knew he was weighing the risks and the debts, and she hated herself for calling in markers that she had no right asking him to pay. "It's for David," she said quietly. "That's all I can tell you, Stevie, but I need this badly. You can do it, can't you?"

Stephen's chair creaked as he twisted it on its base. "Yeah—maybe," he said at last. "It depends. Some files are easier to get to than others. What do you need?"

"It's a compartmented file code-named CHAU-CER. It started out with some traffic between me and Frank and DDO that I generated when I was in Vienna, and Frank was back in the Soviet section. There may be some subcompartments since then—I'm not sure."

He glanced at her sharply. "Does my father know about this?"

"Get serious! You know him better than I do. Do you really think he'd go along with this? He'd have my butt in a sling." She exhaled heavily. "I can't even believe it myself that I'm asking you to do this. But I need some information and I need it fast. I don't know if this file will be any help, but I don't know where else to start— or who else to turn to. Will you help me?"

He began chewing on a hangnail and his gaze shifted around the room. Then he nodded slowly. "I'll try. It may take a day or so. I'll need to work on it late, after everyone's gone home."

"No one will wonder why you're staying late?"

Stephen shook his head. "I usually work till one or two in the morning. In fact, I'm going back home now. My shift doesn't start till four."

"So late?"

"I always do the late shifts, and they're always glad to have people volunteer. Nobody likes graveyard duty, but I do. It's real quiet—just a handful of people monitoring the computers and doing the daily backups. Nobody to bother you. I get a lot more done then."

Nobody to bother you, Mariah thought. Nobody to talk to, either. "Doesn't give you much time for a social life."

He returned to the job of demolishing his paper cup. "I'm too busy for that stuff right now. There's a distributor waiting for a new game I'm working on and it takes up all my spare time. Anyway," he added, "it's not like I've ever been a party animal."

Watching him, Mariah thought back to her own youth. There's a sadness that runs through some homes like an invisible current. It had run through Stephen's childhood home, just as it had run through her own. David and Lindsay had brought her out of that sad, dark place and into the light, but Stephen was still struggling with it. She could easily understand his love affair with the computer. Machines behave predictably; they don't criticize, and they don't up and disappear from your life when you need them most.

"Are you coming to your dad's annual Christmas bash tomorrow night?" she asked.

He sighed. "Yeah, I guess. I wasn't going to, but then my sister gave me a hard time about it."

She studied him closely. "How is it that you and your father are still on the warpath after all these years, Stevie?"

"We're not really—it's not like it used to be. We're just not close. Mostly we avoid each other, except when Carol gets us together. It's easier that way."

"So how come you went to work for the Company? You can't tell me Frank had nothing to do with that."

He nodded reluctantly. "He got me these summer intern jobs when I was in college, trying to get me to focus on what he called a 'serious career'—as opposed to my games, is what he meant. After I graduated, I just kind of drifted into full-time. I didn't feel like going through a bunch of job interviews, and I already had the security clearances and they knew me at Langley. But I never run into my dad there, except in the cafeteria occasionally. Works out just fine."

Mariah shook her head sadly. "Oh Stevie—don't you get it yet? Whatever happens between people—the many things we've done and can't undo—it isn't worth staying mad about. Because one day it's over, and all we have left are memories and regrets. And it would be the pits if the regrets outweighed the good memories."

Stephen's jaw was clenched and he was silent for a long time. "Maybe," he said finally. "But I think it's too late now for my dad and me."

"It's never too late, Stevie."

He glanced up at her and then away, his expression dubious.

The lunchtime rush at Adam's Rib was in full swing when Gus McCord's entourage swept through the front door. Dieter Pflanz glanced at the statue of the biblical first man situated near the entrance. Original sin, he thought, your doing, pal. Thanks a lot. Look at the messes we've been trying to clean up ever since.

He'd spent the morning at the Smithsonian trailing Gus and Nancy before they dropped Mrs. McCord back at the suite at the Madison Hotel. The President was scheduled to meet with McCord at two.

The restaurant was just off Pennsylvania Avenue, a few blocks from the White House, but the reason Gus habitually went there when he was in D.C. was that it featured the kind of meat-and-potatoes fare that he preferred. There were no unpronounceable words on the menu like that pretentious French place that he'd let Siddon talk him into once. Jerry had said that was where all the big Washington movers and shakers hung out, but in Pflanz's experience, it was always best to meet people on your own turf, not theirs. In the meantime, he was happy Gus liked to eat where they served American food for real Americans.

Charlie Briggs, owner of the restaurant, came rushing out as soon as the hostess had seated McCord and his party. McCord, Siddon and Pflanz were at one table. The bodyguards sat at another nearby, their backs to the stone-tile sculpture of the Garden of Eden adorning the wall, their eyes scanning the crowd, the entrance and Gus McCord.

"Mr. McCord! It's good to see you again," Briggs said.

McCord reached out to shake the owner's hand. "You, too, Charlie. How's business?"

"Can't complain. Is your table all right? I had the usual ones held when Mr. Siddon here called to say you were coming today."

"It's fine. How's your son?"

Three years earlier, Briggs's son, then thirteen, had been playing with acetone and matches—one of those stupid pranks that kids pull, never thinking of the consequences. He had coated the inside of the kitchen sink with the chemical when no one was home, planning to videotape the resulting fire for a horror movie he was putting together as an English term project. He had counted on the sink containing the fire, taking special care to remove all flammable materials from the vicinity—except his own clothing. When he struck the match and the acetone blew up in his face, he had received third-degree burns to thirty percent of his body. McCord had heard about the accident and had personally sent in top burn specialists and plastic surgeons to treat the boy, and had paid for every aspect of the long treatment.

Briggs shook his head. "My gosh, Mr. McCord, we were so lucky. It's a miracle Kevin wasn't killed or blinded." His voice dropped. "I don't know how we would have managed if you hadn't—"

But McCord just patted the owner on the back. "You just concentrate on that boy of yours," he said. "That's all that matters. Tickles me pink to hear that he's on the mend."

"Yes, sir. What can I get for you and your friends? On the house. I've got some terrific filet mignon today—melt in your mouth."

McCord looked up at the owner, his expression wistful, almost pained, then back at the menu. "No, I guess not," he said, sighing deeply. "Cholesterol, you know—my wife'll want to know what I had. Better bring me the trout, Charlie."

"You bet, Mr. McCord. Wine? A nice Moselle, maybe?"

"No, thanks, Charlie. Need to keep a clear head—busy afternoon scheduled. Just soda water for me."

Briggs went around the table, taking orders from Pflanz and Siddon, then snapped his fingers and directed a waiter to take the bodyguards' order on the double.

When the owner had gone, Jerry Siddon reached into his briefcase and pulled out the latest issue of *Newsweek*. On the cover was a photo of Gus McCord sitting behind the big antique oak desk in his wood-lined Newport Beach head office. He was leaning back in the oxblood leather chair—arms extended, palms flat on the desk, staring directly at the camera, his copper eyes piercing, challenging, a hint of a smile playing across his mouth. On a credenza behind him, a bronze Remington cowboy dug his spurs savagely into a wildly rearing horse.

The headline read: *Angus McCord—The Cowboy and the Kremlin.* And then, in smaller type: *How the American Billionaire Helped Harness the Communist Behemoth—and Why Business Has Been Good Since.*

"This just hit the newsstands, Gus," Siddon said.

McCord took the magazine and examined the cover, breaking into a grin. "A little melodramatic, wouldn't you say?"

"Maybe," Siddon said. "But it's a pretty positive piece. You get full marks for being the first American businessman to get close to Gorbachev and tip him toward *perestroika,* and then moving in fast to make sure American business was first to profit when the trade barriers came down."

McCord rolled his eyes. "This is getting to be a little ridiculous. All I did was show him around some farms and stockyards in North Dakota that time he visited in '82, and we just happened to hit it off. Like Maggie Thatcher said, this was a man you could do business with."

"Yeah, but when Gorby decided he could do business with *you,* too, it may just have changed the course of history."

"Unbelievable, isn't it?" McCord said, flipping through the *Newsweek* article. "After that, it was just a matter of time. The old Kremlin guard finally kicked the bucket, Gorby took up the leadership, and the rest, as they say, is history."

He returned the magazine to Siddon as the waiters arrived with their food. The three men launched into their meals, then sat back over coffee to go over the issues McCord was planning to raise with the President in his meeting at the White House that afternoon.

A limousine was waiting when they stepped out of the restaurant a short time later. McCord squinted—it was an uncharacteristically sunny day for December in Washington, but the air was bracingly cold, the kind of brilliant cold that McCord had known during his prairie youth.

"Think I'll walk, guys," he said.

Dieter Pflanz was taken by surprise. "Walk? I don't think so, Gus. Not a good idea. Better take the car."

"No. I need a walk. I've got plenty of time and it's only a few blocks. Can't remember the last time I took a stroll through Foggy Bottom. Vary the routine—isn't that what you always tell me I should do, Dieter?"

"This isn't what I had in mind," Pflanz grumbled.

"Dieter's right, Gus," Siddon said. "You should go in the car. Aside from the security issue, it doesn't look good, arriving on foot at the White House."

Gus looked up, fixing his copper eyes in turn on Siddon and Pflanz, nailing them. "I'm *walking*, boys. And I don't want that damn car trailing beside me, Dieter. Send it on ahead. The driver can tell the guards at the White House gate that I'm on my way."

Behind his dark glasses, Pflanz scowled, then waved the driver on with an exasperated fling of his hand, snapping his fingers for the bodyguards to follow McCord, who had already headed down Pennsylvania Avenue.

"I wish the hell," Pflanz muttered to Siddon as they took off after him, "that he'd make up his mind whether he wants to be General Patton or Jimmy bloody Carter."

"It's not gonna fly, Mariah." Frank Tucker leaned back in his chair and its springs protested creakily. Mariah's paper on the Libyan arms operation lay on the desk in front of him.

"I downplayed the McCord shipping angle," Mariah argued. "But I don't think we should leave it out altogether. This morning there was a cable from Tripoli reporting a rumor of a recent transfer of guns and rocket launchers—a figure of twelve million dollars was cited. I've got a gut feeling there's a link, Frank."

"And I trust your instincts. But George Neville hit the ceiling when he saw the draft and insisted that the reference to McCord be taken out."

"Why should DDO have the final say on what goes into our report?"

"He shouldn't, and normally I'd fight it, but in this case, I happen to think he's right. The evidence is still too flimsy." Mariah began to disagree but he held up his hand. "Gut feelings don't belong in a report to the President, Mariah. If there's proof, we'll nail the bastard. Keep digging. But take it out of this paper."

Mariah frowned, and then she had a thought. Since Chaney's departure the previous evening, she had been debating whether—and how—to broach again the subject of Vienna. Now she saw an opening.

"All right then, I'm going to look into possible links to CHAUCER." If she thought she could slip it by him, she was wrong. Tucker saw immediately where she was headed.

"No way. There's no connection and I don't want you wasting your time."

"How can you be sure? We know terrorist groups have tried to get their hands on a warhead before and we know the Libyans are tied into all the major arms supply lines. There could be a link."

"Goddammit, Mariah!" Tucker tossed his pencil down on the desk. "How dumb do you think I am? I told you yesterday that I want you to leave this alone—and that means CHAUCER, too!"

She set her jaw stubbornly. "CHAUCER's my file, Frank. I started that particular ball rolling."

"It's not *your* file! It's an operations file and you—in case you've forgotten—are an analyst, not some fancy secret agent. You're back home now and those glory days are over."

"It's not that easy."

His bushy eyebrows knit together. "Is there something you want to tell me?"

Mariah's fingers snapped the plastic-coated ID card hanging by a chain around her neck. Telling Frank Tucker something he didn't want to hear had never been high on her list of fun things to do. She could, she supposed, not tell him that Chaney had shown up again and firmed her resolve to look into the accident. For sure she wasn't going to tell Frank that she and his son were planning to break into a restricted file.

"Paul Chaney came to my place last night," she said at last.

"And?"

"He said the driver who rammed David's car had stolen the truck and was using a false identity—that he might have been a Libyan. He thinks the driver was murdered after he was arrested." Mariah took a deep breath. "Chaney thinks David might have gotten mixed up with arms dealers looking to acquire Soviet nuclear weapons."

"Do you believe that?"

"About David? No, of course not. Anyone who looked into his background would realize he didn't fit the profile. He had no ideological axes to grind—never did, even back at Berkeley, when revolution was all the rage. He couldn't be bought because he didn't care about money. Although," Mariah added wryly, "if someone had a formula to turn him into a Wayne Gretsky clone, he might have sold a secret or two." Her expression became sober again. "And he couldn't be blackmailed because his entire life consisted of Lindsay and me and his work, with a little hockey thrown in for good measure. He was basically a simple guy, Frank—brilliant, but uncomplicated. Not the kind of guy who becomes a double agent. And—bottom line— he was committed to nuclear disarmament. He'd never help anyone looking to spread weapons like those around."

"So why are you wasting your time with Chaney?"

"Is what he told me about the driver true?" Tucker's gaze wavered momentarily and his silence spoke loudly. "Then it was me," Mariah said. "I knew something and they decided to shut me up. It could only be CHAUCER. First Tatyana Baranova disappeared, then the attack in front of Lindsay's school. They have to be linked."

"Did you tell Chaney this?"

"I told him David couldn't have been targeted because he wasn't supposed to be in the car that morning. I don't think I convinced him, though. He doesn't suspect that I could be involved in anything to put me in the line of fire. Chaney's other theory is that David was working undercover for the Company and was attacked when he discovered a smuggling operation."

Tucker rocked in his chair for a moment or two, then abruptly leaned forward on his desk. "Okay, look," he said, "here's the story—as much as I can tell you, anyway—and you'll forget it immediately if you know what's good for you." He paused, clasping his thick fingers together, his reluctance obvious. "Your friend Tanya opened a real can of worms. Turns out she was right about the Soviets having developed a mini-nuke a few years back. We think they produced a couple hundred of them. Weighs about fifty pounds—small enough to be carried in a backpack. Limited range, but effective, and highly radioactive. One could completely depopulate a small city. Obviously, this thing would make a very effective terrorist threat. And the problem is, they're so small we can't locate them using overhead surveillance—not like the big intercontinental missiles."

"What happened to Tanya, Frank?"

"The KGB spirited her back to Russia. She might be in Siberia or in a psychiatric institute. Maybe she's dead—we don't know. The players at the Kremlin may have changed, but for sure they don't want news of this to get out. Especially if selling these weapons is a secret government operation to raise cash. Anyway, Mariah," he continued, "there's a very tight little team working on this case."

"Under George Neville in Ops?"

Tucker nodded. "It's a small compartment. Only a few people are indoctrinated. And you," he added, as she began to fidget, "are *not* going to be one of them. I don't even know all the details myself, but we have to assume that your cover is blown, as far as this operation is concerned. Sticking your nose into it now is just going to send the bad guys to ground. You need to stay the hell away from this thing. Do you hear what I'm telling you?"

Mariah could only nod. There was logic in what he was saying, but it wouldn't stop her from looking at the CHAUCER file for herself if Stephen was able to get it. She rose and headed toward the door. Then she stopped and turned back to face him. "One more thing, Frank. What about Katarina Müller?"

A look of shock passed over his face like a sudden thunderhead. "You know about her?"

Mariah felt the blood draining from her own face. Why did she have to ask the question? She knew Frank too well not to realize what his reaction meant. How could she have been so stupid—so willfully blind to what was going on under her nose?

"Oh, God," she moaned. She leaned against the door and stared dumbly at him. "I think I knew about her in Vienna, but I just didn't want to believe it could happen. David was having an affair with her, wasn't he?''

Tucker's eyes dropped to his hands. "She was a swallow, specializing in seduction and blackmail."

"Why David? To get at me?"

He looked up at her, his dark eyes angry. "I don't know. Maybe to cause problems in your marriage, get you out of Vienna early. Or maybe they thought the same thing as Chaney—that David was the CIA operative."

"Was Chaney in on it?"

"I don't know—maybe. Probably not. If this was about CHAUCER, it's possible he may have been targeted, too. Investigative reporters can be as dangerous as intelligence agents to an operation like this."

Mariah stood immobilized, remembering how Vienna had suddenly seemed to turn sour for David. How he'd pleaded, just two days before the accident, for them all to go home. How she had smelled someone's perfume on his clothing, knowing subconsciously whose it was, but convincing herself that he had picked it up at the office from hanging his jacket too close to some over-scented secretary. And as she stood there remembering, she felt on her face the first real tears she had allowed herself to cry since the day after the accident, when she had told herself sternly that she had to be the strong one and hold her family together.

"Aw, Mariah, I'm sorry," Frank said gruffly. He came from behind the desk and put his arms around her, holding her stiffly. "I didn't want you to find out about this."

"He wanted to leave. He begged me to pack it in and go home. But I brushed it off. I told him we only had one more year—we should hang in, finish taking Lindsay to all the sights we had planned. Take a bicycle trip through France." She clenched her fists against his chest and looked at Tucker. "Why did he do it? Why did he let that woman into our lives?"

"I've asked myself that question a thousand times. David loved you, there's no doubt about that. And he loved Lindsay. Why would he risk losing you both over a woman like Katarina Müller? It doesn't make sense. The only thing I can think of is that he felt his family was somehow threatened and he did it to protect you. I promise, Mariah," Tucker said quietly, "I'm going to find out who's behind this. I won't let you down."

"I know. You've always stood by me, Frank."

"You, too. And I don't mean just professionally, Mariah. You're the best analyst I ever saw and I'm proud as hell that I was the one who recruited you." Tucker hesitated. Sentimental words didn't come easily to him. "I mean personally, too—everything you did when Joanne was dying. And taking in Stephen the way you used to do. I've never forgotten how you were there for me, and for my family."

There was a short knock and suddenly the door opened. Pat Bonelli breezed in, almost colliding with the two of them standing just inside the door. She froze, looking from Frank to Mariah and back to Frank again. They pulled apart quickly and Mariah took a deep breath as she wiped her face with the flat of her hands.

"Hi, Patty. Don't mind me. I'm having a rough morning and your guy here kindly allowed me to soak his shirt."

Pat nodded slowly. "Is everything all right?"

"Yeah, fine. I'm okay."

Frank glanced at Mariah one more time and then moved back to his desk. "What's up?" he said, looking over at Pat.

"Sorry to barge in, but your daughter's on the phone, Frank. She wants to know what time you want her to come over and help set up for the Christmas party."

"Whenever she gets there is okay—anytime in the afternoon," Frank said.

"And Mariah," Pat added, "Carol also wants to confirm that Lindsay's still okay to baby-sit tomorrow afternoon while she's at Frank's."

"I'll run her over after we visit David. Just tell me what time Carol wants her."

"Okay. I'll tell her." Pat hesitated, looking at the two of them once more before heading out the door.

"Hang on." Mariah grabbed the handle as it was about to close again. "I'm leaving, too. I'll get that report cleaned up and out, Frank," she added, glancing back at him. Their eyes locked for a moment, and then he nodded and looked away. Mariah closed the door quietly behind her.

Tucker sat down in his chair and rocked slowly back and forth. Then he picked up the phone and punched in a number.

"Mr. Neville's office," a chirpy voice replied.

"Frank Tucker. Is he in?"

"Just a moment, please."

A couple of minutes later, George Neville came on the line. "Frank! What's up?"

"Paul Chaney—he's been back to see her. He's going after the story and he's beginning to put the pieces together."

"I see. Not good."

"Not good. And he's got Mariah upset. She knows about Katarina Müller."

"Damn! How's she taking it?"

"How do you think?" Tucker snapped. "Look, George, this is no good. Chaney's got to be reined in."

"I agree. I'll see what I can do." He hesitated. "Frank?"

"What?"

"What about her? Is she going to leave it alone?"

"Yeah, she's going to leave it alone." A moment later, Tucker hung up the phone and stared at the wall. "Please, Mariah, please leave it alone, for God's sake."

9

It had snowed overnight—just a light dusting, the kind that would disappear by noon. When Mariah stepped from the kitchen into the garage on Saturday morning and touched the door opener, it was like a curtain rising on a set for *The Nutcracker*. Evergreen tree branches were frosted and sparkling in the morning sun, while her driveway lay gleaming white and spotless, an empty stage just waiting for the dance of the Sugar Plum Fairy.

But it wasn't enough to chase away the dark spirits that had dogged her steps since the previous day, when Frank had confirmed what she had subconsciously known but refused to ponder—that David had had an affair in Vienna with another woman. And not just any other woman, but Elsa. No, Mariah reminded herself, not Elsa—Katarina Müller. She moved now through a fog of anger and pain and confusion, struggling to understand how such a thing had come about.

"Lins?" she called. "Are you coming? We haven't got all day."

There was a muffled response from somewhere inside the house that she couldn't make out, and then came the ring of the telephone. Damn, she thought, Lindsay's friends again. Let the machine take it. "Leave it, Lindsay! We're running late. I've got things to do back here after I drop you at Carol's."

Lindsay's head appeared at the kitchen door. "It's for you."

"Can I call back?" Her daughter shrugged. "All right," Mariah said wearily. "Put your stuff in the car. Have you got your dress for Uncle Frank's party? Shoes? Okay, get in, please. I'll be right back."

She slipped past Lindsay and into the kitchen, grabbing the receiver from the counter. "Hello?"

"Mariah? It's Stephen. I've got that game you wanted."

Game? Mariah was taken aback for a moment. Then she remembered—the CHAUCER file, of course. "Already? Great. Did you have any trouble finding it?"

"No, not really."

"When can I take a look at it?"

"I've got it right here, at home. Do you want to pick it up, or should I bring it for you tonight?"

How on earth did he get it home? Mariah wondered. She'd expected him to fix it so she could access the file on her office terminal. All the Company's data files were stored in the banks of its mainframes and couldn't be copied onto floppy computer disks. Printed copies of on-screen documents could be ordered up only by those with the clearances and authorization to do so. But even if Stephen had managed to circumvent those security precautions, surely he wouldn't have printed off the whole file—it had to be pretty hefty by now. Never mind. She'd know soon enough.

"I'll pick it up," she said. "Around eleven-thirty, noon, if that's okay. Give me your address." She wrote down the address of his apartment building in Alexandria, then hung up and headed back to the garage, folding the piece of paper and stuffing it into her jacket pocket.

Lindsay was hunkered down in the car, arranging her schoolbag around her feet in the front seat. She would be spending the afternoon baby-sitting Frank's grandson while Carol and her husband helped Tucker set up for the Christmas party. Mariah was gratified to note that she was obviously planning to do her homework while the baby napped.

She turned the ignition and glanced into the rear-view mirror before shifting the Volvo into reverse. If she saw the new footprints that had suddenly appeared on the pristine, snow-frosted driveway, her brain didn't register them. She backed out, then put the car in forward before remembering to reach for the remote control to close the garage door. Before taking off down the road, she glanced in the rearview mirror just long enough to see it start to drop.

Rollie Burton watched the Volvo pull away, then slipped out of the bushes next to the garage and scooted under the door in the last seconds before it closed. A short time later, he was standing in her kitchen, feeling the still-warm coffeepot, wondering how long it would be until she came back from wherever it was she had said she was dropping her daughter.

Opening cupboards one by one until he found the dishes, he withdrew a cup and poured himself some coffee, sipping thoughtfully as he moved to the front door. He reached up and slid off the dead bolt—a precaution, just in case he had to beat a hasty retreat. Then, turning around, he took another sip of coffee and decided to tour the house. Let's start with the bedroom, he thought, running his tongue over his lips.

Ever since the night he had missed her at the pool, he had been thinking about her—about her body in the curve-skimming nylon swimsuit, about how she had evaded his grasp. She probably thought she was smart, getting away from him like that. Women always thought they were so superior. How many of them had dismissed him with a glance, their eyes sliding past him like he was garbage? They always wanted the pretty boys. Even the streetwalkers hesitated when he approached them, probably hoping something better would come along. Burton fingered the blade in his pocket. But he knew how to get their attention in the end.

He stepped into the hall and opened the closet. His eyes landed on a silk scarf, which he withdrew and held to his face, inhaling her scent, smiling in the knowledge that he'd soon have her begging like the rest of them. The voice on the phone wouldn't care—she'd be just as dead when he was done with her.

Dieter Pflanz had sent the Learjet back to California to pick up Gus McCord's sons. Their mother's condition was uncertain, and Gus wanted them nearby in case the worst happened. The boys were due in by noon.

McCord himself hadn't left the cardiac unit of the hospital since the previous afternoon, when he had returned to the Madison Hotel from the White House to discover his wife collapsed in their suite. Pflanz had the bodyguards doing shifts outside Nancy's hospital room until the sons arrived, at which point both he and Jerry Siddon were hoping to convince Gus to go to the hotel to rest. The two of them were hanging out in the lounge of the cardiac unit, standing by in case anything changed.

"You should have heard the President," Jerry Siddon said wistfully. "He practically guaranteed that he'd back Gus if he decided to enter the race next year. Damn! *This* could ruin everything."

Pflanz glanced over at McCord's exec assistant. "That's real sympathetic of you," he said, eyebrow arched.

Siddon grimaced. "You know what I mean. This is awful about Mrs. McCord, of course. I hope she's going to be okay—she's a great lady. But if anything happens to her, Gus will be devastated. And even if she pulls through, he might decide not to put her through the stress of a campaign."

"So he doesn't run. It's not the end of the world. Anyway, I thought the President was committed to supporting the Vice President when his own term is up."

"That's just what he says publicly." Siddon rolled his eyes. "The Vice President is an idiot. The man's not bright enough to run a candy store, let alone the country. The President knows that. We need a man like Gus McCord to clean up the mess that politicians have made of this country."

"I don't know. It seems to me that Gus can do a lot more acting on his own than tied down to some desk job."

Siddon looked doubtful, but Pflanz's CIA contact had said as much yesterday. He and George Neville had had a private meeting in an anteroom of the White House while McCord, accompanied by Jerry Siddon, was making his call on the Oval Office.

"You realize, of course," Neville had said, "that the President will never acknowledge that he knows what your boss is up to. 'Plausible deniability,' and all. If this ever gets out, there'll never be any hint that he was in the loop. But he really appreciates what McCord is doing for this country. Our hands are tied by the congressional intelligence oversight committees—we're just lucky that there's someone like McCord around who's prepared to take on the dirty work that the puritans on the Hill can't stomach."

"Well, that's all well and good," Pflanz grumbled. "But you'd better keep sensitive eyes turned away while we do what we have to do."

Neville nodded soberly. "It's tricky, though. I'm about the only one who knows all the pieces to the puzzle—safer that way. Thing is, it's hard to tell our people on the inside that they can't look at something without tipping our hand." He bit his lip. "And we've got a small press problem."

"Press? Who?"

"Paul Chaney from CBN."

"Damn! It's always the press—whining, scandal-hungry, bloody reporters!" Pflanz stood and went to the window. Down on the White House lawn, two of the President's grandchildren were tossing a Frisbee, losing it periodically to the First Lady's cocker spaniel. "Leave it to me," he said finally, turning back to Neville. "I know how to take care of Chaney."

The visitors' lounge in the nursing home had a piano. After taking David out for a walk in the crisp sunlight, Mariah and Lindsay had brought him back in out of the frosty air. He was wheezing a little and Mariah worried that he might be coming down with a cold. Lindsay was at the piano now, playing Chopin, one of the *Etudes* that he had always loved and that she had learned especially for him. David's eyes were fixed on their daughter, a smile hovering on one corner of his lips as the music filled the room.

Mariah watched him, feeling the anger rise in her with every bar. She tried to fight it down, telling herself that he had paid a terrible price for his betrayal. Whatever the link between Elsa and CHAUCER and the attack in front of the American School, the fates had seen fit to punish him for his duplicity.

But they didn't punish only you, David, she said silently. They punished me, too. And worst of all, they had wounded Lindsay, leaving physical and emotional scars on their child that she knew would never fully heal.

I don't give a damn about how bad you felt about what you were doing with Elsa, Mariah thought, watching him with bitter eyes. You had no right. I loved you. I trusted you absolutely, in a way I never trusted anyone in my life. But in the end, you abandoned me and Lindsay, just as surely as my father abandoned Mom and Katie and me. And I think I hate you for that.

Lindsay finished playing and looked over at him. David's eyes returned his daughter's smile. Suddenly, Lindsay's took on a mischievous twinkle. "Da-ad," she crooned, glancing at Mariah with a giggle and then again at David. "I think I feel a choc attack coming on!"

He grinned lopsidedly. It was an old joke between them, rabid chocoholics both. One of them would begin to moan and faint, the other would run to take a pulse, then soberly prescribe chocolate for the ailment, which was otherwise sure to prove fatal. Next thing Mariah knew, they would take off, cackling wildly, for the nearest source of chocolate. It could be an hour before dinner or ten minutes before bedtime. It used to drive her wild, and it didn't help that Mariah had an allergic reaction to chocolate that made it impossible for her to even pretend to share their enthusiasm.

She rolled her eyes now. "You two are incorrigible. All right. Here, Lins," she said, reaching into her wallet. "Run down to the cafeteria and see what you can find, and I'll take Daddy back. We need to get going soon. Carol will be waiting for us."

She wheeled him down the hall and into his room while Lindsay went in search of chocolate. Parking him next to the computer, she busied herself dusting the keyboard, finding no words she could trust herself to say in the midst of her black mood.

She felt his uncertain grasp on her arm and turned to find his great, brown eyes riveted on her, questioning, imploring. She tried to resist their mute appeal and turn away, but he gripped her tighter, his eyes never leaving her face. She slumped into a chair beside him and exhaled deeply. She couldn't hate him, however much she wanted to.

"I wish you could tell me how it happened," she whispered. "I need to know why."

His eyebrows knit together for a brief moment, puzzled, and then his expression became vacant and his gaze drifted away. Mariah sighed, then reached out with her free hand and touched his cheek. "Oh, David," she said sadly.

He turned his eyes back to her and she felt him pulling her hand into his lap.

"No!" she cried, leaping up. "Damn you, David. How could you?" She walked across the room, then wheeled around to face him. "Where's your Elsa now?" she hissed. "Let *her* give you what you need, like she did in Vienna!"

She regretted the angry words the moment they escaped her lips. David's eyes went wide, and a deep, guttural moan escaped his throat. Mariah clapped her hand to her mouth and stood rooted to the spot, unsure which gave her more pain—the confirmation of the ugly truth that she saw in his eyes, or the agony it was obviously causing him. She moved beside the wheelchair and put her arms around him.

"David, don't—please! It doesn't matter now." She held him tightly, his head on her shoulder, her fingers laced through his dark curls. He was moaning and his stronger hand gripped her arm. They swayed together until Mariah heard the clip-slide of Lindsay's uneven gait coming down the hall. "Here's Lins," she whispered, pulling back, wiping away her tears and David's. "Come on, David—*please*. We have to be strong for her."

He positioned his head against the headrest of the chair, watching her until Lindsay limped in. Then he shifted his gaze to his daughter.

"Toblerone!" Lindsay cried victoriously, waving the triangular box.

Mariah managed a wan smile while Lindsay got herself up onto the bed, opened the box and broke off a piece. She reached over to put it in David's hand, but he seemed unable to muster the strength to lift his arm. The chocolate rolled out of his fingers and onto the floor.

"Dad! Wasting chocolate—that's a hanging offense," Lindsay said mock-indignantly, echoing the words he had always used with Mariah whenever she tried to confiscate their stash.

"I think Daddy's tired, honey. He sounds like he's coming down with a cold. We should go and let him rest now."

"Okay," Lindsay said. She took one bite of the bar and then refolded it carefully in the wrapper and box. Sliding off the bed, she slipped it into the pocket of his shirt. "You can have it later, okay, Dad?"

He smiled up at her and reached his hand to her face, his finger unsteadily tracing her cheek.

"I love you, too," Lindsay said. She hugged him, then put on her jacket and headed for the doorway.

"Go on ahead, Lins. I'll catch up with you in just a minute."

When she left, Mariah turned back to David and took his face in her hands. "Listen to me, David. I love you, now and always, and I know you love me. I *know* that," she repeated, forcing him to look into her eyes again when his gaze dropped. "Whatever went wrong in Vienna, no one can take that away. Nothing can change what we were together."

His sad eyes held hers, and then he blinked slowly, once.

"I forgot to give you this," Lindsay said, reaching into her school backpack.

They had stopped in front of Carol's house in Alexandria and Mariah was lifting Lindsay's party clothes out of the back seat of the Volvo while her daughter hauled out her schoolbooks.

"What is it?" she asked, glancing over.

Lindsay pulled a manila envelope out of her bag. "I don't know. Some man came up to me in the hall at school yesterday and said I should take this home to you."

"Some man? What man?"

"I don't know. A teacher, I guess—I don't know all the staff yet. Anyway, he said to give this to you."

"Okay, drop it on the front seat. I'll look at it later."

Carol's husband, Michael, opened the front door and took Lindsay's heavy book bag from her, then waved them in. The house was bathed in the scent of evergreen from the Scotch pine Christmas tree twinkling in the living room and the spruce garlands draped over the mantel and winding up the stair rail, all festooned with red-and-green tartan ribbons.

"Come on in," he said, leading them into the living room. "Carol's just putting the baby to bed for his nap. She'll be right down."

A voice rang out, "And here she is!" Carol sailed in and hugged Lindsay warmly, then Mariah. As much as her twin, Stephen, resembled their father, Carol was the spitting image of their mother: slim, tall, light brown hair and eyes. She also had her mother's cheerful, outgoing personality—a habitual brightness that not even her long illness had taken from Joanne Tucker. It wasn't difficult to understand why losing her had been such a devastating blow to them all.

Frank's wife had been in her mid-thirties when Mariah had first come to know his family, and Mariah had liked her instinctively. Watching Carol take Lindsay's jacket, chatting away a mile a minute, she remembered how warmly Joanne had welcomed her the first time Frank had invited her home for dinner. She could have been resentful of a younger woman working closely with her husband—Mariah had seen it happen—but not Joanne Tucker. Mariah had arrived in town knowing not a soul, still hurting from the breakup with David.

Joanne had seemed to recognize Mariah's loneliness instantly and had taken her under her wing like a mother hen. Mariah had quickly become like an extended family member to the Tuckers.

"So you and Michael are heading over to your dad's?" Mariah asked Carol.

She nodded. "He just called. We're supposed to pick up a Christmas tree on the way. Pat's over there and they were going to get it last night, but somehow they never got around to it."

Michael grinned. "Nudge, nudge, wink, wink," he said.

"Oh, shush!" Carol said with a laugh, slapping her husband's arm. "Knowing my dad, he was probably up to his elbows in squid and forgot."

"Squid?" Lindsay looked aghast. "Gross! What's he doing with squid?"

"He's got a new appetizer he's trying out. It's a Thai recipe, I think, called Fire and Ice."

Mariah grinned. "Knowing Frank, it'll be interesting, I'm sure." Lindsay and Michael looked skeptical.

"He's having fun," Carol said. "Poor guy, when we were kids, Dad was always chief cook and bottle washer, trying to take the load off Mom. He'd come home from work and spend his evenings cleaning and cooking. Even back then he tried to make new things, but Stevie never wanted anything but hamburgers and hot dogs. Now Dad can be as creative as he wants."

The mention of Stephen reminded Mariah that her next stop was his apartment to pick up the CHAUCER file. "Well, we'll know soon enough what Frank's created this time," she said. "I'd better hustle. I've got mince pies in the freezer that I need to thaw for tonight. Lindsay brought her party clothes. You're still okay to take her over with you?"

"Absolutely," Carol said, putting her arm around Lindsay. "Michael and I will come back to get dressed and pick up her and Alex. I'm hoping you're going to let me play with that hair," she added to Lindsay, looking wistfully at the russet curls. "It's not as much fun dressing up baby Alex. I need a little girl to fuss over."

Michael rolled his eyes. "No fun? He hasn't got much hair, maybe, but you know what she's putting him in for this party?" he asked Lindsay. She shook her head. "An elf outfit!" Michael said, grimacing. "My son the elf!"

Lindsay giggled and Mariah smiled.

Stephen Tucker's apartment building—a drab cracker box with steel balconies and row on row of identical square windows—was one of those nondescript high rises that sprang up like mushrooms in the early sixties before community activists began to object to the blight on the pretty, northern Virginia landscape.

Mariah stepped through the front door of the building and scanned the directory on the wall next to the intercom. She found his name and pressed the button for apartment 601. When the latch on the door clicked, she walked in and headed for the elevator, casting a wry glance at the droopy ficus tree that filled one corner of the lobby, its leaves yellowing at the tips, its pot sprinkled with cigarette butts. Stepping off the elevator at the sixth floor, she spotted Stephen standing in a doorway just to her left, his bulk blocking most of the opening.

"Hi," she said, heading toward him. "You must be beat. I realized as I was driving over here that you can't have had more than a few hours' sleep the last couple of days. We can't go on meeting like this."

"It's okay. Come on in."

The inside of his apartment was as uninspired as the lobby promised. While the sunlight streaming through the windows made a valiant effort to brighten the place, in the end it only drew attention to the dust on the vinyl blinds and the fact that the off-white Berber carpet needed a good shampooing. There was a sagging brown sofa and armchair in the living room, a stained oak coffee table littered with magazines, a stereo against the wall and little else by way of furniture. The monotony of the white walls was relieved only by a few colorful posters advertising computer games—*Sleuth* and *Super Sleuth, Castle Keep, Dinowarriors* and, of course, *Wizard's Wand.*

Mariah peered at the posters. "Are all of these your games?"

Stephen nodded. "There's another one coming out in a couple of months—*Wizard's Weapon.* It's based on *Wand,* but more complex. They're doing a really sharp poster for that one. The distributor says the advance orders for the game are rolling in like crazy."

"This is incredible, Stevie," Mariah said, suddenly seeing him in a whole new light. "You're a one-man computer games empire. How is it that you haven't been profiled in *People* magazine or *Fortune* or somewhere?"

"No way. I write them under a pseudonym and the distributor handles all the advertising and media hype."

"One of these days, you're going to have to quit hiding that light under a bushel, Stephen Tucker," she scolded. "This is a real talent you have."

"It's only kid games," he said, turning away with a shrug. "No big deal. I just made some coffee. You want some?"

She followed him into the kitchen. "No, thanks—you go ahead, though. It is *too* a big deal, Stephen. I'm not really into computer games, but I know from watching Lindsay and her friends that the competition is stiff. There are a lot of games out there. Yours must be great to be doing so well."

"It's just a stupid hobby," he said dismissively, picking through a sinkful of dirty dishes until he found a cup. He rinsed it briefly under the tap and then filled it with coffee, dropped in three teaspoons of sugar from a canister on the counter and reached into the fridge for cream. As he added it to his cup, Mariah saw Cokes, catsup, the remainders of a pizza and little else in the refrigerator.

"I still think you're too modest by half," she said, turning away. There was an old card table and chairs in the kitchen that she remembered having seen at his parents' house years ago. Then she noticed the oven and stopped cold. "Stevie, why do you have cereal boxes in your oven?"

He glanced at the wall-mounted oven, the Froot Loops and Frosted Flakes clearly visible through the glass door. "Easy to find. I eat breakfast at two or three in the morning when I get home from work, at which point I'm not too alert."

Mariah stared at him blankly, then burst out laughing. "You're a nut, you know that?"

"I'm sure my father agrees with you," he said, frowning.

"It's not a criticism, Stephen. The world needs all the eccentrics it can get. God knows, the so-called normal types haven't done much of a job running things. You're unique, my friend—don't ever change."

His color deepened and his dark eyes shifted away. "Come on. I'll show you what I got for you."

She followed him out of the kitchen, across the living room and into the bedroom. If the decor of the rest of the apartment was early garage sale, the bedroom, aside from the rumpled bed shoved against the wall, was a high-tech warehouse. A quick glance revealed two PCs—an IBM and a Macintosh—a laser printer, a modem, a fax machine, a strange-looking keyboard with dozens of buttons and slides, and several other pieces of equipment that Mariah couldn't begin to identify, with cables running everywhere linking it all together.

"Holy smoke!" she said. "This is an incredible setup. What's this thing?" She ran her fingers along the complicated keyboard.

"Digital sampler," Stephen explained. "I use it to create some of the audio effects and voices for the games."

Mariah shook her head in amazement. Her gaze continued its circuit around the room until it came to rest on two photographs taped over his bed. One was a picture of Joanne, Stephen's mother. The other, Mariah realized as she moved closer to examine it, was a shot that she herself had taken one day when a much younger Stephen and David were playing chess in her dining room. Stevie was grinning mischievously as David pondered his next move, an amused but bedeviled frown creasing his forehead.

"I forgot about this picture," she said quietly. "Those were good times." Stephen came over and smoothed the tape holding up the picture. "You miss him, too, don't you, Stevie?"

He nodded silently, then walked to the IBM and turned it on. As the screen began to glow, he opened a small safe in the corner and pulled out a box of floppy disks. "You said Lindsay plays these games, so I assume you've got a PC with a mouse or joystick at home?" Mariah nodded. Stephen held up a diskette to show her. It had a commercial label on it for *Dinowarriors*. "This is a modified disk—not the off-the-shelf game," he said.

He slipped it in the disk drive, and a moment later an animated prehistoric scene appeared, featuring cavemen riding on the backs of dinosaurs, doing something that resembled jousting. Battle music and loud grunts and roars filled the room.

"Of course, this game is scientifically inaccurate," Stephen said over the noise, watching the battle on the monitor. "Dinosaurs were extinct sixty million years before humans appeared."

Mariah watched his face, the dark eyes locked on the figures on the screen. It was his little world, a world he had created—a world he controlled. But it wasn't what she had come to see. "Stevie, what are we doing?"

"Patience," he chided. "Watch." He reached for the computer mouse and moved the cursor on the screen to the menu at the top, bringing it to stop on the Quit Game command. "You click the button on the mouse and *hold* it down for a count of ten, release, then do it one more time. Got that? Otherwise the system just shuts down."

Mariah nodded, then watched him click the mouse as he had told her to do. A moment later, the dinosaurs disappeared and the noise died away. In their place came the familiar format of a CIA operations file index, with the code name CHAUCER as well as the security classification clearly indicated in the upper right-hand corner.

Mariah gasped. "My God, Stevie! How did you do this?" His grin was subtle and a trifle smug. She folded her arms across her chest. "Look—I'm no expert, but I'm not exactly computer illiterate, either," Mariah said. "I happen to know the Company doesn't use floppy disk computers precisely because if it did, people would be walking out with files every day. How did you copy this stuff?"

"A little creative wiring between my terminal at work and my laptop computer," he said, reaching out with his stockinged toe to tap a case on the floor.

"You can't take a laptop into the building, especially not in your area, I'm sure." She peered at him closely. "Can you?"

"You don't want to know."

"No, I guess not—oh hell, yes I do!"

Tell me about it, Mariah thought grimly. "How about you, Tanya? Do you have children?" A shadow passed over Tanya's pretty, round face, and she turned to watch the players on the ice. "I'm sorry. I didn't mean to pry."

Tanya was silent for a moment. Then she shook her head and sighed deeply. "I had a child," she said quietly. "A baby girl." She looked down at the hands she was wringing. "She died when she was two."

"Tanya, how awful! I'm so sorry."

Their eyes met and Mariah saw an unhappy woman desperate to confide something. Why Baranova had picked her, she couldn't guess.

"She was sick from the day she was born. Her skin was yellow—her liver was damaged. And she was mentally retarded," she added quietly. "It was fortunate she died young, perhaps, because she would have had a very difficult life. But she was still a beautiful baby." Baranova's eyes were bright as she turned her gaze back to the rink. Mariah doubted that she was focusing on the noisy action down there. She waited while Tanya composed herself. "It was my fault," she said finally, looking again at Mariah. "Something is wrong with me—something inside. I had two miscarriages before my baby was born. They said the fetuses were deformed."

Mariah began to protest, horrified at the guilt this woman was inflicting on herself. "But that doesn't mean—"

"No, you don't understand. My father was a nuclear physicist, like me—like Dr. Tardiff. He was involved in designing nuclear weapons for the Soviet military. I grew up in a secret community where there was a weapons facility. I left when I went to university. But many people who grew up in that town have since had health problems—cancers, miscarriages, infertility."

Mariah's eyes grew wide as she realized what the woman was saying.

"It was the radioactive materials they were working with. The safety measures were inadequate. Old nuclear reactors and waste were just dumped in lakes where we swam, or buried in fields where we played as children."

"Oh, no," Mariah breathed.

Tanya's eyes flashed angrily. "Those brilliant scientists! They could build weapons of great complexity and terrible beauty, but they couldn't keep their children safe."

Blue-sky guys, Mariah thought, grimacing.

Tanya turned to her anxiously. "Mrs. Tardiff—"

"Mariah."

"Mariah," Tanya repeated, a smile flickering across her features before being replaced again by a nervous frown. "I wanted to talk to Dr. Tardiff, but I do not dare approach him at the IAEA offices. There are other Russians there. Some of them are KGB—they are everywhere. It was very difficult for me even today to get away by myself."

"Why do you want to talk to David?"

"Because your people need to know. My government is desperate for hard currency. There are powerful people who will do anything—they have no conscience. Our security people," she added, dropping her voice, "they tell us that all Americans in the U.N. are CIA agents. But even if he is, I know Dr. Tardiff is a good man." She glanced at Lindsay and then to Mariah. "A man with a family like yours, I feel I can trust."

Mariah cast her eyes around the arena, studying the few spectators, but they all seemed to be concentrating on the action on the ice. Lindsay was engrossed in the game, too, oblivious to the grave conversation taking place between her mother and Tanya. Mariah looked back to Baranova, who was biting her lip anxiously.

Leaning forward, she pretended to watch the hockey game. She glanced again at Tanya and gave her head a brief nod in the direction of the ice. The other woman also leaned forward.

"Let's pretend we're discussing the fine points of the game here, okay?" Tanya nodded and focused on the rink. Mariah pointed a finger in the direction of the players, as if she were explaining a play. "I can help you, Tanya," she whispered. "You were right not to approach David. Don't—not ever. It could be very dangerous, for you and for him."

She heard Tanya's sharp intake of breath and saw her coat sleeve tremble but, to her credit, Tanya kept her cool, even applauding as David's team scored another goal. When the noise died down, and Lindsay finished clapping them on the back, Mariah carried on.

"Where did you tell people you were going when you came out today?"

"To the Hofburg Museum."

"Good—now here's what you'll do. Do you know the café called *Wienerhaus?* It's a little place, just a couple of doors from your office."

"Yes, I know it."

"All right. Today's Saturday. Starting Monday, make sure you walk past it every morning on your way to work. Look at the doorframe, the bottom left corner. Bottom left, got that? Look for a green thumbtack. When you see it, leave the office early and go to the Hofburg Museum between three and four in the afternoon."

"Where in the museum? It's very large."

"Don't worry about that. You'll be spotted."

"What if I cannot get away?"

"Then go the next day, or the next. But always between three and four, okay? Someone will come up to you in the museum and ask for the time. When you tell them, they'll ask if you've seen Montezuma's feather crown at the ethnological museum. That's how you'll know it's the right person.''

"Feather crown," Tanya repeated. "And then?"

"You'll be told what to do next." Mariah glanced at Tanya, whose eyes were open wide and fixed unblinking on the ice. She reached out and gave the woman's arm a quick squeeze. "Don't be afraid, Tanya. The person who meets you will tell you how to get to a safe place to talk. You'll be fine, I promise."

Tanya blinked and looked at Mariah, then nodded.

Oh, Tanya, Mariah thought bitterly as she turned into her driveway, who was I to promise you'd be safe? I turned out to be as bad as the blue-sky guys. In the end, I couldn't protect you or my family.

Up in her bedroom, Rollie Burton heard the hum of the garage door opening.

After Mariah left with Lindsay, he had gone through every room in the house, checking the layout. Eventually, he had gone back to her bedroom to wait, amusing himself by rummaging through her drawers, fingering her lingerie, holding it up against his acne-scarred face, breathing it in.

He moved to the window now. Standing at the corner, out of sight, he watched as the Volvo pulled up the driveway below and disappeared into the garage. A moment later, the car door slammed. From the kitchen, he heard the inside door close and then a series of beeps. He froze at the sound of voices until he remembered that the phone had rung twice since he had entered the house a couple of hours earlier. She was playing back the messages on the answering machine—the callers had sounded like kids, he recalled.

Reaching into his pocket for the ivory-handled knife, he padded silently across the carpet to the door of the bedroom, listening to her movements downstairs. He would wait, he decided. With luck, she would come upstairs soon. If not, he'd go down and get her.

10

After checking the messages on the answering machine, Mariah went to the front hall to hang her coat and then returned to the kitchen. There was a cup sitting on the counter next to the sink. She picked it up and opened the dishwasher, which was empty except for the dishes she and Lindsay had used at breakfast. She glanced at the cup that she had used that morning, which sat in the rack, then at the cup in her hand, a puzzled frown creasing her forehead. It seemed out of place. Then she shrugged and loaded the second cup in the machine, shutting the door.

Her purse was sitting on the kitchen table, Stephen's diskette inside. Mariah checked her watch—almost one o'clock. She went to the freezer and pulled out the mince pies she had baked earlier in the week for Frank's party. She had been planning to spend the afternoon making a *Bûche de Nöel*—a Yule log cake—as an added surprise, but the CHAUCER file was more pressing. First the file, then the cake, she decided. The computer was up in Lindsay's room.

As she picked up her purse, her glance fell on the large manila envelope that Lindsay had brought home from school. She put her handbag down again and took up the envelope, examining her name on the outside, then moved to the drawer near the telephone to find the letter opener. The blade sliced the flap cleanly. Giving the envelope a tip and a shake, she held out her hand to catch the contents as they slid out.

During the few months she had lived with David in New Mexico, Mariah had often seen tarantulas on sale in tourist shops. They were usually embedded in Plexiglas, mummified souvenirs of one of the desert's less lovable residents. The only live ones she had ever seen were in exotic pet stores, but she had never gotten over the dread that one of the arachnid monsters would show up in their Los Alamos apartment one day. Even now, a mere photo of the hairy beast would send shivers down her spine.

So when the black, hairy thing fell out of the envelope and landed on her outstretched hand, she screamed and leaped back, dropping both the envelope and the creature. The envelope landed on the floor on top of it. Mariah stood wedged against the kitchen counter, staring at the floor in openmouthed horror, waiting for it to crawl out.

When nothing happened after a few seconds, she slipped around the walls to the broom closet, her eyes never leaving the manila envelope. Pulling out the broom, she gripped it by the handle with both hands and raised it to waist level, bringing it down hard, over and over, on the envelope. Then, cautiously, she turned the broom around in her hands, using the handle to slide the envelope off the remains of what lay underneath. She expected a sticky mess, but the paper slid easily away from the black, hairy whorl. Mariah gripped the broom and frowned, then peered more closely. Finally, she bent down and prodded it with the broom handle before her fingers reached out and picked it up.

It wasn't a tarantula. It wasn't a spider at all. It was hair—a few curls of black hair flecked, she saw as she examined it, with gray. Mariah stared at her palm and at the familiar dark locks lying there. It was David's hair, she was certain. Then her gaze drifted back to the envelope. Shifting the broom handle under her arm, she picked up the envelope and stood again.

She turned it over and looked at her name typed on the outside: MARIAH BOLT. Not Tardiff. Not Mrs. Bolt-Tardiff, as mail from Lindsay's school usually came addressed, but her own name—the name she used professionally.

She peered into the open end of the envelope and realized that there was something else in there—several stiff sheets of paper, which she gripped between her thumb and forefinger and withdrew. They were three eight-and-a-half-by-eleven photographs. Grainy, the kind shot under low light conditions. A man and a woman, naked, on a bed, in various positions of love-making. She had long blond hair. His was dark, curly. In all three photos, both faces were clearly identifiable.

David and Elsa.

Upstairs, Rollie Burton had heard her scream and his senses had gone on full alert. The blade snapped open in his hand as he edged out into the hall, listening. He crept toward the top of the stairs and peered down, but there was no way to see into the kitchen from that vantage point.

A repeated banging noise brought him to a halt again, straining to hear over the sound of his heart pounding in his ears and the muffled shouts of children playing on the road outside. Downstairs, the banging stopped and then there was silence again.

He gripped the blade tightly and started down the stairs, balls of his feet descending silently onto the treads, one by one, pausing to listen after each step, his back plastered against the wall.

When she cried out again—a deep, primal, choking sob, like an animal mortally wounded—he felt his blood run cold. *What the hell is going on down there?* he wondered.

* * *

Mariah swallowed the anguished scream that had risen in her throat and slumped into a chair, dropping the photographs on the table. They lay there, splayed out, mocking and sinister.

It was one thing to know that David had been having an affair with Elsa. To feel the hurt. To imagine how it had happened. To remember the lies she had told herself the nights David had said he was working late, when she had known instinctively something was amiss.

It was another thing altogether to be confronted with the tangible evidence of his betrayal. To see David touching that woman in ways he should never have touched anyone but her. To see Elsa's smug smile as she wielded her power over him. To see, in one photo, David's beautiful eyes looking up at her crouched over him, pleading with her for something that Mariah apparently had not been able to give him.

She closed her eyes and clenched her fists, fighting down nausea, pushing away the pain and anger, willing herself to put it into the compartment where she had locked the other hurts in her life, reaching instead for the strength to analyze what this meant. Why had she been sent the envelope? Why now? Her eyes snapped open. How had a teacher at Lindsay's school come into possession of these photos?

No, she reminded herself, not a teacher—a man Lindsay hadn't recognized. But who? Why did he want Mariah to see the pictures? And why have Lindsay deliver them, instead of sending them directly to Mariah herself?

To prove a point, Mariah realized. To prove that they knew where to find her child and that she was vulnerable. And not just Lindsay, she thought, looking at the dark locks still clasped in her fist. David, too.

It was a game of terror they were playing with her, teasing, threatening. But *who?* And what did they want her to do? Or not do, she suddenly thought. What are the rules here? How do I know how to play along if I don't know the rules or objectives of the game?

There was only one objective as far as she was concerned, Mariah thought grimly. To protect her family. Lindsay was probably safe for the moment, over at Carol's, but she should call Frank anyway, ask him to go and get her and take her back to his place.

And David. David was a sitting duck in the nursing home. Someone had been there once already, she realized, tightening her hand over the hair in her fist. It was easy enough to do. There was no security to speak of at the home. Getting past the receptionist and the nurses' station was simple—Mariah had often passed by unnoticed when staff was preoccupied with the telephones or a patient or visitor.

She rose from the chair and went to the trash bin under the sink, dumping the hair into it. Then she propped the broom against the counter and turned to the phone. Before she phoned Frank, she would call the nursing home and ask if anyone had noticed any new visitors over the last couple of days. Ask them to keep an eye on David—maybe move him closer to the nurses' station. She picked up the phone and searched for the number of the home.

"Hang it up, pretty lady."

At the sound of the voice, Mariah dropped the receiver. It clattered on the counter as she spun around.

"I said, hang it up," Burton repeated. He was standing in the doorway between the kitchen and the front hall. Mariah stared at his pockmarked face. Then his hand moved and she spotted the glint of the blade. She reached behind and her hand groped along the counter, her eyes never leaving him. When she located the receiver, she hung it back in the wall cradle.

"Who are you?"

But he just smiled.

"Do you want money? I haven't got much cash on hand, but there are credit cards in my purse right beside you. Help yourself and then get out."

"Get out? Aren't you the bossy one?" He shook his head. "I don't think so."

"What do you want?"

"I want you, Mariah."

Her stomach dropped as she watched his eyes move down her sweater. Strange eyes, mismatched, she realized. One blue, one green. "How do you know my name?" she whispered.

His eyes moved up to her face and he licked his lips. "I know a lot about you, Mariah. I know where you go. I know what you do. Seen you without all those clothes on."

"You followed me from the pool the other night."

"Yeah. I almost had you, too. That old man—I was real annoyed."

"What do you want?"

But he only smiled again. Then his gaze fell on the photos on the table. He stepped closer to them, keeping the knife in front of him where she could see it. "Nice pictures," he said, picking one up and examining it. "You like looking at pictures like these, Mariah?"

"No."

He snorted. "Sure you do. You buy these, or is this someone you know?" She said nothing, only glared. His head snapped up. "I asked you a question!"

"Someone sent them to me."

"Kinky friends you've got. But a woman like you, Mariah, I bet you'd rather do it than look at it, wouldn't you? Me, too." She gritted her teeth. He put the picture back down on the table and turned to her. "I know what you need, Mariah," he said, a slow grin rising on his thin lips. "You're all alone. You need a man."

The fury exploded in her so suddenly that she caught him off guard. Her hand grabbed the broom, still propped next to her against the counter, and she lunged. As the end of the handle embedded itself in his solar plexus, he doubled over. The knife fell out of his hand and clacked along the floor. She pulled back and then lunged again. It was a mistake—he dodged and the broom handle glanced off his shoulder. He reached up, grabbing it before she could pull it away. There was a split second when they stood face-to-face, and Mariah saw the cold anger in his terrible, mismatched eyes.

"You bitch! I'm gonna kill you!"

She slipped her hands down the broom handle and shoved it sideways at him, knocking him off balance for a second. He stumbled, then regained his footing and threw the broom aside.

Leaping back, she grabbed the glass coffeepot off the counter and hurled it at him. He ducked and it smashed against the wall, coffee and glass shards flying.

Mariah turned to the door to the garage, yanking at the handle. The door started to open, but he threw himself against her back and it slammed shut again. She gasped, the wind knocked out of her. He held her for a moment, pinned to the door.

Then she felt him grab her hair at the crown. He yanked so hard that she lost her balance, falling backward against him. She felt him start to go down with her, then he slipped his body out of the way and she hit the floor with a bang on her tailbone.

"Get up!" he growled, still pulling on her hair. He grabbed her sweater with his free hand and dragged her across the floor. When he stopped, he let go of her sweater, but before she could move to try to loosen his grip on her hair, he yanked her head back farther. She felt his knee in her spine and the blade at her throat.

"You're dead, lady!"

"Don't! Please!" She winced as he pulled her hair harder, but he hesitated. "I have a child," Mariah pleaded breathlessly. "She needs me—she doesn't have her father anymore. I'll do whatever you want, but please don't kill me." She closed her eyes, chest heaving, praying that his rage would subside. He loosened his grip slightly but the blade stayed at her throat.

"Get up!" he said finally.

He held on to her as she scrambled awkwardly to her feet, the knife nicking her throat. She closed her eyes and waited, shaking uncontrollably, feeling a warm trickle of blood slide down her neck and into her sweater.

He slammed her up against the table. His hot breath was on her neck, coming hard and fast, his body pressed up behind hers. Even without seeing his face, she knew he was looking over her shoulder at the photos.

"Upstairs," he rasped in her ear. "Now—in the bedroom. And if you try anything else, I'll kill you."

He yanked her back and turned her toward the hall, pushing her ahead of him up the stairs.

When he heard the siren behind him and saw the red light flashing in the rearview mirror, Paul Chaney glanced at the speedometer. He was doing almost eighty. "Damn!"

He took his foot off the accelerator and applied the brake, pulling onto the shoulder of the beltway when his speed had dropped to a safe level. He turned off the ignition and reached for his wallet, glancing in the mirror as the police car came up behind him and the patrolman got out. Chaney lowered the window and removed his sunglasses.

"'Afternoon, sir," the officer said, ominous behind his own black shades. "May I see your license and registration, please?"

"Right here, Officer." Chaney held up the wallet.

"Take your license out of the wallet, please. And pass me the registration papers, as well."

"The car's rented. I think the papers are in the glove compartment."

"Get them, please."

Chaney nodded, withdrawing his license and passing it over, then leaned toward the glove compartment. He rummaged around and found the rental folder. As he sat up once more, he noticed the officer was standing with one hand on his hip. No, Chaney thought, not on his hip—on his gun, the eyes behind the dark glasses no doubt watching his every move. What a job these guys had, never knowing when some wacko might pull a gun on them.

"Sorry, Officer. Guess I was going a little too fast."

"Yes, sir. I clocked you doing eighty-one miles an hour."

"Eighty-one? Really? I didn't think it was that fast. Speedometer must not be working right."

"The limit's fifty-five, sir," the cop said dryly. Chaney sighed and nodded. "Wait in the car, please." The patrolman returned to his cruiser to check the computer for priors.

Chaney leaned back in the seat and rubbed his eyes. What else could go wrong? he wondered.

His meeting to discuss his next assignment with Mort Rosen, CBN's news and current affairs VP, had been postponed the previous day. Then Rosen had called Chaney early that morning at his hotel and asked to meet for breakfast. He had headed to the restaurant, confident that Rosen was going to offer him the Washington bureau chief job that he'd been lobbying for. Instead, Rosen had dropped a bombshell. They were letting him go.

"You can't fire me!" Chaney had protested incredulously. "I'm one of the best reporters on this network. I've won more awards than you can shake a stick at and have one of the highest recognition factors in the business."

Rosen had shifted uncomfortably in his seat. "It's a boardroom decision. I'm sorry, but they want to re-think the look of the network."

"The *look?* What the hell are you talking about, Mort?"

"There are new people running things these days. They've got different ideas about the news and current affairs lineup." Rosen glanced up from the napkin he was wadding in his hand. "Look, Paul, this isn't my idea. I wanted you for the job but I lost the battle."

Chaney's eyes narrowed as he studied the other man's face, lined and drawn from too many years of bureau-cratic wrangling. "Who did I piss off this time?" he asked.

"I'm not sure. But you must have done something a lot bigger than some of the stunts you've pulled in the past." Rosen grinned. "Like that time you were sup-posed to be covering the environmental conference in Vienna and the next thing we knew, we were getting video feed from Tunis—you with Yasser Arafat."

"Yeah, but I was the first reporter he saw after he was nearly killed in that plane crash. I had the contacts and I got the scoop. We beat every other network and newspaper in the world."

"I know," Rosen said. "You've pulled a few good ones out of the hat. But it wasn't enough to save you this time."

"This stinks, Mort. I want to know what it's all about."

"Paul, do yourself a favor. Take the severance money they're offering," Rosen advised, naming a figure that made Chaney whistle. "Move on to another network. They'll be fighting over you when word gets out." He sighed wearily. "It's not as much fun around CBN these days, anyway. It's not about good journalism anymore—it's all about profit margins and politics. Get out while you can."

I'll go for the moment, Chaney thought grimly as he waited for the patrolman to come back. But I know there's more to this than just network image. He glanced at the seat beside him, where he had the previous day's *Washington Post* and the latest issue of *Newsweek*—the latter featuring the defiant features of Angus Ramsay McCord smiling from the cover.

The patrolman's voice at the window made Chaney jump. "Here you are, Mr. Chaney. I didn't recognize you. I see you on the news all the time. Hell of a job you did, covering the Gulf War. Flak was really flying over there, wasn't it?"

"Sure was. Thanks," Chaney said, retrieving the license and car rental papers the man held out. He grimaced up at the big cop, backlit by the sun. "You're still going to ticket me, though, aren't you?"

"'Fraid so, Mr. Chaney. Sorry," the cop said, ripping the ticket from his pad and handing it over with a broad smile.

Chaney didn't think the patrolman was sorry at all.

This can't be happening, Mariah thought as Burton pushed her though the doorway into her bedroom. The sunlight was streaming in at the window and she could hear the laughter and shouts of the neighbors' kids playing street hockey outside, their sticks slapping the concrete as they chased the ball up and down the road.

"Hold it," Burton growled.

She froze in the center of the room, her stomach tightly knotted. The knife came up against her throat again, and she felt the heat of his body close behind her as he slipped his free hand under her arm and around her waist. She closed her eyes, fighting down disgust as the hand moved up to her breast and began to knead it.

"I saw you, Mariah," he whispered hoarsely. "I watched you. You thought you'd gotten away, didn't you? You shouldn't have done that—you shouldn't have run from me."

His breath was hot and moist in her ear as he pushed his groin against her back. His hand slid down her stomach and reached between her legs, pulling her tighter against him, groping and exploring. Suddenly, she felt his tongue in her ear, and then his lips moved down on her neck, wet and sucking. Only the cold steel on her throat held her rage in check. I can't die, she told herself. Please don't let me die. I'll let him do anything he wants, but please don't let him kill me. Let me be with my little girl.

She felt him begin to grind against her back, his free hand abandoning exploration in favor of holding her tight to him as he moved. "Hell!" he breathed. "You got me so worked up, I can't wait."

Good God! He's going to come right here in the middle of the floor, Mariah thought as he pounded against her backside. Through fear and disgust, she felt an irrational, almost irrepressible urge to giggle at his squalid ineptitude. But then she felt the cold blade and remembered his deadly fury in the kitchen. She bit her lip and clenched her hands, waiting. He moved a few more times, then shuddered and was still, his hand still wrapped in her slacks as he panted into her neck.

Please, let him leave now, Mariah prayed, knowing that he wouldn't.

Chaney watched the police cruiser pull onto the beltway and speed off. Sure, fella, he thought, frowning, go get some other sucker. Make your day.

He waited for a couple of cars to pass, then moved the Buick out onto the road, reminding himself to watch his speed. A moment later, a green overhead sign announced the McLean turnoff.

He was sneaking up on her again, he realized. He didn't mean to, it just always seemed to happen that way. Today he needed to talk to her badly—not the bloody answering machine that she would ignore, anyway, if she heard his voice on it. Needed to talk to her, he thought ruefully, wanted to, as well.

How many women are there in the world, Chaney? he asked himself. Couple of billion, maybe? Eliminate the underage ones. That leaves maybe a billion—and more than one of them had shown an interest. God knows, I've made a valiant effort to research the alternatives. So why did I have to fall in love with the wife of a friend and the one woman who always looks at me as if I were something she should scrape off the bottom of her shoe?

He hadn't planned it that way. The first time they met had been at a large dinner gathering hosted by a British diplomat in Vienna. She was there alone. Later, Chaney had found out that David had had a conflicting engagement that night, attending an IAEA reception. The two of them were newly arrived in Vienna.

Chaney had found himself seated next to her at dinner. She was attractive and he knew the woman at his other elbow to be a tedious gossip, so he had decided to occupy Mariah's attention before the evening turned into a total disaster. He had picked up the place card beside her wineglass and read the name.

"Hello, Mariah Bolt," he said, holding out his free hand. "My name's Paul Chaney."

Mariah glanced at him and at his hand, then took it in hers. "Yes, I know. How do you do?"

"You're American?" She nodded. Chaney took a closer look at her features. "You look familiar. Have we met before?"

Her eyebrow rose. "Now, *there's* an original line," she said, her mouth turning up at the corners.

"No, I'm serious. You look like someone—a picture of someone. Who?" He puzzled over the place card in his hand and then slapped his forehead. "Of course! Benjamin Bolt."

The wry smile vanished from her face, a frown replacing it as she turned to take up her napkin. A server appeared at her elbow with a bowl of soup. When he had finished serving her and Chaney, and had moved on down the table, Chaney turned back to Mariah. She was stirring her broth slowly, appearing to be intensely focused on the swirling vegetables in the bowl.

"*Are* you related to Benjamin Bolt?"

Mariah pushed a carrot around the bowl with her spoon for a moment, then sighed and put it down. She looked around the table but the other guests were engrossed in different conversations. She turned a reluctant gaze back to Chaney. "I'm his daughter."

"His daughter? That's terrific! I read his books in college—they'd just been discovered. The critics were raving about the lost member of the American Beat Generation. Some of them thought his work left Jack Kerouac's in the dust."

Mariah nodded. "I remember."

"They were right. His work was powerful. I used to carry *Cool Thunder* with me everywhere I went." Chaney grinned. "Women loved it—it was better than walking a puppy. Talk about opening lines—that book was the best conversation opener I ever saw. A girl saw you reading *Cool Thunder*, she'd gravitate right to you."

"How nice for you."

"I *also* appreciated it for its literary merits," Chaney said sheepishly. He watched her as she took up her spoon and began to pick at her soup again. "I didn't know he had a family. I thought he was living alone in Paris when he died."

"He was." Mariah put down the spoon abruptly and fixed him with her cool gray eyes. "Could we change the subject, please? I never really knew my father and I have no interest in discussing him."

She hadn't been interested in discussing much else with him, either, Chaney thought as he pulled up to a stoplight, remembering how she had soon turned her attention to the dinner companion at her other elbow. By the end of the meal, after one or two more fruitless attempts to engage her in conversation, he had her neatly pigeonholed in his mental classification of female types. She was the Ice Maiden: attractive, intelligent and frosty as hell. Pity the poor bastard who married that one, he had thought when he noticed the wedding band on her finger.

And there it would have remained if he hadn't become friendly with David Tardiff, hadn't seen her when her guard was down. Hadn't heard the soft laughter that David could evoke in her. Hadn't seen the gentle touch she had with him and their daughter. Hadn't learned that her smiles were breathtaking in their warmth, even if she only doled them out very selectively. Hadn't begun to sense that behind the reserved exterior, Ben Bolt's daughter was a shy and somehow wounded woman—a woman who came to haunt Chaney's daydreams and undermine his own grim determination never to be vulnerable again.

"Take off your clothes," Burton ordered.

He had turned Mariah around to face him and was holding the knife against her stomach while his other hand gripped the back of her neck. He pulled her head toward him, his breath sour when he kissed her lips. Mariah squeezed her eyes tight, repelled by the feeling of his tongue as he forced her lips apart and began exploring her mouth. Finally, she could stand it no longer and turned her head away, his lips smearing across her cheek. She winced as the point of the blade pricked her skin through her sweater.

"C'mon, Mariah," Burton growled. "You better cooperate if you know what's good for you." He pulled her close again and nuzzled her neck. "Think about those pictures—about that broad. She was hot. I wanna see you just like that. Understand?"

"Shut up!" she cried, pushing at him. He looked up in surprise, holding the knife ready as he watched her face. "Shut up, you bastard! Don't you talk about those pictures!"

"Who's in them?"

"None of your business!"

He stared at her and then slowly nodded as the realization sank in. "Your old man—is that it, Mariah?"

"Shut up, I said!" She closed her eyes and stood, swaying, her body racked with shuddering fear and pain. "Leave me alone," she cried. She opened her eyes and looked at him, pleading. "Please, go away."

He held up the knife and touched her with its wicked point, running it lightly down the knit ridges of her sweater from her breastbone to her groin and then back up again. "'Fraid I can't do that, Mariah."

She caught her breath as a slow grin rose on his lips. She knew then that he wasn't going to leave her alive.

11

Chaney stood at the front door, leaning on the bell. He knew she was home—the garage door was open and her car was there. He put his ear close to the door, listening, then rapped on the wood paneling. "Come on, Mariah, open the door!"

But the door remained stubbornly closed. He turned around on the front porch, glancing at the sidewalk. A couple of teenage boys were walking by, snapping each other with towels. The pool, he thought, that's where she'd been the other night. David had once said that she was a serious swimmer.

"Hey, guys! Are you going swimming?"

The boys stopped their horsing around and stared at him suspiciously. "Yeah. So?"

"So nothing." Chaney cocked his thumb at the house. "I'm looking for a friend, figured she might be there. Where's the pool?"

The teenagers relaxed visibly. "Down this way," one of them said, pointing. "Follow the path—you can't miss it. It's in the rec building."

Chaney's eyes followed the direction the boy indicated. "Thanks," he said.

"Sure, man." The kid and his buddy headed off down the path, towels snapping once more.

Chaney went down the front steps and out to the walkway.

At the first ring of the doorbell, Burton had shoved her against the wall and clamped his hand over her mouth. He leaned his body into hers and put the point of the blade to her throat. "Not a sound," he hissed. Mariah blinked and they stood, frozen, while the bell rang several more times. "Who is it? Who were you expecting?"

Mariah shrugged and shook her head as best she could. The sweaty hand he had clamped over her mouth was also blocking her nose and she was having difficulty breathing. As the sound of banging on the front door drifted up the stairs, her lips under his hand wanted to smile at the welcome persistence. But she looked at Burton and realized it was making him extremely nervous—the mismatched eyes were flitting around the room. Please, she prayed, just let him run.

The banging stopped and there came the muffled sound of male voices. Paul Chaney? It sounded like Paul Chaney. He was talking to someone outside—and then he wasn't. She strained her ears, but there was only the slap of hockey sticks and the droning of distant traffic. No, she wanted to scream, don't leave, please! But it was hopeless. He was gone.

Mariah's eyes closed and she felt tears welling up again while the intruder waited for what seemed like an eternity. Then, slowly, she felt his body relax. His hand slipped from her mouth, and he kissed her hard on the lips, then moved his mouth down her neck. She pressed herself into the wall, clenching her fists as his free hand began to travel over her body, exploring. When it reached her hips, he gripped the bottom of her sweater and tugged at it. "Take it off." He took a step back, moving the knife away from her neck, flicking it impatiently. "Now—hurry up!"

Mariah stared at the weird eyes, knowing that there was nothing about her that they were seeing—not a woman, not the mother of a child, not even a human being. Those eyes were fixed on nothing but a toy and a victim, the way a cat watches a fluttering sparrow hooked on its claws, playing with it a little before the killing pounce. There was an inevitability about what was happening in this room, she realized. He was going to rape her, and then he was going to kill her. His strength and the knife in his hand gave him the right to do it. All that was required of her was that she bow to the forces of primitive nature being played out here—submit and get it over with.

She crossed her arms in front of her and grasped the bottom of her pullover, drawing it up and over her head. Bringing her arms back down, she began slowly untangling them from the wool. His eyes were focused on her bra and his chest rose and fell heavily. "Good," he breathed, a grin stretching out his lips. His face was shiny, sweat shimmering unevenly on the pockmarked surface. He waved the knife over her body. "Now the rest."

She nodded, and even managed a small smile, as she extracted her hands from the sleeves and lightly shook out the bulky sweater. And then she lunged, holding the sweater before her, driving it into the knife and wrapping it quickly around the blade and his hand. As he dropped back and struggled to free himself from the tangle, she raised her right hand and extended the heel of it, driving it into his nose, connecting so hard that pain shot up her arm to her elbow.

He staggered, a tiny trickle of blood seeping from each nostril, and then his knees buckled. His hands reached to grab her as she leaped past him toward the door, but one was still tangled with the sweater and the knife. His other hand wrapped around her arm, but she yanked herself free before he could lock on. He hit the floor with a thud.

Mariah ran out the door, pulling it shut behind her and then flying toward the stairs. As she started down, she heard the door slam against the frame and then rapid footsteps. She took the steps two at a time.

When she reached the bottom, she turned and glanced up. He was on the landing, his eyes wild with fury and the lower half of his face dripping scarlet from the nose, which was bleeding heavily now. He raised his right arm behind his ear, then brought it down with a snap. She saw the knife in slow motion as it flew out of his hand and spun toward her, the blade rotating over the ivory handle until the killing point was aimed directly at her.

At the last split second, she jumped aside, diving for the floor. When she scrambled to her knees and turned around, she saw that the blade had quietly stopped— Paul Chaney's eyes went wide as the knife buried itself in his gut. He looked from his stomach to Mariah to the stairs. And then he stumbled back against the wall.

"Paul!" Mariah screamed.

But Burton was already down the stairs and on him, fumbling for the knife. Chaney grabbed the man's wrist and the two of them grappled while Mariah cast her eyes desperately around the hall for a weapon of some sort. Finding none, she pounced on Burton's back, wrapping her right forearm around his windpipe. She gripped her wrist with her other hand, squeezing as hard as she could until she finally heard him gurgle and he released the knife. His knee came up and connected with Chaney, who crumpled with an agonized groan into a ball on the floor.

Burton threw himself backward against the opposite wall, slamming Mariah into it. She slid off his back limply, collapsing on the floor. He turned and fixed her with a look of infinite hatred on his bloodied face. Then, with one last glance at Chaney, who was slowly unfolding himself on the floor, Burton flew to the front door. A second later, he was gone.

Mariah got to her feet and staggered to the door, slamming the dead bolt home. She moved toward Chaney, who had pulled himself to a sitting position, his knees still tucked into his chest. On the floor beneath his body appeared the ivory-handled knife.

"Are you all right?" she asked.

He looked at his left hand, the palm bleeding. Rolling his fist, he poked two fingers tentatively through the gaping hole in the front of his leather jacket. The knife had entered at the center, on the placket where the two sides overlapped, its lethal intent foiled by multiple layers of cowhide. He withdrew his fingers and nodded, stunned and unable to speak, his eyes closing again on the other pain that Mariah knew hadn't dissipated yet.

She ran into the kitchen and locked the door to the garage. Placing her palms to the wood and pressing her cheek against its cool surface, she leaned into the door, eyes closed, willing herself to become just another part of the unfeeling architecture. The sound of Chaney calling her name from the hall brought her back among the living. She turned and examined the kitchen. Long, dark spatters stained one wall, the floor beneath it littered with the remains of the coffee carafe. The broom lay wedged into a corner, while on the table the scattered photos of David and Elsa provided mute testimony to still another aspect of the human capacity for cruelty. She picked her way past the glass on the floor and returned to the hall.

"Mariah—oh God, you're bleeding!" Chaney cried, leaping to his feet.

Her eyes drifted to her chest, where a line of blood ran down between her breasts and into her bra. She touched her throat. "It's just a nick," she said numbly, examining the blood on her fingers.

He moved forward and she felt his arms go around her, but she recoiled from him and from the cold touch of leather on her bare skin. She crossed her arms in front of her chest and stood pressed against the wall for a moment. Then, shivering, she went to the hall closet and reached in for David's old hockey jacket. Her hand froze in midair. She stared at the jacket, remembering the countless times she had seen him wear it—and the times she had snuggled into it as he pulled her close. She looked at the fuzzy crest of his college team stitched on the breast and remembered how she used to trace it with her finger, lying against him in parked cars or under autumn trees. Looking away from the jacket, she pulled down a fleece cardigan, zippered herself into it and shut the door.

"I almost left," Chaney was saying behind her. "I was going to go and look for you at the swimming pool, but then I decided to check the garage. I tried the kitchen door. I saw—" He hesitated. "I saw everything in there—the broken glass and everything. Then I heard pounding on the stairs and I just ran into the hall."

Mariah turned around and leaned against the wall, sliding down to a sitting position. "You saved my life. He was going to kill me."

"Who was he?" She shook her head. Chaney watched her for a minute, then said, "I'll call 9-1-1."

She pulled up her knees and buried her head in her arms as Chaney went into the kitchen. She heard his voice vaguely, but it seemed to be coming from somewhere a long way away, down a long tunnel. Then it was closer, and she looked up to see Chaney crouched in front of her.

"The police will be here in a few minutes," he said. She nodded dumbly. "Mariah, those pictures—"

Her head snapped back. "Oh, God! I've got to get rid of them!" She scrambled to her feet.

Chaney grabbed her. "No, Mariah! The police will want to see them. They're evidence. You can't touch them."

"No! They don't have anything to do with him! I have to get rid of them! No one can see them!" She struggled against him, but he held her tightly. "Let me go!"

"Mariah, what are you talking about? Where did they come from?"

"From Lindsay."

"What?"

"Lindsay—someone sent them home with her from school. Someone's trying to terrorize me. I don't know why."

"Someone *did* terrorize you, Mariah. He nearly killed you!"

"No, he didn't know anything about the pictures. He was in the house, waiting, when I got back from dropping off Lindsay. She gave me the envelope in the car. I had just opened it when that—" she hesitated, then spat out the word "—that *bastard* came into the kitchen."

"They could be related."

"He was a stalker," Mariah argued. "The one who followed me from the pool the other night."

"He could have been a hired thug."

Mariah glared at him. "And who are you, Chaney? What's your role in all this?"

"What?"

"You heard me! This is about Vienna again, isn't it? About whatever game you and Katarina Müller were playing there."

He was stunned. "How do you know her real name?" He blanched as the truth dawned. "It was you! You're CIA!"

"Never mind how I know! What were the two of you up to?"

"I was never in league with that woman! She used me—maybe to get to David, I don't know. I was an idiot. I knew what she was, but I played along for a while, thinking there was a story in it."

"What are you talking about?"

"She approached me out of the blue at a reception one night—came on hot and heavy. I didn't much like her, but there was something about her."

"Yeah, I'll bet."

"No, I mean I was suspicious of her. I'm not sure why. Maybe it was just because she was so damn calculating. Anyway, I've got a friend in the German embassy—an intelligence officer. He told me she had been an agent for the other side during the Cold War. He was curious to know what she was up to now and so was I, so I played dumb." Chaney sighed. "You have to believe me, Mariah. I didn't realize until too late that she was going after David. I never would have let it go on if I had known."

"You knew about them." It was an accusation.

He bit his lip, watching her closely. Then he nodded. "I saw them together one night, going into her apartment building. It was the evening of the ambassador's reception." He sighed again. "That's why I did what I did on the terrace that night, Mariah. You looked so unhappy. I thought you must have suspected that David was cheating on you. I just wanted to hold you and make the hurt go away."

Mariah stared at him and then slid back down the wall. "Oh, God, what happened? How could he have done it?"

Chaney crouched in front of her. "I don't know, but we're in this together, Mariah."

"What's it got to do with you?"

"David was my friend...and I care about you, too," he said quietly. "Ever since David and Lindsay were attacked, I've been following up leads, trying to figure out who was behind it. Someone seems to be real annoyed about my snooping."

"Annoyed?"

"I got fired this morning."

From off in the distance, they heard a police siren. As Mariah stared at Chaney's sober face, the siren grew louder. She glanced around nervously. Suddenly, she grasped his arm. "All right, listen, we'll work together. Maybe we can figure this out. I have some information that might help. But we've *got* to get rid of those pictures." He started to shake his head, but she gripped his arm tighter. "Please," she pleaded. "I want the police to get that bastard who attacked me. But if those pictures become part of the investigation, they could come out in court eventually and Lindsay would find out about her father's affair. She adored David. I could kill him for what he did, but I can't let her be hurt any more than she already has been. Please, Paul, help me."

The wailing of the siren was piercing now. Then it whined to an abrupt halt, and they heard the sound of a cruiser crunching to a stop on the road outside. Chaney hesitated briefly, and then leaped up and ran to the kitchen. At the sound of a knock on the front door, Mariah rose to her feet. She watched in the kitchen doorway as Chaney stuffed the photos into the envelope, and then jammed the envelope down the back of his pants. He looked up at her and nodded. She opened the front door.

For the next five hours, Mariah recounted the horror of what had happened, stunned to realize that it had been barely twenty minutes that she had been terrorized by the intruder—it had seemed agonizingly longer than that. Over and over—first for the patrol officer, then for the investigators, then later in the hospital emergency ward where she and Chaney were taken to have their cuts and bruises examined and photographed and treated, and to receive tetanus shots for the knife wounds—she described the sequence of events that had begun when she returned to her house that afternoon. The only detail she left out was any reference to the envelope and its contents.

One officer took Chaney out to a police van to question him separately, while Mariah walked through the house with the officer heading the investigation, Sergeant Albrecht. She pointed out the places where she had struggled with Burton, describing his pockmarked face and mismatched eyes, shaking again as she recalled the moment she had understood that he was going to kill her.

"You say he was in the house when you got home?" Albrecht asked. Mariah nodded. "How did he get in, do you suppose?"

"I'm not sure. The dead bolt was on the front door when I left. I usually come and go through the kitchen."

"That's the door to the garage?"

"Yes."

"Did you lock it when you went out?"

"No, but I always close the garage door with the remote."

The sergeant grimaced. "Those things aren't secure, you know. They operate on a few common frequencies—any amateur hacker can defeat them." He sighed. "Did you close the garage door when you left this morning?"

"Yes, I'm sure I did. But I was running late and in a hurry. I don't think I stayed to see it close completely." She buried her head in her hands. "This was my fault, wasn't it? I should have been more careful."

"It wasn't your fault, Ms. Bolt. Maybe you made it a little easier for him, but an animal like that, he'd have found a way in sooner or later, especially if he was stalking you, as you said. Don't worry—we'll get him. My people are dusting for prints now and we've got his weapon. And blood samples for DNA typing," he added appreciatively. "Do you think you broke his nose?"

Mariah looked at the heel of her hand, which was already showing signs of a bad bruise. Her wrist ached and felt swollen. "I'm not sure, but he was bleeding like a pig and I sure as heck hurt my hand when I hit him."

"That's a mean right hand you've got there, ma'am," Albrecht said. She smiled a little. "We'll alert the hospital emergency wards in the area to watch out for broken noses attached to mugs fitting your description of this creep. Chances are he'll lie low, but we might get lucky."

Mariah nodded. Then her head snapped up. "I just remembered something. There was a cup on the counter when I came in. I thought it was out of place at the time. I didn't leave it out this morning and I'm pretty sure my daughter didn't."

"Where is it now?"

"I put the cup in the dishwasher—navy blue. There's a white one in the machine, but that was mine from breakfast."

"Okay, good. I'll have one of the officers check it for prints. We'll also want to get your fingerprints and Mr. Chaney's so we can know whose prints are whose." He took her by the elbow and led her to the door of the bedroom. "Here," he said. "Put these on."

Mariah puzzled over the tinted goggles he handed her, but she did as she was told and then they went in. The room was dark, the heavy drapes drawn. Someone was moving slowly around the room with a light, pausing now and again to place markers and take samples before moving on.

"This is Officer Harmon," Sergeant Albrecht said. "She's using a portable laser to search for fibers and fluids."

"Almost done," the officer said. "Two secs, and then we can turn the lights back on."

"Just stand against the wall here and try not to move or touch anything," Albrecht instructed Mariah. She stood in the corner, watching the laser illuminate minute fragments that she knew would never have been picked up by the naked eye, grateful for the officers' thoroughness, but feeling the anger rise in her again as she remembered the reason for it.

"Okay, all done. You can hit the lights, Sarge."

Albrecht flipped the switch and took Mariah's goggles from her. "I'll leave you with Officer Harmon now, Ms. Bolt, while I see how the boys are doing outside."

Mariah nodded, wincing in the light. She looked over to see Officer Harmon, a young black woman, coiling up a cable on the light wand. Mariah's pullover was still lying where her attacker had thrown it after untangling the knife. As she glanced around the room, she noticed that a drawer—her lingerie one—was open, a few items tumbling out. There was a pair of panties on the floor. She stared at them.

"You said you never removed your clothing," Officer Harmon said, "except for the sweater." Mariah nodded. "Then it appears the creep was examining your undies while he waited. I assume you don't usually leave things scattered like this?"

Mariah looked over at her. "No, I don't." She stared again at the drawer, feeling nauseated and furious at yet another violation. "I didn't see this before. My back was to the dresser."

The other woman nodded. "Ms. Bolt, this isn't easy, I know," she said gently. "Every time I see a case like this, it makes me sick that so many creeps do this to women and get away with it. But we're gonna get this one—I can feel it in my bones. Will you help me?"

Mariah looked around the room one more time and then nodded. "Yes, whatever it takes. Just tell me what you want."

"Okay. I checked the underwear for possible semen residue, but there doesn't seem to be anything there. Since the creep never managed to get his pants off—which is okay by you, I'm sure—chances are we won't find anything. But just to be certain, I'd like to take in the clothing you had on—the sweater and the pants—to examine them. We might find fibers from his clothes or hair samples on them, too. Also, if you can tell me where he kissed you—" She grimaced. "Sorry, that's sure not the word for it, is it?"

Mariah shook her head. "Not in this case—unless you call what a leech does kissing."

The other woman snorted. "Ain't it the truth. Anyway, I'd like to take some swabs for saliva. This is just double-banking the evidence, of course, since we've got the bloodstains here on the carpet and all the way to the front door from that bloody nose you gave him." She grinned. "Way to go. Hope you broke the son of a bitch's face, pardon my French."

"My sentiments exactly."

"Okay, if you could slip those slacks off very carefully, I'll bag 'em. Then we'll go in the bathroom and take some swabs and a couple of pictures, if you don't mind. I've already finished examining the bathroom, but I need to dust for prints in here, so I don't want to disturb anything."

"Then can I take a shower?"

Officer Harmon shook her head. "Better wait till you get back from the hospital. The car's waiting downstairs to take you and Mr. Chaney. We'll want you both to give blood samples there, too, by the way."

"Why?"

"So we can tell your bloodstains from the perp's."

Mariah nodded. She unzipped her slacks and stepped carefully out of them, dropping them in the paper bag that the officer held open. The policewoman sealed and labeled the bag, then put it aside and slid open Mariah's closet.

"Does anything look like it's been disturbed in here?" Harmon asked. Mariah glanced at the neatly arranged racks and shelves and shook her head. "Okay, let's get you something to put on after we're done."

It was already dark when the police car drove Mariah and Chaney back to her house from the hospital. Yellow plastic barrier tape was still strung around the yard, but the command van that Mariah had seen when they left for the hospital was gone now, as were most of the curious onlookers. Only one other police cruiser remained on the road outside.

They were led into the living room, where Sergeant Albrecht was sitting on the couch, making notes and drinking coffee from a disposable cup. The radio on his belt crackled periodically. When he looked up, his eyes were bloodshot and weary-looking, but he managed a smile. "Almost done here," he said, "and then we'll be out of your way."

"How's it going, Sergeant?" Chaney asked.

The sergeant's lower lip jutted out and he nodded. "Not bad. We found a footprint in the bushes outside the garage and some matching muddy prints on the floor inside—looks like that was the point of entry. We're going for a make on the shoe now. And there were some kids playing hockey outside who saw the guy—saw his bloody face and watched him drive off. They were able to describe the car—Japanese, sounds like a Nissan or a Toyota maybe, green, beat-up. We've got an APB out on it."

"Is there anything else we can do?" Mariah asked.

"Not really. Oh, one question. We came across some hair in the kitchen trash can—black, curly. It's obviously not yours or Mr. Chaney's, and you said your attacker had thinning white hair. Any idea how it got there?"

Mariah froze, staring at the sergeant, then her gaze shifted to the photograph on the wall unit of Lindsay and David. "It's my husband's," she said at last.

The policeman frowned and looked down at his notebook, flipping through the pages. "You said your husband's an invalid in a nursing home," he said, looking up.

"That's right."

"So how did his hair end up in your kitchen trash?"

Mariah turned to face him. "I visited him this morning. I trimmed his hair and when I got home, I found some on my clothing. I put it there."

The sergeant said nothing for a moment, then nodded and snapped his notebook shut. He stood up. "Okay, I guess that's it then. We'll try to keep an eye on your house until we find this creep, Ms. Bolt. You should be careful in the meantime. I don't think he'll be back, but you wouldn't want to take any chances. We'll be in touch."

Mariah shook his hand. "Thank you, Sergeant. I'm grateful for your hard work."

Albrecht nodded and headed for the door. Chaney followed and let him out, while Mariah slumped into one of the wing back chairs in the living room. Chaney came back in and dropped onto the sofa. They listened until the cars outside pulled away and then he reached behind him and pulled out the envelope from his pants, dropping it on the table. It was curled and wrinkled.

"How did you manage to keep that hidden at the hospital?" Mariah asked.

"I wrapped it in my clothes when they left me to undress. It stayed in the examining room with me the whole time." He leaned back on the couch and massaged his temples. Then he looked over at her. "What was that about David's hair?"

Mariah exhaled heavily. "I forgot about it. It came in the envelope, with the pictures."

"What?" Chaney exclaimed, sitting up with a start.

"It's a message. They're telling me they can get to Lindsay or David anytime they want." She closed her eyes for a moment, then continued. "Those phone calls I made while we were waiting around at the hospital—I asked the nursing home to move him closer to the nurses' station. I also called a friend of mine—Lindsay's baby-sitting his grandson—and asked him to go and get her." Frank Tucker had been determined to come and get Mariah, as well, but she had convinced him that she was fine and to carry on with his Christmas party preparations.

"A friend of yours? One of your spook friends?"

Mariah sighed. "I'm no spook, Paul, at least not the kind you're obviously imagining me to be. I'm just your garden-variety Company analyst."

"Really," Chaney said dubiously.

"Really. Most of us are just average Americans, you know, with kids and mortgages and flabby muscles. Ordinary people—not James Bond. Trust me," she added, frowning, "if I had been a fully trained covert operative, that creep wouldn't have walked out of here alive this afternoon."

Chaney watched her for a moment, then nodded. "No, I guess not," he agreed. "So where do we go from here?"

Mariah checked her watch—it was almost eight o'clock. "How do you feel about going to a Christmas party?"

"What? You're not serious! I thought we were going to work on this thing."

"We are, but I want to see my daughter first—she's there. I want to take her some overnight things so I can get this place straightened up before she sees it." She glanced around at the powder-laden surfaces of the room and at the bloodstains on the hall carpet that were visible even from where she sat. "And I need to talk to someone," she added.

"This is a Company party?"

"Not exclusively, but the host is my boss."

"Is he going to be happy about seeing me there?"

Mariah rolled her eyes. "Not particularly." That was an understatement if ever there was one.

"What'll you tell him?"

She studied him briefly. "That you saved my life. And do me a favor and don't say anything else, okay, Chaney?"

He nodded. "Okay."

12

Tucker had obviously been watching for her because the front door flew open while they were still at the bottom of the walk. His heavy black eyebrows were locked together and his endless forehead was corrugated with anxious wrinkles. He stepped back to admit them, nodding briefly to Chaney before closing the door and turning to Mariah.

She attempted a smile, then gave up the effort and stepped into his awkward bear hug. She rested there a while, listening to the sounds from the living room of a party in full swing—music, tinkling glasses and laughing voices. The happy aromas of Christmas evergreens, good food and wine wafted down the hall.

Finally, Tucker pulled away and looked down at her. "Bloody hell, Mariah," he said gruffly. "Are you all right?"

She nodded halfheartedly. "I'm okay. But I almost missed this shindig, Frank—that, and the rest of my natural life. If Paul here hadn't shown up when he did—"

Tucker turned to Chaney, his hard, black eyes scrutinizing the reporter. Chaney had lost his leather jacket to the police for evidence and was wearing the sport coat and tie he habitually carried around in his car for his stand-ups before the television cameras. He had regained his composure after the afternoon's trauma and bore his usual air of calm self-assurance. He handed

Tucker the mince pies that he had carried in from the car.

Frank took them and set them on a hall table, then held out his hand grudgingly. "Frank Tucker," he said. "I guess you're the hero of the day."

"Not me. Mariah was doing a good job of fighting off the creep. If anything, she saved *me*—we were struggling for the knife when she attacked him like a she-lion. In the end, I think, he just didn't like the odds, so he took off."

"You didn't say anything to Lindsay, did you, Frank?" Mariah asked.

Tucker shook his head. "No," he said. "Carol and Michael and Pat know. We just told Lindsay we needed her help with the decorating."

"Good. I'll tell her we had a break-in, that's all. Carol's okay to keep her tonight? I need to get my place cleaned up before she sees it."

Tucker nodded. "She could have stayed here, too, but Carol thought she'd have more fun with the baby. Come in and have a drink," he added to Chaney as he helped Mariah out of her coat.

"I think we could both use one," Chaney said. He stepped out of the way, standing in the living-room doorway, waiting while Tucker hung the coat in the closet.

When Frank turned back to face her, Mariah saw him frown at the wrap they had put on her sprained right wrist at the hospital. She was wearing a slim, black velvet skirt, but the bandage on her throat had obliged her to trade the scooped silk blouse she had originally planned to wear that night for a sequined turtleneck sweater. She could tell by the warmth in her cheeks that her color must be feverishly high.

She patted his arm reassuringly. "The other guy looks worse, believe me," she said.

Tucker's frown only deepened. He glanced at Chaney, then again at Mariah. "I want to talk to you," he whispered. "Alone."

She nodded grimly. "Me, too. But first, I want to see Lindsay."

He scooped up the pies, and led them both into the living room, where forty or fifty people were standing around in small groups, laughing and talking. Pat Bonelli was with a crowd from the office, but she detached herself as soon as she spotted Mariah, strode over and threw her arms around her. The two women hugged tightly. When Mariah stepped back, she could see that Pat had tears in her eyes.

"Oh, Mariah! I can't believe it," she cried.

"It's okay, Patty," Mariah said, touching her friend's arm. "I'm not hurt, just really angry, that's all." She glanced around. "Let's don't make a big deal of it, okay? I don't want to broadcast this, and I particularly don't want to scare Lindsay."

Pat nodded, but Mariah could tell by her tightly pressed lips that she was overwrought. The tough ones are always such big softies, she thought, giving the secretary another affectionate hug. "This is Paul Chaney. Paul, this is my friend Pat Bonelli. We've been working together for years."

Chaney stepped forward and they shook hands. Pat was obviously impressed by what she saw, Mariah noted wryly as the other woman straightened and smiled, blinking away the tears in her eyes. Mariah shook her head. The Chaney charm—someone should bottle it. Tucker was standing off to the side, one pie balanced on each hand. He cleared his throat roughly and Pat's eyes snapped away from Chaney.

"Here, let me take those," she said quickly, relieving Tucker of the pies.

"I *had* planned another surprise," Mariah said ruefully, "but somehow it didn't get made—can't imagine why."

"These look great," Pat said, sniffing appreciatively. "And there's food for the multitudes here. Our Frank really outdid himself. Come take a look at this buffet."

"In a minute. I want to see Lindsay. Do you know where she is?"

"In the bedroom with Carol, changing the baby."

"I'll go find them. Patty, could you show Paul the buffet? He must be starving. I forgot to offer him any food at my place."

Chaney smiled. "I wasn't up for eating before, but I think I could be talked into it now. It sure smells good in here."

Pat held out her elbow for him as she balanced the pies, and Chaney looped his hand through. "Let's go," she said cheerfully.

They headed off toward the dining room while Tucker stood at Mariah's side, scowling. "I guess I'll just fetch drinks," he grumbled.

Mariah looked up at him. "Be nice, Frank," she warned. "I'm feeling unusually charitable toward him today, under the circumstances."

"Yeah, I suppose," he conceded. "But you're not going home tonight, are you? You should stay here, or at least with Carol and Michael."

She shook her head. "No, I want to go home. I'm not letting some creep scare me out of my house."

"It's not a good idea. He might come back."

"I don't think so. Neither did the police, but they're keeping a close watch on the place. And," she added, "I won't be alone. Chaney's going to camp out on my sofa."

"Get serious! That guy?"

"*That* guy saved my neck, Frank," she whispered, eyes flashing. "And that guy came clean with me about Vienna, which is more than I can say for some so-called old friends."

"I was trying to protect you, Mariah. There's nothing you can do to change what's past, and the rest is being taken care of, I told you that."

"What does that mean, Frank, 'taken care of'?"

Tucker glanced over at a couple approaching them. Mariah recognized George Neville, deputy director for the Agency's operations arm, and a woman she presumed was his wife. Mariah hadn't been to one of Frank's annual Christmas bashes since before Vienna, but this was the first time she could remember seeing anyone from Ops—let alone the deputy himself. "Later," Frank whispered.

"Well, well! Mariah Bolt, it's good to see you," Neville said heartily, giving her a peck on the cheek, which she had the immediate urge to wipe away. She'd only met him once or twice and was surprised that he even remembered her name—although, come to think of it, she thought darkly, maybe it wasn't so strange. Neville's manner was unfailingly smooth, his dress impeccable, his silver hair swept back like chrome fins, his smile permanently fixed. But the gray eyes above the smile were cool and appraising. The couple of times Mariah had met him before, she had always left his presence feeling that she had been probed and x-rayed.

When he introduced the woman as his wife and she extended her hand, Mariah took it in her left. "This looks painful," Neville said, delicately picking up her bandaged right hand. "Been beating off the media, have we?" Mariah felt a flash of anger but his expression was neutral, even faintly amused. "I noticed your date."

"He's not my date. As for my hand, I slipped and sprained my wrist, that's all. Nice to meet you," she added, smiling briefly at his wife. Then she turned and gave Neville a hard look, retrieving her hand. Under the circumstances, she decided, this was as polite as she was obliged to be—rank be damned. "Would you excuse me? I need to find my daughter."

She made her escape and went in search of Lindsay. She found her in the master bedroom with Frank's daughter, both of them occupied with baby Alex on the bed. Lindsay was stretched out beside him, tickling his fat little belly, while Carol busied herself with the diaper. Lindsay jumped up when she saw Mariah in the doorway.

"Mom! You made it, finally! Where were you? I thought you were coming at seven." Mariah hesitated, then crossed the room quickly, wrapping her daughter in her arms. She held her tightly and closed her eyes, not trusting her voice. Lindsay hugged her back, then looked at her, puzzled. "What's the matter, Mom? Are you crying?"

"Just a little, honey. I'm glad to see you, that's all."

Lindsay spotted the bandage on her hand. "What happened? How did you do this?"

Mariah took a deep breath, then grimaced. "I hit somebody." Lindsay's eyes went wide. "Don't worry, sweetie. It's like I told Uncle Frank—the other guy looks a lot worse."

"Who did you hit?"

"A burglar."

"Mom!"

"It's okay, Lins. Some guy broke into our house and I surprised him when I got home this afternoon, that's all. I'm not hurt and he didn't get anything. Mr. Chaney showed up and we chased him off."

"Mr. Chaney? No kidding."

"Nope, and under the circumstances, I decided I'm going to stop being so rotten to him—for a day or two, anyway," Mariah added, smiling. "I brought him along to the party."

"He's here? Cool," Lindsay said. But then a shadow crossed her features again. "Did you call the police?"

"Yes. That's why I was late. We had to tell them fifty or sixty times what happened and they took a bunch of fingerprints and stuff. They'll get the bum, don't worry."

Lindsay nodded. She lifted Mariah's hand and examined the bandage, then looked at her with anxious eyes. "You're really okay?"

"Honest. But I'm pretty beat. I may not stay too long tonight."

Lindsay's face fell. Carol reached out and touched her arm. "Lindsay? Would you like to sleep at my house? You could stay longer at the party."

Lindsay brightened, but then looked back at her mother and shook her head. "No, I'll go with you, Mom."

Mariah held her by the shoulders and kissed her cheek. "I'm okay, honey—really. I brought an overnight bag for you. Why don't you spend the night at Carol's? That would give you a chance to play with this little guy in the morning." Lindsay hesitated, then nodded.

They leaned over the bed, where Alex was happily waving his chubby arms and legs. Lindsay dropped back down beside him, and he grabbed her hair, gurgling in delight. "Isn't he cute, Mom? He calls me La-la. At least, we think he does—he says it whenever he sees me."

"La-la," Alex obliged, giggling and kicking excitedly.

"He's beautiful. I can't believe how much he's grown!" Mariah exclaimed. "And look at the hair!"

Tight auburn curls covered the head that had once sprouted only peach fuzz. As Carol snapped his outfit together and Lindsay picked him up and bounced him on her lap, Mariah was struck by how much the two children resembled a Victorian postcard: Lindsay in her high-necked, lace-trimmed dress of deep green velvet and the baby in a matching velvet outfit trimmed with red, the pointed toes of his cloth booties jingling with bells. Carol picked up a little peaked elf cap off the bed and placed it on his head, but he pulled it off again and happily waved it around. They laughed and headed back into the party.

"You must be hungry, Mariah," Carol said. "Let's get you some food."

"I could use something. Have you two eaten?"

Lindsay shifted baby Alex onto one slim hip. "I have," she said. "I even tried that squid thing Uncle Frank made." She curled her lip, leaving no doubt as to her judgment on the recipe.

"I think it's an acquired taste," Carol said, laughing. "You should try it, Mariah. It's...interesting." They watched as Lindsay carried Alex over to the Christmas tree to show him the shiny decorations. Then Carol turned to Mariah and laid a hand on her arm. "Are you really all right?" she asked quietly.

"Yes," Mariah said slowly, watching the children backlit by the dancing flames in the fireplace behind them. "It seems like a bad dream now. This is real," she said, waving her arm around the room, "and that was just a nightmare that happened to someone else." She touched her hand to her throat and looked at the woman by her side. "But I really thought I was going to die this afternoon, Carol. And it was weird, because all I could think was, I can't let him kill me—I can't leave Lindsay all alone. I have to be there to help her grow up."

Carol put an arm around her shoulder. "That doesn't sound strange to me. Before I had Alex, I don't think it would have made sense. But then this little person comes along, and you love him so much and he depends on you so totally that you know nothing could ever be as important as keeping him safe—not even your own life.'' Carol's gaze drifted off for a moment. When it returned to Mariah, her eyes were bright. ''Now that I have a child of my own, I can't help thinking about my mother, and how hard it must have been for her to know that she wouldn't be there for Stevie and me one day—how that must have hurt her.''

Mariah nodded soberly. ''Speaking of Stephen, did he come?''

''Yes, he's here somewhere. I had to threaten to disown him before he finally agreed to show, though. Honestly, Mariah,'' Carol said, exasperated, ''he may be my twin, but sometimes I just can't figure him out.''

''He's not gregarious, is he?''

''Tell me about it.''

''Here, I made you a plate.'' Hearing Pat Bonelli's voice behind her gave Mariah a start. She smiled and thanked her as she took the food and utensils Pat was holding. Then Mariah glanced over at Paul, who was patting an empty spot on the sofa beside him. She excused herself and went over to join him, balancing the meal on her lap as she settled in, wincing at a sudden stab of pain in her wrist as she lifted the fork.

''Just ignore me if I end up with this all over my lap,'' she warned, trying to figure out how to proceed.

''Not a chance,'' he said. ''You're the only one here, aside from your friend, Pat, who isn't avoiding me like the plague. I find your clumsiness charming, I can assure you.''

Mariah looked around the room. She could see by the furtive glances in their direction that Chaney's presence was unsettling to some people and was the object of considerable curiosity.

''We all spend too much time together, and it's hard to talk to outsiders sometimes,'' she said. ''But it's not difficult to understand. If you ever want to know what it feels like to have a communicable disease, try telling someone that you work for the CIA and see how fast the conversation dies. Also," she added, "a lot of these people don't have much use for the media. They've been burned too often. The Agency's mistakes get blown up all the time, but we never get good press when we do something right."

"Well, whose fault is that?" Chaney asked. "To know you may be to love you, but it's not like the Company encourages familiarity."

"It's changing—slowly. A lot of what gets done at Langley is pretty basic political analysis, and we've got some really bright people. We're trying to get them to circulate a little more, especially among the media and academics."

"Maybe, although I think your friend, Tucker, would like to circulate me right out the door." Chaney launched hungrily into his food. "But you should see that spread, Mariah, it's unbelievable. I think your boss could give you a run for your money in the cooking department."

"Oh, no. He's the grand wizard—I'm just his humble apprentice."

"Tucker taught you to cook?"

"In a manner of speaking. Let's say he challenged me to learn." She winced again at the effort of cutting into the beef roulade on her plate, finally ceding the utensils to Chaney, whose own hand, despite the bandaged cuts, was functioning better than hers. He put his dinner aside momentarily and cut up hers. "Thanks," she said, taking the fork awkwardly in her left hand.

"What do you mean, 'challenged you'?" Chaney asked, retrieving his plate.

"Frank was my first boss when I joined Langley," she explained, poking at the food. "He and his wife kind of adopted me—she died a couple of years later.

Anyway, I was young and on my own and my eating habits were pretty awful—I think I told you that my mother wasn't exactly Betty Crocker. Frank used to give me a hard time about it. He started bringing me the same leftovers that he brought himself for lunch. Incredible stuff—chicken cordon bleu, lamb curry, you name it. If I liked something, he gave me the recipe. Pretty soon, I'd collected a lot of recipes, and I started feeling guilty about not reciprocating, so I learned to cook in self-defense."

Just then, Tucker himself appeared, carrying two glasses of wine, which he handed to Mariah and Chaney. The reporter raised his glass. "To the chef and grand wizard."

Mariah also raised her glass to Frank, then clinked it against Chaney's and took a deep swallow. Tucker frowned, clearly puzzled. "I was just telling Paul how you forced me to learn to cook," Mariah explained. She took another long sip of wine, welcoming its anesthetic effect on her throbbing emotions.

"There's Lindsay. Don't you look pretty!" Chaney said as she squeezed between them on the sofa, the baby on her lap. She blushed. Chaney shook Alex's little hand. "And who's this? If I didn't know better, I'd say you'd suddenly acquired a baby brother. He looks just like you."

"It's their outfits," Mariah said, smiling and stroking Lindsay's hair. "I was just thinking how much they look like a couple of characters out of Lewis Carroll."

"This is Alex," Lindsay said. "He's Carol's baby— Uncle Frank's grandson," she added, looking up at Tucker.

"Mariah?" Frank said. "Could I have a word with you when you're done eating?"

Mariah glanced at Chaney and Lindsay, then drained her glass and nodded. "I think I'm finished. Great food, Frank, but I haven't got much of an appetite to-night."

Tucker led her into the bedroom and shut the door. Mariah sat down on a chair while Frank paced.

"I don't like it," he growled.

"What?"

"Chaney being here. Showing up out of the blue like that."

"Frank!" Mariah protested. "A few hours ago, the guy took a knife in the gut for me. It's a miracle he wasn't killed."

"How do you know it wasn't staged? He could have been working with that creep."

"That's crazy! I saw that knife coming at me—it was meant to kill. No sane person would have stepped in front of it on purpose."

"I still don't trust him," Tucker said, scowling darkly. "And neither should you. You know he was in-volved with that Müller woman in Vienna."

"He's got an explanation for that."

Tucker's black eyebrows shot up. "You called him on it?"

"Yes. He knows I'm with the Company, Frank. I told him I knew about Katarina Müller and it didn't take him long to figure it out." She sighed. "Chaney's not stupid—and it's not like it's a national secret, you know. I'm obviously not going on any more overseas assignments and our side of the house doesn't hide it-self. This is the age of the new, open CIA, remember?"

But Tucker just shook his head. "I don't like it. Something's wrong here."

"You don't know the half of it."

"What do you mean?"

She rubbed her eyes with her hands, feeling the rough bandage on her wrist scratch against her cheek. Then she told him about the envelope containing the photos and David's hair, gritting her teeth to keep her emotions in check. She was determined not to cry for David anymore—he had made his fate when he slept with Katarina Müller.

Tucker slumped onto the bed. "Bloody hell!" he breathed, staring at the floor. "What are they up to?"

Mariah's head snapped up. "Who? Who, Frank?"

But Tucker only glared. "You need to lie low. Get away for a while. It's only three weeks till Christmas— why don't you take Lindsay on a vacation? Maybe back to California, show her your roots."

"Are you out of your mind? In the first place, my family's gone, so what I am going to show her? Some crummy rented cottage where my mother and sister and I lived after my father ran out on us? I couldn't get away from that place fast enough, and I have no desire ever to see it again." Mariah shook her head. "And in the second place, Frank, I'm damned if I'm going to just sit back and be victimized! I want to fight back. Just point me in the right direction, for God's sake!"

"No," he said firmly. "I'm going to put a stop to this once and for all, I promise, but I want you out of the way."

"Is it Neville and his boys in Operations?"

Tucker wasn't listening. He stood up and started pacing again. "You and Lindsay can stay here. Someone will keep an eye on both of you around the clock and I'll—"

Mariah leaped out of the chair and grabbed his arm. "No, Frank! Listen to me—I'm *not* hiding!"

His own hands came up and he shook her by the shoulders, bringing his face to within centimeters of hers. "*You* listen to *me*, Mariah! I want you out of the line of fire! Leave it alone—for Lindsay's sake, if not your own."

"What are you talking about, Frank?"

He turned away, scowling. "It's one of Neville's covert operations. I was providing some technical advice, but you should never have gotten caught up in it like this. The thing's gone sour. Someone's out of control and it has to be shut down. I can get Neville to do it."

Mariah studied his face. She had never seen Frank look so worried. "It *was* the CHAUCER file, wasn't it, Frank?" He hesitated, then nodded. "Was betraying Tatyana Baranova part of the operation? Did we sell her out?"

He dropped his hands and shook his head. "No, I don't think so. I'm not sure," he said. "I don't know what the hell happened, but that's when it started to go bad—the day she disappeared."

The CIA station in Vienna had a safe house—with an attached garage through which visitors could be taken in and out unobserved—in one of the city's suburbs. It was there that Tatyana Baranova was driven three days after the rendezvous with another station operative at the Hofburg Museum. When she was led into the paneled study of the old house, her face registered both shock and relief at the sight of the officer assigned to debrief her.

"Hello, Tanya," Mariah said, stepping forward, smiling warmly.

"Mrs. Tardiff! Mariah, I mean," Tanya exclaimed. "It's you? You are CIA?"

"Me? No, I'm just a friend, Tanya," Mariah said. "They thought you might prefer to talk to someone you know." She signaled to the officer who had driven Baranova to the safe house. He stepped out of the room and closed the door behind him.

Tanya watched him go and then turned to Mariah. "Just the two of us?"

"Just us," Mariah said. There were two other case officers watching and listening from the next room, recording everything, but she had convinced the station chief that their presence in the study would only frighten the Russian woman. "Here, let me take your coat. Would you like some tea or coffee? I've made both."

She folded Tanya's coat over a chair, then led her in front of a warm fire crackling in the hearth, where cups and carafes were laid out on a low table between overstuffed armchairs. Tanya stood before the fire, warming her hands. "Tea would be very nice, thank you," she said.

Despite the warmth of the fire, Tanya was trembling, Mariah noted. She busied herself with the cups, giving the younger woman time to compose herself. "It feels like it's going to snow out there, doesn't it?"

Tanya turned, startled, and then nodded. Mariah smiled and indicated one of the big chairs. When Tanya sat down, Mariah handed her a cup of tea and held out the milk and sugar. There was also a plate of sandwiches and pastries on the table, but Tanya declined these, obviously too nervous to eat. Mariah fixed up her own cup and sat back in the chair across from the Russian, sipping the tea, gauging how far to take this first meeting.

"Did you have any trouble slipping away?"

"No. I said I was going to do some shopping on my lunch hour, as the man at the Hofburg Museum told me. Things are quiet at the office today, and no one will notice if I am a little late—everyone takes long lunches."

"We'll get you back in good time," Mariah promised. "And we'll have a shopping bag with a few things in it for you to take back to the office—just biscuits and a couple of jars of jam and such." It was a reminder to the boys in the next room to make sure they had something pulled together to support Tanya's alibi. They kept on hand a stock of plastic carrier bags and little goodies for just this purpose.

Baranova seemed to relax a little.

"Tanya," Mariah said, beginning slowly, "when we met at the hockey rink, you said there was something my people needed to know. You were worried about something that your government might be planning to do. Can you tell me what that was?"

"Perhaps not my government," Tanya said quietly.

"Who then?"

Tanya shrugged. "I am not certain. But people here—in the West—you do not understand how it is in my country now."

"In what way?"

"There is a struggle for power going on. Gorbachev has broken up the old guard, but he is not fully in control. There are those, especially in the military, who would like to destroy him and the changes he has made, and they have the power to do it. He will not last long in the Kremlin."

"Are you aware of something in particular?"

The younger woman traced the pattern on the china cup, her finger following the complex ins and outs of the old Royal Doulton design. "There is a secret research facility in the southern part of my country," she said at last.

"The town where you were raised?"

"Yes. I told you that my father was a weapons designer. He has been involved in a project to perfect a small, portable nuclear weapon. Like—what do you call them? The big guns soldiers rest on their shoulders?"

"Bazookas?"

"Yes, bazookas—maybe a little smaller, but like that," Tanya repeated, smiling. "It is a funny word in English—bazooka."

Mariah smiled back briefly. "What about these weapons, Tanya?"

The younger woman's face sobered. "They are very dangerous. Their explosive effect is not very large, but they emit a high level of radiation. They are a modified version of the neutron bomb that your own government was working on a few years ago."

"But we agreed to cease work on that weapon," Mariah said.

"Yes, I know. But my government never acknowledged that we were doing similar work. And because these weapons are so small, they are difficult to detect. Your spy satellites are useless against them. They can be transported in a suitcase."

Mariah stared at the woman, realizing full well the implications of what she was saying. A small weapon like that could be smuggled easily into any city in the world, or aboard an aircraft and set to explode at a predetermined time, raining a deadly radioactive shower on the population below.

"The weapons were never acknowledged to exist," Tanya went on, "and so they have never been included in any of the arms reduction talks my government has held with yours."

Mariah watched her closely. "There's something else, isn't there?" Tanya nodded slowly but seemed unable to speak. Mariah leaned forward and touched her arm. "Tell me," she said softly. "You've come this far, Tanya. It was the right thing to do. Now tell me what we need to know."

Tanya put down her cup and stared at her hands. Finally, she looked up. "No one seems to know who ordered it, but the weapons are going to be shipped out—very soon, perhaps."

"Where, do you know?"

"Astrakhan."

"On the Caspian Sea?" Mariah asked. Tanya nodded. And from there by boat to Iran, Mariah thought, and right into the international terrorist arms bazaar. And wouldn't they fetch a pretty price?

"She risked her life to tell us about those weapons, Frank," Mariah said. "How did we let the KGB get her? Why didn't we protect her?"

Tucker stood by the bedroom window, looking out. "She knew the risk she was running."

"Oh, come on, Frank! She was a sweet, kindhearted young woman!"

He turned to face her. "I'm not trying to be coldblooded, Mariah, but Tatyana Baranova is lost—probably dead. You don't have to like it, but it's a fact you have to accept. If you're not careful, you could be next."

She stared at him angrily. "Get him in here, Frank."

"Who?"

"George Neville."

"Did I hear someone calling my name?" Mariah spun around to see Neville standing in the doorway of the bedroom. He stepped into the room and closed the door behind him. "You people are missing a good party," he said. "What seems to be the problem?"

Mariah stared at the operations deputy, unsure of herself in the face of his cool smile and calculating eyes. But then she remembered the attack in her house and the photos and Lindsay, and her fury rose anew.

"I'm glad you're here, Mr. Neville," she said. "Maybe you can explain to me why my husband and daughter were attacked in Vienna and I was told it was nothing but a traffic accident. And why someone is playing psychological terror games with me now, threatening my family again here and sending me incriminating photos of my husband with a former East

German spy. And why someone tried to kill me this afternoon.''

"Photos? Frank told me you were attacked," Neville said, frowning at Tucker. "I don't know anything about photos. And surely you don't believe—''

Mariah pulled down the collar of her sweater, revealing her bandaged throat. "I spent my afternoon with six inches of cold steel cutting into my neck, Mr. Neville, while a disgusting creep tried to rape and murder me. You'll forgive my disregard for protocol, I hope, but I'm in a really bad mood and I want to know what the hell you people think you're up to!''

"Mariah!''

"No, Frank, it's all right," Neville said, holding up his hand. "Mariah, I know what you've been through is terrible. You have a right to be angry. But you have to believe me when I tell you that we had nothing to do with this—absolutely nothing, I swear.''

"I don't believe you.''

"Why not? Because that Chaney guy is looking for conspiracies under every rock? Come on, Mariah! You know how the media feel about the work you and I do.''

"Oh, no," Mariah said, shaking her head. "Not you and I, Mr. Neville. I don't know what *you* do, but I'm just a simple analyst trying to make sense of a confusing world. What I do doesn't get a child mauled and a brilliant man destroyed. It doesn't get a young woman like Tanya Baranova kidnapped and probably murdered for trying to do the right thing.''

"What are you saying?" Neville asked incredulously. "You joined up with our troops when you went to Vienna, Mariah. You recruited Baranova, for chrissake! What did you think you were inviting her to do, if not put her neck on the line?" Mariah stared at him, then sighed and closed her eyes briefly. "And as for your husband and daughter, well, hell. I'm sorry about your little girl. I mean it," he added as she glared at him. "I've got kids, too, you know. But you should be asking yourself what part your husband played in this."

"He was set up!"

"He had free will, Mariah! He could have walked away from that woman."

"Oh, God," Mariah said, slumping onto the bed. "Why didn't he?" She glanced up at the two men. "And don't tell me it was about sex. He didn't even like her when Chaney brought her around. It used to give him the creeps when she fawned over him—he said so. And we had a good marriage. I've thought and thought about it, and I can't believe he'd have done what he did if she weren't holding something over him."

Neville pulled up a chair and sat down opposite her. "Did your husband know you had recruited Baranova?"

"I never discussed my work with him—especially on this case. It would have put him in an awkward position. Although," she added, reflecting, "he might have seen us together, that first time, at the IAEA office party, and then when she came to the hockey rink."

"So he could have guessed."

"I suppose, if someone had suggested it. But otherwise it wouldn't have occurred to him, I don't think. He never mentioned her to me."

"What about Chaney?"

"What about him?"

"Did he know about Baranova?"

Mariah shook her head. "I don't think so. He was playing that day at the rink, but she left before the game was over. They never met."

"He introduced David to Katarina Müller?"

"Yes, but we thought Elsa—Katarina—was just another one of his girlfriends. He had a few," Mariah said dryly.

"Was Chaney in love with the Müller woman?"

"He says not—just the opposite. He knew she was a former East German agent and he was looking for a story."

"Why is he still dogging this?"

"Because he and David were good friends. And because—" She hesitated.

It was Tucker who finished the sentence. "Because he's in love with you. Has been for a while, hasn't he, Mariah?"

Neville peered at her closely. "Is he?" Mariah shrugged. "This is important, Mariah. If he's in love with you, he might have set up David to get him out of the way."

"There was nothing between us. I never encouraged him in any way. He had no reason to believe I could be interested in him, even if David weren't around. In fact, just the opposite. He was convinced I couldn't stand him. And he was genuinely upset about David—they were friends. When he discovered it was no accident, he wouldn't let it drop. Now it looks like he's been fired for his persistence."

"He has?" Neville said, sitting up straighter.

"This morning, apparently. At least, he seems to think that's why he was fired. Look, never mind Chaney. I want to know who sent me those pictures. And what they're supposed to mean."

"Have you got them with you?"

She looked at him with utter disgust. "They're not the kind of family snaps I keep in my wallet. I left them at home."

"What was in them?"

"David and Elsa—Katarina Müller."

Neville nodded, no further explanation was necessary. "I'd like to have them. I'll have them analyzed, see what we can find out."

"Are you saying you don't know anything about them?"

"Of course that's what I'm saying! For crying out loud, woman, think! Tatyana Baranova disappears. The Müller woman is assigned to compromise your husband. Frank here tells me David tried to talk you into leaving Vienna. That didn't work, so someone tries to kill you instead—" Mariah's eyes went wide. "Yes, you. I've always believed it was you they were after. Now Chaney starts reopening old wounds and suddenly they try again. What does all this suggest to you?"

Her gaze went from Neville to Tucker and back again. "KGB—or their successors."

"Bingo!" Neville said, sitting back in the chair. "Now that wasn't so hard, was it?"

"Don't patronize me!" Mariah said angrily.

"Well then, stop acting like a sophomoric CIA conspiracy theorist!" Neville snapped. "Why the hell would we do something like this to one of our own?"

Mariah glanced up at Tucker, who was watching Neville closely. She turned back to the deputy. "My daughter was given those photos at school yesterday. The creep who attacked me has been stalking me at least since Thursday night—he admitted it. Why would they try to blackmail me into silence if they had already decided to do the job permanently?"

Neville frowned. "It doesn't make sense," he agreed. "Unless your stalker is just that—your basic, all-American, murderous pervert who has nothing to do with this Vienna business."

"A little too coincidental, wouldn't you say?"

"I don't much like it as a theory, either, but in the absence of more evidence, it's all I can figure for now. In any event, they won't get a second chance, Mariah. I've assigned protection for you and your daughter until we get to the bottom of this."

Mariah shook her head. "I already told Frank I'm not going into hiding."

"Good. I don't want you to," Neville said. "We're going to be very discreet. I'd like to flush out whoever's behind this."

"You're hoping they'll try again?" Mariah said.

"For your sake, no. But if they do, we'll be there."

Mariah went to the window and stared out for a moment. A light snow had begun to fall, shimmering against the backdrop of bright Christmas lights strung on homes up and down the street. On the roof of a house across the street, tiny white lights spelled out the perennial message of Christmas hope, *Peace on Earth*—as if the mere act of stringing up the lights could make it happen. "Maybe I should send Lindsay to David's parents in New Hampshire," she said quietly.

"You might want to consider it," Neville said. "You might also want to consider losing the reporter, Mariah. At best, he can't do you any good. And given what's happened since he showed up this week, I'd suggest that his company is positively dangerous for you."

Mariah turned to study his face, but it was a mask. "Can't do *me* any good, Mr, Neville? Or the Company?"

But Neville had risen and headed for the door. "We should get out to the party now, before someone misses our charming company. Are you two coming?"

Mariah glanced at Tucker and she saw that he was watching Neville darkly. Frank nodded almost imperceptibly, and then followed him out the door.

13

Mariah circulated through the party for a while, but her heart wasn't in it. Leaving Chaney in a group debating the subject of media responsibility, she went in search of Lindsay to say good-night. Carol was sitting on a chair in the corner of the living room, rocking her sleeping baby, and Mariah's daughter was nowhere in sight. She moved from room to room until she finally discovered Lindsay in the den with Stephen Tucker. The two of them were hunched over Frank's computer, eyes transfixed on the screen, their faces bathed in its flickering bluish glow. Lindsay's hand was toggling a joystick to direct the action on the monitor.

"There you are, you two."

"Hi, Mom," Lindsay said, glancing up brightly. "Look at this, it's Stevie's new game. He's letting me test it!"

Stephen sat up straighter in the chair and watched Mariah approach, his eyes dropping to her bandaged hand. When he looked up, Mariah met his frown. She smiled and waved her hand, attempting to make light of the injury. She had spotted Stephen earlier, deep in conversation with Frank's secretary, and Pat's anxious glance in Mariah's direction had left no doubt as to what they had been discussing.

Lindsay sat back, beaming at the medieval parade of dragons, knights and wizards on the screen. "This is even better than *Wizard's Wand*," she said excitedly. "Wait'll my friends hear about it!"

"Sounds like you've got a hit on your hands, Stevie," Mariah said. Lindsay nodded in rapid agreement. From the girl's rapt expression, Mariah could see that Stephen had moved up into a category usually reserved for rock stars in the adolescent hierarchy of idols—a plump and unlikely heartthrob, maybe, but no less a hero for that.

The hero blushed profusely, the effect vaguely purplish under the computer's blue light. "Still a few kinks to work out," he mumbled. He glanced at Lindsay and his discomfort was apparent. Mariah thought back to the boys on the school steps with their skateboards and wondered whether, if he were younger or she ten years older, Stephen, too, would be doing handstands to earn the approval of those pretty dark eyes. The next few years are not going to be easy, she thought ruefully, regretting that David wasn't going to be there to intimidate the inevitable parade of suitors.

After watching the game for a short time, she kissed Lindsay good-night. Stephen followed her out into the hall.

"You're all right?" he asked. Mariah nodded. "Did it have anything to do with that operation in Vienna?"

She glanced around quickly, then shrugged. "I'm not sure, but your dad and some other people are looking into it. I didn't tell anyone about the file," she added, noting his sudden tension, "and I won't, Stevie, I promise. But now I'm really grateful that you got it for me." He looked dubious.

"Mariah?" They turned to see Paul Chaney coming down the hall. "Hi," he said. "Sorry to interrupt. I was just escaping a conversation in there that was showing signs of turning into a lynching. Some guy's had a bit much to drink."

"That's okay. I'm about ready to leave. This is Frank's son, Stephen Tucker," she said. "Stevie, this is Paul Chaney. He's a friend of David's from Vienna."

Stephen averted his eyes, mumbling some indistinct greeting as he shook Chaney's outstretched hand, his shyness painful to watch. He stepped back and followed at a distance as Mariah and Paul moved toward the front door.

Frank was already in the entrance, standing by the closet with her coat in his hand. He spun around as they approached. Mariah's eyes narrowed and she reached out for the garment. "I was just coming for that. We're going to head off now, Frank. It's a great party, but I'm beat."

Tucker glanced at Chaney and then held up Mariah's coat. As she turned and directed her arms into the sleeves and he lowered it onto her shoulders, she was struck by the heaviness of it, as if it were being dragged down by lead weights. She slipped her hands into the pockets and froze. Her eyes locked on to Frank, who was fixing her with a dark warning look.

In the left pocket, her hand wrapped around something hard, metallic and rectangular, the top side of it open. Along the open edge she felt the first bullet spring-loaded in a clip. She depressed the bullet with her thumb—by the resistance she felt, she knew the magazine was fully loaded. The fingers of her bandaged right hand traced the outline of the pistol that Frank had planted in the other pocket of her coat—a 9 mm semiautomatic, by the feel of it. He knew she didn't own a gun and under any other circumstances would have refused to have one in her house. But he also knew that she'd received enough basic training to be able to use the weapon if the need arose.

"Are you sure you won't reconsider and stay here?" Tucker asked. She shook her head firmly and his frown deepened. "Be careful."

Chaney stepped forward and cupped his hand under her elbow. "I'll keep an eye on her," he said. Tucker's frown shifted to Chaney, then to his hand on Mariah's elbow and back to her face.

"I'll be fine, Frank. Let's talk tomorrow," she said soberly. "I'm exhausted right now."

Chaney shook hands with Frank and Stephen, and he and Mariah headed out the door. At the bottom step, as she glanced up at Tucker and his son, Mariah was struck by the identical dark frowns on the faces of the two big men watching them leave.

She was silent as they drove back to McLean, feeling physically exhausted and buzzed at the same time, thinking about the conversation with George Neville. As much as she distrusted the smooth manner that belied his reputation for ruthlessness—you didn't get to be head of covert operations by being a Boy Scout—she knew there was some truth in what he had told her in Frank's bedroom. He was as mystified as she was about some of this. But at the same time, she realized, he hadn't told her what he *did* know regarding the whole ugly business.

Katarina Müller's targeting of David looked to be a simple case of blackmail to get him and Mariah out of Vienna. How David had let himself get into such a compromising situation, though, was something she couldn't begin to comprehend. Mariah's refusal to leave the post when David had pleaded with her to pull out early had probably pushed Müller's employers to up the ante, leading to the attack in front of Lindsay's school.

But now it was starting all over again. Why?

She glanced over at Chaney, frowning at the road ahead of him as he drove, clearly lost in thought. His persistence in dogging the case obviously had something to do with it; someone wanted them both to back off. But she knew by his stubborn expression that he had no intention of doing that. She also knew that he alone had been straight with her, and that the two of them were allies now. The realization was tinged with more than a little irony, given the way she had felt about him in Vienna.

"Are you okay?" he asked quietly. Mariah nodded. "Did you tell Tucker about the envelope?"

"Yes." She couldn't mention Neville.

"And? Does it make sense to him?"

"No. But I have to believe that whoever ordered Elsa—Katarina Müller—to set David up for blackmail is obviously trying to shut me up, too. And you, as well, I guess."

"Did Tucker tell you that Katarina Müller is dead?"

"What?"

Chaney pulled up to a stoplight and faced her. "Her body washed up on the banks of the Danube three months ago—what was left of it, anyway. My friend in the German embassy told me about it. I looked for her after the attack on David and Lindsay, but she had disappeared. They identified her by her dental work— she'd been in the river for quite a while."

Mariah shook her head. "No, he didn't tell me," she said, turning away to watch the road. "I can't say it breaks my heart to hear it, though."

When Chaney drove up to her house, they were surprised to see two Fairfax County police cruisers and an ambulance parked at irregular angles against the curb. The command van that had been there earlier that afternoon was back, as well as a vehicle whose side door was marked "Coroner." A small crowd had gathered once again, their faces and the surrounding houses and trees flashing in the red strobe of spinning lights. A new pathway of police barrier tape had been strung, but this one extended from the curb to her front door and along the asphalt walkway leading toward the center of the condominium complex.

They approached the yellow line and spotted a police officer whom Mariah recognized as the patrolman who had been first to arrive at her house that afternoon. He lifted the tape for them to pass under. "Ms. Bolt, Mr. Chaney—glad you're back," he said. "Sergeant Albrecht's been waiting to talk to you."

"What's the matter?" Mariah asked. "What's happened now?"

"There's been a body found."

"Who?"

The cop shrugged. "Not sure, there's no ID. Been there a couple of days, looks like. Come this way, please."

They followed the officer down the path until they came to the junction where it turned toward the recreation center. A couple of people wearing vests stenciled POLICE in large white letters were taking measurements along the path and into the wooded ravine that dropped steeply from its side. Mariah recognized Officer Harmon, the policewoman who had been gathering evidence in her bedroom earlier. Portable floodlights were angled down into the ravine and a small generator throbbed noisily. Paramedics were milling around a white-draped stretcher.

The officer tapped Sergeant Albrecht on the shoulder. He glanced at Mariah and Chaney and nodded briefly, then turned back to his conversation with a man whose jacket identified him as being from the coroner's office. A moment later, the sergeant walked over. As he approached, Mariah was conscious of the weight of the gun in her pocket and felt decidedly uneasy. She slipped her hands into her pockets.

"Busy day we're having in your neighborhood, Ms. Bolt."

"The officer said you'd found a body."

"Some guy walking his dog came across the old guy when the dog suddenly took off into the ravine."

"Your man said there was no ID on the body," Chaney said.

Albrecht nodded at Chaney, then addressed Mariah. "You said your stalker followed you from the pool on Thursday night."

"Yes, but I was walking with—oh, no!" Her eyes went wide. "He killed him!" she whispered. "Oh, God—oh, God, no!" She felt Chaney's arm go around her shoulders. She leaned against him and closed her eyes, her hand across her mouth.

"That's what it looks like, I'm afraid," Albrecht said. "You mentioned a stalker. And Laughlin, the old guy at the pool?"

"John Laughlin," she replied dully.

The sergeant shuffled his feet, waiting as she took a deep breath. When she looked up at him, he said, "Do you think you could manage to take a look at him and see if it's the same man? We've already determined that Laughlin lived alone and his neighbors haven't seen him for a couple of days. We're tracking down next of kin now. Dollars to doughnuts it's him, but a positive ID would help us a lot."

"Whatever you need," she said.

He took her gently by the arm and led her to the stretcher. As they approached, Mariah was conscious of a strong, cloying odor. Unpleasant. Like the nursing home, but worse, much worse.

"Brace yourself, now. It's not a pleasant sight."

"How?" Mariah whispered.

"Cut his throat." Albrecht signaled to the paramedics and one of them rolled down the top half of the sheet covering the body.

The eyes were wide and dull, the mouth gaping. The white hair, so neatly combed after his swim, was mussed and tangled with dead leaves. His skin, even in the poorly illuminated night, shone a pearly gray-green color. A dark port-wine stain spread from his neck down the pigeon chest that he had pounded so heartily that night.

"Oh, poor Mr. Laughlin. I'm so sorry," Mariah whispered. She tore her eyes away and looked up at Sergeant Albrecht and nodded, as the paramedics pulled the sheet over the old man.

At that precise moment, old John Laughlin's killer was well on his way to getting blind drunk.

Rollie Burton stretched forward on the sofa, reaching for the bottle of whiskey on the table in front of him. He made a halfhearted attempt to pour another glassful, scowled at the glass in his hand and let it drop to the floor. Leaning back on the sofa, he grasped the neck of the bottle and took a long gulp. He held the burning liquid in his mouth for a second or two, then swallowed and reached up to massage his aching head. Black pools of blood had formed in the hollows under both eyes, leaving them raccoonlike, puffy and swollen. His nostrils were packed with cotton, and he breathed noisily through his mouth.

After leaving the condominium complex that afternoon, he had driven straight back to the underground garage of his dingy apartment block in Arlington, knowing he had to get the Toyota and himself off the road quickly. He had made good time in the early Saturday-afternoon traffic.

In the garage, Burton had stuffed his nose with tissues, cleaned up his face as much as possible and slipped a windbreaker over his bloody sweatshirt. He had pulled on his baseball cap and dark glasses as extra precaution before bounding up the stairs to his second-floor apartment, avoiding the elevator, but no one had been around to see him. He had spent the rest of the afternoon lying down with ice on his nose, knowing it was broken, knowing there was no way he could chance having a doctor look at it. Knowing he was going back to kill the bitch the first chance he got.

Taking another swig of whiskey, he was startled by the jangle of the telephone. The liquor went down the wrong way and he coughed spasmodically, rolling himself over and off the sofa, stumbling toward the kitchen and the phone. His voice, when he finally recovered enough to pick up the receiver, was hoarse and dusky. "Hello?"

"Burton?"

Burton froze at the tinny, slightly garbled sound of the familiar voice. "Yeah?" he said cautiously.

"You screwed up." The voice knew his phone number—whoever it belonged to probably knew where to find him, as well. The kind of people who had Burton's number and made use of it were not the kind to tolerate mistakes.

"What are you talking about?"

"Don't play games with me," the voice hissed. "You were supposed to take her out, not get your jollies, you idiot!"

Burton leaned against the wall, the burning liquor in his stomach barely counteracting the profound unease that this high-pitched voice was rousing. "I was doing what I was supposed to do—making it look like something else. It was a professional decision." He winced at his own audacity, praying the voice would buy it.

When he heard only silence at the other end of the line, he decided to plunge ahead, taking the offensive.

"And you neglected to mention some critical facts—like she's got a kid. What the hell am I supposed to do, take out a kid, too, and have every cop in the Commonwealth of Virginia looking to strip my hide? And how about the reporter, for chrissake? He tails her everywhere! You want me to do this under television lights?"

Burton shook his head vigorously, his courage mounting along with his whiskey-primed indignation. "I'm a professional! You want me to work under these kinds of conditions, you bloody well better give me all the facts—not to mention a hell of a lot more money. Otherwise, this contract's just a piece of garbage!"

He held his breath, waiting for a reaction. For a long, agonizing moment, there was only silence.

"What do you want?" the voice asked.

"A few more days—and more money."

"What?"

"You heard me. This isn't as straightforward as you led me to believe. We're talkin' high risk here—real high risk. That's gonna cost."

"How much?"

Burton was feeling decidedly courageous now. "Double," he said, "including another ten grand up front before I move again." There was a squeaky hiss on the other end of the line that he took to be an intake of breath. Buy it, he prayed.

"All right," the voice said at last. Burton slumped with relief. "It'll take a day or so. Be at Tyson's Corner—same place as before, the Dumpster—after 2:00 a.m. Tuesday morning. The money'll be there."

"Got it."

"And Burton?"

"What?"

"No more screwups. Is that clear?"

"Yeah, sure. It's in the bag."

He hung up the phone and leaned against the wall, holding his hand to his throbbing head. Then he moved back to the sofa to finish the bottle and drown the nagging feeling that he might finally be getting too old for this game.

"The good news," Sergeant Albrecht said, "is that we think we know who this guy is."

Mariah and Chaney glanced up sharply. They were sitting in Mariah's kitchen while the officer posed more questions about the night the stalker had tracked her from the pool.

"Already?" Chaney said. "How did you manage that?"

"Dumb luck. That, and the fact that my next-door neighbor works on the FBI's national fingerprint ID system. We ran the prints we picked up here through our own computers this afternoon, but came up blank. I gave my buddy a call, and he happened to be working today and agreed to run them right away. Usually it takes weeks to get anything back from those guys," the cop added, grimacing.

"And they found something?" Mariah prodded.

"Yup." Albrecht reached into his notebook and pulled out a photo. He laid it on the table. "Is this your guy?"

Mariah and Chaney examined the picture of a white-haired man sitting at a sidewalk café, glass in hand. A sign in a window behind him advertised food and beverages in Spanish—*vino y cerveza, tapas y platos combinados*. Having seen many such pictures, Mariah guessed that it was a surveillance shot taken with a telephoto lens. She shuddered, then glanced over at Chaney. The two of them looked up at the sergeant and nodded.

"Looks like the guy's a professional hit man named Roland Norman Burton," Albrecht said.

"Professional?"

The cop nodded, watching her closely. "You got any enemies, Ms. Bolt? Been involved in any CIA funny business?"

When he had asked her that afternoon where she worked, Mariah had said that she was with the Central Intelligence Agency. As she had told Frank, it wasn't a national secret, although she had always preferred to maintain the public fiction of a State Department job—there was always someone who wanted to take you on when they found out you were with the Company. Where the police were concerned, however, she had decided to come clean.

"I'm just a political analyst, Sergeant. I told you that. Why do you ask?"

Albrecht looked over at Chaney. "Mr. Chaney," he warned, "since you're involved in this case and a friend of Ms. Bolt, I'm letting you sit in. But you understand that none of this is for public consumption until we nail this bastard?"

"My interest here is personal, not professional, Sergeant."

"Okay, good," Albrecht said, turning back to Mariah. "It seems Burton works for various employers, mostly the mob and international drug cartels. Both the FBI and the Drug Enforcement Agency have files on him a mile long, but neither one's been able to get enough evidence to make anything stick. They were surprised to hear he was even in the country—seems he operates mostly in the Far East and Latin America. Guy's getting on, though. He's in his fifties and he could be slowing down, coming home to retire."

"I don't understand why he would be after me, then," Mariah said. "The Company has a narcotics unit that works with DEA on international cases, but I've never been anywhere near that part of the outfit."

"Well, I said Burton does *mostly* drug-related hits, but he's not choosy. He'll free-lance for anyone who comes up with the price. And," Albrecht added, "he's one of yours—used to be, anyway."

"What? CIA, you mean?"

The sergeant nodded. "Covert operator from the days of the old Phoenix operation in Vietnam. Trained assassin—*well* trained. Word is, the Company booted him out after a year or so, though—bastard was too mean, even for those guys. Seems he kept getting picked up for sexual assaults on local women over there, some of the attacks pretty vicious.''

Mariah shuddered again. She got up and went to the kitchen sink for a glass of water, then leaned back against the counter as she drank it. Putting the glass down, she noticed the flashing light on the telephone answering machine.

''So where does this leave us, Sergeant?'' Chaney asked.

''A little further ahead. We're contacting the CIA Office of Security to see if they might have any recent information on Burton or contacts he might have in the D.C. area.'' He snapped his notebook shut. ''Meantime, folks, you should be extra careful. I'm going to keep a patrol car close by, but this is one mean S.O.B. we're dealing with. We can't underestimate him. Normally, I wouldn't expect a stalker to be back after a close call like the one he had here, but if he's on a contract, all bets are off. If you did break his nose, though,'' he added, looking up at Mariah, clearly reaching for some sort of encouragement, ''he may lie low for a few days. That might give us enough time to track him down. We can hope, anyway.'' She didn't feel encouraged. The sergeant got to his feet. ''I'd better be going now. We'll be in touch.''

Mariah nodded and Chaney followed him to the front door. She stood thinking for a moment, then turned to the answering machine and hit the playback button.

''*Mrs. Tardiff, this is the Montgomery Convalescent Care Home. The time is 11:15 p.m. Please call the night duty nurse as soon as possible.*'' Mariah frowned and glanced at the clock on the stove—just after midnight. She searched her phone list for the number and dialed.

When Chaney came back into the kitchen a couple minutes later, she was just hanging up the phone. He stopped dead when he saw her face. "Mariah? What's the matter?"

Her eyes drifted slowly up to him. "Has the sergeant left?"

"The car's still outside," Chaney said, glancing out the window. "What's wrong?"

"Get him back in here, Paul."

"What is it? What happened?"

"I just spoke to the nursing home," she said numbly. "David's dead."

"I want an autopsy," Mariah said when Sergeant Albrecht came back in and had been told what happened.

"What did the nursing home say?"

"They were doing evening rounds about two hours ago and found he had died in his sleep. His doctor came in and signed the death certificate. He listed a probable aneurysm as the cause of death—apparently, that's common after head injuries like my husband's."

"You don't buy it?" Albrecht questioned.

Mariah glanced at Chaney and then dropped her gaze, picking at the bandage on her wrist. "I don't know what to think," she said quietly. "Maybe there's something more." She looked up to see Albrecht watching her closely through narrowed eyes. "After everything that's gone on today, I'd just feel better if we ruled out any other possibility."

The sergeant hesitated, then nodded slowly. "Okay. I'll get on the radio and catch the coroner's people— they just left with Laughlin."

"Can you wait just a little?" she pleaded. "I'd like to see him first. Please. I'll go over to the nursing home right now."

Albrecht flushed as he watched her. "Sure," he said, "I understand. I'll have the coroner's people go by first thing in the morning."

"I'll take you, Mariah." Chaney led Albrecht to the kitchen door. "How soon will you have the autopsy results, do you think, Sergeant?"

"By noon or shortly thereafter." Albrecht turned back to Mariah. "I'm sorry, ma'am. This has been a truly awful day for you." He reached out and placed a card on the table. "If there's something else you think you'd like to tell me, call anytime, day or night. The dispatcher can reach me at home if need be."

She nodded, unable to speak.

14

"Remember Rollie Burton?" George Neville asked.

He and Dieter Pflanz were strolling by the fifty-eight thousand names inscribed on the black granite walls of the Vietnam Veterans Memorial. They had paused briefly near the vertex of the walls—each, because of the other's presence, resisting the impulse to reach out and finger names of friends who had sunk in that quagmire, young men, in most cases, hardly more than boys. Even hardened as the two of them were now, after too many years spent doing too many dirty jobs, resisting the impulse to touch the wall and the memories those names evoked was almost as difficult as resisting the impulse to breathe.

Ramming his fists deeper into his pockets, Pflanz glanced over at Neville, then stepped back from the wall and turned to walk up toward the reflecting pool. The morning had dawned dull, gray and cold. Now, close to noon, the heavy sky threatened snow. The trees along the Mall were bare and uninviting, and the few tourists who had ventured out walked quickly, hunkered down in their coats.

"Yeah," Pflanz said as Neville caught up to him. "Guy was borderline psycho. What about him?"

"Our security people had a call from the Fairfax County police. They believe Burton was the man who attacked Mariah Bolt yesterday. Wanted to know if the

Company had any recent information on his where-abouts.''

"So?"

"So do we, Dieter?"

"Why are you asking me?"

"I'm just wondering if you know anything about it."

"Why would I know anything about an attack on one of your people?"

"Come on, Dieter!" Neville snapped. "Don't be cute! I know you've never been happy about that screwup in Vienna. But I told you she was okay—neutralized. If you're involved in this, I'm gonna have your hide, because it's completely unnecessary and counter-productive."

Pflanz stopped cold and spun around, his beaked nose bearing down hard on the other man, one fist wrapped in Neville's lapel. "Don't you mess with me, George," he growled. "If anybody's hide gets nailed to the barn door, it's not gonna be mine. You called me in here, remember? We've done one hell of a job for you, so don't give me this butt-covering bureaucratic garbage!"

"Take it easy," Neville said, glancing around quickly and then turning back to Pflanz's angry face. "I know what you've done. But the woman's asking hard questions. And she's got friends, all of whom seem intent on protecting her. If she gets hurt, there'll be hell to pay."

"Then you should keep an eye on her."

"We are."

"Fine."

Neville hesitated. "You really don't know anything about Burton?" he asked. Pflanz had loosened his grip on Neville's lapel, but he glared at him so severely that the deputy backed off. "Okay, okay. I just needed to be sure."

* * *

"Do you want some more tea, Mariah?" Chaney asked quietly.

She shook her head slowly. "No, thanks."

She was huddled on the sofa in the living room, her arms wrapped around her knees, a blanket hugging her shoulders. The house was warm enough, but she couldn't seem to stop shivering. She regretted that she had launched herself so obsessively into cleaning the place after she and Chaney had returned from the nursing home the night before—in the wee hours of the morning, really. Now there was nothing to do but wait.

When she'd refused his offer of help, Chaney had withdrawn to the living room, leaving her alone, knowing she needed time. She had scrubbed and dusted and vacuumed until every trace of the attack and subsequent police investigation had disappeared. It had been 4:00 a.m. when she finally fell into her bed, physically and emotionally exhausted.

But there was to be no escape from pain and self-recrimination. Sleep was denied. The last image of David was burned on her mind's eye—his tortured body finally at ease but cold to her touch, stretched out lifelessly in a glaringly bright, tile-lined room. Mariah was sentenced to hear the nurse's words reverberate over and over in her head: "aneurysm...bursting brought on by stress."

Stress, her mind shrieked accusingly, like the emotional stress of her outburst in his room that morning, when David had reached out to her for comfort and instead she had thrown Elşa's name in his face.

When she finally tiptoed downstairs again at eight to make some coffee, Chaney was already up, looking as if he had passed a night almost as restless as hers. She had made him tea and breakfast—the coffeepot was smashed, she remembered grimly—and she had sat with him. But they had said little. She knew he was waiting for her to make the opening. She knew she should make use of these few hours—the calm before the storm of telling Lindsay and calling David's family and making funeral arrangements and going through the whole awful ordeal. She knew she should pull out Stephen's diskette and get on with examining the CHAUCER file. She knew she should find out what else Paul had learned during his investigation of the attack in Vienna. But paralysis had set in—she just couldn't bring herself to deal with anything right now.

Mariah glanced at her watch. "I wish they'd call."

"Sergeant Albrecht said noon or thereabouts. He told me he'd be in touch as soon as the procedure was over."

She had decided to wait for the autopsy results before calling David's family, and to leave Lindsay with Carol for the morning, as planned—let her have a little fun with the baby before her young world was shaken yet again.

"I'm going to have to leave to pick up Lindsay soon," Mariah said. She closed her eyes. "Oh, Paul, how am I going to tell her?"

Chaney sat down on the couch and touched her arm lightly. She didn't flinch, they were beyond that now. The past twenty-four hours had destroyed both the wall between them and her energy to maintain it. The quiet support he offered was the only point of relative calm in the turbulent waters raging around her.

"It won't be easy," he said softly. "But in a way, maybe she's already said goodbye to him. To part of him, anyway, the part that didn't come back after the accident."

Mariah frowned and then nodded slowly. "It's true," she said. "We really lost him last January. But I'm afraid she'll start blaming herself again."

"Blaming herself? Why?"

"It doesn't make sense, I know. But for a long time after the accident, she felt it was her fault because he was taking her to school when it happened."

"That's an awfully heavy burden for a kid to carry."

"I know, and I think I finally had her talked out of it. But I understand where she's coming from. I blamed myself for years after my father left us."

"You were seven years old, Mariah!"

She shrugged. "Guilt is a precocious emotion. It develops early."

"Why would you think your father's leaving was your fault?"

She pressed her lips against her knees for a moment. "My mother worked to support him while he wrote. But she didn't mind—she believed in him." Mariah shook her head. "She spoiled him, but then, women always did, I think. He was good-looking and talented and they used to fall all over him. I was conscious of that even as a little kid." The corners of her mouth lifted in a small smile. "And, of course, they'd fuss over me, too. I used to be so proud to go out with him. I remember walking along the beach, holding his hand, feeling like a fairy princess."

"But the fairy tale didn't last, did it?" Chaney said quietly.

"No. One night, my mother was working and there was a party on the beach. There was no money for baby-sitters, so he took me with him. I remember the big bonfire, people singing, laughing. I thought it was a hoot, being out so late at night, dancing in the sand. He picked me up in his arms and swung me around and we laughed and laughed. I thought he was the greatest daddy in the world."

She hugged her knees tighter. "And then, at one point, he said he was going for a walk and that I should stay with the people near the fire. After a while, when he didn't come back, I got nervous. No one was paying any attention to me, and all the faces started to look scary in the firelight. So I wandered off down the beach, looking for him. No one even noticed me leave. I remember the blue light of the moon on the water, the rumble of the waves. It seemed so ominous—I got really frightened. I remember running in the sand, stumbling and crying, calling for him. I almost tripped over them in the dark.''

"Them?''

"Him and the woman he was with. 'Having a rest,' he said. He was annoyed—she was embarrassed. I remember thinking they were going to catch cold with their clothes all undone like that.''

Chaney shook his head. "Then what happened?''

"He took me home and put me to bed, but I woke up later when my mother came in. They were shouting at each other. 'How am I supposed to get any work done,' he said, 'when I've always got the kid on my neck?' ''

Mariah pulled the blanket tighter around her shoulders. " 'The kid,' '' she said bitterly, looking up at him. "Nice, huh? Anyway, next day he was gone, leaving a pregnant wife and a seven-year-old child. We never saw him again.''

"What a creep!'' Chaney breathed. He studied her face. "And you thought it was your fault?''

She nodded. "For years, until I finally got old enough and smart enough to come to the same conclusion as you—that the guy was a first-class heel, end of story.''

"Was that when he went to Paris?''

"Yes. Some rich woman he had met—seduced, naturally—financed him to 'further his art.' At least, she financed him until she caught him cheating on her, too. Then she pulled the rug out. He was living in some dive in Montmartre when he died of hepatitis a year later.''

"And his landlady packed away all his stuff in an attic and the writing was lost for years,'' Chaney said, quoting the press stories that had come out when some college English professor had gone searching for the rumored Bolt manuscripts and discovered them in Paris. "He never knew your sister, I guess."

"No. Katie was born six months after he left. From there on in, about all I can remember of my childhood was sandy floors in a crummy cottage, taking Katie everywhere I went and trying to keep her quiet while my mother rested on the sofa between shifts."

"That must have been rough on you."

"I didn't really think about it. I figured it was the price I had to pay for driving our dad away. As I got older, school and the water were the only escape I had from all that, so I threw myself into the books and competitive swimming. I got academic and athletic scholarships after high school and a chance to finally get away from those memories."

"It made you the person you are today, didn't it?"

She shrugged again. "I guess."

"I know it couldn't have been easy, Mariah, but that little girl turned into a pretty impressive woman." She glanced at him and then away, uncomfortable. "What happened to your sister?"

"She died when she was twelve. I was up at Berkeley. Katie was fooling around with some kids on the Newport pier and fell off—broke her neck and drowned. I blamed myself for that, too. I thought that if I'd been there to keep an eye on her, it wouldn't have happened. I felt so bad. I decided to quit school to stay with my mother, but she threw me out. I thought she blamed me, too. We didn't speak for almost a year. Then she got sick—ovarian cancer. I went back to be with her at the end, and she told me that she wanted me to finish my education, be independent—make better choices than she had made. That's why she hadn't let me come home. She knew I'd go back to the only place I felt safe—buried in the books."

"Your mother sounds like a good woman."

"She was. She didn't deserve the life she got."

Chaney was quiet as she tucked herself wearily into a corner of the sofa, pulling the blanket around her and closing her eyes, her mind's eye watching the parade of loved ones who had been wrenched out of her life, one by one. She must have dozed off because when the telephone rang, she leaped up, startled and disoriented, eyes flashing around the room until Paul appeared and put a hand on her shoulder, and she remembered where she was. She stood rooted to the spot as the phone jangled again.

"Do you want me to take it?" he asked.

She looked up at him and nodded dumbly. He turned and headed for the kitchen. She followed, waiting in the doorway, watching as he picked up the receiver, listening to his half of the conversation, first with Sergeant Albrecht, then, apparently, with the pathologist. When he hung up the phone a few minutes later, he seemed stunned.

"What? What did they say? There was something else, wasn't there?" Chaney nodded and she blanched. "Was David murdered?"

"No," Chaney said, turning to face her. "It was an aneurysm. But he also had cancer—thyroid cancer. Anaplastic carcinoma, the pathologist said. They don't have biopsy results yet, but he was absolutely certain. It had spread to the trachea. When he was lying down in bed, they figured the windpipe became blocked. It looks like he went into respiratory distress and the strain of that caused the aneurysm to burst."

Mariah watched him, the words sinking in slowly, remembering David wheezing when she'd visited him the day before. Then her knees buckled, and the next thing she knew, she was on the floor and Chaney was holding her up. "I thought I did it," she whispered.

"Did what?"

"Killed him. Yesterday, when I saw him. I told him I knew about Elsa. I was angry and hurt. He understood what I was saying. His reaction—oh, Paul! I thought it was the stress of that that did it.''

''No, Mariah, listen to me,'' Chaney said firmly, lifting her chin. ''David was very sick. The pathologist said that the kind of cancer he had spreads like wildfire and is virtually always fatal. He couldn't have lived more than a few more months. Maybe,'' he added quietly, ''this was the kindest way for it to happen.''

Mariah stared ahead, nodding but seeing nothing. Chaney pulled her shaking body closer, and they sat together in the middle of the kitchen floor, rocking slowly while she cried.

''She's not completely out of the woods,'' Gus McCord said, ''but the doctors say we can probably move her back in a few days. Her specialist in California is lining up round-the-clock nursing care so she can be at home. She's going to need to take it easy. 'Course,'' he added, grinning and shaking his head, ''I may need to tie her down to accomplish that.''

He was hyper, Dieter Pflanz noted, rambling and elated at the news that his wife was going to pull through from the heart attack. It had been a mild one, the specialists had said, a warning sign that she was going to have to slow down a little, ease up on her activities. McCord was pacing nervously across the floor of the hospital lounge, his strained features really showing his age—and then some—for the first time since the security chief had known him.

Pflanz nodded. ''That's good, Gus. Now maybe you can slow down, too? Get some rest.''

McCord grimaced. ''Don't you start, Dieter. I get enough of that from Nance and the boys.''

''Yeah, well, they're right. You're no good to anybody if you collapse from exhaustion. Have you slept at all in the last two days?''

''Some. I catnapped.''

Pflanz snorted. "I'll run you back to your room when the car gets here. The boys are on their way now from the hotel. Let them sit with Mrs. McCord for a few shifts—they've been cooling their heels for the past twenty-four hours. You need to quit hogging her."

"Since when did you add mother hen to your list of security duties, Pflanz?"

"Since Jerry Siddon got on the plane to California this morning. He left me in charge of that department."

"You could go back, too, you know. There's no point in hanging around, wasting time, when there's nothing you can do here."

"I've got some business to take care of."

McCord frowned, studying the big man. "Is there a problem with New Mexico?"

Pflanz hesitated. "Not really. A minor glitch. I'm taking care of it."

"I thought we already did, Dieter," McCord said. "Is it this Chaney business again? I thought I took care of that."

"He's out. He's still snooping, but he's neutralized. He can't do any damage now."

"Then what's the problem?" Just then, the four McCord sons came through the door of the lounge.

"It's no big deal, Gus," Pflanz said quickly. "Leave it to me."

"It wasn't because of the accident, Lins," Mariah said gently. She was holding Lindsay in her arms, sitting on the bed in Carol's guest room where she had taken her daughter to tell her about David. Lindsay was crying softly. "He was very sick. We probably would have lost him, anyway, even if the accident had never happened. They said he had a kind of cancer that's not curable."

"How did he get it?"

"I don't know, sweetheart. It's always hard to know with cancer. It just seems to happen to people sometimes."

"I can't believe he's gone."

"I know. Me, neither." Mariah stroked her daughter's red curls. Then she had a thought and sat back a little. "Do you remember the last thing you said to Daddy, Lins?"

"No."

"Think about it. What was the very last thing you said, just before you kissed him and left his room yesterday?"

Lindsay frowned as she struggled to remember. Then the lines in her forehead softened. "I told him I loved him."

Mariah gathered her up in her arms again and held her tightly, kissing the top of her head. "Yes, you did, sweetheart," she said quietly. "And you know what? So did I."

15

At first he thought he'd been double-crossed.

Rollie Burton had driven into the parking lot of the Tyson's Corner Mall after 2:00 a.m. as the voice had directed, keeping the old Toyota back in the shadows on the edge of the lot until he saw the mall security patrol car go by. Then he pulled up alongside the big Dumpster. Leaving the engine running, Burton climbed out of the car, glanced around quickly, then looked into the Dumpster. Last time, the briefcase with the money had been sitting right on top of the pile. This time the Dumpster was only half-full, but there was no case to be seen.

"What the hell...?" Burton cursed under his breath.

He pulled a penlight out of his pocket and shone it in. And then he spotted it. The case had slid down the pile of trash and lay deep in one corner of the box, on the far side at the back where the Dumpster stood wedged against a wall of the building and the loading dock.

"Great," he mumbled.

He stood on tiptoe and reached in as far as he could, but his arms were too short to make it. He tried to squeeze his body into a small opening between the loading dock and the big steel box, but the space was too narrow, even for his lean frame. Finally, with an exasperated sigh, he pocketed the flashlight and hiked himself up onto the lip of the Dumpster and over the edge. He scrabbled on the loose pile of cardboard and slid down onto his butt, cursing again. Working his way over to the corner, he squatted, breathing heavily through his mouth.

He pulled the penlight out of his pocket again and opened the briefcase on his knees. Picking up one of the banded stacks of twenties, he flipped it between his fingers, starting to sniff before remembering that he couldn't. He had packed his nose again, not wanting to risk its starting to bleed all over the place. It wouldn't be the nice, crisp smell of new bills, anyway, he thought, dropping the stack back in the case. But these were safer. He ran his fingers lightly over the rest, then closed the lid, clicking shut first one lock, then the other.

At the sound of a third click, he froze. His eyes rose to see the head and torso of a large figure standing beside the Dumpster, silhouetted against the parking-lot lights. Burton lifted his flashlight to the face.

"Kill that!" the figure growled.

A gun rose in the circle of light. It looked like a Smith and Wesson, Burton thought, the old Hush Puppy from their Vietnam days, fitted with a silencer. He lowered the flashlight and snapped it off. "You?" he said, stunned.

"Long time no see, Rollie." The silhouette shook its head. "You got old, but you didn't get any smarter. Still can't do a job without your dick getting in the way, can you?"

"Hey! A guy's gotta have some fun," Burton said, his grin nervous. "Gimme a break, will you? I'll take care of it." He squinted at the figure. "Who is she, anyway? How come you want her taken out?" No reply. "Okay, sure—none of my business. And I never saw, never laid eyes on you. Hell! I didn't have a clue. That voice on the phone—you guys got electronics now, I guess, hey? Real effective."

He went to rise but slipped on the loose trash underfoot and fell against the corner of the Dumpster, the briefcase flying out of his hands. "I'll just climb out of here and get on with it, okay?"

"No, Rollie, you've screwed up for the last time."

Burton's mismatched eyes grew wide. "Dieter, please! Don't!"

The plea was lost in the sharp hiss of compressed gas escaping from the silencer, followed by a dull clang as the bullet passed through his brain and lodged in the steel walls of the oversize box that had become his coffin. One green eye and one ice blue stared blindly at the huge hand that reached in and lifted out the briefcase. The Toyota was still idling when the rent-a-cop security patrol pulled around the corner again twenty minutes later.

Mariah had taken David home to be buried in the Tardiff family plot in Dover, New Hampshire. Dozens of Tardiff sisters and brothers and aunts and uncles and cousins showed up at St. Charles Catholic Church, where one Mass a week was still said in French for the benefit of a few old parishioners who took comfort in the language of their childhood—immigrants who had come from Quebec to New England in waves over the past hundred years, seeking work in the region's textile mills. The mills were mostly gone now, and the language would be, too, when the last of the ancient ones died off. Only the names in the telephone book—the Leducs and the Cléments and the Tardiffs and others—would be left to remind generations to come of their heritage.

Mariah moved through the wake and the funeral as if sailing through a North Atlantic fog, greeting people and receiving expressions of sympathy, but experiencing it all through a dense filter. She was grateful, though, for the cushion of support that the big family provided for Lindsay, with its aunts and uncles and cousins by the dozens, not to mention the all-enveloping love of David's mother and father.

Watching David's mother cluck over Lindsay, Mariah smiled. She had never known her own grandparents. Her father had been an only child, his parents divorced and long dead. Her mother had been estranged from her family for years, cut off after running away to California at eighteen with the irresponsible beatnik, Ben Bolt. The Illinois banker and his wife had never forgiven their daughter, nor she them for their continuing coldness even when they knew she was struggling alone with two young daughters. Mariah had called them when her mother was dying, hoping for a reconciliation at the end. The timid woman's voice that had answered the telephone had been replaced quickly by the bluster of her husband, who had taken the news as coolly as if she were a defaulting client seeking to fend off a foreclosure. Mariah had never been tempted to seek them out again.

Standing in the bitter cold at the cemetery, her arms around Lindsay and her in-laws' arms around both of them, Mariah wondered what David's family would have made of his last actions in Vienna. Like all large families, they had their share of eccentric characters and their little peccadilloes. But there was nothing in the simple, family-centered traditions of these good people to prepare them for the mind-boggling personal and professional lapse that David had suffered at the hands of Katarina Müller.

Mariah stared at the casket suspended over the open grave, barely hearing the drone of the final rites being pronounced by the priest, her wet cheeks turning to ice in the cold wind. This isn't over, David, she promised. I know who you were and what you were. And I know that no matter what you did in Vienna, you were victimized and frightened. Stephen Tucker was right—you were a good man and you didn't deserve this. I'm going to get to the bottom of it, I swear. So rest easy now.

Most of the people from the cemetery came by David's parents' house afterward. Frank Tucker and Pat Bonelli stopped by briefly before heading back to Logan Airport and their late-afternoon flight to Washington.

"Carol wanted to come so much," Pat told Mariah over coffee, "but she couldn't leave the baby with this awful croup he's picked up. And Stephen was going to come, too, but then he got cold feet at the last minute—you know how he is with strangers," she added apologetically.

Mariah shook her head. "It doesn't matter. I know how he felt about David. Poor Stevie. I guess David was one of the few people he ever felt really comfortable with. He was broken up after the accident. And Carol's been nothing but supportive ever since we got back from Vienna. So have you two," she added, looking up as Tucker came over with Pat's coat. "I don't know what Lindsay and I would have done without you."

"How long are you going to stay in New Hampshire, Mariah?" Tucker asked.

"Through Christmas, I guess, if that's all right with you and the office. I think Lindsay needs to be with David's family right now. It's not going to be an easy holiday season, but she's got a lot of support here."

"I think that's a good idea."

Mariah knew he had more in mind than just Lindsay's needs, but she also knew from his opaque expression that he wasn't about to discuss it.

"Hello, Paul," Pat said, looking up at Chaney, who had drifted over from a conversation with a group of Tardiff cousins. "Nice to see you again, although I wish it could have been under happier circumstances."

Chaney nodded and smiled briefly, then extended his hand to Tucker. "You two are heading back now?"

"That's right. Are you?"

Chaney shook his head. "Not exactly. My son lives in Connecticut. I'm going to run down to see him tomorrow."

"That's nice," Pat said. "Are you spending Christmas with him?"

"I'm afraid his mother's not prepared to be *that* generous," he said. "I'm going to spend the holidays with my parents. They're retired out in Phoenix."

"Well, you have a good Christmas, anyway," Pat said warmly. "Mariah, I'll call you in a couple of days to see how you and Lins are doing, okay?"

Mariah hugged her. "Sure. And thanks for coming up, Patty. You, too, Frank."

"Just take it easy, Mariah," Tucker said. "The office will survive and the only important thing is for you and Lindsay to relax. Forget about everything else for a while."

Mariah nodded slowly.

She had set the alarm on her watch for six-thirty, but when it went off the next morning and Mariah rolled out of bed, she noticed that the house was already full of warm cooking smells. She pulled on jeans and a sweatshirt and went down to the kitchen, where David's mother was just pulling bread out of the oven. The older woman glanced up, startled, as Mariah approached.

"What are you doing up so early?" Mrs. Tardiff scolded. "You should sleep in. Poor thing, you looked exhausted yesterday."

Mariah gave her a hug. "Me? What about you? How long have you been up, for goodness' sake?" She sniffed at the fragrant loaves.

"Oh, I can never sleep in the morning, you know that. I'd just as soon get up and get busy."

"Nothing worse than just lying there in bed, remembering, is there?" Mariah said softly.

David's mother put the loaves on a rack to cool and slipped two more into the oven. Then she straightened and wiped her hands on her apron, gazing out the window. "I used to bake six loaves, three times a week, when the children were at home. I could have given them store-bought, of course, but they liked homemade better—especially David. He was such a little devil. If I didn't keep an eye on him, he'd polish off a whole loaf all by himself as soon as it cooled."

Mariah smiled. "He didn't change. I never knew how a small guy like that could eat so much and not gain an ounce."

"It was all that energy he had. Always on the go, into something." David's mother's eyes were bright. She sniffed and pulled out a tissue from her apron pocket, leaning into the arm that Mariah put around her shoulder. "I have—had—six children," she said quietly, "and I love them all. But in my secret heart, David was always special. He was born premature, you know, almost didn't make it—such a scrawny little thing. They said he'd always be sickly, maybe a bit slow-witted, too. But he showed them. He was like a little terrier dog—such a scrapper. He'd go after what he wanted and not rest till he had it. And heaven help anyone who tried to take anything of his away from him."

Mariah nodded as the two of them stood watching the bare trees outside the window swaying in the gray, early-morning light. They turned at the sound of footsteps in the doorway behind them.

"Everybody up already?" David's father asked. Watching his warm brown eyes, Mariah was struck once more by how much he resembled David—or vice versa, rather. The older man's hair was pure white now, the dark curls of his youth gone, but Mariah knew that this was what David would have come to look like if they had been allowed to grow old together.

She smiled at his kind face. "All except Lindsay," she said. "I wouldn't expect to see her up much before ten. Suzanne and her kids are coming by to pick her up at noon." David's sister had promised to drive Lindsay and her cousins to the mall that afternoon.

"Well, you two sit down and I'll get you some breakfast," Mrs. Tardiff said, beginning to bustle again.

"Not for me, thanks," Mariah said. "I'm going to go for a drive, if that's all right with you. I feel restless—I think a little air might help."

"Of course it's all right, Mariah," David's father said. "Do you want some company? I'll come with you."

"No, thanks. I need to be on my own for a little, do some thinking. I'm fine, really," she added, noticing the worried look on both their faces. "I just need to blow off excess energy. I might go for a walk down by the ocean."

"Have something to eat first," Mrs. Tardiff said. "It won't take a minute."

"No, thanks, really. I'm not hungry right now. I'll have something when I get back. I won't be too long, I promise."

Backing her rented car out of the driveway a few minutes later, Mariah noticed the gray Ford parked down the street a little way. As she headed off, she glanced in the rearview mirror. Sure enough, the Ford was pulling out. Keeping her speed down, she debated her options. Then she headed for Silver Street and the Spaulding Turnpike on-ramp.

David's hometown was in that little neck of New Hampshire that abuts on the Atlantic Ocean—eighteen narrow miles of coastline wedged between Maine and Massachusetts. Ever since they were married, she and David—and then Lindsay—had come up for a week or two every summer to spend time with the Tardiff multitudes at the old, rambling cottage they maintained in York Beach, Maine, just across the state line from New Hampshire. David's parents would move in for the summer, riding herd on the sons and daughters and in-laws and grandchildren who would drift in and out of the cottage, camping out on beds and sofas and, when those ran out, on the floor. It had taken Mariah a couple of seasons before she finally figured out which kids went with which parents. Somehow, amidst all the happy confusion, it didn't seem to matter much.

She smiled at the memory as she approached the turnpike toll plaza, slowing and glancing in the rear-view mirror. The early-morning traffic was heavy, but she spotted the gray Ford, part of Neville's surveillance team, a couple of cars back. As the road widened to double the number of lanes at the toll plaza, the Ford veered off to the far-right wicket. Textbook perfect, Mariah thought, smiling grimly. He knew that she had no choice but to go through the toll plaza, so he could allow himself to get a little ahead of her now, diverting suspicion, and pick her up again farther down the road.

But Mariah had gotten to know this part of the country well enough over the past fourteen years to believe that she could shake him here. She joined the longer line of traffic at one of the manned booths for those without exact change. As she neared the wicket, she watched the driver of the Ford drop a quarter in the basket of his lane and pull through the plaza. He headed off at a sedate but respectable speed.

Mariah rolled down her window as she edged forward, smiling at the man in the booth.

"'Mornin','' he said cheerfully. "Twenty-five cents, ma'am."

She reached for her wallet. "Am I going the right way for Rochester? I'm not from this area and I get so turned around," she added sheepishly.

"No, ma'am—you're going to Maine here. You wanna go west."

"Oh, no! And I'm running late," Mariah said, checking her watch and letting a frantic note creep into her voice. "I've got an eight o'clock appointment. Can you tell me how to get back in the right direction?"

The man in the tollbooth looked at the line growing behind her. "Tell you what," he said, leaning out the door of his booth, "there's an emergency-vehicle turn-around here on the other side of the toll plaza. You turn in there and you can head back the other way. Just be careful pulling out into the traffic."

"Oh, thank you! You're a lifesaver."

"Ayuh," the man said, his Yankee drawl pronounced. "Just drive safe now."

Mariah grinned as she slipped around the toll plaza and headed in the westbound direction. She took the next exit off the turnpike and doubled back to the eastbound on-ramp, pulling over to the side of the road to wait. It took ten minutes but, sure enough, the gray Ford sped by, heading west. She pulled onto the turnpike once more, being careful the second time she went through the toll plaza to pick one of the exact-change lanes, avoiding the nice man in the booth.

Paul Chaney was waiting for her when she pulled up to the little coffee shop in York Beach.

"Hi," she said, stepping out of the car and looking him over. "You replaced your jacket, I see. You should let me reimburse you for it."

He shook his head. "It was time for a change, anyway. I'd had that old one for years."

"Well, I can see how this is a whole new image," she said ironically. The new leather bomber was virtually identical to the slashed one the police had taken. "Did you have any trouble finding this place?"

"No, but I had some company to shake first."

"Me, too. Lost him at the toll plaza."

"Ran a red light in Portsmouth and shook mine. Any idea who they are?"

"Baby-sitters, but I'm not in a mood to be baby-sat right now."

"Want some coffee?"

Mariah nodded and followed him inside. After they had found an empty booth and the waitress had taken their order, she glanced at his hand. "How are the cuts?"

"Healing nicely. I'll get the stitches taken out in Phoenix. How about your wrist?"

She clenched her fist lightly and pivoted the wrist, which she had left unwrapped. "Coming along. It's getting mobile again." She scanned the coffee shop and then leaned toward him. "I had a phone call from Sergeant Albrecht after you left last night. They found Burton."

"Great. And? Did he say who hired him to go after you?"

She sat back abruptly as the waitress arrived with their coffee. When the woman left, Mariah stirred milk into her cup, then sipped thoughtfully. Finally, she looked up at Chaney again. "He wasn't in a position to say much," she said. "He was dead."

"What?"

"Shot through the head. He was in a Dumpster behind the Tyson's Corner Mall."

Chaney whistled softly. "Sounds like an execution."

"That's what Albrecht thought, too. Burton was already inside the Dumpster when he was shot—the bullet was lodged in the side of it. The police figure he was lured there, maybe for a payoff, which would explain why he would have climbed into the thing. His car was still running when they found him. Whoever shot him just picked him off like a fish in a barrel."

"This doesn't look good, Mariah."

"I agree. So does Sergeant Albrecht. He had more questions about my line of work, *and* about that lock of David's hair that they found in my kitchen trash. He said the pathologist noticed that a clump of hair had been whacked off the back of his head. Didn't think much of my alleged barbering skills, it seems."

"Why don't you come clean with him, Mariah? It can't hurt Lindsay now. Burton's never going to trial."

"Because the police aren't going to be able to get to the bottom of this," she said. She reached into the tote bag she was carrying and pulled out the back issues of *Newsweek* and the *Washington Post* that Chaney had left with her the previous day. "I read these and I think you're right—there could be a link to Vienna. I missed that article on the accident in New Mexico in the *Post* last week, with everything that was going on."

"Well, they really buried it," Chaney said. "Two paragraphs on page thirty-two. But I guess the real news is that it got reported at all. I'll bet the feds had a major campaign on to keep it under wraps."

"I haven't looked at a newspaper in days. Has there been any follow-up?"

"Nope. Incredible, isn't it? Five nuclear weapons experts—two Americans and three Russians—get blown to kingdom come in the New Mexico desert and nobody bats an eyelash."

"I knew Kingman."

"The deputy director of the Los Alamos lab?"

Mariah nodded. "David worked for him. When I was living with him in Los Alamos, we often got together with Kingman and his wife. She's a medical doctor. I heard they got divorced, but she's still there, as far as I know."

"Do you know anything about the Russians?"

"Sokolov, Borodin and Guskov. Of the three, Sokolov was the star. Their best physicist. The other two were lesser lights. Borodin was a nuclear engineer involved in their testing program at Semipalatinsk. Guskov I don't know much about—also an engineer, though."

"The other American, Bowker, was an engineer, too," Chaney mused aloud. "What did you tell me that night when I came to your house and said I thought someone had tried to recruit David? That you'd want mostly engineers and technicians for an illicit weapons program?"

"If I recall correctly," Mariah said, "these guys had something else in common. They were all single—or widowed or divorced. No families.

"No one to ask questions."

"Exactly."

"Did you read the *Newsweek* article on McCord?"

Mariah nodded, her eyes narrowing. "Why are you suspicious of McCord, Paul?"

"Two reasons." Chaney took the magazine from her and opened it to the profile on Gus McCord. He flipped until he found a picture of McCord and his entourage touring a factory in Russia. "Look at this picture. See this big guy in the background? Have you ever seen him before?"

Mariah peered at the photograph and at the beak-nosed figure towering over McCord in the rear of the group. She shook her head.

"I saw him in Vienna," Chaney said.

"Where?"

"In front of Katarina Müller's apartment building. He was also watching David go in with her that night when I saw them together."

Mariah felt the blood run out of her face. "Do you know who he is?"

"His name is Dieter Pflanz. He's head of security for McCord Industries. And Mariah," Chaney added, "he's also ex-CIA."

"It figures," she said, examining the photo again. "You said you had two reasons for suspecting a link to McCord. What's the second?"

"McCord owns forty percent of CBN. Not a majority, but he is the largest shareholder and makes his influence felt when he feels strongly about something. The guy who told me I was getting the ax said it was a boardroom decision."

"I still can't believe they fired you, given the ratings your awards must pull in for them."

"McCord's got enough dirt on every member of that board that he could easily get them to go along with canning me. And they're paying me off handsomely, I can assure you."

"To buy your silence," Mariah said. "So how come you don't stay bought, Chaney?"

He grinned. "Just plumb dumb, I guess."

Mariah smiled and glanced around. The place was filling up. "Did you bring your laptop computer?" she asked.

"It's in the trunk of my car."

"You won't miss it for a while?"

"I happen to be between assignments. Why do you need it, Mariah?"

"It's getting a little crowded in here. What do you say we get our bill and go for a walk on the beach?"

They scrambled down wooden steps and over the rock-pile breakwater that protected the shore road from high storm tides. Mariah wrapped her woolen scarf tighter around her neck and rammed her hands deep into the pockets of her coat.

"Not much like the beaches of your youth, is it?" Chaney said, watching the waves crashing on the sand.

Crusts of ice covered the rocks strewn at the edge of the beach. The sky was overcast and the North Atlantic wind blew cold.

"No. It even smells different—saltier, somehow," Mariah said. "I've been coming here with David for years, but I've never been able to enjoy swimming in this water. Even in August, it's freezing—to me, anyway, although the locals think it's fine. All the same, this beach carries a lot of happy memories for me. A lot more than California ever did."

She stood quietly for a moment, staring at the surf slamming against the beach, her lips pressed tightly together. Then she looked at Chaney and headed up the beach at a brisk pace. His long legs pulled him up beside her in a few strides.

"I think you're right about McCord," Mariah said. "I think he's involved in some kind of funny business."

"Why? What do you know about him, Mariah?"

"I stumbled across something last week. I was doing a quick paper on terrorist arms suppliers after those three bombings in London, Paris and New York. Our satellites had picked up a possible shipment of arms out of Libya. We couldn't prove it because the arms—if that's what they were—disappeared en route somewhere. But there was evidence of involvement by a shipping company that a McCord subsidiary bought up last year."

"What happened to your paper?"

"It was sanitized. The information on the McCord link never made it past the front office. They were right, I suppose—the evidence was flimsy. But I've still got a gut feeling something's going on there."

"This is serious, Mariah. McCord's being touted as presidential material. He was at the White House last week, and there are rumors that the President might pull the rug out from under the Vice President and support McCord if he decides to run next year.''

''I know.''

''Why would McCord get into running arms? The guy's got more money from legitimate sources than ten men could spend in a lifetime. He's Mr. Philanthropy and he's got political ambitions. It doesn't make sense. But then,'' he mused aloud, ''why was Dieter Pflanz spying on David and Katarina Müller in Vienna? And what's the link to the attack in front of Lindsay's school?''

Mariah frowned and kicked at a piece of driftwood. ''Some people in the Company think the attack in Vienna was meant for me.''

Chaney stopped cold. ''What do *you* think, Mariah?''

''It could have been,'' she said quietly, tracing a line in the sand with her boot.

''Why? What were you into over there?''

''Not much, for the most part. That's the irony of it,'' Mariah said. She walked on and Chaney followed. ''I'm from the analytic side of the Company and we don't get to go overseas as a rule. I wangled a station assignment because I wanted to go to Vienna with David. But I wasn't part of the covert ops brotherhood and they barely tolerated my presence in the station. Most of what they had me doing there was paper handling— sifting through intelligence reports. They also gave me a couple of very low-priority assets to handle—nothing earthshaking.''

''There must have been something else, though.''

She nodded. ''I met a Russian physicist at one of David's office parties. It turned out that she had knowledge of a secret Soviet nuclear weapons program.''

''And she spilled her guts to you?''

"It was a sad story. She had grown up near a nuclear weapons research facility and may have suffered damage from exposure to radioactive waste. When she volunteered to provide information, I was allowed to debrief her because I had more expertise in the area than anyone else in the station and she and I had already established a rapport."

"What happened to her?"

"We ran her for about a year and a half, and then she just disappeared. Failed to show up for a meeting one day and never returned to the IAEA offices. Vanished. When the IAEA made inquiries, the Russian embassy said she must have defected in the confusion when the Soviet Union was breaking up, but neither we nor any of our allies could find her. We're pretty sure the KGB got her. They've never really ceased operations, despite the cosmetic changes they've gone through since the Soviet breakup."

"And then your car was attacked in front of Lindsay's school and you were supposed to be in it." Chaney stopped walking and pulled on her sleeve, turning her to face him. "Mariah, how could you not have seen a possible link? Why didn't you suspect earlier?"

"I did!" she said angrily, shaking her arm loose. "It was the first thing I thought of! But taking care of David and Lindsay was my priority, so I turned to the one person I trusted to keep watch on the follow-up investigation."

"Frank Tucker."

"Yes. He's been with the Company for thirty years. He started out in Operations, but he switched to the analysis side of the house when they discovered his wife had leukemia—they couldn't travel anymore. He's been my mentor and one of my best friends for sixteen years. I would trust him with my life, Paul."

"But he lied to you."

"I don't think he did—not exactly. At first, he believed it when he told me it was an accident. Later, when he began to suspect the truth, he kept it from me to protect me. That's what he said, and I don't think he's lying. After you showed up at the nursing home that night, I tried to get into the Company files on CHAUCER."

"CHAUCER?"

"That was the code name for the Russian source I was running."

"And? What happened?"

"I was locked out. And I think Frank was, too—from part of it, anyway."

Chaney watched her for a moment. "Mariah? Why did you ask me to bring my laptop up here?"

She sighed deeply and turned to watch the waves again. "I stole the CHAUCER file," she said finally. "Don't ask how, I just did. I haven't had a chance to read it yet. Before I left home, I glanced at it long enough to see that there were subcompartments set up after I opened the original. I'm guessing that Frank doesn't have access to them and that's why he's in the dark about what happened. But I need to study the file to be certain."

"And then what?"

"I'm not sure." She turned her gaze on him. "Are you really going to Phoenix?"

"Yes, after I see Jack, my son. I'm flying from New York to Phoenix tomorrow afternoon."

"Do your parents really live in Arizona?"

"Yup." Chaney watched her watching him and the corners of his mouth rose slightly. "And yes, I'm planning to backtrack to New Mexico, if I can give those baby-sitters the slip again."

She nodded. "I think I should go to New Mexico, too."

"Why?"

"Because there's a link there, I'm sure of it. I know the area and I know some people who could be helpful," she said.

"You'd leave Lindsay?"

"For a few days. She's fine here with David's family and until I know what's happening, I'd feel better if she was out of the line of fire. Whatever's going on, it's me they're after, not her. Let's see if we can't distract them a little."

"How will you slip away?"

"I've got an idea. If it works, I'll meet you in Albuquerque in two days. At noon on Sunday, in the plaza of the Old Town. Is that all right with you?"

"It's fine with me, but are you sure?"

"I'm sure. I'm tired of having to walk around with this in my pocket." She half pulled out the pistol that Frank had left in her coat the night of his party. Chaney's eyes dropped and then grew wide as he watched her shove it back inside. "Enough is enough, Paul," Mariah said grimly. "Let's nail these bastards and get them out of our lives."

He nodded. "I'm with you."

16

Two days later, Mariah stood in an early-morning line-up at Logan Airport in Boston, waiting to purchase a ticket for Washington, D.C. There were two weeks to go until Christmas, but the rush was already beginning, with students and grandparents traveling in great numbers to take advantage of sale fares before the high-season blackouts.

Glancing around casually as the line inched forward, Mariah spotted her watcher leaning against a wall down the concourse a little way, reading a newspaper. It was one of the two who had been trading shifts in front of the Tardiff home in Dover for the past several days. Now that she was on the move, she knew he would keep her under surveillance until she boarded her flight and then call ahead for a pickup watch at the other end.

She had told Lindsay and the Tardiffs that she was going home for a few days to clean up some work at the office and to pick up some Christmas things that she had forgotten in the rush of making the funeral arrangements. David's parents, sensing her restlessness, had thought she simply needed the time alone. Lindsay had found Mariah's plans a little surprising, but she was snuggled into the pampering environment of her grandparents' home comfortably enough not to mind her mother's absence for a short time.

"I have a reservation on the seven o'clock flight to Washington-Dulles," Mariah told the ticket agent when she finally reached the counter. "Mariah Bolt." She pulled out her credit card and handed it to the agent.

"Bolt—Bolt, yes, here it is," the agent said, looking up from her computer screen and smiling. "Any baggage today, Ms. Bolt?"

"Just a carryon," Mariah said, indicating the briefcase in her hand.

"Fine." The agent handed Mariah her ticket and credit card. "That's flight 381, boarding in about five minutes. You should go straight through security to gate 21. Have a good flight."

"Thanks very much."

She headed off down the terminal toward the gates, slipping into the women's rest room just before the security control area. Inside a cubicle, Mariah set her case on the floor and took Frank's semiautomatic out of one pocket of her trench coat and a roll of duct tape from the other. Pulling the plastic bag out of the waste receptacle on the wall, she slid the gun into the bottom of the bin and secured it there with a strip of duct tape, then replaced the liner bag. She reached in with her hand to arrange the bottom of it around the form of the gun, then wadded up some tissue paper and dumped it on top. Depositing the duct tape into the briefcase, she gave the toilet a diversionary flush, then headed out of the cubicle again.

After passing through security control, Mariah paused at a newsstand, observing out of the corner of her eye as the watcher flashed an identity card to one of the guards in the security area and walked around the electronic gates—he was obviously armed. She was still at the stand when he walked by her, seemingly oblivious, and settled himself into a chair near the gates, taking up his newspaper again.

By the time she reached gate 21, the flight to Dulles was boarding. She held back until all the passengers had come forward, then joined the end of the line. An attendant at the gate ripped the stub off her boarding pass. Mariah trailed the crowd slowly working its way down the ramp until they turned the last corner leading to the aircraft door, out of sight of the departure lounge. At a moment when the attendants' view was blocked by the oncoming line of passengers, she slipped out the ramp service door, down the steel staircase and onto the tarmac. She walked under the aircraft and toward the terminal baggage handling area, then stood against the building, looking back at the plane.

"Hey, lady! What do you think you're doing?"

Mariah glanced over to see the ground maintenance supervisor approaching. She ignored him until he was standing right in front of her.

"Ex-*cuse* me, lady, but just what the hell do you think you're doing out here?"

"Do you mind?" Mariah said coolly. "You're blocking my view."

"Oh, pardon me!" he said sarcastically. "Lady, you better have a good explanation for being down here or the airport cops will be here in exactly thirty seconds."

Mariah reached into the pocket of her trench coat, keeping her eyes on the aircraft, and withdrew a small plastic folder. She snapped it open and held it up in front of his nose. "Central Intelligence Agency," she said. "We have a VIP on this aircraft. A defector, actually, but I'd appreciate it if you'd keep that to yourself. We're just making sure he gets off safely to Washington."

The supervisor took the folder from her and examined it, looking back and forth between her face and the photo on the card.

Mariah held up her thumb. "Would you like to compare my fingerprint to the one on the ID, too?"

He handed the folder back to her and she replaced it in her pocket. "No." He peered up at the aircraft and then down at her. "CIA, huh? So how come nobody told me about this?"

Mariah looked briefly at the oval name tag on his jacket and then turned to the plane once more. "Well—Mr. Figueroa, is it? I'm sorry, Mr. Figueroa. We appreciate your vigilance here, really we do." She leaned a little closer to him and lowered her voice, never taking her eyes off the plane. "But we're moving this guy very quietly. He's already survived two assassination attempts—barely—so obviously we don't want to advertise his movements."

He stood beside her and joined her in her surveillance of the aircraft. "Jeez, you don't say!" Then he glanced down at her again. "You don't mind me saying so, miss, how's a little thing like you gonna stop some assassin?"

She smiled mysteriously. "Dangerous things come in small packages, Mr. Figueroa. I'm well trained, I can assure you. And anyway, I'm just one of a team here. This airport and that plane are crawling with our people this morning. We won't breathe easy till this bird's off the ground."

"No kidding." Figueroa turned to the aircraft just as the ramp rolled back and the doors were closed. A moment later, a tractor began backing the Boeing 737 out of the gate and toward the taxiway.

Mariah let out a deep sigh. "Thank God! Gone—and good riddance! He's someone else's headache now." She turned and smiled at Figueroa. "There are days, you know, when I ask myself why I didn't just take up circus tightrope walking if I wanted this kind of stress in my life."

The supervisor returned her smile. "Well, I don't know, sounds like a real interesting job you've got. I'd never have guessed it to look at you, though. CIA," he said, shaking his head. "Who'd have figured?"

"Could you point me to the service elevator, Mr. Figueroa? I've got to be getting back to the office now."

"Sure, no problem." He led her into the baggage area.

Mariah heard a whistle. "Hey, Fig!" someone shouted. "Who's yer girlfriend?"

"Just ignore them," Figueroa said, bending toward her. "These guys don't got a clue about the stuff you gotta deal with these days." He pulled out a key and called the service elevator, then leaned in and turned the key in the lock on the control panel. "This'll take you back to the main concourse. Nice talkin' to you."

"You, too. And by the way," Mariah added, her finger to her lips, "not a word about our defector, please." Figueroa shook his head solemnly and Mariah smiled. "I'll be sure to make a note of your cooperation, Mr. Figueroa." When the door closed, she slumped against the wall of the elevator and exhaled sharply.

Stepping out onto the concourse again, she noted that the overhead monitors were flashing the departure of Flight 381 to Washington-Dulles. Keeping herself in the middle of a traveling group of high school basketball players, Mariah headed toward the security control area. She arrived just in time to see her watcher come through from the gates, dump his newspaper in a trash can and head out the main exit. Mariah turned back down the concourse and approached the Air West ticket counter.

"Good morning," the agent said. "Can I help you?"

"Yes, I'd like to fly to Albuquerque. I understand you have a connection this morning."

The agent punched in the information on his keyboard and peered at the screen. "That's via Dallas-Fort Worth, departing at seven-thirty, arriving in Albuquerque at ten forty-five, local."

Plenty of time, Mariah calculated, as long as there were no flight delays. Otherwise, she'd miss the rendezvous with Chaney at noon in Albuquerque's Old Town. "That's fine. I'd like a ticket, please."

"One way or return?"

"One way. I'm not sure about my return plans yet."

"Name?"

"Diane Tardiff."

"How do you spell that last name?"

Mariah handed him an American Express card that she had been carrying around in her wallet since David was injured in Vienna, having never gotten around to cutting it up. The name on it said "D. J. Tardiff." David's signature was a trademark scrawl that she had long ago learned to forge to facilitate household bill-paying. As long as the AmEx bill was paid, she knew, no one would ever examine the charge slip closely.

"Okay, Ms. Tardiff," the agent said a few minutes later. "That's flight 292, gate 47, boarding shortly."

She thanked him and headed back down the concourse to the women's rest room, cursing under her breath at the sight of a yellow plastic sign propped in the rest-room doorway—*Closed for Cleaning*. She hesitated, debating her options, then pulled a tissue out of her pocket. Reaching under the collar of her sweater and loosening the bandage covering the cut she had taken from Burton's knife, she scratched at it until it began to bleed. After dabbing at it with the tissue, she replaced the bandage. She ran into the rest room holding the bloody tissue over her nose. The attendant looked up in surprise.

"Sorry," Mariah said, her voice muffled. "I've got a nosebleed."

The wizened old woman nodded. "Sure, sure. Dat's okay, lady." She watched as Mariah soaked a paper towel in cold water and held it over her nose, tipping her head back, keeping the bloody tissue in view. "You okay?" she asked. Mariah nodded.

The woman returned to cleaning the cubicles, rolling her cleaning cart in front of the one where the gun was stashed. Mariah watched in the mirror as she wiped down the toilet and lifted the flap on the wall receptacle, peering in. She pulled out the half-full plastic bag and dropped it into the trash bag on her cart, then shook out a fresh liner and slipped it in, folding the edges over the sides of the bin. As her hand reached in to push down the bottom of the bag, Mariah dropped her briefcase. The bang of its brass hinges reverberated in the tiled room. The cleaning woman spun around, then bustled over as Mariah slumped against the sink.

"Lady! You okay?"

Mariah straightened and gave her an embarrassed smile. "I'm fine. I just felt a little dizzy, that's all."

"Maybe I get a doctor?"

"No, no, that's not necessary. I just need to sit for a second," Mariah said, slipping by the woman and perching on the edge of the toilet seat she had just cleaned. She looked up and smiled. "Really, I'm fine. It's just the sight of blood—always does this to me. But look, the nosebleed's stopped now. I'll be okay in just a minute."

The woman watched her dubiously for a while, then handed her the briefcase.

"Thanks. Don't let me keep you from your work. I'm sorry to be such a nuisance."

"No problem." The woman moved on down the line of cubicles.

Peering around to see her disappear into the next cubicle, Mariah quietly closed the door and took a deep breath. As the cleaning lady began to clatter in the next stall, Mariah pulled the liner out of the waste receptacle. Reaching in, she peeled back the duct tape and lifted out the gun, then replaced the liner bag. She slipped the wadded-up tape into the bin and the gun into her pocket, then walked out of the cubicle, flashing a wave of thanks to the old woman as she headed back out to the concourse.

At the security control area, she hesitated for a moment, then pulled out her ID card again, took a deep breath and headed for the side gate of the security area that her watcher had passed through not long before. Her expression was sober and her step purposeful as she walked through the gate.

"Ma'am?" A guard approached, his hand raised.

She held up the ID. He glanced at it, and then turned at the sound of a sudden, piercing wail coming from one of the electronic gates. An exasperated mother traveling with a small baby and two other children was trying to push a balky toddler through the security gate. He was clinging to her leg, screaming. A long line of passengers fidgeted behind the mother, anxious to get to their flights. The security guard turned back to Mariah and took one last look at her face and the picture on the card, then waved her past, going back to help coax the toddler through the electronic gate. Mariah headed for gate 47, thankful for small mercies and the terrible twos.

"We have a customer," Dieter Pflanz said.

He and George Neville were standing on the tarmac at Washington's Dulles Airport, watching as Nancy McCord's stretcher was transferred from an ambulance to the McCord Industries Learjet under the close supervision of Gus McCord and her cardiologist. The whine of engines along the taxiways provided effective cover for their conversation.

"Who?"

"A new fundamentalist group with a political agenda. Apparently, they're looking for a spectacular stunt to gain attention for themselves. Ghaddafi's people are impressed with our Madeira operation and recommended us as a supplier of special orders."

"Good. Are your people in place?"

"Everything's ready. There's a meeting set for to-morrow to negotiate the deal and let the customer examine the goods."

"My God," Neville said, shaking his head. "We might actually pull this off."

"We will if nobody gets cold feet. *And* if you keep things under control at your end. What's happened to the Bolt woman and the reporter?"

"She's on leave in New England until after Christmas. Chaney's in Phoenix with his parents. We're keeping tabs on them." Neville decided not to mention that the watchers had lost them both for a couple of hours a few days earlier. Nothing had happened, and each of them had been under continuous surveillance since, without incident. "You heard what happened to Rollie Burton?"

"I heard. Couldn't have happened to a nicer guy."

Neville eyed him closely, then turned away. "I suppose," he said. He waved his hand toward the medical people milling around the Lear. "What about all this? Is it going to affect the operation?"

Pflanz shook his head. "McCord's following it closely, but I've got the day-to-day responsibility. He's committed to seeing it through."

"Good. I guess this thing with his wife has been pretty rough on him," Neville said, watching McCord bark orders at the aircraft crew.

"Yeah, but he's a tough old guy."

"Think he'll still throw his hat in the political ring?"

"Dunno. Up until a few days ago, I figured he would, but I wouldn't put money on it now. Not if his wife can't handle it."

Neville nodded. "God only knows why anyone would want to deal with those idiots on the Hill, anyway. I'd say he's more effective doing just what he's doing now."

"Yup," Pflanz agreed.

* * *

Mariah picked up the peaked cap and turned it around in her hand. It was brown plaid, the sort often worn by old duffers on the golf course, and it had been lying on the front seat of the car when she got in, next to a lemon yellow polyester windbreaker. Neither item of clothing looked like anything Paul Chaney would be caught dead in.

"Did you get a new tailor?" she asked, positioning the hat on his head. "Your fans are going to love this look."

He glanced at his reflection in the rearview mirror and grimaced before pulling the hat off. As he did, a cloud of white powder fell from the hat and encircled his head. Chaney ruffled his hair to shake it out. "It's my father's. I wore this stuff and a pair of his glasses when I slipped away from Phoenix last night. Put some talc in my hair to whiten it and then drove out of my parents' garage after dark. Worked like a charm."

"This is their car?"

Chaney nodded. "They kept my rental. My dad agreed to stay inside until today. I phoned this morning and my mother said the watchers were still in the street outside the house."

"The phone might have been tapped, you know."

"We had a code. I disguised my voice and pretended to be a carpet cleaning outfit. She said they'd just had their rugs done. If she'd agreed to a cleaning, I would have known the watchers were on to me."

Mariah rolled her eyes. "Don't they find this cloak-and-dagger stuff a little strange?"

"They love it—most fun they've had in years," Chaney said, grinning. "My mother's always been a community activist and she loves frustrating the authorities. My dad's an old newspaperman and he knows what it takes to get a story sometimes."

"Is that what you're after here, a story?"

"You know it's not," Chaney said soberly. Mariah nodded. "So which way?" he asked, pulling out of the Old Town parking lot.

"Right." Mariah peered at the map he had handed her. "We need to pick up Interstate 25 north to Santa Fe, then Route 68 toward Los Alamos. But before we hit Los Alamos, I'd like to see where the five scientists were killed."

"The managing editor of the *Phoenix Star* is an old friend of my dad's," Chaney said, heading for the freeway. "I spent yesterday morning in their morgue. They had a little more information on the accident than what appeared in that *Washington Post* article."

"And?"

"It happened just south of Taos. Report said they'd been drinking in a bar there beforehand."

"They went all the way to Taos for a *drink?*"

"Apparently. There'd been an official dinner of some sort in Los Alamos for the visiting Russian scientists. After the dinner, Kingman and Bowker, the two Americans, took three of the Russians out."

"It's over sixty miles from Los Alamos to Taos. Why would they go all that way?"

"Maybe there are no decent bars in Los Alamos?"

"The place isn't famous for its nightlife," Mariah agreed. "But they could have gone into Santa Fe if they were looking for something better. It's half the distance."

Chaney shrugged. "Does seem a little strange," he agreed, yawning.

"Why don't you let me drive? You've been on the road all night."

"I napped in the car for a couple of hours after I got in this morning. I'm okay for a while. We'll switch in Santa Fe." He glanced over at her. "Did you read the CHAUCER file?"

"Yes, finally. But there were gaps. There's reference to some calls on the secure line between DDO and the station chief in Vienna, but no record of what they talked about."

"DDO—that's the deputy director for operations, right? George Neville?" Mariah's head spun around. "I've seen him testify before the Senate Intelligence Committee. And I saw him at your boss's party that night," he explained, obviously pleased with himself.

"You did? Why didn't you say anything?"

"Because you asked me to play dumb, so I did. But guess what, Mariah? That friend of my father's at the *Phoenix Star?* He was in Saigon during the early days of Vietnam and he tells me that Neville and McCord's man, Dieter Pflanz, were stationed there at the same time. My dad's buddy drank with both of them. That was about the time Burton, your attacker, was thrown out of the place. Just one big happy family, those guys."

"I *knew* I didn't trust that snake Neville," Mariah fumed. "But this is beginning to make a little sense."

"How so?"

"Well, first of all, after Baranova, the Russian woman, told me about the secret nuclear weapons research facility, our satellites and local agents were tasked to confirm the existence of the facility. They were able to confirm her story. I knew that in Vienna—that's why I was assigned to continue her debriefing. What I didn't know is that DDO called in an outside agent—the file refers to him by the code name PILGRIM—to do some follow-up work. Exactly what isn't clear. One of the telex messages between Neville and the station chief confirmed the arrival of PILGRIM in Vienna and ordered the chief to render any assistance requested, but otherwise to stay out of his way."

"I'll bet Pflanz is PILGRIM. It would explain why I saw him lurking around there."

"I think that's a good bet." Mariah paused, biting her lower lip.

"What?" Chaney asked when he noticed her hesitation.

"They knew about David and Katarina Müller," she said grimly. "They all knew. The station chief. Neville. PILGRIM. Frank Tucker." She glanced at him, her expression cold. "I guess that makes it unanimous, doesn't it? All of you knew, and nobody told me."

"Mariah—"

"Never mind. It wasn't your place to tell me. But those bastards should have." They rode in silence as Mariah raged over the multiple betrayals.

"It seems strange that they didn't," Chaney said finally. "And that they let you carry on with your Russian source. I would have thought they'd pull you out as a security risk."

"That's what I thought, too. But according to the file, they bugged our apartment and our car—and David's office. Then they confronted David. Apparently, he told the station chief that Müller had blackmailed him into the affair."

"Blackmailed? How?"

Mariah shrugged. "That's one of the gaps in the file. I can only assume that Müller must have threatened Lindsay and me. I can't see what else she could have had on David to get him to go along."

"So what happened after they called David on it?"

"They told him to carry on, find out what she was after. And here's something interesting—David had taken a trip to Moscow on IAEA business a couple of months earlier, and guess who he met there?"

"Who?"

"Yuri Sokolov, the nuclear physicist who was killed here a few weeks ago."

"Bingo!"

"Yup. David never mentioned this to me because he knew I would have felt honor-bound to report it, but it seems Sokolov expressed regret over his work on the Soviet nuclear weapons program. Thirty years later," Mariah said, grimacing, "and the guy's conscience starts to bother him. David did discuss it with some IAEA people, though, and one of them—surprise, surprise—turned out to be an agent that another of our people in the station was running."

"Aha! So, when Katarina Müller went after David, your people figured she was tasked to find out whether Sokolov's loyalties were suspect."

"Exactly."

"Seems funny that the Russians would have let Sokolov come to the States if he was under suspicion, doesn't it?" Chaney said.

Mariah nodded. "Not only that, but Borodin and Guskov—the other two Russians who were in the accident with Kingman and Bowker? Handpicked for this conference at Los Alamos by Sokolov himself."

"Curiouser and curiouser."

"If you want curious, try this—I don't think Katarina Müller's targeting of David had anything to do with Sokolov."

"Why not?"

"Because apparently she never tried to get a darn thing out of him. There was one telex from the station chief to DDO, really pissed off because David kept insisting that Müller wasn't pumping him for any information at all."

"You think she just had the hots for him?"

"Who knows? Dammit, Paul! David wanted out, but they wouldn't let him break off the contact. They just left him twisting in the wind. And so did I, when he tried to get me to leave Vienna. If he had told me what was going on, we would have been gone like a shot. They couldn't have forced us to stay."

"But how could he tell you, once it started? By then, he was in over his head. And I knew David," Chaney added quietly. "The last thing in the world he would have wanted was for you to find out. He would have been terrified of losing you and Lindsay if you did."

"He should have trusted me," she said glumly. "We could have worked it out. In the end, he lost everything, anyway."

Dieter Pflanz was back in his Newport Center office when the secure telephone jangled in the cabinet behind his desk.

"They're missing," Neville said as soon as Pflanz picked up and the machine went to scramble.

"Who?"

"Mariah Bolt and Paul Chaney."

"Oh, for chrissake! Where? When?"

"Chaney gave our people the slip in Phoenix—last night, we think. The woman got on a plane from Boston to Washington this morning and never got off."

"Whaddya mean she never got off? Are you telling me she parachuted out in midflight?"

"No...I don't know. We're still trying to track her. We've got a credit-card trace on, but the only transaction that shows up so far is the ticket she bought to Washington. If Chaney hadn't disappeared, too, I might think she'd been kidnapped."

"What about Chaney?"

"No paper trail there, either. He left his parents' home by car. On his own—that we know."

"And your guys didn't see him go?" Pflanz asked, incredulous. "You got blind watchers these days, George? Equal employment opportunities or something?"

"It was dark and Chaney was disguised as his father," Neville snapped, obviously just as furious. "The watchers didn't tumble until the old man himself walked out the door this morning and waved to them."

"Laughing his head off, no doubt. Dammit, George! What kind of outfit are you guys running these days?"

"I don't need this from you, Dieter! Those watchers are in deep shit when I get them on the carpet. Meantime, I called to let you know so your people could be on the lookout. We're searching the Phoenix airport for the old man's car and checking passenger logs, just in case Chaney paid cash for a ticket and flew out. If he's driving somewhere—"

"If he's driving, he could be anywhere by now—including New Mexico," Pflanz said angrily. "Could the woman have flown there, as well?"

"We're checking that, too. Meantime, you might want to head out."

"I'm on my way. You've got the number for the phone in the Lear. Call me as soon as you know anything."

"Roger."

As they left the Albuquerque plains and traveled north toward Santa Fe, following the old Camino Real-Chihuahua Trail, the flat, scrubby terrain gave way to the increasingly rugged peaks that mark the southernmost tail of the North American Rocky Mountains. The air grew crisp and clear as the road climbed steadily upward, until at Santa Fe, Mariah and Chaney found themselves breathing deeply to capture the thin air.

When Chaney pulled into a gas station, Mariah climbed out of the car and stretched limbs cramped from too many hours spent sitting. Her day had begun eleven hours and two time zones earlier, and they still had a long way to go before it would be over. There would be another hour's drive until they reached Taos at about three that afternoon, she calculated as she slipped off her watch to make the adjustment for local time.

While Chaney filled the gas tank, Mariah went into an adobe café for coffee and sandwiches. Waiting in line at the cashier, she scanned a front-page article in a newsstand copy of *U.S.A. Today*. It was an interview with Libya's Moammar Ghaddafi, denouncing what he called Washington's efforts to dictate to the world, now that Moscow no longer blocked its way.

"Freedom-loving peoples everywhere," Ghaddafi was quoted as saying, *"must use any tactic—any weapon—to repel the Yankee dictator and bring him to his knees. If acts of so-called terrorism are what is required to teach a lesson to America and its global pawns, then so be it."*

Mariah added the paper to her purchases and tossed it to Chaney as she slipped into the driver's seat a few minutes later. "Ghaddafi's saber-rattling again," she said, pulling back onto the highway and heading north toward Taos.

Chaney perused the front page of the paper as he sipped his coffee. "When he says 'any weapon,' you know he means it, too," he said. "God! Twenty thousand Soviet warheads in a rickety cupboard guarded by people who can't get enough to eat—that's a pretty tempting target for lunatics like this."

Mariah nodded. "It's insane, that kind of firepower. And the worst of it is, *we* started this stupid deadly game and God only knows what price we'll end up paying for it."

Chaney refolded the paper and munched thoughtfully on his sandwich. "I always found it strange that David could have been involved with nuclear weapons. He was such a conscientious guy. How did he ever get into it in the first place?"

"Those guys just seem to drift into it. It's like a scientific Mount Everest that they can't resist climbing just because it's there. They start out fascinated by the beauty of the atom, and the next thing you know, they're completely caught up in the challenge of developing a physics package and engineering a mechanism for a desired effect. They don't even call them bombs—in the lab, they're just referred to as 'gadgets.' 'Getting the gadget to work'—that's the name of the game."

"But they must think about the consequences of what they're creating."

"Oh, sure, sometimes. But by the time they do, they're so entrenched in the organization and seduced by the salaries and state-of-the-art equipment that they find ways to justify it in their minds. Defending democracy. Doing unto others before they do it to us. Whatever."

"Why did David quit?"

"I like to tell myself that it was because of me. I came with him when he first got the job at Los Alamos, but I wouldn't stay there. The fact is, though, he kept at it for almost two more years before he finally followed me to Washington."

"What changed his mind?"

"There was an accident in his lab, a fire. One of his technicians got caught in it and suffered massive radiation exposure. He was just a kid—twenty-three years old. It took him two weeks to die, and I guess it was pretty horrible. David was really shaken and walked away from the job not long after."

"They say radiation sickness is an awful thing to watch. The victim just sort of rots from the inside out."

Mariah nodded. "Radiation destroys the body's ability to regenerate cells. Since our cells are dying off all the time, this creates something of a problem, to say the least. David said that when they pulled the kid out, he looked fine, aside from suffering smoke inhalation. But they knew when they checked his dosimeter badge that he was a dead man. He started getting sick a few hours later. Over the next several days, his gums and then his face blistered and started peeling away. Ulcers spread all over his body. The membranes lining his intestines and blood vessels eroded, and he started hemorrhaging and swelling up like a balloon until, finally, his skin just split open. There was nothing they could do except give him morphine for the pain. When he died at last, David said, it was a blessing."

"What a horrible way to go," Chaney breathed.

"After that, David just couldn't stomach the work anymore. He quit and moved back in with me and got a university teaching job." A shadow of a smile passed briefly over Mariah's face, then faded. "The day he showed up on my doorstep was one of the happiest of my life. I just can't understand why it all had to end the way it did."

Dieter Pflanz was sitting in the copilot's seat of the Lear, when a beep from the cabin indicated an incoming telephone call. Flipping a switch to transfer the call to the cockpit, he picked up a headset. "Hello?"

"It's me."

"This is not a secure line," Pflanz warned.

"I know," Neville said. "We've traced one of those missing items we were discussing. It was misfiled under another name. The cargo was shipped to Albuquerque this morning."

"All right. I'll alert our receiving office to watch for it."

"I'm going to head out there to pick it up. I'll meet you this evening. In the meantime, you should try to locate it, but you are to take no further action until I arrive."

Pflanz scowled.

"No action," Neville repeated sternly. "Is that clear?"

"Clear," Pflanz grumbled.

17

"Are you sure this is the place?" Mariah whispered. As she and Chaney walked through the front door of the Trinity Bar, she squinted while her eyes adjusted to the dim, windowless room after the midafternoon sun outside.

Except for a languid pool game going on in the corner, the place was largely deserted. Two men in perspiration-stained cowboy hats moved around the table while another three or four lounged nearby, watching, their boots tapping on chair rungs to the rhythm of Garth Brooks on the sound system. A bartender was wiping glasses, chatting with a woman leaning on the bar. Her teased blond hair and white ruffled blouse reflected the roseate glow of a neon beer advertisement on the wall above her.

"Unless there's another Trinity Bar in Taos, this is it," Chaney said, sounding dubious himself.

Years of accumulated beer, sweat and cigarette odors permeated the walls and carpet of the room, the smell heady. With its Formica tables and scuffed wooden chairs, the place was decidedly untrendy as watering holes went, Mariah thought. It didn't look like the kind of place that anyone would spend an hour driving to in order to impress foreign visitors.

Several pairs of eyes watched as Mariah and Chaney approached the bar. "Help you?" the bartender asked, never pausing in his wiping.

Chaney settled his lanky frame onto a bar stool and nodded. "I'll have a beer," he said, glancing at Mariah. She hiked herself up beside him and nodded, as well. "Make that two—Coors, I guess."

"Coming right up."

Mariah studied the room in the reflection of the mirror behind the barman. The woman at the end of the bar, she noticed, was standing straighter, examining herself in the mirror. A forefinger with a long magenta nail subtly wiped lipstick at the corner of her mouth as the woman's gaze shifted almost imperceptibly from her own image to that of the new arrivals. The game of pool continued in the corner, but the conversation dwindled. Mariah had the distinct impression that ears were tuned in their direction.

"Not much snow out there," Chaney observed, taking one of the cans the barman laid down on the counter. Mariah took the other and watched a head mushroom as she poured the beer into a glass.

"Not so far," the barman agreed, returning to his wiping. "Had some a few weeks ago."

"Must be rough on the skiers."

"Guess they've been using the snow-making equipment on the hills, trying to get 'em ready for the Christmas rush. Don't see too many skiers in here."

"How about people from up the mesa?" Chaney asked, taking a sip from his glass.

"Los Alamos, you mean?"

He nodded. "Do they come in much?"

The barman pursed his lips as he shook his head. "Nope. We get local people here. The tourists, they like the fancier places in town and at the resorts. And those lab people—don't see them ever. They're kinda in their own little world up there, I guess."

"But you did get some, didn't you? One night, a few weeks ago?"

"You federal agents or something?"

"Reporter," Chaney said, pulling a business card out of his wallet. "Paul Chaney, CBN News. This is Mariah Bolt."

Ex-reporter, you mean, Mariah thought. Of course, Chaney stood a good chance of being recognized, and there wasn't much to be gained by saying that he was unemployed—nor by revealing her own affiliation.

"I thought I'd seen you before!" the woman at the end of the bar exclaimed.

Chaney smiled at her, then addressed the barman. "We're looking into that accident where the five scientists got wiped out by the gasoline tanker. Wondered if you could tell us anything about the night they came in here."

The bartender shrugged. "I never spoke to 'em. Cheryl here waited on 'em, though."

Chaney turned and held out his hand to the woman down the counter. "Hi. Could we talk with you for a minute—Cheryl, is it?"

The woman moved up beside him, blushing as she took his hand. She nodded briefly at Mariah before turning her gaze back on the reporter. "C-H-E-R-Y-L. Miller—M-I-L-L-E-R," she said, articulating the letters as if he were holding a pen poised for the information. "I talked to the police, too. Told them I remembered those guys real well. Funny bunch, they were. Really stood out, you know? Not the type we usually see in here."

"Did you know they were from Los Alamos?"

"Oh, yeah. They all had these briefcases, see. I tripped over one of them—nearly lost a whole trayload of drinks—and I saw the name of the lab written on them."

"There were some Russians in the group?"

"Yeah," Cheryl said, rolling her eyes. "Real dudes— new Levi's and cowboy hats. Guess they can't get that stuff over there, huh?"

"Guess not."

The woman glanced around. "You got cameras outside? Is this gonna be on TV?"

"We're doing background research. I'm not sure if there's a story here or not. Could I count on you for an interview later, if necessary?"

"Sure!"

"Great," Chaney said, nodding. Cheryl moved a step closer. The barman was leaning on the bar now, listening intently.

Mariah suppressed the urge to gaze heavenward. Here was vintage Chaney, doing his thing, weaving the spell. And the amazing thing was, it worked on both men and women—Mariah had seen it in Vienna. She had always found it difficult to handle the casual banter with strangers that was the stock-in-trade of the diplomatic cocktail circuit. She would listen to the babble and the laughter, feeling shy and awkward, wondering why it was that everyone in the room seemed to be in on some secret joke that no one had ever told her. But Paul, she had noticed, could talk to anyone about anything— make them feel significant, like their lives counted for something. Even the most suspicious and taciturn would eventually warm up to him, open up to him. It was probably the secret of his success as a reporter. And yet, watching him now, she saw that there was respect there. He genuinely liked people, and he telegraphed the promise that he wouldn't abuse their trust. It was a promise, she realized with sudden shock, that she had come to believe in herself.

"So," Chaney said, looking from Cheryl to the bartender and back again, "you guys know your clientele and you knew these characters from Los Alamos were out of place. Did you talk to them, Cheryl?"

"Not really, just kinda chatting, you know?"

"How did they seem?"

"They were okay. Especially the old guy—the American. Good tipper, sweet guy. The Russians, too. Kinda corny, but nice, you know?" She shook her tousled head sadly. "Really awful what happened to them. Eddie Ortega there said they never stood a chance."

"Eddie Ortega?" Chaney asked. He glanced over her shoulder to the group by the pool table that she had indicated with a cocked thumb.

"He's one of the firemen who went out that night." Cheryl swiveled to face the men across the room. "Hey, Eddie! Come over here a minute, will you?"

A barrel-chested man with a long black braid running down his back looked over at them and then around at his friends. With a shrug, he detached himself from the group and ambled slowly toward the bar, the wooden heels of his cowboy boots thudding hollowly on the carpet-covered plywood floor. Mariah watched the black eyes over high cheekbones as they assessed her and Chaney, one after the other. Eddie Ortega, she knew, had deep roots in this land, far deeper than those of the skiers or artists—or scientists—who had made New Mexico their home in recent years. His voice, when he spoke, was a contrabass rumble, possibly the deepest voice she had ever heard.

"What can I do for you?"

"Mr. Ortega, my name's Paul Chaney. I'm a reporter for CBN News. This is Mariah Bolt. We're looking into that tanker accident where the five nuclear scientists died a few weeks back. Cheryl here tells me you were one of the fire fighters on the scene."

"Yeah, that's right."

"I understand it was a pretty bad accident."

Ortega nodded. "Closed the highway for a whole day until they could resurface the road."

"Were the bodies brought here to Taos?"

"What bodies?"

"The bodies of the scientists and the driver of the tanker."

"Weren't no bodies."

"No bodies?"

"Nope. Vaporized by the fire."

"Nothing left?" Chaney asked. *"Nothing?"* Ortega shook his head. Chaney frowned and took a long, thoughtful sip from his glass, then looked up at the man again. "Mr. Ortega, how long have you been a fire fighter?"

"Seventeen years next March."

"That's about how long I've been a reporter," Chaney said, nodding. "Covered some pretty hairy places. Africa. The Middle East. Seen wars, plane crashes, terrorist bombings. Covered a volcano eruption once. Personally, I've never seen a fire where a bunch of people died and they didn't find a single trace of *any* of them." The fire fighter shifted and watched the floor intently. "Have you, Mr. Ortega? Seen many fires where absolutely *nothing* was left?"

The room was silent.

"Teeth," Ortega rumbled finally. "Tungsten pins."

"What?" Mariah said.

"Tungsten pins. They said the older American guy— Kingman, his name was?" Ortega asked, glancing at Cheryl. She nodded. "Said he had bad knees. Had pins in 'em. Those pins are usually made of tungsten. Just about indestructible. Fire wouldn't have melted 'em."

"Or the teeth, right?" Chaney prompted. Ortega shrugged. "Mr. Ortega, there were six men in those two vehicles. That means one hundred and eighty or so teeth among them, give or take a few that might be missing. Have you ever seen a case where a fire was so uniformly hot that not one of those teeth would have survived? Even after a plane crash, they usually find *something*—teeth or bone fragments or porcelain dentures. Or tungsten orthopedic pins, as you say."

"We tried," Ortega protested. "We was siftin' through the debris when they made us pull out."

"They?"

"Feds. FBI, maybe, I'm not sure. Coroner should know—if he's sober this week. Once the feds move in around here, you get the message pretty quick that you should just back off and shut up."

"What exactly happened?"

"Feds came in, said it was a national security issue and they was takin' over the investigation." Ortega snorted, shaking his head. "Never saw nobody destroy a scene like that before."

"What do you mean?" Mariah asked. "What did they do?"

"Just bulldozed it and carted it away—ashes, twisted steel and all." Ortega looked at Mariah and Chaney in turn. "You know, them feds, they figure we're all just rubes or dumb Indians or somethin' up here. Well, this may not be the Big Apple or nothin', but we know how to do a job right. I been takin' courses to get my fire inspector's certification and I'll tell you this—any of us suggested that's how you handle forensic evidence, we'd be shot."

"Park here and we'll walk back," Mariah said.

Chaney pulled the car into a parking lot at one of the few spots on the highway where the valley widened a little. For most of the way between Taos and Española, NM 68 was a narrow, winding two-lane road wedged between the Sangre de Cristo peaks on one side and the Rio Grande and the Jemez Mountains on the other. But at Pilar, about twelve miles south of Taos, a parking area had been leveled next to the river, allowing access for hikers and the river-rafting companies that every summer launched daily loads of tourists looking for a white-water thrill.

Racing against the sinking sun, Mariah and Chaney quickly hiked back up the highway a thousand yards or so to the place where the accident had happened. Although Eddie Ortega had marked the spot on their map, they realized that it was pretty hard to miss. About five hundred feet of roadbed had been recently resurfaced, and the hills and scrub beside the spot were scorched and blackened. Mariah shaded her eyes from the sun, dropping rapidly now behind the Jemez Mountains, and scanned the highway in both directions.

"An open stretch," she said. "Good visibility in either direction."

"They said it was snowing that night," Chaney recalled. "And those guys had had a few drinks, according to Cheryl at the Trinity."

"Maybe one of the drivers dozed and drifted over the centerline?"

"Or swerved to miss an animal and skidded, maybe."

Mariah shook her head. "No visible skid marks, Ortega said, not from the van or the tanker truck. They must have just flown into each other."

They poked around the site a little more, but there was nothing to see—new black asphalt and scorched piñon bushes, that was it. In a few months, when the fresh asphalt faded to match the rest of the road and new spring growth overtook the burn damage, no sign would remain that five of the world's best nuclear weapons experts had lost their lives here.

They walked back down the highway toward the Pilar parking area. Chaney started to head to the car, but Mariah veered off toward the river, walking to the bank. The river was narrow, only about thirty feet across, and maybe ten feet at its deepest point. This time of year, its flow was relatively sedate. But in late spring and early summer, when the melting runoff from the mountains was at its peak, experienced rafters would thrill at the river's untamed rapids. The wildest stretches were in the gorges upriver, including the Taos Box Canyon, one of the best white-water runs in the country. Mariah and David had done it not long after arriving in Los Alamos, and she would never forget the heart-stopping excitement as the inflatable raft dropped precipitously through the churning waters and rugged terrain. But an easier course started right here at Pilar, she knew, a relatively manageable sluice through narrow drops· and massive boulders that even families with kids could enjoy.

"What are you doing, Mariah?" Chaney called.

She picked up a flat stone and attempted to skip it across the water, but it sank unceremoniously on first contact. "Nothing. Thinking."

"It's getting dark," he said, walking toward her. "We should get going."

She nodded but walked farther along the bank, picking up a long stick and prodding between the rocks on the shore, then using it as a walking stick while she ventured out onto some boulders that jutted into the river near the end of the clearing. She stood on a large boulder, looking first up and then down the winding river, and took a few soundings with the stick. Finally, with a sigh, she turned back and began to pick her way across the boulders to the bank. She was only a step away from terra firma when her eye, watching the water flow over the rocky streambed, caught sight of something wedged in a crevice just at the edge of the bank.

Mariah reached down to try to pick it up, but a scrubby juniper branch hanging over the riverbank caught on her sleeve. She yanked her arm to free it from the bush's grip, but with the sudden movement, her footing gave way on the slippery rocks. Her hands flailed but found only air, and she fell backward into the stream.

She heard Chaney yell as she plunged her hands into the freezing water to break her fall. The edge of the riverbank dropped away sharply, but she managed to spin herself around and regain her balance on the narrow ledge before the current could grab her and carry her off. When Chaney ran up, she was sitting in a shallow, ice-cold pool, thoroughly soaked. She glanced up. Seeing that she was unhurt, Chaney folded his arms across his chest and broke into an amused grin.

"Oh, shut up!" she said, disgusted.

"I didn't say a word. Far be it from me to tell Mariah Bolt where and when to take her daily swim." She gritted her teeth.

Chaney held out a hand and Mariah stretched out to take it before remembering what she had been trying to do when she fell. She ignored him and scanned the rocks, but the object she had seen was gone. Then she spotted it where it had fallen into the river. She reached behind her, plunging her hand back into the icy water.

"What are you doing, crazy woman?" Chaney put his hands under her arms, pulling her to a standing position. The cold wind on her wet clothes sent Mariah into immediate and uncontrolled shivering. "Come on, you lunatic. You're going to get pneumonia."

"I found something," she declared, holding up her clenched fist.

"Get out of the water, Mariah!" He helped her out and up the bank toward the road. "Come on, there's a blanket in the car. Let's get you wrapped up before you freeze to death."

Mariah nodded and they broke into a run. Chaney grabbed her arm as she stumbled across the rocky parking lot, her freezing muscles sluggish and unresponsive. Water squished in her sopping boots. When they reached the car, Chaney opened the trunk and withdrew a woolen blanket. He threw it around her shoulders, then led her to the passenger seat, where he sat her down and pulled off her waterlogged boots and socks.

"Get in and I'll get the heater going," he said.

While he started the car, she pulled the blanket tighter and tucked her feet up underneath herself. Only then did she peer at the object still clasped in her hand.

"What have you got there?" Chaney asked, putting the car in gear.

"Part of a buckle."

"What?" She held up a bit of black nylon webbing to which was attached half of a plastic buckle. "You took a swim in icy water for *that?*"

Unable to keep her shivering hand still, Mariah slipped the thing into her pocket. "Pretty stupid," she agreed, "but I hadn't planned to go in. God! I'm freezing!"

"The heat's kicking in. We'll get to a hotel as fast as we can so you can dry out."

"Hilltop House in Los Alamos," she said, her jaws clattering. "That's the best bet."

Chaney hesitated at the edge of the highway. "We should return to Taos. It's faster."

"No, let's carry on. I'll survive. Go south. The Los Alamos turnoff is just past Española."

Chaney nodded and they headed back down NM 68 as the last light faded. Mariah huddled down into the blanket, cold and wet and miserable despite the raging car heater. At one point, she reached over and held the steering wheel while Chaney shrugged out of his jacket and draped it across her. When they finally turned off NM 68 and began the steep ascent up the five-fingered mesa that constitutes Los Alamos, Mariah was feeling sluggish and dopey.

"You'd better wait in the car," Chaney said, casting a wry glance at her. "I don't think the management will be too impressed by you sloshing across their lobby."

Mariah nodded as Chaney climbed out, leaving the engine running and the heater pumping. A few minutes later, he was back. "All set. We can move the car around the building and slip in the side door."

When they entered the hotel, a family was leaving and cast curious glances at the blanket-wrapped woman going in. "Mommy!" Mariah heard the youngest child cry. "That lady's all wet!"

"Hush!"

Chaney grinned at Mariah as they climbed the stairs to the second floor. She only shook her head ruefully.

"Here you go," he said, slipping a key in a lock and stepping away to let her pass.

She flicked on the light. "Thanks. What room are you in?"

Chaney closed the door behind him. "This one."

"Excuse me? I don't think so. You get your own room, bub."

"I was lucky to get this one," he said, dropping their bags. "There's some kind of conference going on, but fortunately they had a last-minute cancellation. Unless you want to drive around until you turn into the Snow Queen, we're just going to have to make do. Relax," he added, catching her stern gaze. "You'll sleep on that bed over there and I'll take this one here, light-years away. I promise to behave."

Mariah frowned but conceded. There wasn't another large hotel in the town, and she knew that their chances were slim of finding accommodation in one of the few small inns.

"Why don't you take off those clothes?" Chaney suggested.

On the other hand, maybe she should just make him sleep in the lobby.

"I *mean*," he said, slowly and deliberately, "why don't you go into the bathroom, run yourself a hot tub and throw those wet things out to me? The clerk at the desk said there's a laundry room downstairs. I'll dry your stuff and get us something to eat while you warm up.''

Mariah glanced down at the drip marks she was beginning to make on the carpet. ''I guess,'' she said. ''I'm traveling light. I don't have much else to wear.''

She emptied her coat pockets on the dresser, sliding Frank's gun into the bureau's top drawer, then slipped out of the coat and handed it to him before heading to the bathroom to fill the tub. As she tossed out the rest of her wet things, she heard a thump on the floor.

''I left my duffel bag outside the door, Mariah,'' Chaney called. ''There's an extra sweater in there that you can use when you get out. I'll be back in a while.''

''Okay, thanks. See you.''

She stepped into the tub and sank gratefully into the warm bath, submerging herself up to her ears until the shivers finally melted away and the numbness left her hands and feet. Closing her eyes, she let her mind float, listening to the steady hum of the building through the water. This was her element. All her life, whenever she had needed escape from pain or confusion, she had sought out the peaceful, buoyant calm of water. It cleared her mind, washing away the debris until she was once again able to think. Somewhere nearby she heard footsteps clumping along the hotel's thin floors. Hilltop House, like most of Los Alamos, had the cost-conscious, jerry-built feeling of a military base despite the fact that the hotel, like the town, had long been open to the public and run on a normal commercial basis.

It felt strange to be back here, Mariah thought, remembering how isolated she had felt when she had moved here with David after Berkeley, cut off from the world on what the Soviet propagandists had always liked to call the mesa of doom.

Los Alamos had remained a closed town for two decades after the Manhattan Project conducted the Trinity Test in 1945 that launched the atomic age. Access during that period had been limited to the scientists who continued to perfect the nuclear arsenal as the American defense focus shifted from Japan and Germany to the Soviet Union. But by the time Mariah and David had arrived, the town of Los Alamos had long been opened up, only the actual lab site off-limits and invisible to outsiders. Despite the proliferation of fast-food restaurants, movie theaters and bowling alleys, however, there was no escaping the fact that it was a one-industry town engaged in an arcane and deadly business.

She reflected on the irony of the Russian scientists who now apparently visited the lab in great numbers. With the end of the Cold War, the scientific fraternity had reasserted its primacy. Former enemies had become worthy colleagues, like the five who had driven to Taos that night, Mariah thought, dreamily trailing her fingers through the warm water. Driven sixty-five miles for a few drinks in a seedy bar and then vanished off the face of the earth.

Water sloshed on the floor as Mariah shot upright in the tub. "Holy smoke!" she breathed. She lifted herself out of the water. Snatching a towel off the rack, she wrapped it quickly around herself before running into the room and over to the bureau where she had dropped the contents of her coat pockets. She picked up the buckle she had fished out of the Rio Grande and turned it around in her hand. It was the sort of plastic buckle normally attached to life vests, among other things. The black webbing was frayed and the buckle could have been ripped off after becoming snagged in the bushes next to the river, just as her sleeve had. Even frayed nylon is strong, however. The person wearing this buckle would have had to be moving pretty quickly to have had it ripped off like that.

"Holy smoke," she repeated.

* * *

The clerk at the front desk of the Hilltop House Hotel examined the photos the stranger handed him.

Brian Latimer had already worked a full shift that day, and he had an essay to finish before English class tomorrow. But the guy who was supposed to have taken the Sunday-evening shift had called in sick with the flu, and Brian was stuck there for two extra hours until the manager got back from dinner. Mrs. Peterson had apologized when she'd asked Brian to stay on and had said yet again that he was the most responsible student she had ever had the pleasure to employ at Hilltop House. Yeah, right, Brian mused ruefully. I'm so responsible, I'll probably flunk English for not getting this paper in on time. Come on! he thought, glancing at the clock before turning back to the stranger at the desk.

The man was conservatively dressed in a suit and tie, and he had presented some sort of government ID, which Brian didn't find surprising. He had lived in Los Alamos all his life. His father was now chief of security at the lab, and Brian had heard endless lectures about how you had to be security-conscious. The old man could get really uptight when strangers showed up on the mesa. Los Alamos might look like any other small town, Brian thought, but a person could become real paranoid living in this place. As soon as I graduate, BAM! I'm outta here. He glanced nervously at the clock one more time. *If* I graduate.

"So, have you seen them?" the man asked.

Brian shook his head. "Not the lady." He flipped to the other photo. "But this guy, yeah. Checked in a while back. I just saw him go out again—five, ten minutes ago maybe."

"He was alone?"

"Yup." Brian handed back the photos. "Who is he?"

"Nobody special. It's just a routine check. What room did you say he was in again?"

"I didn't. But it's...let's see..." Brian consulted the register. "He's in 303. You want to leave a message?"

"No," the man said, turning to leave. "And there's no need to mention I was here, if you happen to be talking to him. You understand about security, don't you, son?"

"Yes, sir." Do I ever, Brian thought, watching the man go. It's the story of my life. He turned back to the clock. Come *on*, Mrs. P. I gotta get that paper finished!

"Speedy Delivery—laundry and pizza our specialty!" Chaney called as he unlocked the door and slipped into the room.

Mariah leaned on the jamb of the bathroom door, arms folded. "You don't look like the Mr. McPheely I remember from 'Mr. Rogers' Neighborhood.'"

Chaney put his load on the table before looking over at her. Then he froze, taken aback. "Yeah, well, you're no Mr. Rogers, either," he said finally.

Mariah glanced down. Wanting to travel light that morning, she had been able to fit only a change of socks, underthings and an extra cotton turtleneck in her briefcase, along with her toiletries. On her feet now were her heavy woolen socks. Her legs were bare, but Chaney's oversize sweater, which she had pulled on over her own things, came halfway to her knees. She tugged at it self-consciously, wondering why it should suddenly feel so much more revealing than the thin nylon Speedo suits she had spent half her life in. She felt her cheeks go warm.

"Looks better on you than me," Chaney said, a smile mounting.

"Oh, quiet! Can I have my slacks?"

"Right here." He handed them over, neatly pressed and folded.

Mariah went into the bathroom to put them on. "Nice job. Thanks."

"My one domestic talent. I've done more laundry in hotel rooms than I care to think about."

"Paul?"

"What?"

Mariah came out of the bathroom holding a black hardbound notebook. "This was on top of your bag when I went to get the sweater."

Chaney stared at the notebook for a moment, then walked over and took it from her hand. Squeezing past her, he picked up his duffel bag, dropped the book inside and zipped the bag shut.

"I didn't read it. Honest. Well—the flyleaf," she confessed. "Nothing else, I swear. *'Letters to Jack, Volume XII?'*"

He regarded her briefly, then threw the duffel bag in a corner and started fidgeting with the pizza box.

"I'm sorry, Paul. I didn't mean to be nosy."

He sat down in a chair, contemplating the wall. "It's a journal," he said quietly. "I started it after I lost him. He was just a baby." He tore the bill off the the top of the pizza box and began folding it and refolding it in his hands until it was a tiny, irreducible square. "Phyllis had remarried. I realized that someone else was going to be his dad—teach him to ride a bike and throw a baseball. I wouldn't be there when he hurt himself or lost his first tooth. Someone else would commiserate with him when some little girl broke his heart for the first time."

Mariah moved quietly into the room and sat on the edge of the bed nearest him, watching the tight lines around his mouth and the deep creases in his forehead.

"I realized he'd never really know me," Chaney went on. "Not the way he'd know that other father he saw every day."

"So you started writing letters to him?"

He nodded. "I send postcards and things when I'm traveling. But this is different—letters to the man he'll be one day. From a guy who just wants to tell his son what he's seen and pass on a bit of what he's learned about this world, for what it's worth. I don't know. I'll hand them over to him one day, I guess. He can read them or burn them or do whatever he wants with them. I just want him to know that I never stopped thinking about him, even if I couldn't be there." Chaney looked over at her. "I guess that doesn't really count for much, though, does it?"

Mariah reached out and laid her hand on his. "It counts for a lot, Paul. I would have given anything to have something like that from my father. Just to finally know that he did care, after all."

He leaned forward, his elbows on his knees, and cupped her hand in both of his, examining it closely. "Mariah—"

"What?"

He hesitated, then shook his head. "Nothing. Never mind."

"No. Tell me."

"I don't want you to start hating me again."

She withdrew her hand and sat back on the bed. "I never hated you, Paul."

"I made you uncomfortable."

"Yes, you did. But it was more than that."

"What do you mean?"

"You reminded me of him."

"Him?"

"My father."

"I'm not Ben Bolt, Mariah."

"I know. You're nothing like him, but I didn't know you then. I'm sorry."

Chaney was silent for a moment. "You have to let it go," he said at last. "One of these days, Mariah, you're going to have to forgive your father."

"Forgive him?"

"I'm not excusing what he did, to you or to your mother and sister. It was despicable. But if I recall correctly, Benjamin Bolt was twenty-eight years old when he died in that Parisian flophouse. Most of us make stupid mistakes when we're young that we spend the rest of our lives regretting. Maybe, if he had lived, he would have realized that he'd blown it, big time. I can't believe he wouldn't have regretted losing you."

Mariah clenched her jaw. "He should regret in hell."

"He probably is. But you're suffering, too, Mariah. You have been all your life. And you'll continue to do so, until you recognize him for the immature jerk that he was and then forgive him and let him go."

She watched him dubiously, then shook her head slowly. "Even though you might be right, I'm just not sure I can."

They sat in silence for a moment. "Come on," Chaney said. "This pizza's getting cold."

She took a deep breath and nodded. "I'm starving." She curled into a chair across from him and took the slice he held out. They ate in silence for some time. "I made a phone call while you were out," Mariah said finally.

"To?"

"Rachel Kingman. She's the ex-wife of Larry Kingman, the deputy director of the lab who disappeared in the accident."

"When did you last see her?"

"About sixteen years ago."

"She must have been surprised to hear from you."

"Very. I told her David had died and that I'd heard about Larry—asked if we could talk. She had dinner guests tonight, but she agreed to see us in her office tomorrow morning before her patients start arriving."

"You said she's a doctor?"

Mariah nodded. "Paul? You know that buckle I fished out of the river? I think it might have come from a life jacket."

"So?"

"It got me thinking about rafting."

"I don't get it. What's the point?"

"Why do you think those scientists went all the way to Taos for a drink?"

He frowned. "I think it's so they would be seen and noticed. Why else would they go to a place where they stood out like five sore thumbs? They even took their briefcases in with them, so there would be no doubt in anyone's mind where they came from."

"Right. And then there's a messy accident in which nothing survives except the license plate of their van. No bodies to ID, but that's okay, because everyone knows who was in it."

"What's this got to do with the buckle?"

"Well, it comes back down to, why Taos? I think it's because of that spot in the river where I fell in. It's one of the best places around here for launching a raft, and there's easy access to the highway. If you had an experienced guide, you could easily float downriver from Pilar to any one of several pickup points farther south. And guess what, Paul? Larry Kingman was an experienced rafter. He took David and me out when we first came to New Mexico."

Chaney whistled. "You know what this means, don't you?"

"Yup. It was all a big setup. Those guys aren't dead, they just went to a lot of trouble to make it look that way." She watched him closely through narrowed eyes. "But you've suspected it all along, haven't you?"

"I wasn't sure. I just felt something wasn't right and the more I looked, the more not right it seemed."

Mariah nodded. "All the emergency vehicles came from Taos, to the north of the crash site, so no one would have noticed them slipping away below the scene at Pilar. And even if someone had checked down there later, it snowed that night—their tracks would have been covered."

"They arranged it so it would look like a collision, but the tanker was probably rigged to blow once everyone was clear. Which explains Eddie Ortega's comment about the truck," Chaney said.

"Which comment?"

"Just before we left the bar—maybe you were in the rest room at that point. Ortega said he didn't know which oil company the tanker belonged to. Whatever markings it might have had were erased by the fire, and he didn't know who in Taos was scheduled to receive a delivery that night. Since the local authorities were pulled off the investigation, nobody pursued it."

Mariah munched thoughtfully on her pizza. "If those were real federal officials who moved in, then this has got DDO written all over it."

"And if they weren't," Chaney said ominously, "then it could be anyone. Anyone with the desire and the dollars to buy themselves five of the world's top nuclear weapons experts."

Dieter Pflanz was waiting when George Neville came through the arrivals gate at Albuquerque airport. The two men strode quickly to the main entrance, where a car was waiting. They climbed in the back seat and the vehicle sped away.

"We've located Chaney at the hotel in Los Alamos. He was alone when he checked in," Pflanz said. "We haven't spotted the woman yet, but she might be meeting him there."

"We did a credit-card trace on car rental agencies in Albuquerque but came up blank," Neville said. "She flew out of Boston under the name Diane Tardiff, but the AmEx card she used was issued to her husband. We couldn't find anything else under Bolt or Tardiff except the plane tickets. Are you sure she didn't meet him here in Albuquerque?''

Pflanz shrugged. ''We're watching the hotel. Might be a good idea to set up electronic surveillance.''

Neville nodded, then leaned forward toward the driver. ''Pass me the phone, will you?'' he said. The driver handed back a cellular phone and Neville punched in a series of digits. ''What's the room number?'' he asked Pflanz as he waited for the call to be picked up.

''It's 303.''

''Code alpha-seven-two-seven,'' he said into the mouthpiece. ''Site ninety-four, Priority One—full coverage, unit three-zero-three.''

When the order was confirmed from the other end, he passed the phone to the driver. Arrangements were now in place for Chaney's room and telephone to be bugged. Site ninety-four was Hilltop House, the usual stop-off point for anyone—domestic or foreign—with an interest in the Los Alamos National Laboratory. More than one visitor had been monitored at that location, so surveillance resources were easily activated when the need arose. Some Russian visitors at the hotel were, in fact, under surveillance at that very moment.

In theory, the CIA has only limited authority to undertake domestic surveillance, and then only on foreign targets, with the FBI taking the lead where surveillance is required on American citizens. Neville felt confident that they could be in and out in a matter of hours, before anyone noticed that DDO had authorized domestic surveillance on a room occupied by an American citizen.

''We'll just watch him for now. With any luck, he'll come up empty and back off. In the meantime,'' Neville added, ''it's time to come clean, Dieter. I want everything you know and I want it now. I mean it—it's 'need to know' time, fella. I've given you loose rein so far, but this is it.''

"And if I say I don't know what you're talking about?''

"Then we're all going down in flames together, my friend. You know that, don't you? Whatever went wrong here, you haven't managed to plug the leak, despite your extracurricular activities. Oh, yes,'' Neville said, as Pflanz glanced at him sharply, "I know what you've been up to. It doesn't take a rocket scientist. I've looked the other way up to now, but it's no good anymore. Either we work together or this party's over.''

Pflanz stared gloomily at the passing headlights. Almost two years of work and it was all coming unhinged on some sideshow, because a nosy reporter couldn't leave well enough alone. At this point of the operation, Pflanz knew that damage control called for extreme measures, but he didn't think Neville would go for it. On the other hand, the man had as much to lose as they did if the thing fell apart. The deputy might yet be persuaded.

18

Chaney's breathing was deep and regular. He had spent the previous night driving from Phoenix to Albuquerque, managing to snatch only a couple hours' sleep in the car while waiting for her to arrive from Boston. No wonder he was exhausted, Mariah thought. She'd thought she was, too.

They had both been ready to pack it in as soon as they finished the pizza, hardly able to keep their eyes open. Paul had graciously given her first crack at the bathroom, and she had been under the covers in her own bed, half-asleep, by the time he turned out the lights. But almost against her will, Mariah's eyes had opened and she watched his silhouette against the window as he slipped out of his trousers and into the other bed. The last thing she remembered before falling asleep was the striking contrast between his long, smooth torso and David's compact, bristly one.

She glanced now at the luminous readout of the digital clock on the table between them—nearly midnight. They had been sleeping for almost four hours.

Chaney turned onto his side and Mariah stared at his sleeping face in the light from the window, remembering its surprising vulnerability when he spoke of the journal he kept for his son. She felt a sudden urge to touch him, to brush aside the cowlick that tumbled across his forehead and feel his skin under her fingertips. Her eyes followed the long curve of his arm on the bedclothes, the fair hair on his forearm glistening in the pale light. He took up an inordinate amount of space, she thought, studying the hills and valleys in the covers that rolled down to the foot of the bed and beyond. Her hand fought against the impulse to run over those planes and come to rest on the plateau of his hip. She shifted onto her back and closed her eyes, working to block out his image and the urges it was arousing in her. Had *always* aroused in her, she suddenly knew.

It was true what she had told him, how he had reminded her, with his frank good looks and easy charm, of the father who had abandoned her. But that was only part of the reason she had been so uneasy with him in Vienna.

As time went on and Paul's attentions toward her remained undimmed, what she had subconsciously feared was that she might be capable of giving in to it, that she might have inherited from her father some "infidelity gene" that preordained her fate, despite David and everything he meant to her. It wasn't supposed to work that way, she told herself. When you chose a mate, you were supposed to be oblivious to all others—like a cable television box, unwanted signals scrambled. That she had never succumbed to the temptation Paul represented was small comfort to her, and in the end, it had been easier to relegate him in her mind to some philanderers' dustheap rather than to admit to a simple mutual attraction.

And now, she was feeling his pull again, compounded by deprivation, by not having been held or caressed for—how long? Too long. Too long without a warm and trusted person on the other side of the bed who would draw her close and, just for a while, hold the cold world and her cold fears at bay.

But even as she thought about it, darker images came rushing in. The only man who had put his hands on her in all that time was that animal, Burton. She felt again his groping, brutal explorations, the foul lips and the look of hatred and contempt in his strange eyes. How could she ever let another man touch her without remembering the ugliness of that experience?

And how would she ever forget those photographs and David's eyes pleading with Katarina Müller as she crouched over him? How could she trust anyone if even David could betray her?

The hardest thing she had ever done in her life was learning to trust him. Every instinct had told her not to, not because it was David, but because experience had taught her that this was a recipe for getting hurt. People left or they were ripped away, and so the safest course was to stand aloof. And then David had come along, with his goofy humor and his wild enthusiasms. He had pursued her with the same dedication that he devoted to all of his passions—his work, his hockey, his family—until his persistence had finally broken down the wall of her defenses.

It had taken Mariah a long time to admit to herself that when she left David in Los Alamos, it was due to something much, much deeper than philosophical opposition to his work. She had left in a panic over the realization that she had come to depend on his being there. Terrified by her vulnerability, she had pushed it away by leaving him. But the period they were apart had been—before now—the worst of her life. She had finally understood that living in an emotional bubble was living without meaning. It had taken David to teach her that, and he had felt it, too, she knew. In almost fourteen years of marriage, they had never made love, never touched, never passed a day together, without his regarding her with the same expression of gratitude that she had always felt toward him.

She shivered and moved onto her side, pulling her knees up and the blankets tighter around her shoulders. When she glanced over at Paul again, she realized with a start that his eyes were open and that he was watching her. "Are you all right, Mariah?"

"Yes. Just wrestling with ghosts."

"The demons of the dark. Who's winning?"

"They are. Don't they always?"

"Not necessarily. Sooner or later, the dawn comes around again—if you give it time and if you let it." She shivered. "Are you cold?"

"Freezing. I think I'm still feeling the effects of the swim in the river."

Chaney rolled to a standing position and picked up the bedspread from the foot of his bed, throwing it over her. "Better?"

"Thanks."

He crouched beside her. "I'd offer up my warm body, too, if I didn't fear grievous injury."

"Injury?"

"I've seen you fight, remember?"

As Mariah returned his smile, Paul's hand came up and stroked her hair softly, then moved lower, his thumb lightly tracing the line of her cheek and her lips. Mariah's eyes closed, but snapped open again as she felt a subtle shift in the air current around them. His face was now close above hers. She laid her palm briefly against his chest, then took his hand in hers, easing it away—wanting to leave it where it was, wanting to let him go on, but knowing it would be a mistake. "I can't," she said.

He watched her for a moment, then gave a reluctant nod. "I know. It's all right." He squeezed her hand and stood up.

"Paul?"

"What?"

"You're a good man, you know that? How come I never saw it in Vienna?"

"Beats me."

"Maybe it was that Casanova image."

He waved his hand dismissively. "Never believe the image of a media person. I'm not suicidal, you know."

"Yeah, well, somehow I don't see you as monk material, either."

"Never claimed I was."

"Would have been a pretty hollow claim," she said wryly.

"We all have our defense strategies—'once burned' and all that. It's hard to do damage to a moving target."

"It's one way to keep the demons at bay, I suppose."

"It's lost its appeal, frankly. I don't much like waking up with strangers."

Mariah lifted herself onto her elbow, suddenly frowning. "Paul? Would you answer an awkward question for me?"

"Awkward?"

"About Katarina Müller."

"Mariah, don't—"

"Please, Paul. I want to know what she had that could make him do it." He shook his head. "You won't tell me?"

"Not won't—I can't, Mariah. I don't understand it myself. Except—"

"Except what?"

"Once, just once, I confronted her, asked her what she thought she was up to with David."

"And? What did she say?" He hesitated, his reluctance obvious. "Come on, Paul. Nothing could hurt more than what I already know."

"I asked her how she could justify trying to destroy such a good marriage. And she said to me, 'You think you know them so well, their charming little family, but it's all a sham, a big lie. You don't know anything about David and Mariah.'"

"What!" Mariah sat straight up in the bed. "How could she say that?" She crumpled the edges of the blankets in her fists. "I can't believe David *ever*, ever said anything to her to justify such a lie. We *did* have a good marriage, dammit!"

"I know that, Mariah. That's why I didn't tell you this before. She was a professional liar and cheat. Don't let it upset you, please."

She pulled her knees up tight, rocking slowly. "I suppose she was a sexual gymnast?"

Chaney glanced back, frowning, but his eyes softened when he saw her face. He sat down beside her and wiped her wet cheek. "I wouldn't know," he said. "I never slept with her."

"Come on."

"I mean it. I didn't find her attractive. I was curious about her, but not that curious."

Mariah took a deep breath and reached for a tissue to blow her nose. "Well," she said grimly after a couple of honks, "David obviously couldn't say the same. I guess that makes you the better man."

"No, Mariah, that's exactly the conclusion you shouldn't draw. I've got no claim to the moral high ground here. I walked away from every woman who ever cared for me, only to fall hopelessly in love with the wife of one of the best friends I've ever had. If that doesn't make me the jerk of the century, I don't know what does. But I want you to know," he added, "I never meant to do anything about it. I would never have touched you if it hadn't been for... what happened."

"I know that."

"You do?"

She nodded. "I do now."

He took her hand in his. "Then know this, Mariah—I still love you. No, listen to me," he said as she glanced down uncomfortably. "I want you, but I'll never try to force myself on you again. I'll be there, whenever and however you want me—or not, as you wish. You only have to tell me."

Mariah studied his sober face in the half light. She knew what she wanted to tell him. She wanted to tell him how grateful she was that he was there. She wanted to tell him she was sorry for every nasty thought she'd ever entertained about him—and there had been plenty. She wanted to ask him to put his arms around her and hold her for a while. She wanted very much to kiss him, and maybe more. But she couldn't. Not now. Maybe not ever.

"I don't know what to say, Paul."

"You don't have to say anything, except maybe, 'Good night, Paul.'"

She gave him an attempt at a smile. "Good night, Paul."

"Good night, Mariah." He squeezed her hand one last time, then returned to his bed, light-years away, as promised.

Mariah lay back on her side, pulling the blankets tight. Closing her eyes, she focused once more on listening to his breathing and wrestling with the demons, pretending to sleep until finally, at long last, she did.

George Neville and Dieter Pflanz were less than a mile away, on the top floor of a low-rise office building in downtown Los Alamos. The sign on the front door of the suite indicated that it was leased to McCord Industries, a defense contractor well known locally. Most of the offices in the suite were occupied during working hours by marketing and engineering staff, but none of these employees was present when Neville and Pflanz arrived late Sunday night. Nor, when the employees returned the next morning, would they be aware that the two men had ever been there.

The two covert operators were in a securely locked set of rooms at the end of a long hallway, one with its own separate entrance near the building's stairwell. The rooms housed an elaborate communications complex linked up by satellite to the company's headquarters in California and, from there, to McCord operations worldwide.

It was nearly ten o'clock when they arrived at the ComCenter and settled in for the night. The listening device in Paul Chaney's hotel room had been functioning for about an hour, the receiving end set up at the McCord office. So far, it had been transmitting only silence, the technician monitoring the bug said. At Neville's order, the technician had amplified the sound until they finally were able to hear breathing sounds and concluded that Chaney was asleep.

"Apparently, the switchboard logged one outgoing call earlier this evening, local," the man said.

"To?"

The technician shook his head. "It was before we got the tap activated."

"We can track it through the phone company records first thing in the morning," Neville said.

"Why don't we just move in now?" Pflanz asked, turning to the deputy. "He hasn't had a chance to do any damage. We should take him before he does."

"Take him *where,* Dieter? We don't know whether Chaney really knows anything or whether he's just fishing."

"He suspects! Why else would he be here?"

"Suspecting is one thing. Proving is another. You can't just go snatching citizens off the street!"

"What do you think he's doing in Los Alamos if not looking for proof? And suppose he finds something?"

"There's nothing to find!"

"You hope. But suppose he does? And suppose he tells the woman, wherever the hell she is. What are you going to do, appeal to their patriotism? Chaney's a muckraker, George. He'd like nothing better than to blow this all over the six o'clock news!" Pflanz rolled his massive fists into wrecking balls. "There are bigger things at stake here than this guy. We should take him now."

Neville's voice was low and dangerous. "We *watch*. We listen. And we do nothing—do you get that?—until *I* say we do." They stood eye to eye, neither blinking nor moving, fixing each other with the hard stare of those accustomed to having their orders followed, warriors whose long alliance was showing dangerous signs of fraying.

"This is a tactical mistake and you're going to regret it, Neville," Pflanz told him finally. "We're *all* going to regret it."

"Maybe," Neville said, "but it's my call. We keep him under surveillance for a little longer, see if he meets up with Mariah Bolt, and find out what she's been up to. With luck, they'll both come up empty and back off."

"And if not?"

"We'll cross that bridge when we come to it. Meantime," Neville said, "let's get some shut-eye." He turned to the technician monitoring the bug in Chaney's room. "You shout if you hear anything." The man nodded as Pflanz and Neville moved to an office next to the ComCenter and stretched out on a couple of couches.

It was around midnight when the technician called them to report that there was a conversation going on in the hotel room. As they grabbed up headsets to listen, Neville recognized the second voice. "She's there with him!" he said, punching the air with his fist. "We've got them both!"

They listened to the conversation between the reporter and the analyst, and then replayed it again on tape after the targets went back to sleep—in separate beds, it seemed.

"Okay," Neville said. "This is good."

"Good? How do you figure?"

"Because they're both where we can see them. They won't find out anything poking around Los Alamos. No one at the lab knows anything, and even if they did, they sure as hell wouldn't talk to any hotshot television reporter." Pflanz did not look reassured. "Interesting," Neville mused aloud. "If he's not lying to her about his involvement with the Müller woman, then I guess it confirms what you learned, Dieter. That Chaney was just the vehicle she used to get to David Tardiff."

Pflanz nodded. He had never had any doubt that Katarina Müller told him the truth before she died. He had long since learned what death-row priests have always known—that the confessions of the condemned are nearly always truthful.

"Rachel, this is Paul Chaney," Mariah said, stepping back from a hug. She and Chaney had risen early that morning and ordered a room-service breakfast before driving down the road to arrive at the medical building at precisely seven-thirty.

Dr. Rachel Kingman closed the door of her office and turned to face them. She was wearing a white lab coat over a navy sweater and slacks, sensible oxfords on her feet. Her steel gray hair was arranged in a no-nonsense helmet, and she wore not a speck of makeup. Only the sparkling green eyes gave away the humor and warmth that Mariah knew lay under that efficient exterior.

In this small community, where the men worked and most of their wives stayed home with children, it had been difficult for a young graduate student to find friends with similar interests. During her brief stay in Los Alamos, Mariah had felt socially as well as physically isolated, her only kindred spirit being the wife of David's boss at the Los Alamos National Laboratory.

Rachel Kingman had been on the lab's medical staff at the time, although she had confided to Mariah even then that she was considering switching to private practice.

The Kingmans were childless—whether by choice or circumstance Mariah never knew. All she knew was that Rachel Kingman had wide interests that extended to history, politics and philosophy, and that the older woman had been good company over many evenings when Larry Kingman and David had disappeared into the intellectual thickets of high energy physics. Seeing her again after all these years, Mariah regretted that she hadn't made an effort to keep in touch. She had left Los Alamos and David under unhappy circumstances, and social niceties had been the last thing on her mind at the time.

Mariah watched Rachel's warm features now as shook hands with Paul. "Mr. Chaney, how do you do?"

"It's good to meet you, Dr. Kingman. And call me Paul, please."

"Paul. And I'm Rachel. Only my patients call me Dr. Kingman. I presume you're not here for a checkup." Chaney smiled. The doctor glanced at Mariah and then studied Chaney. "You're a reporter, aren't you?"

"That's right. But I'm off duty at the moment—unemployed, as a matter of fact."

"Unemployed?"

"It's a long story."

"Paul's a good friend, Rachel," Mariah said. "David's and mine. He was with us in Vienna."

"Well, then, you're welcome here." She turned away from Chaney and her expression became sober as she took Mariah's hand. "How have you been? I was so sorry to hear about David."

Mariah pressed her lips together and nodded. "I'm trying to deal with multiple shocks. First the accident, then finding out that he had cancer when he died. And there have been some other things, too. It's been a horrible year, to tell you the truth, Rachel.''

"What a tragedy. He was a fine young man. I wasn't surprised, of course, to hear about the cancer, but how awful that his last months should have been wasted because of a senseless traffic accident.''

"What do you mean,'' Chaney asked, puzzled, "'not surprised about the cancer'?''

Rachel Kingman had been patting Mariah's hand but she glanced up when Chaney spoke, then waved them to some chairs. She herself took up a perch on the edge of her desk. "A professional hazard, I'm sorry to say. I'm seeing all too much of it here.''

"Because of the lab?''

She shrugged. "The jury's still out. The few epidemiological studies done so far have been inconclusive, and officials, of course, deny any link. But the fact is, here in Los Alamos, we seem to have very elevated rates for certain cancers—brain tumors, leukemia, thyroid cancer.''

"Like David's,'' Mariah said.

"Exactly. They're better equipped now to handle radioactive materials at the lab, but you just have to look at the photos in the historical museum to see how naïve they were about the dangers back in the early years of this place. You may not have heard about this, Mariah, but there's been radioactive waste found in one of the canyons around here. People go horseback riding and kids have been playing there all their lives. We're talking about waste that will be deadly for thousands of years to come.''

"This sounds just like what's happened in the former Soviet weapons sites,'' Mariah said, astonished.

"On a lesser scale, perhaps, but no less worrisome.''

Chaney shook his head. "Fifty years of tinkering with radioactivity and we still haven't worked out a satisfactory way to handle the deadly garbage that's left over. And even if we figure out how to store it permanently, how are we going to warn future generations away from dump sites? There won't even be any common language in a thousand years, but this stuff will still be lethal."

"Our gift to the future," the doctor agreed grimly. "Of course, David didn't have to go horseback riding in the canyon to develop his cancer."

"What do you mean?"

"It was the accident in his lab, I would think."

"The accident?" Mariah asked. "The fire, you mean, where the technician died?"

"David told you about how that poor boy suffered?" Mariah nodded. Rachel shook her head sadly. "It was terrible—*terrible.* No one should ever have to die in that kind of agony."

"Awful," Mariah agreed. "David had nightmares about it for years. But what's that got to do with his cancer, Rachel?"

"Well, unlike the technician, David took a sublethal dose of radiation that night, but we knew that he was at an extremely elevated level of risk for cancer as a result." Dr. Kingman stopped short as she glanced up and caught sight of Mariah's face. "I suppose the two of you never enjoyed talking about this, did you?"

"Talking about *what,* Rachel? He told me about the fire and about how the tech died a lingering death from radiation sickness. What else was there to tell?"

Rachel sat back on the desk, frowning. "David didn't tell you that he was the one to find the technician that night and get him out of the building?"

"What!"

"Oh, dear," the doctor said quietly. She massaged her temples wearily for a moment. "I suppose he might have feared your reaction, Mariah. We had some long conversations during his recuperation. He told me you'd lost all of your family. He missed you terribly after you left Los Alamos, and perhaps he feared you wouldn't take him back if you knew the prognosis."

Mariah was too stunned to speak.

"Exactly what happened that night?" Chaney asked.

Rachel shifted her gaze to him. "David's lab was in one of the old buildings left over from the war. Those buildings have pretty much all been torn down now. They were never meant to be more than temporary but, typically, some had remained in use long past their normal lifespan. They were rickety wooden things and the wiring was inadequate for all the new equipment they had put in there. My ex-husband was always ranting about lost time when the fuses blew and experiments were ruined."

"Faulty wiring—is that what caused the fire?"

She nodded. "That's what I heard, although the investigation was never made public. David and the technician were working late that night, running some sort of experiment on a cesium source. I don't know the details—that's all classified, of course. Anyway, David had run out to pick up some dinner. When he returned, he found the building in flames. He ran inside and found the technician, who was unconscious by then. Apparently, the fellow had grabbed the radioactive source with a pair of tongs and was trying to get it out of the building, but he was overcome by smoke. He dropped the source and collapsed right on top of it."

"Giving himself a lethal dose of radiation."

Dr. Kingman nodded again. "I was working in the laboratory's health complex at the time, and I was on duty when the two of them were brought in. We treated them both immediately for smoke inhalation, but we knew from the technician's dosimeter badge that he had taken a supralethal dose of gamma radiation. David had taken off his badge when he went out to get dinner, so there was no way of knowing how severe the damage might be in his case. All we could do was monitor. As it turned out, he developed a milder case of radiation sickness. He recovered, but—''

''But there were long-term ramifications,'' Mariah said. ''Damn him! How typical!''

''Typical?''

''That he never told me this.'' She looked up at Dr. Kingman. ''You might be partly right about why he didn't, but it was more than that. He never wanted to be the bearer of bad tidings. We were a great team. I always anticipate the worst, David refused to ponder it— the eternal optimist. He seemed to think that if you shut your eyes to the ugliness in this world, it wouldn't touch you. He just sailed through life, ignoring the bad things.''

''Maybe that's not such a bad way to live.''

''*Que sera, sera?*'' Mariah said bitterly.

''Sort of. Live today to the maximum and let tomorrow take care of itself.''

Just then, there was a knock at the door. When Rachel walked over and opened it, Mariah saw a young woman in a nurse's uniform standing on the other side. '''Morning, Dr. Kingman,'' she said cheerily. She glanced at Mariah and Paul, then at her boss. ''Sorry to disturb you—just wanted you to know I'm here. I didn't realize you had patients already.''

''Not patients—visitors. An old friend. We won't be too long. The Marshall twins are still due to come in for their allergy shots at eight?''

The young woman in the doorway nodded. ''On their way to school, and then you're giving flu shots at the seniors' center this morning, remember?''

''I remember. Buzz me when the twins arrive, okay, Beth?''

''Okeydokey,'' the young woman said, bowing out.

When the door was closed again, the doctor turned back to see Chaney studying Mariah. Then he leaned forward in his chair, turning his attention to the older woman. "Rachel, we shouldn't hold you up, but we wanted to ask you some questions about the accident involving the other Dr. Kingman, your ex-husband."

"What about it?"

"Mariah and I have been looking into David's car accident in Vienna and we've uncovered strong evidence that it might have been a deliberate attack. When we heard about the accident here involving your ex-husband, we became curious about possible links between the two. Among other things," Chaney continued, "David had recently been in contact with one of the Russians who was with Larry that night. And this Russian—a Dr. Sokolov—apparently went to some extraordinary lengths to ensure that the other two Russians killed that night were included in the delegation that was visiting the lab."

Mariah jumped in. "And now we think we've uncovered some anomalies that suggest that the tanker accident wasn't what it appears to be."

"What kind of anomalies?"

"For one thing, the fact that Larry and the others drove all the way to Taos for a drink that night," Mariah said. "We went to the bar. Frankly, Rachel, it's kind of a dive. Not Larry's sort of place, from what I recall of him. And then there was the way the investigation was handled."

"What do you mean?"

"Federal officials claimed jurisdiction," Chaney said. "Pushed the local police and fire authorities off the case."

"That's not surprising, is it? Given Larry's work? And the death of the Russians?"

"But there *was* no investigation, Rachel," Mariah explained. "The locals said the feds just bulldozed the evidence. You know how meticulous the security people are here. Does that sound like something they'd allow?''

"No, it doesn't."

"Had you spoken to Larry recently—before the accident?"

"Yes, of course." She caught their exchange of glances. "We split up about five years ago. It was just one of those things. Other people were involved, but that really wasn't the reason. We just seemed to have drifted into a state where we couldn't live together anymore. But once we had established a little distance, we found we could enjoy each other's company again. In fact, I had dinner with Larry only two days before the accident."

"Did he mention any recent rafting excursions?" Chaney asked.

"No," the doctor said, looking puzzled. "I would have been surprised if he had. This isn't rafting season—too cold and the water's too slow for a decent run. Besides, he couldn't enjoy it the way he used to."

"His bum knees," Chaney said.

"Yes, ski injuries. He'd had pins put in. But how did you know that?"

"We spoke to a very conscientious fire fighter in Taos," Chaney explained. "They'd received information on the suspected victims and were trying to make a positive ID. He was sifting through the wreckage, looking for evidence—dental remains, orthopedic pins, anything—when the feds pushed him off the case. Tell me, could Larry still manage a raft if he had to?"

"Oh, sure, I suppose he could. It would be uncomfortable, but he could do it."

"How did Larry seem when you last saw him, Rachel?" Mariah asked. "Was there anything unusual about his behavior?"

"Not particularly. He was a little pensive, perhaps, but it was a nice evening. We spent it reminiscing about the good old days.'' She shook her head. ''It's funny, because after I got word about the accident, I almost felt that he'd had a premonition something was going to happen.''

''A premonition?''

''It's silly, I know. It's just that he seemed to want to make amends, apologize for any mistakes he felt he'd made. You know how it is. Every relationship has unexplored reefs that eventually hang us up. But that was one of the most honest conversations Larry and I had had in years, and we laid a lot of old issues to rest.'' At that moment, the telephone on her desk sounded. Dr. Kingman reached back and picked it up. ''All right,'' she said after a pause. ''Get them prepped in the examining room, will you, Beth? I'll be there in a few minutes.''

When she replaced the receiver and turned to Mariah and Paul, they were making moves to get up. ''We don't want to keep you, Rachel.''

''But where is this all heading?''

''Maybe nowhere,'' Mariah said. ''It's still too sketchy to jump to any conclusions.''

''What about Scott Bowker,'' Chaney asked, ''the other American who was in the van that night? Did you know him, Rachel?''

''No, I never met him. I had heard of him, though.''

''How so?''

She shrugged. ''This is a small town and a lot of these people are my patients. I hear the gossip.''

''What gossip?''

''Bowker was relatively new at the lab, had been there only about eighteen months. He was brilliant, they say, but prickly. Didn't fit in very well, made no friends.''

''Do you know why?''

She nodded. ''There's a lot of anxiety in this town. With the end of the Cold War, some people are wondering if there's a future for places like this. The lab is struggling to shift gears, cut back the nuclear weapons work and find a peacetime mandate.''

''Swords into plowshares?''

''Something like that. But it's not as easy to do as you might imagine. It's like turning around an oceangoing supertanker—takes a lot of time and maneuvering. Apparently, Bowker had been brought in to help define the 'new look' of the lab, but he had a tendency to lay guilt trips on people when he thought they weren't shifting gears fast enough. Gave them the 'mesa of doom' line once too often, I think. People don't like being told that their life's work has been immoral.''

''So no one was brokenhearted to see the end of Scott Bowker?'' Chaney asked.

''Well, no one wished him dead, if that's what you mean, but the mourning period for Bowker was brief, I'm sure. Not that he'd have cared. I don't think he was any happier with the lab people than they were with him.''

''What about Larry, Rachel? How did he feel about the changes at the lab?'' Mariah asked.

''He felt they were long overdue. Larry had stayed on because he was getting close to retirement, but he had long ago lost his fascination with the destructive potential of the atom and recognized the arms race for the insanity it was. He was a real 'atoms for peace' proponent, in the end.'' She sighed deeply. ''He could have done a lot of good here. I miss him.''

From the other side of the wall, they heard a bump and then a couple of childish, high-pitched giggles.

''We should let you get to your patients, Rachel,'' Chaney said.

Dr. Kingman nodded, frowning. ''But I still don't comprehend what it is you're after. If I understand you correctly, you think Larry was involved in some sort of murder-suicide plot. That just doesn't seem credible.''

''No,'' Chaney agreed. ''It doesn't.''

"And so?"

"We can't prove anything. But personally, I don't think those five men are dead. I think their services have been bought, and the accident was staged to make it look as if they had died. Covering their tracks so they could disappear."

"Bought? Who would want to buy their services?"

"There are any number of nasty customers for the kind of skills those men could offer, Rachel," Mariah said. "That's the really scary thing about all this."

"It doesn't fit, Mariah. Larry would never do something like that."

"Are you sure? There are a lot of things I thought David could never do, but I was wrong."

Dr. Kingman shook her head firmly.

"All we have at the moment are gut-level suspicions," Chaney said, "and pieces of a puzzle that don't fit together. If there *is* another explanation, I'd like to know what it is. In the meantime, Rachel, could we ask you to keep this conversation to yourself? We wouldn't want to get anyone up in arms over what may be nothing more than paranoia on our part."

Dr. Kingman studied him and then Mariah, and finally nodded. "All right," she said. "But I think you're chasing illusions, to be perfectly honest."

"Maybe so," Mariah agreed as she and Chaney headed for the door. "And if we are, then I for one will be happy to go home to my daughter and try to put our lives back together."

"Your daughter?" Dr. Kingman broke into a smile. "I didn't know you and David had adopted a child. That's wonderful!"

"Adopted? No, Lindsay was our reunion gift to each other," Mariah said, her own smile a little sheepish. "She was born nine months after David came to Washington. She's thirteen now. I wish you could have seen them together, Rachel. They were just crazy about each other. Losing him has been awfully hard on her."

Dr. Kingman had her hand on the door but stood there, not moving and looking troubled, studying Mariah's face.

"Rachel? What's the matter?" Mariah asked. The doctor glanced at Chaney and then looked back to Mariah, obviously hesitant. "It's okay. You can say whatever it is in front of Paul."

The older woman's discomfort was apparent. "It's just that—"

"*What*, Rachel?"

"Forgive me, Mariah, but that's just not possible."

"What's not possible?"

"That you and David could have a child."

"But we do. She's with his parents right now. Believe me, Rachel. I carried her for nine months and I was there when she was born. Whatever else may or may not be going on here, I can assure you that she, at least, is not a figment of my imagination."

"That may be, but—"

"But what?"

"I'm sorry, Mariah, but don't you see? David Tardiff couldn't have fathered a child—with you or anyone else. After the accident in his lab, David was left sterile."

19

Leaving Chaney to bid a quick farewell to the doctor, Mariah stormed out of Rachel Kingman's office building and into a park across the street. She broke into a run, her mind reeling as she raced down the asphalt walk. Paul's voice, calling her name, followed her across the park, but she ran on and on. When he finally caught up to her, she had come to a halt outside Fuller Lodge. Chaney slumped against a park bench, gasping.

Before 1942, when the federal government had taken over the private boys' school at Los Alamos for the Manhattan Project, Fuller Lodge had been the school's main dining room. After the scientists moved in, the lodge was the site of intense brainstorming sessions, as Robert Oppenheimer, Enrico Fermi, Edward Teller and other brilliant minds of the day earnestly debated the most efficacious method to produce a massive nuclear blast. Mariah stared at the building, its rustic chinked-log construction belying its lethal history.

"Well?" she said stonily. "Aren't you going to ask?"

"Ask what?" Chaney said, still breathing hard.

"Who Lindsay's real father is?"

"No, not unless you want to tell me."

Mariah gripped the back of the bench, closing her eyes as she swayed unsteadily, feeling the earth disappearing from under her feet, her whole world swept away. The sense of vertigo was overwhelming, producing intense nausea.

Opening her eyes suddenly, she lurched toward a clump of bushes and threw up violently, her stomach continuing to convulse long after it had been emptied. When the wrenching heaves finally ceased, her ribs ached.

Feeling Chaney's hand on her back, she straightened shakily. He handed her a handkerchief dampened with snow, which she held against her face, forcing herself to breathe deeply until the trembling slowed. Paul put his arm around her shoulders and led her to the bench. They sat there quietly for a long time, the sun warm on their faces as it turned the light snow to puddles on the sidewalk.

"It all makes sense now," Mariah said at last.

"How so?"

"David. The way he was after he left Los Alamos and showed up on my doorstep. With Lindsay. In Vienna."

Chaney said nothing, but she knew when she glanced up at his face that she wasn't making the least bit of sense.

She exhaled sharply. "I hadn't heard from him in months before he came back into my life. I missed him terribly, but he wasn't answering my letters or phone calls. I thought he must be involved with someone else. Then one day he showed up—thin, tired-looking. It was the only time, except for those last weeks in Vienna, when I ever saw David depressed. He told me about the fire, how the tech died, but nothing about getting hurt himself." Mariah wrapped her arms across her chest as the tears started flowing freely. "I would never have turned him away. He should have known that. He should have told me."

Chaney was quiet as she rocked slightly back and forth.

"He had always wanted children," she said finally. "It may be one of the reasons I left him in the first place—after the rotten childhood I'd had, I couldn't face the thought of bringing a baby into the world. Then, a few weeks after David moved in with me, I discovered I was pregnant. He seemed very subdued about it—I guess now I know why. But after a few days, he seemed to get used to the idea, and there was no looking back after that. He bonded so tightly with the baby—even before she was born—that I convinced myself he was the father."

A kaleidoscope of images suddenly flashed across her mind, images of David and Lindsay. David in the delivery room, holding the tiny wet bundle, earnestly introducing himself to his new daughter as the nurses exchanged amused glances. The baby and David stretched out on the sofa sleeping, her little fingers wrapped in the comfy fur of his bare chest. David leading a two-year-old Lindsay out on the ice on her first pair of double-bladed bobskates. David stubbing his toe in her darkened bedroom as he laid a trail of gold glitter from the window to her pillow where she had left her offerings for the tooth fairy. Lindsay's red ponytail bouncing joyously above her perch on David's shoulder when her team won the Midget Softball Championship.

"But you must have known he might not be the father," Chaney said quietly.

Her eyes snapped up. "Of course I did! I'm not an idiot, you know! Don't you think I agonized over it? For nine months, I had nightmares about giving birth to a bald baby with bushy eyebrows." Mariah's eyes went soft and a small smile tugged at the corners of her lips. "And then Lindsay was born, and she was so beautiful and she looked like nobody except her tiny, perfect self and David loved her so much." She glanced up, realizing she was rambling again. "It might sound crazy, but from the moment she was born, I never, *ever* considered the possibility that she could be anyone's child but David's. Because he *was* her father, in every way that mattered.''

Chaney nodded and turned to watch two mothers and their young children strolling across the quiet park. "Frank Tucker," he said at last.

"Yes. Are you shocked?"

"No. I could see the night of the party that the two of you have a special bond."

"It's not what you think. He's a very dear friend, but there's never been anything between us. Except once. It's hard to explain—it just happened." Mariah groaned and slammed her fists into her thighs. "Oh, hell, that's so lame! I *never* let Lindsay get away with an excuse like that. Things don't 'just happen,' I always tell her. We're responsible for our actions."

"We're human, Mariah. We make mistakes."

"Frank and I made a mistake, a terrible one. One we both regretted as soon as it happened."

"His wife was still alive, wasn't she?"

"Yes, it was just before David came to Washington. Joanne Tucker was dying, *really* dying, after fighting so hard and for so long. Her leukemia had been in remission, but she was getting weaker all the time and they knew she wouldn't pull out of the next relapse. One night, Frank and I were working late. My car battery was dead when we went to leave, so he gave it a boost and then followed me to make sure I got home all right. Joanne and the kids were away at her parents' place in Pennsylvania for a couple of days. It was her last visit home. Frank was leaving the next day to bring them back."

Mariah and Chaney watched as a squirrel ran across the walkway toward the lodge, coaxed out of hibernation by the unusual springlike weather. It paused, its tail flicking joyously, then darted off again.

"It had been a crazy day at work and we hadn't eaten, so when we got to my place, I invited him in. It was innocent. I've always liked Frank Tucker. He's a gruff old bear, but he's honest, a real straight-shooter. Nothing phony about him. And I was one of the few people who wasn't afraid of him—I guess that's why we got along. Anyway, we ate, we drank a bottle of wine. We talked, about nothing much at first, but it was comfortable, you know? Neither of us had had anyone to unburden ourselves on for a long time. I was lonely. Frank was the rock in his family, trying to hold it together by sheer force of will."

She closed her eyes briefly as if to block out the memory. Finally, she opened them again.

"Frank started talking about Joanne, how he'd spent most of his marriage living in fear of losing her. But strong as he was and hard as he'd tried, he couldn't stop it from happening. He was hurting so much, Paul, and so scared about what was coming. And then, all of a sudden, he just crumpled. That tough old bruiser just sat there in my kitchen, tears flowing down his face."

Mariah was crying now, too.

"I didn't mean for anything to happen. Neither of us did. I just put my arms around him and held him while he cried. And then, God forgive me, I kissed him. He held on to me, like a drowning man grasping for a rope. Before we knew what was happening, we were in my bed." Her nails bit into the palms of her hands, clenched on her thighs. "Afterward, we felt terrible. Joanne had been so good to me. And Frank was in agony over what he had done—to her and to me. He blamed himself, but it wasn't his fault."

Mariah held Chaney's wadded-up handkerchief against her aching chest. When she exhaled, a long, shuddering sigh came out.

"For a while, it was awkward," she said, "but eventually, Frank and I managed to revert to our old relationship. A couple of days later, David showed up. And then I found out I was pregnant."

She stood abruptly and began walking along the path. Chaney followed and pulled up alongside her. "So there you have it," she said. "The whole ugly story."

"You shouldn't be so hard on yourself, Mariah. You reached out to comfort a friend in pain. Caring is not an indictable offense, in my book."

"I condemned you for the same thing after that night on the ambassador's terrace."

"I suppose. The difference is, of course, that when I kissed you, you didn't respond."

She hesitated. "A part of me did," she confessed. "I'm not a stone, you know."

"I know that. But you resisted," Paul said, "which still makes you the better man, Gunga Din."

"No. Look what a mess I made of things."

Chaney stopped walking and grabbed her arm. "Just hold on a minute, Mariah. Maybe you made a mistake, although I'm not convinced what you did was so awful, under the circumstances. But the result of that mistake was Lindsay. And not only is she a joy in her own right, but the two of you made David happier than he would ever have expected to be, given what happened to him here. So let's keep this in perspective, shall we?"

"But don't you see? The lie came back to destroy us in the end. She knew—Katarina Müller knew the truth. She must have. That's what she meant when she told you our family was a sham. And that was what she used to blackmail David."

"How could she know?"

"Someone must have gone digging into his past, found out about the accident in the lab and put two and two together. Whoever that is would be the most likely person to have hired Katarina Müller."

"But even if she had threatened to expose the truth, David couldn't have believed he would lose you over it. After all, you had played a part in building the illusion."

"Not *me,* Paul! It wasn't *my* reaction David was afraid of—it was Lindsay's. Her daddy was her hero. If she found out he wasn't her biological father, who knows what might have happened? David would never have let her be hurt like that. And what if she'd wanted to know her real father? David would have been terrified of losing her, or of being in any way diminished in her eyes. I think he would have done anything to avoid that, including letting himself be compromised by that woman."

Chaney shifted his gaze across the park, frowning thoughtfully. "Rachel Kingman might know."

"Know...?"

"Whether anyone had come fishing for information on David. She was his doctor. If someone had found out about the accident at the lab, they might have approached her for information on his medical history."

"You're probably right. I should have asked when we were in there, but after she dropped that bomb about David's sterility, I couldn't bear to hear another word."

"I know, it was a shock. But we should find out, Mariah. I'll go back, if you want. You can wait here."

"No, it's all right." She nodded toward a phone booth on the edge of the park. "But I think I'll call rather than go up. I can't handle facing her just now."

"Are you sure you don't want me to do it?"

She shook her head wearily. "Have a seat while I use the phone. I'll be right back."

Standing in the phone booth, listening to the ring at the other end, Mariah watched Paul across the park. He was bending down to gather clumps of wet snow, which he packed into balls and pitched at a nearby tree trunk, his expression grim. One after another, they smacked against the bark, exploding in a soggy, white shower. Last night, in the dark, he had told her he loved her. Now, in the harsh light of this day, he must be feeling like a fool, knowing what kind of person she really was. And even though she had never let herself seriously contemplate the possibility of having him in her life, she felt, amidst all the other emotions raging inside, a deep sense of loss that came from knowing he, too, would soon be gone. That sense of loss, she realized, was a measure of the distance they had traveled since that first tense night at the nursing home—and since Vienna.

She turned away from him as the phone was picked up.

"Dr. Kingman's office."

"Is this Beth?"

"Yes."

"Beth, this is Mariah Bolt. I'm the friend who was with Dr. Kingman when you came in this morning. Could I speak with her?"

"Oh, hi. I'm not sure if she's still here. She was about to leave for the seniors' center."

"Can you catch her?"

"I'll try, but she was running late. Someone else showed up after you left."

"Please try, Beth. It's urgent."

"Hold on."

As Muzak wafted across the telephone link, Mariah rifled through the pages of the phone book in the booth, looking for the address of the seniors' center. She had just found it when Beth came back on the line, obviously out of breath.

"Hi," she said. "I caught her. She was just about to get on the elevator. She'll be right here."

"Thanks, Beth."

"No problem."

The Muzak returned briefly, and then Mariah heard an extension click followed by Rachel Kingman's anxious voice. "Mariah? Where are you? Are you all right?"

"I'm fine, Rachel. I'm sorry I rushed out like that. It was just such a shock."

"I'm so sorry. I shouldn't have said anything. But when you mentioned your daughter, it took me completely by surprise. I shouldn't have blurted it out the way I did."

"It's not your fault. It's just that David never told me. I had been briefly involved with someone else before he came back into my life, but for all these years I really believed David was Lindsay's biological father. I believed it because I wanted—desperately—for it to be true. I think what hurts most is that he knew, but he never let on. He just swallowed his pride and took on another man's child."

"All he wanted was to be with you, Mariah. Like most people who have confronted their mortality, David had a clear sense of what was really important to him. If you felt the same way about him, I think that's all he would have cared about."

"I did, Rachel. But our secrets undid us in the end. And I need to know who else knew the truth, because I think that person was responsible for the attack on David in Vienna."

"How can you be sure?"

"I'm not, but it's the only thing I can figure at the moment. How about it, Rachel? Who else would have been aware of his condition?"

"No one here would have known that he was permanently sterile. During the recuperation period in the lab's medical facility, his sperm count was checked and was initially noted as being very low, which is quite common in these cases. Human beings are about the most radiosensitive creatures on the face of the earth, and no part of the human anatomy is more sensitive than the reproductive organs."

Mariah felt her stomach flip. "Initially low, you said. You mean maybe the damage wasn't permanent?"

"Hold on, I'm not finished. There are documented cases where the sperm count has returned to near-normal levels after a trauma like this, but the recovery period is generally a year or two."

Mariah's hopes crashed. "So there's no chance David could have fathered Lindsay?"

"No, I'm afraid not, but not just for that reason."

"What do you mean?"

Rachel Kingman's sigh was audible. "David was a scientist, Mariah. He may have had an exuberant personality, but he wasn't one to kid himself. As a scientist, he knew the risks of gene damage after exposure to radiation. Even if the organism manages to reproduce, there's a high probability of genetic mutation that could be passed on to offspring. The mutation might not manifest itself for two or three generations, but it would be random and potentially deadly. David wasn't prepared to take that risk where unborn children were involved."

"What are you saying, Rachel?"

"I'm saying that David insisted on being sterilized—permanently. I performed the vasectomy myself."

Mariah put her hand to her forehead and leaned against the wall of the phone booth. "Oh, my God," she breathed.

"The thing is, Mariah, I didn't do it at the lab complex, so it's not in their records. I was just in the process of setting up my practice. David was self-conscious about it and didn't want the whole lab to know, so he asked me to do it quietly here. Maybe it wasn't the soundest professional decision I've ever made, but after everything he'd been through, I felt he deserved the dignity of a private decision on this."

"And you never told anyone? Not even Larry?"

"Aside from the fact that I respect patient confidentiality, my husband was David's boss, and David had asked me not to tell anyone at the lab. So, no, I didn't tell Larry. But I did tell someone, I'm afraid, Mariah. Afterward, I regretted it, but at the time, I still had the lab security ethic deeply ingrained."

"Security? What do you mean?"

"It was not long after David left Los Alamos. I had a visit from a CIA officer. David had confided to me that you'd gone to work there. Apparently, the two of you had decided to get married and the CIA man said he was doing a routine security check."

"That's normal when employees marry," Mariah said, nodding.

"Well, he had already been to the lab. He knew about the fire and he knew that I had been David's physician. For a security man, he seemed to know a great deal about the effects of radiation. He kept asking questions and in the end, I'm afraid, I told him everything."

"And?"

"It was strange, his reaction. He seemed stunned. And then he told me never to tell anyone else what I had told him, that I should treat the information as top secret. Destroy any written record, in fact. Doesn't that strike you as odd?"

"Very," Mariah said, frowning. Alarm bells were ringing furiously in her brain. "Do you remember the name of this security man, Rachel?"

"No, I'm afraid not. It was such a long time ago. But I do remember what he looked like. You don't forget a character like that."

"What did he look like?"

"Very big—tall and broad. And completely bald, except for these great dark eyebrows. Quite a fearsome fellow, actually."

"Frank."

"What?"

"Frank Tucker," Mariah said dully. "Was that the name, Rachel?"

"I'm not sure, Mariah, but that rings a bell. Tucker—yes, I think that was it."

Mariah pounded the wall of the booth. "Did anyone else make inquiries, Rachel? More recently, maybe, a year or so ago? Or could someone have seen David's medical file?"

"His file is locked away in a safe. I couldn't bring myself to destroy it, but it's been sitting on the bottom of that safe for fourteen years. I just noticed it there the other day, in fact. Until this morning, I'd never discussed his case with anyone but that Tucker character. But—"

"What?"

"Maybe I shouldn't be telling you this." Rachel sounded hesitant, but then she plunged ahead. "Oh, look, I know you and I know you wouldn't be up to anything you shouldn't be."

"What is it?"

"A man came up here not long after you left. Knew you had been to see me. Wanted to know what you were after."

"Did he give his name?"

"He said his name was George Sanders."

"Sanders? What did he look like?"

"In his fifties, well dressed, silver hair. Very smooth."

George Neville, Mariah thought, her heart pounding. "And? What else did he ask?"

"Mariah, he knew—about your daughter. Wanted to know about the lab accident and who else might have been aware of it."

"Did you mention Tucker's visit?"

"No, I'm not sure why. I just didn't like his style. I told this Sanders fellow that you and I were old friends and were just having an 'old friends' kind of chat. He didn't buy it, though. He wanted to know if you'd asked about Larry. I said you'd just expressed condolences. Mariah," Rachel asked anxiously, "what on *earth* is going on?"

"God only knows, Rachel. Look, I have to run, but I'll be in touch again, I promise."

"Mariah, wait—"

But Mariah had already dropped the phone. Turning around, she spotted Paul across the park just as he was jumped by two men. One was a stranger, but the other, she realized as she struggled to get the door of the phone booth open, was the hawk-faced man in the *Newsweek* photo of Angus McCord in Russia—the man Chaney had identified as Dieter Pflanz.

When she finally managed to wrestle the door open, Mariah ran, plunging her hand into her coat pocket as she went. But as her fingers wrapped around the butt of Frank's gun, a voice from behind stopped her in her tracks.

"Hold it, Mariah!"

She withdrew the weapon and wheeled around to confront George Neville emerging from behind a tree on the other side of the telephone booth. He stopped when he saw the gun in her hand.

"Is that really necessary?"

"Yes, it is. Tell those goons to let him go, Neville."

"My, my, your little stint with our side of the shop certainly toughened you up, didn't it?" Neville shook his head in mock dismay. "Another angel falls."

"I'm not kidding! Tell them to let him go, now!"

Her eyes followed Neville's glance across the park, where Pflanz and the other man were working to subdue a struggling Chaney. Neville turned back to face her. "Calm down, Mariah. We need to talk."

"I'm losing patience!"

"No doubt. But you're not going to shoot me. We both know it, so why don't you just give me that gun before someone gets hurt?"

"Don't count on it, buster! I'm sick of lies and deceit. Tell them to leave Chaney alone and then maybe we'll talk. *You'll* talk, I should say. You'll tell me exactly what the hell you and Tucker and Pflanz and his boss have been up to."

Neville seemed taken aback. He cocked his thumb in Pflanz's direction. "How do you know who he is?"

"Tell them to release Paul. Now!"

Neville looked at the others. "Well, I'd like to, Mariah, really I would. That does look painful, doesn't it?" He winced and turned to her again. "But we have a small problem, I'm afraid. You see, Pflanz there would like nothing better than to break that reporter's neck, and whether or not you shoot me is immaterial. I think the only chance we have to save the amorous Mr. Chaney is to hustle over there and try to convince Pflanz that the two of you will listen to reason."

"Reason? What are you talking about?"

"We made a mistake, Mariah. We should have brought you up to speed long before now, but Tucker didn't think you could handle it. I think he's wrong. I think you not only have a need to know but a right to know. Chaney presents something of a problem, but maybe if we had brought you in sooner, things never would have gotten to this point. So why don't we just go and rein in those fellows before that reporter loses an arm—or worse."

From the corner of her eye, Mariah noticed at least two other men approaching cautiously from the edges of the park, watching her and Neville, their hands hidden deep in pockets that no doubt held more than handkerchiefs. Somehow, she didn't think they were there to rescue her and Paul.

"You're going to have to hand over the gun, Mariah," Neville said, confirming it. "There are some jumpy people here this morning and they frown on this sort of bravado, I'm afraid."

Still she hesitated. Frank had given her the weapon for self-defense after Burton's attack, despite Neville's promise of protective surveillance. Tucker, it had been apparent, didn't altogether trust Neville, and neither did Mariah. But at the same time, she realized, she had been living a lie for fourteen years, a lie that Frank had helped to perpetrate and that had destroyed her family in the end. Worse yet, Frank had been the only person who knew how the lie had made David vulnerable to blackmail—the only person who could have used the secret to betray them. She couldn't begin to understand why Frank would have wanted to do that, but the evidence of his involvement was unavoidable.

All she really knew for certain, Mariah thought as she saw Pflanz slam Chaney to the ground, was that Paul had landed in trouble because he cared for her and David. He had become entangled in the consequences of their past deceptions, and she couldn't stand by now and watch him be injured—or worse—for it. She dropped her arm and reluctantly handed the gun to Neville.

"Attagirl," he said, slipping the weapon into his coat pocket and taking her firmly by the elbow. "Let's go rescue your friend."

A few minutes later, Mariah and Chaney were hustled into the back seat of a dark sedan, locked in while Neville and Pflanz launched into an obviously tense debate a short distance away.

"Looks like they aren't entirely agreed about what to do with us," Chaney noted as he rubbed his upper arms.

"Neville's playing good cop to Pflanz's bad," Mariah said, "but I wouldn't trust either one as far as I could throw them. Are you all right?"

"Fine, aside from having my arms nearly ripped out of their sockets."

Mariah massaged his shoulder. "Oh, Paul, I'm sorry you got dragged into this mess."

"No one dragged me. I walked in with my eyes wide open. I cared too much for you, and for David, to let it drop when I knew the attack in Vienna was deliberate."

Mariah turned and stared out the window. "Oh, David," she said softly. "What did I do to you? What did I get you into?"

Chaney took her hand in his. "Mariah, listen to me. I know how much this hurts. But you're just as sinned against as sinning. David should have told you about his injuries."

"Why did we do it, Paul? How could two people who loved each other so much keep secrets like that?" She exhaled deeply. "I never even considered telling David about what had happened with Frank that time. It was such a mistake, I just wanted to pretend it never happened."

"And I'm sure that once he had you back, David didn't want to risk losing you again. He let you believe the baby was his, knowing it would bind the two of you together even more tightly."

"That's more or less what Rachel said, too. But Paul, she also told me that Frank Tucker was here asking questions after David and I got back together. He knew. And Neville was just up to see her and he knows, too. No one else did. Do you know what that means?"

Chaney nodded. "This doesn't look good at all, Mariah." He glanced out the window at Neville and Pflanz, who had evidently come to an agreement and were heading for the car. "Moreover," Chaney added,

"I think that Pflanz fellow has a very personal dislike for me, for some reason."

"When did you begin to suspect?" she asked wryly.

A rear door opened and Neville slipped in beside Mariah. Pflanz dropped into the front passenger seat, while the second man who had jumped Chaney got behind the wheel and started the engine.

"Where are we going?" Mariah asked.

"Back to work. Holiday's over," Neville replied.

"Some holiday. Now how about telling us what's going on, as you promised?"

"In the fullness of time, my dear," Neville said, nodding in the direction of the driver. "Little pitchers have big ears, as they say."

They drove in silence to a government airfield on the outskirts of town, where a Learjet stood parked on the tarmac. Mariah recognized it as the latest thing in corporate jets, another example of military technology going civilian. Nicknamed "the Hummingbird," the plane could take off and land almost vertically and could hover nearly as well as a helicopter. Its price tag put it out of the reach of anyone but the Gus McCords of this world, however.

The driver of the car left as soon as they got out. As they walked across the tarmac, Mariah could see the pilot in the cockpit. He had evidently been alerted to their arrival because the engines were running and he seemed to be making final preparations for takeoff. Sure enough, the plane began to taxi as soon as they were inside and Pflanz pulled the door shut.

Neville indicated a group of four deeply upholstered club chairs that encircled a low Plexiglas table. He took one himself as Mariah and Chaney buckled themselves in across the table from him. Mariah glanced around the cabin. The interior had been custom-finished with oak paneling and plush carpets. A desk built into one corner was fitted out with a computer terminal, fax machine and telephone. Farther back in the cabin, there was yet another grouping of chairs opposite a sofa that ran along the far wall of the cabin.

Ignoring the fourth chair in the group where the others were sitting, Dieter Pflanz settled himself into the high-backed leather desk chair, buckling his seat belt as he swiveled to face them. His hooded, beadlike eyes flitted about as he brooded over them, shoulders hunched, fingers clenched around the carved wooden arms of the chair.

Mariah turned away from his hunter's gaze to Neville, but he was preoccupied with folding his overcoat and laying it on the empty seat beside him. Chaney was watching out the window as the plane rolled onto the runway. As sunlight streamed in, warming the cabin, Mariah shrugged out of her own coat, slipping it over the back of her chair. There was a fierce roar of engines, and then the plane rose, hovered for a few seconds, then hurtled forward. As the aircraft climbed and banked steeply, brilliant shafts of sunshine traveled through the cabin. When the pilot leveled off, the sunlight was falling in narrow slits through the starboard windows; they were headed east.

"We're going back to Langley?" she asked Neville. He nodded. "Whose plane is this?"

Neville glanced at Pflanz and then to Mariah and Paul, who was watching them now and listening quietly. "It belongs to a friend."

"McCord," Mariah said.

Neville frowned, then leaned forward, elbows on his knees. Pursing his lips, he studied his hands for a moment. With a quick glance at Chaney, he turned his gaze to Mariah. "I wonder whether it wouldn't be better if we didn't burden Mr. Chaney with more information than he really needs to know. Nothing personal, you understand," he added to the reporter, "but there's sensitive material involved, and I wouldn't want to put you in the position of having to compromise your journalistic principles."

"That's awfully kind of you," Chaney said dryly.

Neville shrugged. "We try to cooperate with the fourth estate."

"Much appreciated, I'm sure, but I'm having a little trouble figuring out what you intend to do once we land, since your friend here seems to think I know too much already."

"Well, that's really the question, isn't it? What exactly is it that you think you know?"

"He doesn't know anything," Mariah cut in. "He's just been fishing, but he hasn't learned a thing and I haven't told him what little I know. Let him go on his way and he'll drop this investigation. Won't you, Paul?"

"Don't bother perjuring yourself, Mr. Chaney," Neville said, holding up his hand. "Sorry, Mariah, but that's a little disingenuous, since we already know that he's aware of what happened in Vienna when your family was attacked, and Mr. Chaney doesn't have a reputation for backing off. What I want to know is why the two of you came to New Mexico and what you found out here."

"Noth—"

"Forget it, Mariah. These guys aren't going to let us walk, so what's the point?" Chaney turned to Neville. "As you say, I knew about Katarina Müller in Vienna and that she had compromised Mariah's husband. I figured it had something to do with his efforts within the IAEA to limit the spread of nuclear weapons. When I found out the truth about the truck driver who had attacked David, that pretty much clinched it in my mind. Then I saw a news item about the five nuclear arms specialists who were involved in that tanker accident outside Taos. I knew that one of the Russians, Sokolov, was their best mind in the field."

"How did you know that?"

"David Tardiff told me he'd met Sokolov in Moscow. He also told me that Sokolov was slated to visit Los Alamos under the Russia/U.S. Nuclear Cooperation Pact."

No, Mariah thought, that was on the CHAUCER file. He's covering for my theft.

"I see," Neville said. "Go on."

"Well, the accident in New Mexico seemed entirely too coincidental. If it wasn't an accident, I thought, there were two possibilities. Either those guys were eliminated by our side because they were smuggling arms, or their deaths were staged by a well-organized terrorist group who wanted them to disappear without a trace so they'd be free to help build a secret arsenal."

"And which theory is correct? Have you decided?"

"Neither."

"Neither?"

"Nope," Chaney said. "I found out in Los Alamos that both of the Americans, as well as Sokolov, were disenchanted with the nuclear arms race. I have to imagine that the other two Russians were, as well, since they were handpicked for this trip by Sokolov. So I don't think any of them would have been involved in spreading nuclear weapons. We followed their trail to Taos, to the bar and then to the site of the accident. There were no bodies after the accident—no identifying evidence of any kind. But lots of people had noticed them in the bar, so that was supposed to suffice for an ID of the victims. The feds—your people, I'm guessing—moved in quickly to squelch any in-depth investigation."

"Why would we want these scientists dead?"

"I didn't say you did. You just wanted it to look like they were dead. But those men weren't killed in that fire. They slipped away in the confusion after rigging the tanker to destroy their van. Picked up a raft down the road at Pilar and floated down the Rio Grande under cover of darkness. Were met by your people, I would imagine."

"I see," Neville mused aloud. He glanced at Pflanz, whose glower had deepened. "An interesting speculation. Anything else?"

"Well," Chaney continued, "there is the matter of Pflanz here. I saw him keeping an eye on Katarina Müller in Vienna." Pflanz's eyes focused directly on the reporter. "I know you two are old comrades-in-arms and I know Pflanz now works for Gus McCord. And I'm pretty sure that McCord got me fired from CBN. That was stupid, if you don't mind me saying," Chaney added, looking up at Pflanz. "Very unsubtle and it really pissed me off."

"And I was right about McCord running arms, wasn't I?" Mariah said angrily to Neville.

"Mariah!" Neville and Chaney admonished in unison, spinning to face her.

She looked at them in turn. "Oh, the hell with it," she said. "I told Paul about that report of mine that you squelched, Mr. Neville, and about CHAUCER—so sue me. And you said it yourself, Paul, they're not going to let us walk. Let's just get all the cards out on the table, shall we?"

Neville sat back in his chair and drummed his fingers on the armrest. "So what's your conclusion? You think that Dieter here and Gus McCord and I have gone into peddling nukes for our own profit. Is that it?"

Mariah studied the deputy closely. He was arrogant—too used to operating in the shadows, too used to ignoring the rules that others are bound by, writing his own, instead. It was the kind of professional deformity that plagues the world of covert operations, where the name of the game is violating other countries' laws and where ends too often come to justify any means. Moral standards become blurred, ethics a matter of relativity—do unto others lest they do unto us. It was why CIA covert operations had so often landed the Agency in hot water, obscuring its defensive surveillance and analytic work.

The question was, had Neville also fallen prey to the most banal kind of personal corruption—simple criminality in pursuit of the almighty buck?

"Why don't you stop playing games and tell us?" Mariah said impatiently. "You wanted to know if we would listen to reason. Well, let's hear a reasonable explanation for all of this."

Neville paused, his focus shifting to the middle distance, apparently weighing his options. Then he nodded and looked at Mariah.

"It was CHAUCER that started it," he said. "We located those weapons that Tatyana Baranova told you about. Management at the research facility was corrupt. As long as the Soviet Union was functioning, workers in the weapons program had elite status and received the best consumer goods available. But when the country unraveled, Moscow's preferential treatment of them disappeared and people in those isolated communities were cut off from even the most basic commodities. It didn't take some of them long to figure out that they had something valuable that they could trade for what they needed, something for which outside buyers were willing to pay a premium price."

"And McCord's gunrunning?" Mariah asked.

"The shipping company that McCord bought had for years been engaged in a profitable sideline peddling surplus East bloc weapons—Kalashnikovs and such—to various guerrilla groups and terrorist organizations. McCord took over the operation, with our knowledge, to use it as a front for acquiring illicit Soviet nukes."

Chaney shifted forward in his chair. "Why did he need this shipping company?"

"*Bona fides,*" Mariah said. Neville nodded.

"What?"

"You don't just walk into the illegal arms bazaar and start peddling, Paul," she explained. "You have to have a legitimate—if that's the word—reputation as a reliable dealer before sellers or buyers are going to trust you. You have to establish your *bona fides.*"

"Especially if you're going to get into the very tricky specialty of nuclear weapons," Neville added.

"Okay," Chaney said. "So McCord and his buddy Pflanz buy their *bona fides* in the arms market through the acquisition of a company that's been dealing in arms for a long time. Then what? They corner the market in smuggled former Soviet nukes, is that it?"

"That's the general idea," Neville said.

"Well, gee, why didn't you just say so?" Chaney said, leaning back in his chair. "It's the epitome of the American entrepreneurial spirit—exploiting new commercial markets. Who could object?"

Neville scowled at the sarcasm and Mariah could have sworn she heard Dieter Pflanz actually growl. She shook her head thoughtfully.

"There's more to it," she said. "The five experts who disappeared in New Mexico were obviously needed for the safe handling of the smuggled Soviet nukes. But we already determined that they were philosophically opposed to spreading these things to terrorists and other crazies. So how do they fit in?"

Neville sighed. "It's a double sting operation," he said. "First we try to get our hands on the weapons whenever we hear about a corrupt Russian source. After we do, a team goes in and plugs the leak that we've identified. That's sting number one. A few former KGB officers are cooperating with us on this."

"The KGB!" Mariah exclaimed. "But it was they— or their successors—who kidnapped Tatyana Baranova!"

"A case of the right hand not knowing what the left is doing, I'm afraid. One of their more traditional operators in Vienna found out she was in contact with us and had her spirited away. We tried to locate her, but our trusted sources inside the Russian security apparatus are limited, and we have to be careful not to compromise this other business."

"You said a double sting," Chaney said. "Does that mean you're tapping the buyers, as well as the sellers?"

Neville nodded. "The team of scientists from New Mexico has been set up in a secret offshore facility. There they disable the weapons' detonators and remove the radioactive fuel, then plant an electronic tracing device. Once the dud nukes are transferred to buyers, the bug will send an intermittent signal too brief to be detected by them—a signature pulse once every two hours that only lasts a millisecond. Long enough, though, to be picked up by one of our satellites. We track the location of the dud and, by extension, the baddies."

"Taking them out at your leisure," Chaney said.

"That's our hope. We haven't actually transferred any yet, although we've acquired several of the portable nuclear weapons that CHAUCER put us onto. And we've recently had some nibbles from potential customers."

Mariah and Paul stared at Neville, stunned by the audacity of the thing—and by the realization that this elaborate scam might actually work. But there was no escaping that it had one glaring, fatal flaw. It was Chaney who pointed it out.

"And while you're waiting for customers for the dud nukes, McCord and Pflanz peddle conventional weapons to these same crazies," he said.

"A few deals here and there to keep up appearances," Neville said with a shrug. "It's a small price to pay."

"Oh, come on!" Mariah exclaimed.

"Come on yourself, Mariah!" Neville protested. "You've studied this, you know how many conventional arms dealers are out there. The market's wide open. If a terrorist wants to buy guns or explosives, there's no end of willing suppliers. We have to establish the connections somehow, and dealing in arms is a language they understand."

"Not to mention the fact that it underwrites the costs of the sting operation," Mariah said dryly. "Even Gus McCord's pockets aren't bottomless."

"But it's highly illegal under U.S. law," Chaney said. "The congressional intelligence oversight committees go nuts over unauthorized CIA arms dealing, regardless of the motive. They'd throw a fit if they knew about this operation. That's why you need McCord, isn't it? To keep it off the Company's books."

"Gus McCord is a patriot and a humanitarian." They all looked up at Dieter Pflanz, who was now perched on the edge of his chair. "He's not doing this for himself. He's doing it for the good of America, to keep it safe."

"He's in flagrant violation of American law," Chaney argued. "The law is designed to keep this country safe, too."

"What do *you* know about it, Chaney?" Pflanz spat. "You never fought for this country. Where were you when the rest of us were slogging through the jungles of 'Nam?"

"In college, drawing a high draft number, thank God," Chaney countered. "Because I'm not sure what I would have done if I had been called. I didn't support that war and I make no apologies for it—I think our leaders made a drastic mistake there. But that doesn't make me any less a patriot than you or Gus McCord,

Pflanz, so don't give me this garbage! You guys hold in contempt the laws and institutions of this country, the same country that Gus McCord wants to lead as President. What kind of patriotism is that?''

Pflanz rose from his perch, his shadow falling across them. For a moment, he said nothing and the roar of the plane's engines seemed deafening. "I told you," he said finally, turning to Neville. "I told you it was pointless. He doesn't want to see reason, he just wants a goddamn exposé to get his face on the tube!''

"Take it easy, Dieter. He's simply expressing an opinion. He has a right. Why don't you go up to the cockpit for a while and let me talk to these people?''

Pflanz hesitated, watching them glumly. Then he turned and disappeared into the cockpit, pulling the door shut behind him. The others sat in silence for a second.

"Now what?" Chaney said.

Neville glanced up, then sighed and ran his hands through his hair. "I was really hoping I could make you see the importance of keeping this under wraps. We could make it worth your while, you know."

"Are you trying to bribe me?" Chaney asked, incredulous.

"No, no, nothing like that. I'm just suggesting that the Agency has a policy now of trying to be helpful to the press—especially its more sympathetic members. We need people to understand what we're doing, and you could develop some contacts that would make you the envy of your colleagues in the press corps. We're not monsters, you know. If we occasionally get carried away in our zeal to accomplish an objective, it's with the best of intentions, I can assure you."

"Tell that to the families of the forty-seven people who were killed in those terrorist bomb attacks in New York and Paris and London," Mariah said. "Tell them you let McCord sell weapons to terrorists—with the best of intentions.''

"There's no link between McCord's operation and those attacks!"

"You hope not," Chaney said. "But it doesn't really matter whether you sell to terrorists in Africa or the Middle East or Europe or wherever. Those groups are interlinked and trade amongst themselves."

"If we don't put a lid on the spread of nukes," Neville said, "the next time a bomb goes off, it could wipe out Paris or London or New York City."

"I know that, but making the world safer for conventional terrorism is not the answer. You can't get in bed with the bad guys and expect to keep your virtue intact."

"You don't know what it's like out there," Neville said angrily. "Neither do the good congresspeople on the Hill. Gus McCord does, and that's why he volunteered to step in and help us, in spite of the constraints that Congress would put on us."

"You're wrong, Neville," Chaney said. "I've spent my life out there on the front lines, trying to make Americans aware of the issues so they can make informed choices about what they want their government to do. I've seen plenty of rich, powerful dictators who operate in secrecy, megalomaniacs like Gus McCord who think only they know what's best. In the end, it's ordinary people who always suffer."

"You think the American people care how we do this job, as long as it gets done?"

"We have checks and balances on covert action for a reason, Neville. Churchill used to say democracy's the worst system in the world—except for all the others. Nobody in America elected Gus McCord to 'save' them, especially at the cost of trampling on the law and doing deals with terrorists. Not yet, anyway. God help us if we do."

As Chaney spoke, Mariah was conscious of a change in the sound of the engines. She glanced around the cabin and noted that the sunlight was traveling around the walls in a steady path. "Why are we circling?" she asked, watching out the window. "We're losing altitude." Below them stretched vast, empty tracts of eastern New Mexico.

Neville and Chaney looked out as the aircraft moved into a hover pattern. Neville unbuckled his seat belt. "I don't know," he said. "I'll find out."

As he rose and turned toward the cockpit, the door opened and Dieter Pflanz emerged holding a gun. He stepped up next to the closest chair—Mariah's—and spun it around to face the others. The fingers of one hand gripped her shoulders tightly, like talons, and she felt the cold, hard steel of Pflanz's gun against her temple.

"What's going on here, Dieter?" Neville asked.

"Nothing," he said. "We're going to shed some cargo, that's all."

20

"You can't do this, Dieter," Neville said slowly.

"No? Watch me. You!" he said to Chaney. "Get up!"

Chaney's eyes were large and blue as robin's eggs as he unbuckled his seat belt and stood up. "Don't hurt her, Pflanz. I'll do what you want, but leave her out of this. I'm the one who dragged her into it."

"She should have stayed away from the likes of you. I tried to warn her."

"Warn me?" Mariah said. "What are you talking about?"

"That envelope I gave your daughter at school. I tried to warn you it would be dangerous to reopen this can of worms. But you couldn't leave it alone. You had to follow this jerk down the garden path."

"You bastard! How could you threaten a child and an invalid?"

"I just wanted you to back off and mind your own business."

"You hired Katarina Müller."

"No bloody way."

"Then how did you get those pictures?"

"I took them from her—before she died."

"You murdered her!"

Pflanz's voice was a deep rumble in his chest just behind Mariah's head, and she felt his fingers digging into her shoulders. "She was blackmailing your husband and she set up the attack in front of your daughter's school. You should be thanking me for giving her and that mercenary truck driver what they deserved."

"What about Burton, the guy who attacked me in my house? Was he another of your warnings?"

"No, but I took him out, too."

"Gee, Pflanz," Chaney said. "You're a regular guardian angel."

"I don't believe in diddling around while the system lets the bad guys get away. People like you, you talk so much about democracy and protecting people's rights. And then you just sit on your hands, afraid to act, while the crazies take over the world."

"Dieter, listen to me," George Neville said. "*This* is crazy. I know how you feel. But Chaney and Mariah here, they're law-abiding American citizens. You and I may not agree with their view of things, but we're on the same side, for God's sake."

"I'm not on *his* side. Muckrakers like Chaney, they're the kind that destroyed America's will to fight during Vietnam. They suck the spirit right out of this country. What we're doing is right, George, you know that. We can't let the same mistakes happen again. This time, we finish what we started, and no reporter's going to stop us until we win this war."

"I won't go along with this," Neville said emphatically.

"Then just stay out of my way. I'm not afraid to do what has to be done."

"I'm telling you no, Dieter." Neville's hand moved to the front of his jacket.

Mariah gasped as Pflanz's fingers slipped up into the soft flesh under her jawbone, wrapping around her windpipe. It would take nothing for those fingers to crush it like a paper straw. "Don't make me do it," he growled.

Neville lifted his hands. "Take it easy."

"You—Chaney!"

Chaney tore his anxious eyes from Mariah's face. "What?"

"Get Neville's gun—inside his suit jacket. And mind, lift it out real careful. One false move and you can kiss the woman goodbye."

Chaney nodded and reached inside Neville's jacket, lifting the weapon out of a shoulder holster, holding it up with two fingers where Pflanz could see it.

"Take out the clip and toss the gun onto the sofa. All right, now take the bullets out of the magazine and drop them on the floor." The bullets disappeared into the thick carpet in a series of soft thunks. When Chaney had thrown the empty clip aside, Pflanz released his grip on Mariah's throat and tapped her on the shoulder. "Get up," he instructed. He kept one hand on her shoulder and the gun at her head while she unbuckled her seat belt and scrambled to her feet. Pflanz guided her backward toward the door of the aircraft. When they reached it, he stopped. "Get over here, Chaney. Open the door."

"Dieter, for God's sake. Don't do this!" Neville cried.

"Shut up, George. Chaney, I said unlatch the door!"

Chaney stared at him for a second, and then came over and reached for the lever in the big door, yanking it up. There was a hiss of escaping air as the seal was broken and the hatch lifted up and away, opening the side of the aircraft to a gust of frigid wind. A few bits of loose paper whipped around the cabin. The floor was tilted toward the open door, the aircraft hovering low over the barren landscape.

Pflanz shoved Mariah into Chaney's arms and stood back against the open hatch. "Okay. One by one or together—your choice," he yelled above the drone of the engines and the rush of the wind. Mariah gripped Chaney's jacket and stared at Pflanz, unable to believe that he was serious. "Come on!" he hollered. "I haven't got all day. Step out or I'll shoot first and push later. Move it!"

"No!" Mariah shouted. "You go to hell, Pflanz! You can't get away with this!"

"Really? Who knows where you are? Nobody. And by the time the vultures and coyotes are finished with your bodies, there'll be nothing left by spring."

Still they stood frozen to the spot. Pflanz waved his gun impatiently.

"I'll go first," Chaney said finally.

"Paul, no!"

He regarded the open door grimly. "Let me get this over with—I hate long goodbyes. By the way," Chaney added, looking down at her and touching her cheek, "I still think you're the finest woman I've ever known." He pried her fingers from his jacket and moved next to Pflanz in the doorway, turning briefly to give her a halfhearted salute.

The next move was as sudden as it was unexpected. As he turned again toward the door, Chaney's hand made a rapid, slicing arc down on Pflanz's wrist. Pflanz stared in disbelief as the gun fell, bounced once on the floor and disappeared into the void. But he recovered quickly, reacting with instant reflexes, grabbing Chaney's lapel with his left hand as his right smashed into the reporter's face. Chaney fell backward against the bulkhead but Pflanz pulled him to his feet again. The two of them stood poised in the open hatch. Chaney was stunned by the blow but managed to grab Pflanz's shirt, hanging on tenaciously, evidently deter-

mined to take the bigger man with him when he went
out the door.

Pflanz brought his arms up hard between Chaney's,
breaking his grip, then grabbed the reporter's jacket
once more and prepared to heave him out the door like
a rag doll. But for some reason, he hesitated. At first,
she thought that Pflanz had been distracted by her
scream, but Mariah realized that there had been another loud noise and she noticed a small red spot beginning to flower on his chest. Pflanz's wild gaze
traveled down to his shirt, then from Chaney to Mariah and beyond. His scowl deepened as he looked back
to the reporter, the two of them locked together as
Pflanz began to list toward the blue sky.

Mariah leaped forward, grabbing Paul by his belt and
pulling backward with all her might, but Pflanz was too
heavy and her feet skidded on the deep pile of the carpet. As the three of them slid together toward their
doom, Chaney struggled to pry open Pflanz's fingers on
his jacket. Finally, with the crimson bloom spreading
across his shirtfront, Pflanz's grip went slack. Mariah
gave one last yank on Paul's belt and the two of them
collapsed on the cabin floor. Pflanz flailed desperately
for a perch of some sort. Finding none, he fell back into
the blue, his beaded eyes bright and furious, his arms
outstretched like great wings as he sailed off in the
bright morning light.

From their tangled heap on the floor, Mariah and
Paul tore their eyes away from the open door and
looked back at Neville. He was crouched behind one of
the club chairs, his forearms propped on the armrest,
the left hand supporting the outstretched right in which
he held a gun. It was the gun that he had taken from her
in the park in Los Alamos and stuffed in his coat
pocket, Mariah realized—Frank's gun. Neville got to
his feet and moved to the door, peering out briefly be-

fore pulling it shut with a grunt and ramming the locking bar home. Then he turned to face them.

"Are you all right?" he asked. They nodded dumbly. "Make yourselves comfortable. I need to have a little chat with the pilot and then make a couple of calls. We're going home." Neville disappeared into the cockpit. A moment later, the aircraft began to climb, resuming its eastbound trajectory.

Mariah turned to Chaney and wordlessly threw her arms around him, burying her face in his neck. He held on tightly for a very long time. "Thanks for hauling me back in," he said at last, his voice husky. "I thought I was a goner for sure."

"You can thank a low center of gravity. Being short finally paid off."

Chaney tried to smile but it turned to a wince at the angry welt that was rising on his cheekbone. Mariah touched it gingerly, then planted a light kiss, first on his cheek, then, tentatively, on his lips. The next kiss went much deeper, unrestrained by doubt or hesitation on either side.

When Neville returned to the cabin a while later, they were sitting together on the couch at the rear, hands clasped, heads bent together in quiet conversation. The deputy's expression was weary as he settled into a chair across from them. "I've arranged for a search party to go out and look for his body," he said.

"It's more than he would have done for us," Mariah said bitterly.

"I'm sorry for what he tried to do. I don't excuse it, but I want you to know that Dieter Pflanz wasn't really an evil man. He never sought money or personal power for himself. His mind wasn't particularly subtle, but he believed in the rightness of what he was doing. In the end, he got confused by the blurry lines that divide right from wrong—maybe we all did. He couldn't tell anymore who the real enemy was.''

''He was a personal friend of yours?'' Chaney asked.

''We'd been through a lot together. He saved my life more than once.''

''It must have been hard to do what you did,'' Mariah said.

''It was what I had to do. I'm not an evil man, either, Mariah. I know you don't think much of me or some of the things I do, but in a dangerous world, we don't always have the luxury of ideal choices. Nobody wants nuclear weapons landing on their doorstep, but nobody wants our troops out there playing policeman all the time, either. Faced with a danger, I had to make the best choice from a poor range of options. That's my job.''

''What happens now?''

''Well, this operation is obviously wound up, if for no other reason than we can't run it without Pflanz—he was the linchpin. And anyway, if you stumbled across it, Mr. Chaney, it was probably only a matter of time before someone else did, too, and Congress, as you say, will not be amused. My career, I think it's safe to say, is about to come to an end. I have only one favor to ask,'' Neville added.

''What's that?''

''It's not for me, but rather a humanitarian gesture. We have people out there in the field who are negotiating with buyers for those dud Russian nukes. If this story gets out now, they're dead. Do you think you could delay just a little before going public with this?''

''Can you assure me that there won't be any more arms running by McCord?''

''You have my word,'' Neville said. ''That side of the operation is shut down as of this moment.''

"Well, I don't have a job, as it happens, so I guess I can sit on this." Chaney glanced at Mariah. "In any event, I didn't get into this investigation for its news value."

"I appreciate your cooperation, Mr. Chaney."

"Then appreciate this—I'm going to be watching, Neville. And I won't hesitate to raise holy hell if I find evidence that your people have stepped over the line again into illegal activities, however noble the cause. That's *my* job."

"I know. And despite the fact that you in the media also overstep the bounds of morality sometimes, I've seen enough closed regimes to know that your job is important. So, we have an understanding?" Chaney nodded. Neville turned to Mariah. "What about you, Mariah?"

"It's not over yet. Not for me."

"What do you mean?"

"Who really hired Katarina Müller to blackmail my husband, Mr. Neville?"

"We've always assumed it was the same Russian intelligence faction that kidnapped Tatyana Baranova. I still think so, despite what Müller told Dieter Pflanz before she died."

"What did she tell him?"

"She said she never met the people who hired her for the job. The assignment came by telephone, with the payoff money transferred electronically. She said the person who hired her spoke English with an American accent."

"And you don't find that strange?"

"The method, no. It's common enough—funds get transferred electronically through numbered accounts, difficult to trace. As for the accent, many KGB agents were trained to speak English with an American accent. When Müller and the truck driver she hired were murdered, I thought that was Russian handiwork, too, until Pflanz told me that he himself had been mopping up.''

''What if it wasn't Russians who hired Müller?''

''Why would you think it wasn't?''

''Do you know how Müller blackmailed my husband? I mean before she dragged him into bed with her?''

Neville nodded. ''When my guys in Vienna found out about it, your husband told them Müller had threatened your daughter. The bedroom pictures, it seems, were simply to add insult to injury—extra ammunition. It was his child he was trying to protect.''

''Do you know *how* she threatened our daughter?'' Neville hesitated, glancing at Chaney. ''Never mind Paul,'' Mariah said. ''He knows everything.''

''I gather that David Tardiff wasn't your child's true father. Before she died, Müller confessed to Pflanz that she got her hooks into your husband by threatening to tell your daughter she was illegitimate.''

''And where did the information come from?''

''From whoever hired her, I guess.''

''Your people, Mr. Neville.''

''What!''

''It had to be. Only one person knew, besides David and his doctor, and that was Frank Tucker. He told you and you used the information. What I can't figure out is why you wanted to do this to us.''

Neville sat back in his chair and stared at her, dumbfounded. ''This is paranoia, Mariah! I didn't know about your daughter until Pflanz told me last night. If Frank Tucker knew, he never told me. For that matter,'' he added, frowning, ''how do I know it wasn't you yourself who set up your husband? Maybe you and Chaney cooked this up to get David out of the way.''

Chaney grabbed Mariah and held her back as she leaped out of her seat toward the deputy. "Back off, Neville!" he said angrily. "That's not true and you know it!"

"It makes more sense than what she's suggesting," Neville snapped. "Dammit, Mariah! You persist in painting me as the villain in this piece. I'm no angel, but I do protect my own people and I count you among them. I swear, I didn't know anything about this until Dieter told me yesterday."

Mariah slumped down in the sofa again. "Neither did I."

"Excuse me? *You* didn't know?"

"I never knew David had been injured in Los Alamos and couldn't have children. When I became pregnant, I knew there was a chance he might not be the father, but I hoped he was. As time went on, the hope became the reality, in my mind."

"But Tucker knew? All along?" She nodded. Neville's eyes narrowed. "Mariah, is Frank Tucker the father of your child?" She looked away and nodded again, reluctantly. "Oh, shit," Neville breathed. "I'm going to have to have him investigated, you know. This doesn't look good."

"Let me talk to him first."

"That's not a good idea."

"Please. God knows, Frank Tucker owes me some sort of explanation. But in spite of everything, I can't believe that he's corrupt, or that he would deliberately put me or my family in harm's way. Give me a chance to find out what's going on."

Neville drummed his fingers on his knee. "All right, I'll let you approach him first. But I want you to wear a wire. If Tucker has been turned, he could be dangerous."

"Not to me. He wouldn't hurt me. Whatever else he's done, I'm certain of that."

"You're not going to him without surveillance, Mariah. That's my condition. Take it or leave it."

"I'll take it."

When they arrived back at CIA headquarters at Langley, it was early evening and the security watch reported that Frank Tucker had already signed out for the day. George Neville took Mariah down to the boys in technical services and had her fitted with a concealed mike and transmitter, then driven home to pick up her car. Chaney waited at the Agency with Neville. It was about seven-thirty when she rang the doorbell of Frank's home in Alexandria.

"Mariah! Where have you been?" Tucker pulled her inside and shut the door, then turned to face her. "Patty was trying to call you yesterday but David's parents said you'd come back here. Then Neville called to say you'd disappeared—wanted to know if I knew where you might have gone. What's going on?"

"I took a trip."

"A trip? Where, for Pete's sake?"

"Los Alamos." Frank stepped back and Mariah saw the color drain from his face. "We need to talk," she said.

Tucker nodded and followed as she headed down the hall and into the living room. The lights were winking on the Christmas tree and the floor was covered with books and toys.

"What are you doing?" she asked.

"Sorting the kids' things. Carol wanted her old books for the baby, so I started going through this stuff, separating hers from Stephen's. Let me take your coat."

She shook her head as she stared at the juvenile paraphernalia spread across the floor, realizing the accumulated family history that it represented—a history of Frank's and Joanne's life with their two children. It was a life into which she had been a frequent and welcome visitor, with privileged knowledge of some of its ups and downs, good days and bad. But it was essentially alien to her own existence, outside the protective cocoon she had built for her own life with David and Lindsay. Even now, knowing the link that bound those two worlds together, it was impossible to really feel their connectedness.

"Mariah? Why don't you sit down?"

She turned around to look up at him. "I spoke to Rachel Kingman in Los Alamos, Frank."

Tucker sank into a chair but his eyes never left her face. "And?"

"She remembered you."

"Mariah—"

"All these years, Frank—all these years you've known Lindsay was your child. And you never said a word. How could you do that, just walk away from her?"

"How could I not?"

"Oh, Frank! I know how hard things were for you. But didn't it bother you that another man claimed your flesh and blood?"

"Yes, it did. But aside from my own situation, how could I step forward and stake a claim when it was obvious who you wanted the father to be?"

"David knew, and he kept silent, too. All these years, I thought I knew you both, but I don't understand either one of you."

"Don't blame David. It was my idea."

"Your *idea?* You discussed this? The two of you actually conspired to keep quiet about this and then left me in ignorance?"

''What would it have accomplished for you to know the truth?''

''Ignorance is not bliss, Frank!''

''Maybe not, but knowing the truth is no picnic, either. Listen, Mariah. I knew from the time my kids were babies that we were going to lose Joanne one day. It hung like a sword over our life together. I didn't want that for you. I didn't want anything to spoil whatever time you and David had.''

''Why didn't he tell me?''

''He was afraid. He knew you understood radiation well enough to know what it probably meant for him in the long run.''

''What made you go to Los Alamos that time?''

''When the two of you started living together again, I asked the Office of Security to do a background check on him. I knew he had a high-level security clearance since he'd worked on the nuclear weapons program, but I was suspicious when he showed up out of the blue like that. Suspicious,'' Frank admitted, ''and maybe a little jealous, too. Not that I expected anything more between us. What happened was a mistake. You felt sorry for me. I knew that. But it did something for me, Mariah. It gave me hope. Up to then, I'd felt like my life was over. It sounds selfish and I'm not proud of this, but for the first time, I began to believe that I could go on after Joanne was gone. I *would* survive, hard as it was losing her.''

Mariah closed her eyes and nodded. This was something she could understand. Ever since David had been injured in Vienna, she had been just barely functioning in a cold, dark void. Not even Lindsay could alleviate the fear and loneliness she had felt since she had lost him. No one would ever be to her what David had been, but Paul Chaney's presence these last few days had sparked a tiny glimmer of hope that perhaps one day there could be light and warmth in her life again.

"Anyway," Frank went on, "just as you announced that you were pregnant, the security report came back explaining why David had quit the lab. Nothing about the situation felt right—even putting aside my own feelings. So I went to check it out for myself. I met with Dr. Kingman. Then I came back here and confronted David with what I knew."

"Did he know, Frank, that it was you?"

Tucker shrugged. "I'm not sure—he might have guessed. I just told him that the baby's father was married and would never interfere with your lives. David seemed satisfied with that."

Mariah slid down onto the couch and stared at the floor. The cushions sank as Frank came over and sat next to her.

"Mariah, please understand. I didn't mean to abandon you or the baby. But you were never really mine to have—either of you. I never kidded myself about that. Stepping aside for David seemed the right thing to do."

"David saved our butts, didn't he, Frank?"

"Maybe. What could I do, tell Joanne? Tell Carol and Stephen, 'Gee kids, tough luck about your mom dying, but guess what? Dad's got a new girlfriend and, as an added bonus, she's pregnant'? I was a forty-three-year-old guy with a sick wife and two kids, one in the throes of teenage rebellion. You were twenty-five and in love with another man, your whole life ahead of you. It was just no contest. David was a better father for Lindsay than I ever could have been, better than I ever *was*."

Mariah watched his agonized features, then sighed deeply and put her hand on his arm. "Oh, Frank, I'm so sorry for the mess I caused."

"I'm the one who's sorry, Mariah. You gave me strength to go on, but you got hurt in the end for your kindness. I wish I could go back and change everything."

"I don't—not if it would mean not having Lindsay. David understood that." Mariah looked him in the eye. "I think you made the right decision, Frank, even though this hurts right now. But you were a good father, too—you *are* a good father. Don't ever think differently."

There was a contemptuous snort from the front hall. Mariah's stomach plunged at the sight of the bulky figure that moved into the doorway. "Stephen!"

"How long have you been sneaking around?" Frank growled.

"Long enough. I saw her car outside so I came in quietly."

"What are you doing here? Why aren't you at work?"

"I'm off tonight. Carol said you were sorting through our stuff so I dropped by to make sure you didn't chuck out my things."

"I wouldn't do that."

"Sure, Dad. You wouldn't do that—not a model father like you." He snorted again, looking from one to the other. "You're a great pair, you two. I figured you'd find your way back together, sooner or later."

"What are you talking about?"

"I always suspected, you know. Even back then, I thought you acted weird whenever she came over here. Mom was too good-hearted. She didn't see what was going on right under her nose. But I always wondered if you were diddling Mariah."

Frank jumped to his feet. "That's enough!"

"And then I find out the truth. You cheated on Mom. And you," he continued, turning on Mariah, "you foisted *his* kid on David. David was such a great guy, and you just made a fool of him."

"I'm warning you, Stephen!"

"Frank, don't!" Mariah said. "It wasn't like that, Stevie. You don't understand."

"Oh, please! Spare me!"

"We made one mistake. And it was my fault, not your father's. He loved your mother very much. You must know that."

"He loved *you*. He had the hots for you back then and he still does."

"That's it, Stephen! You stop that right now and apologize!"

"The hell I will! Tell her, Dad, tell her you can't forget her. You still think about her. Tell her about your password."

"What?"

"Your password on the computer system at work. That was when I knew for sure."

"What are you talking about?"

"I was hacking on the system one night, about a year and a half ago. I broke into the main password file and I found your password—MARIAH. Now there's an unforgettable one, huh, even for a byte-hater like you? And then, when it came time for a new password a few weeks later, I checked again." Stephen turned to Mariah. "You'll never guess what he'd changed it to," he said, shaking his head incredulously. Mariah shrugged. "Guess!"

"I don't know, Stephen!"

"LINDSAY—surprise, surprise. And you know what it was the next month? MARIAH again." He wagged his finger at his father. "That's a no-no, Dad. You're supposed to use a new word every time. But you never do. It's just MARIAH-LINDSAY-MARIAH-LINDSAY—month after month."

"It doesn't mean anything, Stephen, an old man's preoccupation, that's all. Don't read more into it than you should."

"You were preoccupied, all right. So preoccupied about it that last year, you changed your will."

Frank was stunned. "How do you know that?"

"When I started selling my games, I needed a lawyer, so I used yours. I was in his office one day to see about a contract. He had a new secretary and she didn't realize that Stephen F. Tucker wasn't the same person as F-for-Frank Tucker. She was supposed to give me some papers to read over, but she gave me more than I bargained for. It wasn't till I started reading that I realized what it was."

"Oh, no," Frank breathed.

"I never let on. I didn't want her to get into trouble with her boss."

Frank passed his hand over his dome and exhaled sharply.

"What is it?" Mariah asked. "What did you do?"

Stephen turned to her. "He wrote Lindsay in. Changed his will so that one-third of his estate would go to a trust fund to be disbursed anonymously. Only the lawyer would know the name of the beneficiary—his bastard child by one Mariah Bolt."

"Oh, Frank, no! Why did you do that?"

"It was little enough, but I wanted to provide something for her."

"She doesn't need your money. That's the last thing Lindsay needs."

"What do you mean?"

"She's going to be a wealthy young woman one day. After my mother died, I became sole heir of the great Benjamin Bolt. His damn books keep selling and the royalties keep coming in, but I never wanted *money* from him! When Lindsay was born, I had it put in trust for her. Being Ben Bolt's daughter was no gift, as far as I was concerned, but I thought she might at least derive some benefit from being his granddaughter."

"It wasn't about money," Frank said quietly. "There isn't even much there. It was just the right thing to do."

"What do you know about doing the right thing, either of you?" Stephen asked. "You made fools of the two best people I ever knew—my mother and David Tardiff. They didn't deserve that." Mariah watched as Stephen's round face became twisted with hatred, wet with tears. He met her look. "David was so good to you—took you when you were pregnant with another man's child, raised her like she was his own. And how did you repay him? By throwing yourself at that Chaney guy while David lay dying."

"That's a lie!"

"The hell it is! I saw you at the Christmas party the night David died all alone in that nursing home. Chaney couldn't keep his eyes or hands off you. You left Lindsay with Carol so the two of you could be alone."

"No, Stephen! You're wrong!" Mariah cried. "I loved David. How could you say such a thing? How could you even think it? That wasn't why I left Lindsay that night. I needed time to clean up. Our house was a mess after I was attacked and I didn't want her to be frightened."

"Rollie Burton should have done what he was hired to do."

A stunned silence filled the room. The clock on the mantel ticked thunderously. Outside, a set of tires swished on the wet pavement.

"How do you know that name?" Frank asked.

Stephen shifted his bulk from one foot to the other, his dark eyes flitting around the room, his mouth opening and closing. Finally, he was saved by the rattle of a key in the front door and his sister's voice in the hall.

"Don't get up, it's just me! I came to help sort through that junk." She was shrugging out of her coat as she came in from the hall, smiling broadly. "Hey! The gang's all here. Mariah, hi. I didn't know you were—" Carol stopped as she caught sight of their faces. "What's going on? Dad? What's the matter?"

Tucker glanced at her and raised his hand, then turned to his son. "I want an answer, Stephen. How do you know the name of the man who attacked Mariah?"

"You told me."

"No, I didn't."

"Then Mariah did, at the party."

She shook her head. "I didn't know his name then. The police only told me later, after I got home. And I haven't seen you since."

"Well, then, I must have seen it on a file when I was hacking on the system."

"There's nothing about the attack on any Company file," Frank said. The two big men, so alike and yet so unalike, stared at each other across the room, no bridge of comprehension linking them despite the family tie and their outward physical resemblance. "*You*, Stephen? *You* hired Burton to kill Mariah?"

"Dad!" Carol cried. "Good God! What are you saying? He'd never do such an awful thing. Tell him, Stevie. Stevie? For God's sake, tell them!"

"I shouldn't have had to. If she had been where she was supposed to be that morning, instead of David—" Stephen's voice suddenly broke, rising to an agonized wail as his eyes skirted the ceiling. "Oh, hell! You weren't supposed to be there, David. I'm sorry! I never wanted to hurt *you!*"

Mariah watched Stephen's swaying body and listened with astonishment to the keening voice, suddenly recognizing the symptoms of the corrosive, angry bereavement that comes with the worst losses in life—of a parent, a child, a mate. And as she watched, she knew that it was something more than friendship, more than hero worship of David that underlay the agony they were witnessing.

He rammed chunky fists into his jacket pockets and looked back at them, his eyes glistening. "I told David once how I felt about him," he said, confirming her suspicion. "He wasn't disgusted. He didn't turn me away. He said he couldn't love me that way, but we could still be friends. He was still willing to be my friend," Stephen repeated, his voice filled with wonder.

"Stevie, I loved him, too."

"You didn't deserve him! When I found out what you did to him, and to my mother—I decided to give you a taste of your own medicine."

"Katarina Müller."

"Who's Katarina Müller?" Carol asked.

"A woman who seduced and blackmailed David and then tried to have me killed in Vienna—only David and Lindsay got hurt instead. She was working for Stephen."

"What? Mariah, no!" Carol protested. "That's impossible. He doesn't know people like that, he doesn't really know *anyone,* for that matter. He doesn't even go anywhere, you know that. Stevie's got problems, I admit, but he doesn't hire killers!"

Mariah studied this unlikely employer of assassins. Stephen's face was flushed and shining, his breathing audible as the rounded shoulders rose and fell laboriously. He lived detached from human contact in a world of personally programmed fantasy, his mind-set dominated by the simplistic good guy-bad guy scenarios that he created for his computer games, where villains were dispatched with a few keyboard punches.

"He could do it without leaving the comfort of his bedroom," she said. "He has everything he needs right there. A computer, a modem, a telephone. Access to all the billboards, I would imagine."

"Billboards?"

"Computer billboards—information services available to anyone with a computer and a modem to link up to them. You've heard of the ads for mercenaries in magazines like *Soldier of Fortune?* Well, there are computer billboard variations on the theme. If you want somebody blackmailed or murdered, it's a buyers' market out there, especially now, with the end of the Cold War. Some people have even set themselves up as agents, brokering for out-of-work spies and assassins. That's how he found Katarina Müller—and Burton, I would imagine. With the earnings from his computer games, he could easily afford their services."

"Why would you do this, Stephen?" Frank asked. "Murder? For God's sake, why?"

"I didn't start out to have her killed. At first, I just thought it would be poetic justice if David had an affair with another woman. Mariah would have to find out about it, of course, so we needed pictures. But the problem was, it wasn't easy to get David to go along. That Müller woman said she tried everything, but he wasn't interested—until I gave her the ammunition she needed."

"Why did you have to drag Lindsay into it?"

"She was in it from the start, wasn't she?" Stephen snapped. Then his features softened just a little. "I didn't mean for Lindsay to get hurt—this wasn't her fault. She's okay. She just got caught in the middle. I didn't know they'd do it the way they did."

"Why, Stephen?" Frank repeated. "If you didn't set out to kill Mariah, what changed? Why did you up the ante?"

"Because I was monitoring the cables from Vienna and I knew David was trying to leave. I thought she'd luck out again, not get what was coming to her. And then I saw the report on the CHAUCER file about that Russian informer disappearing. Oh, yeah, Mariah, I knew about that file all along. And I figured that if anything happened to you, everyone would just think the Russians were responsible for that, too. It was a golden opportunity. But then it all went wrong and David got hurt instead. That was your fault, Mariah. *You* should have been in that car. When I saw David in the nursing home—what he had become—I wanted you to pay. I wanted it so bad! So I decided to hire Burton to finish the job."

Stephen took another step toward the door and withdrew his hands from his pockets. In one hand he held a revolver, which he pointed at her.

"But Burton screwed up, too," he continued. "I should have known. You can't trust anyone. People always let you down, in the end. Well, no more. This time, I'll take care of it myself."

"Put it down, Stephen," Frank said evenly. "It's all over. You can't possibly get away with this—you know that."

"I don't care anymore, not after what happened to David. It's her fault and I just can't stomach the thought of her getting off scot-free again."

"Free?" Mariah cried. "Do you think I got off free, Stephen, seeing my husband and child hurt like that?"

"It's not enough!"

"It's me you're really angry with, Stephen," Frank said. "Leave Mariah out of it."

"Oh, right—protect her. No, Dad, I'm more than angry with you. I hate your guts. I want to see you hurt, too, for what you did—hurt bad. And I know the best way to do it." He raised the gun toward Mariah.

"Stevie, no!" Carol cried. "This is insane!"

"You don't know what they did, Carol! Stay out of this, because you just don't understand!"

"What don't I know, Stephen? What don't I understand? That Lindsay is our half sister? I know that!"

Stephen froze and his head snapped toward his sister. "What?"

"I know it," Carol repeated. "For God's sake, Stephen, put that thing away."

"Carol," Mariah whispered. "How do you know?"

"I suspected it after you came back from Vienna and I saw Lindsay. She'd grown incredibly, and changed. She was a little girl when you left but she'd turned into such a young lady."

"But how—"

The other three stood motionless as Carol walked over to a bookshelf by the fireplace and shuffled through it, finally finding what she was looking for. It was an old leather-bound album, and she opened it to reveal sawtooth-edged photographs held in place with black corners. Carol flipped the pages and then brought it over to Mariah.

"I used to love these old pictures when I was a little girl," she said.

Mariah took the album and examined the page Carol tapped with her finger. On it was a black-and-white photograph of a wedding party. The bride and groom were seated, surrounded by a half-dozen other people, the men in high starched collars and dark suits, the women in dropped-waist dresses, shirred, tucked and lace-trimmed, their hair pinned up in the Edwardian style that preceded the bobs of the twenties. Mariah's eyes moved along the formally sober faces arranged around the couple. When she came to a young girl in the upper right-hand corner of the photograph, she froze. The girl had pale skin and dark eyes. Her curly hair was twisted and coiled on top of her head, but unruly wisps escaped at her cheeks. Although the photograph was black-and-white, there was no mistaking that that hair had to be red. Her gauzy linen dress had a high lace neckline, but she looked as if she would have been more comfortable in jeans and a sweatshirt.

"It's Lindsay," she whispered.

Carol smiled a little and nodded. "In a couple of years, I think. Actually, this is Granny Tucker—Dad's mother. She was fifteen when this picture was taken. The bride is her older sister. It's one of the few pictures we have of Gran and the only one of her as a girl. It looks like my Alex got her red hair, too, but Lindsay's a dead ringer. She couldn't be anything but a Tucker."

"Oh, Carol!"

Frank's daughter took back the album and, after one last look, closed it and returned it to the shelf. Then she turned to face the others.

"So you see, Stevie, I *do* know. When I first saw Lindsay again after Vienna, it took me a while to figure out why she looked so familiar. I came over here one day to hunt through the albums when Dad was at work. I don't say I wasn't hurt when I realized what must have happened. But in the end, she *is* our sister, and she's a wonderful young girl. You must see that."

"That's not the point! It's not about Lindsay. It's about these two, and what they did to our mother."

"What did they do to her?"

"Come on! You know this would have hurt her!"

"But it didn't, because she never knew about it."

"Carol, I'm sorry," Frank said. "I loved your mother. When I lost her, it was like losing my own life. I never meant to do anything to hurt her."

"I know that, Dad. She loved you, too. I'll tell you what *did* hurt her, Stevie," Carol said, turning once more to her brother. "It was the thought of Dad being left alone. Do you know what she told me that last time she went into the hospital? It was just after Mariah and David got married. Mom and I were alone, for once not pretending we didn't know what was coming. She needed to talk about it. And at one point, Mom said she was sorry that David had shown up because she had secretly hoped that Dad and Mariah would get together after she was gone. She knew that Mariah is a good person and has been a good friend to Dad."

"I don't want to hear this!" Stephen screamed.

"You need to hear it! Honestly, Stephen! You're my brother and I love you, but you've always been so wrapped up in yourself that you couldn't see anyone else's point of view—especially Dad's. He may not have been the most demonstrative father in the world, but he loved us. He worked hard to make our lives as normal as possible. He took care of Mom, us, the house—everything. How easy do you think that was for him? Why can't you see that he's not Superman and forgive him his mistakes?"

"Because to me he always *seemed* like Superman," Stephen cried, "and he hated me for not being strong, too. I tried to be like him, but I couldn't and so he never approved of me."

"That's not true," Frank protested. "I never wanted you to be like me!"

"You could never accept me for what I am! You never touched me, never told me you loved me. You were always so closed off. You still are."

"I don't mean to be, Stephen. It's the way I was raised. People didn't touch in my family, kept their feelings to themselves. I know it's not good, but I never learned to be any other way. You're my son and I *do* love you. I always did, even if I didn't always understand you."

"Mom understood me. So did David—he was the only real friend I ever had. I miss them. God! I miss them so much!"

"I know you do," Frank said quietly. He stepped closer as Stephen stood trembling. "Give me the gun now, son. It's all over."

"No!" Stephen cried, jumping out of reach with surprising speed, given his size. "She can't get away with it anymore!"

"Stephen, put it down!" Carol cried. "Mom would be very angry if she saw this. You know she would. Think about someone other than yourself, just for once! Think about Lindsay—she's our little sister. She's already lost the only father she ever knew, the father she loved. For God's sake, Stevie," she added softly, "we lost *our* mother. Don't make Lindsay lose hers, too."

Stephen hesitated, his hands shaking visibly. Mariah watched him warily, her peripheral vision taking in the placement of furniture in the room, trying to decide which way to dive if his finger began to move on the trigger. It was then that she noticed a shadow moving across the living-room window behind him. There were people outside—Neville's people, she realized wearily. One way or another, whether Stephen shot her or not, it was all over now.

They stood motionless for what seemed an eternity as he wavered. And then suddenly, he broke, spinning around and thundering out of the room and down the front hall.

"No!" Mariah screamed. "Stevie, don't go outside! Frank! Don't let him go out there with the gun!"

Tucker glanced at her and then at the window, his face registering instant comprehension. He shot toward the hallway like a bullet, but the front door had opened before he was even out of the room. There was a moment of confusion outside: panicky shouts, rapid footsteps. And then a hail of loud retorts, like a fleet of trucks backfiring. Then no sound at all, except a father's anguished groan.

Epilogue

On New Year's Day, nineteen days after Stephen Tucker died on his father's doorstep, a commercial airliner on a regularly scheduled flight from West Africa to Paris was hijacked. Arabic linguistics experts called in to analyze recordings of cockpit conversations with the three hijackers determined from their accents that they were Libyan. The pilot was forced to detour to New York's Kennedy International Airport. Once on the ground at JFK, the hijackers released several of the passengers, mostly nationals of countries deemed "friendly to the cause of freedom." One of the passengers carried a list of demands—along with a chilling threat.

The hijackers were calling for the release of a number of prisoners held on terrorist charges in Western Europe and the extradition to Libya of U.S. military personnel involved in an air raid on the desert encampment of Colonel Ghaddafi in order that they might face a war crimes tribunal. The hijackers also demanded twenty million dollars in gold. If their demands were not met, they threatened to detonate a nuclear device that, although small, would depopulate much of New York City and render a good part of the Atlantic seaboard uninhabitable for decades to come. In a subsequent telephone call to the *New York Times,* the hijackers repeated their threat and claimed to be a suicide squad who would gladly meet Allah as martyrs of the Holy War before they would surrender to the Great Satan.

The standoff at JFK continued for thirty-six hours. Behind the scenes, American and international police and intelligence forces scrambled to confirm the identity and sponsorship of the hijackers and to gauge the validity of their threat. In order to prevent mass hysteria and gridlock on roads out of New York, the possibility that a real nuclear device could be on board was downplayed. Among press members covering the siege, however, rumors circulated that the terrorists had obtained an experimental weapon stolen from a Russian research facility. No credence was given to this report by official sources, who cited the efficacy of arms control agreements in preventing just such a disaster.

At 4:00 a.m. on day three of the crisis, the aircraft was swarmed by a special commando squad. All three hijackers were killed. One hostage died later of gunshot wounds and nine others were hospitalized for their injuries. Although the raid on the aircraft lasted only four minutes and all of the survivors were quickly hustled away for debriefing, a journalist who happened to be near one of the returning S.W.A.T. team members thought she heard him say that the attack was launched after a device was detonated but failed to produce a nuclear explosion. At a news conference later that day, federal officials produced seven handguns, three Uzi submachine guns and several grenades and knives that they said constituted the entire arsenal of the hijackers. Upon further questioning, they denied categorically that a nuclear device had ever been on board the aircraft. The threat, they said, had been a ruse.

For some time afterward, news commentators speculated on the conflicting reports. Some alleged a cover-up. Others doubted this, but suggested that nuclear terrorism was an inevitability. Learned experts were trotted out on both sides of the debate to confirm that crude nuclear weapons were either notoriously easy to manufacture and steal or, alternatively, far too complex and unstable to meet the mobility and ease-of-use requirements of the average renegade with a cause. Some reputable commentators suggested that the Kennedy device had been real, but the hijackers, thankfully, had bumbled.

In the weeks that followed, rumors circulated of a covert operation to wipe out the training facilities and arms supply lines that the hijackers had used. At the same time, the International Atomic Energy Agency in Vienna and various governments, including Washington, declared unceasing vigilance in their efforts to prevent the spread of nuclear weapons.

It was a classic case of announcing that the barn door had been shut after the horses had already escaped.

On a Saturday afternoon in mid-January, Paul Chaney and Mariah Bolt stood just off Constitution Avenue in downtown Washington, watching his son and her daughter race around the circular skating rink between the Museum of Natural History and the National Gallery. The air was crisp and cold. Lindsay's hair flamed out behind her as she lunged ahead, matching the younger boy's energy with her long and increasingly strong glides.

''Lindsay's doing great out there,'' Chaney said. ''Almost got her old form back.''

Mariah gave a satisfied nod. ''She's so stubborn—she won't quit until she's even better than she used to be. She skated every day while we were in New Hampshire.

There's a coed hockey league that she's determined to join next year."

"Jack's starting to play this year, too."

"He's a nice little boy, Paul. The two of you look like you're having a good time this weekend."

"It's a new experience. Up to now, we've never had more than a few hours at a time together. We've got almost ten years to make up for, but this is a real breakthrough. It's dicey, though," he added. "I don't want to tread on his stepfather's toes. He and Phyllis are doing a good job with Jack and this isn't easy for them. But Jack has asked and they've agreed that he can spend occasional weekends and holidays with me."

Mariah glanced up sharply. "Does this mean you're staying in the States?"

Paul turned to face her. "Yup, it's a done deal as of yesterday. You're looking at the new anchor and coproducer for a weekly investigative news program to debut on ABC in the spring. We go into preproduction next month."

"Paul, that's wonderful! Congratulations!"

"Thanks. The concept is exciting and I'm looking forward to it. And," he added, watching her closely, "we're going to base the program here in Washington."

Her stomach did a quick somersault. "Washington?" The calm in her voice belied the gymnastics going on inside.

He nodded. "That was one of my objectives when I went after the CBN bureau chief job. I was really bummed out when I got fired and thought I'd have to go back into the trenches."

"I would have thought you'd want New York. There's a lot going on there and you'd be closer to Jack."

"It's an easy hop from here. Compared to where I've been for the past ten years, this commute will be a picnic. And," he said, looking at her intently, "I was very motivated to try to line up a Washington-based job."

"Ah, yes, the allure of government intrigue."

"There's that, of course," he said, turning back to the rink. "But I had more personal matters in mind." His eyes never left the kids on the ice, but it was obvious that he was practically holding his breath in anticipation of her reaction.

Mariah hesitated, not entirely sure how to react. It was altogether too much, too soon—and yet not a surprise. She had known all along that sooner or later they would have to address the question left hanging since the day after Stephen Tucker's death, when she and Paul had parted for their respective Christmas destinations: whether what had happened between them was an ending or the possibility of a beginning.

After the disaster on Frank's doorstep, Stephen's body had been whisked away, George Neville holding the police at arm's length on some national security pretext when they responded to a call from an anxious neighbor. Frank fell into a dark and self-recriminating silence, and there was no comfort that Mariah could offer him in the immediate aftermath of his son's death. In the end, the only thing she could do was leave the family to grieve in peace.

When she returned home, a car was idling across the road from her driveway. Chaney had waited with Neville's people at Langley while Mariah went to confront Frank, and they had driven him to the condo when word came that it was all over and Mariah was on her way home.

Paul jumped out of the back seat as soon as she pulled into the garage, striding quickly toward her and wrapping an arm around her shoulders as he led her into the house, pausing only to hit the garage-door button. It dropped against the bitter cold as the two of them sought refuge from the night. There was no one else Mariah would have wanted to be with right then—but she very much needed to be with Paul.

There is always a certain poignancy about making love to someone for the first time—the gentle surprises in each new touch, the warm explorations and discoveries as bodies learn to fit together. And with Paul, Mariah discovered, there was the added sweetness of complete trust, made more acute by the intense bond that develops when two people come within a gasp of dying together.

Still, as they pulled apart from one another at Dulles Airport the next afternoon—Paul on his way to retrieve his father's car in New Mexico and return with it to Phoenix, Mariah to New Hampshire to be with Lindsay and David's family and to visit his grave for a long, soul-searching commune about the secrets they had kept from each other—there was an unspoken agreement between them not to try to explore what, if anything, could follow.

They had talked on the phone a couple of times over the holidays, and Paul had told her he was going to New York to see about a job. For two weeks, she had heard nothing. Then, the previous evening, he had called to say he was back in Washington and that his son was with him. They set up a skating excursion for the next day, leaving all questions hanging until they could meet face-to-face.

"Paul," she said now, "I'm not sure I'm—"

"—ready. I knew you were going to say that. I know it's too soon after David and I don't want to put pressure on you—or scare you off—but I'd like to be there when you decide you *are* ready. I just don't know if that's presumptuous on my part.''

Mariah sighed. ''It's not that I don't feel anything for you. You know I do. But it's not that simple. I have more than myself to think about—there's Lindsay, too. She looks happy out there at the moment, but she's still got a lot of pain, both physical and emotional, that she's dealing with. God knows, being thirteen is hard enough, but after everything she's been through this past year, I'm afraid I'll blow it if I'm not careful right now. We need time to stabilize—me as well as her.''

''I can understand that,'' he said, nodding. ''Have you decided about . . . you know?''

''Whether to tell her the truth? Yes, I've decided. Part of me rejects the idea of keeping secrets any longer. That's what got us into trouble in the first place. But I talked it over with Frank and Carol, and they've agreed with me that it would be a mistake to tamper with Lindsay's memories of David. He was the only father she ever knew and his love was the most important pillar of her young life. It would be criminal to undermine that now, when she needs it most. We were lucky that George Neville arranged to keep the details of Stephen's death under close wraps—Lindsay thinks it was an accident. And Carol has been wonderful. She wants very much to stay close to her sister, under any circumstances. Eventually, it might be possible—or necessary—to tell Lindsay everything. I don't know. For now, we'll take things one day at a time.''

''What about Frank? How's he doing?''

''He's in deep mourning for his son. It hurts to see the guilt he's putting himself through, because whatever mistakes he might have made, Frank did everything he was capable of doing for his family.'' Mariah shook her head sadly. "I'd give anything to erase what happened between him and me."

"Except Lindsay," Chaney noted. "And even if you could, it still wouldn't have made Frank and his son compatible. Theirs is an old story, you know. It happens all the time. It sounds like Stephen lived uneasily for most of his life, on the margins and in the shadow of his father. You didn't make him into the unhappy man he turned out to be."

"Maybe. But I didn't help, either. Anyway, it's hard for me to feel too sorry for Stephen after what he did to David and Lindsay, but I worry about Frank. Patty Bonelli has really stood by him through all this, though. She's good for Frank and she won't let him get too far down. I have a feeling that when the dust settles, the two of them might finally get married. Frank's decided to take early retirement—maybe that's good, I'm not sure. He's been working so hard for such a long time, but I have difficulty imagining Langley without him."

"And what about Mariah Bolt? What does she do now?"

"Professionally, you mean? I've been offered a job in the CIA's nuclear nonproliferation unit, helping to keep tabs on the Russian arsenal and all the crazies out there who want a bigger bang for their buck."

"Mariah, what happened to the five scientists from the so-called tanker accident?"

"You're not going to broadcast this, are you?"

"You know I'm not. I just hate loose ends."

"They're resettled under new identities and they'll be doing consulting work as the need arises. No," Mariah added, catching his look, "not that kind. Neville kept his word. Henceforth, CHAUCER is defunct. But their expertise is going to be critical in the next few years."

"That phantom nuke in the New Year's hijacking at JFK—that was their work, wasn't it? It was one of the duds that Neville said they'd already found a buyer for."

She shrugged. "I'm not sure. I was out of the loop while I was on leave. But personally, yeah, I'd bet the farm on it. This disinformation campaign is just to keep all the bad guys out there guessing. They're not to know that possessing the stolen weapon tagged that gang, but they *are* supposed to be very worried about what exactly we're capable of. And you may *not* quote me on that, Paul Chaney."

"Let's get one thing straight, Mariah. I intend, at the very least, to remain your close personal friend. And I promise that nothing you and I discuss will ever find its way into my work, unless you tell me it's all right. Okay?"

"Okay."

"So, are you going to take this new job?"

"I'm not sure," Mariah said. "Part of me just wants to walk away from the whole stinking business. I used to think it was just the cowboys in covert ops who lose their moral compass from time to time and that we analysts were untouched by all that. When I started out, I thought I knew why it was important to do this work. But the more I know about politics and human frustration and all the just and unjust causes out there, the more I know it's not that simple."

"You mean one man's terrorist is another man's freedom fighter."

"It's true, isn't it? The fact is, there are times when we're not necessarily the guys wearing the white hats. And often as not, there are no white or black hats—just a lot of shades of gray."

"Are you telling me there aren't any absolutes in this world worth fighting for?"

Mariah frowned, turning to watch Lindsay and Jack join a line of kids playing crack-the-whip on the ice. "I'll tell you what's absolute for me, Paul—the need to keep them safe. Not just *our* children, all of them. It's what David believed, too. Somehow we have to try to get the genie back in the bottle. Our kids are inheriting the legacy of Los Alamos and the arms race, and there are consequences those blue-sky guys never envisaged when they started tinkering in the lab with their 'gadgets.'"

"Sounds to me like you've just talked yourself into a job."

"Maybe I have," Mariah agreed, turning back with a smile. It vanished as she looked behind him and saw three people climb out of a limo that had pulled up on Constitution Avenue.

Chaney followed her gaze across that park. "Well, well," he said, "look who's here—George Neville and Angus Ramsay McCord. Who's that woman with them, I wonder?"

Mariah had already started walking. "It's Tanya!"

"Tanya?"

"Tatyana Baranova, Paul! The Russian woman who was responsible for CHAUCER."

With her eyes fixed on Tanya, Mariah strode quickly toward the limo. The pleasant round face was now thin and drawn, the once-rosy flush faded to an unhealthy pallor. Deep circles made her eyes look sunken and her blond hair was lank and dull. She was wearing what appeared to be an expensive blue woolen coat, but Mariah could see that she had lost an incredible amount of weight. Still, Tanya smiled as Mariah reached the sidewalk. No one said a word as the two women embraced.

"Oh, Tanya!" Mariah said when she finally stepped back to look at her again. "It's so good to see you, you have no idea."

"It's good to see you, too, Mariah. And very, very good to be here."

"How are you? What happened to you?"

"Someone from our embassy followed me one day when I was on my way to meet you. I know a car pulled up beside me on the street, but I don't remember very much after that—not for a long time. They took me back to Russia. There were drugs, questions—it's all very vague to me. When I finally became aware of my surroundings again, I was in prison. I was there for many months, until three days ago, in fact. And now, here I am."

"Tanya, I'm so sorry! Can you ever forgive me?"

"Forgive *you?* There is nothing to forgive! I came to you of my own free will. Remember once, you said it was the right thing to do? It was. I have never regretted it. Someone had to speak up."

"You're a very brave woman, Tatyana Baranova."

"And you. But Mariah, they told me about Dr. Tardiff, that he died." Mariah nodded sadly. "Oh, the poor, fine man!" Tanya exclaimed.

"Yes, he was, Tanya. We miss him very much."

"And your little Lindsay? How is she?"

"Pretty well, all things considered. But she's not so little anymore. In fact, she's over there skating, working on her hockey moves," Mariah added, smiling. "Come over and see her."

Tanya smoothed her hair self-consciously and shook her head. "I do not want her to see me like this. I am not at my best and she would not understand. Perhaps another time? Perhaps you will visit me in California? You told me once that is where you come from.''

"You're going to California?''

"Yes. Mr. McCord here and his wife have kindly invited me to stay with them for a while.''

Mariah turned to the wiry little man standing beside Tanya. She had seen him dozens of times, of course, in photographs and on television, but she wasn't prepared for how utterly ordinary he looked. Only the piercing copper eyes revealed the man's relentless drive.

"You'll stay with us as long as you like, Tanya,'' McCord said, "and then we'll set you up in a home of your own, wherever you choose and whenever you feel ready.''

George Neville stepped forward. "Mariah Bolt, Paul Chaney—this is Mr. Angus McCord. I'm sure you recognize him, of course.''

"Call me Gus, everybody does,'' McCord said, pumping their hands in turn. "Ms. Bolt, Mr. Chaney, it's a pleasure to meet you. I've been hearing fine things about both of you.''

"We've heard a lot about you, too,'' Mariah said dryly.

"Mr. McCord is responsible for getting Ms. Baranova out of Russia, Mariah.'' Neville's tone was that of a disapproving parent to an ill-mannered child. "We finally managed to locate her, but without his influence, I don't think we could have sprung her. The country's in chaos right now, and there's just no single authority we could appeal to for her release.''

"But money always clears a path, doesn't it?'' Mariah remarked.

"The good Lord's been generous with me,'' McCord said. "I've never been reluctant to spread the luck around by spending money on a good cause.''

"Well," Mariah said, looking back at Tanya, "this was *definitely* a good cause."

"Yes, ma'am, I do believe it was," McCord agreed. "This lady is a genuine heroine and she'll want for nothing for the rest of her days—you have my word on that. We're going to help her get her health back and get her settled where it's warm and sunny, and then she can decide what she'd like to do next."

"Will you come to visit me, Mariah?" Tanya asked. "You and Lindsay? I would like that very much."

Mariah smiled at her and nodded. "It's ages since I last set foot in California. I think it's about time I took a trip home and showed Lindsay her roots. Maybe at Easter."

"Mr. Chaney," McCord said, turning away from the two women, "I was hoping you and I could discuss a little business. I know you're at loose ends these days and—"

"You're wrong, Mr. McCord. I *was* at loose ends—as you well know—but not anymore."

"Oh, I see. Well, that's good to hear. I knew you'd bounce back, resourceful fellow like you. In fact, I told the other members of the CBN board last week that a terrible mistake was made when we let you slip away. We agreed that you were capable of handling any job at the network you might want, any job at all. Maybe we could still persuade you to rejoin?"

"No, I don't think so. And by the way, I sent back my severance check."

"There was no need to do that."

"Oh, yes, there was. You can do a lot with your money, McCord, but you can't buy me. And as for your late buddy, Dieter Pflanz—"

"Mr. Chaney!" Neville protested. "You can't believe Mr. McCord knew or would ever have approved of—"

"Maybe. I wish I were certain of that. In any event, the man *was* in his employ. By all rights, McCord, I should have blown the whistle on you the minute that Lear touched down from New Mexico. But I made a deal with Neville here, and I'll stick to my side of the bargain if you stick to yours." Chaney glanced at Mariah and Tanya. "You're getting a freebie on this one, but don't expect me to keep quiet in future if you pull another stunt like that illegal arms operation."

McCord opened his mouth to say something, then closed it again and nodded soberly.

"There's just one more thing," Chaney added.

"What's that?"

"Tell me you don't really have the gall to run for office after all this."

"There are people lining up out there whose motives are far less patriotic than mine, Mr. Chaney."

"That may be, but frankly, they don't scare me nearly as much as you do."

McCord's eyes bored into the reporter, but Chaney was uncowed. "Ever hear of Webster's Law, Mr. Chaney?" the billionaire asked finally.

"Webster?"

"As in Daniel Webster. He once wrote, 'Nothing will ruin the country if the people themselves undertake its safety, and nothing can save it if they leave that safety in any hands but their own.' Well, that about sums up how I feel. I can't stand back and leave the country's safety in someone else's hands."

"I don't think Daniel Webster had you personally in mind when he wrote that, Mr. McCord. Just the opposite, in fact. I think he meant that *all* of us have to play a part in safeguarding the best things about this country and this world we live in. That means getting involved, not sitting back and waiting for some father figure to come along and do it for us. And it means keeping an eye on people like you who try to *buy* their way past the checks on power that keep a democracy from turning into a dictatorship—however 'benevolent.'''

McCord shrugged and cocked his head in the direction of the Capitol building a few blocks to the east. ''Well, you can rest easy, Mr. Chaney. I'm not really interested in wasting my time on the tomfoolery that goes on up there, anyway. Man would have to be a masochist to want to get into politics. No, I'm thinking more along the lines of retirement. My wife's been a little under the weather and we're not getting any younger. I'd like more time with my family, and we want to get Tanya settled in. So here's an exclusive for you—Gus McCord has ruled out running for elected office. It's time to pass the torch to you young ones now.''

''And on that note,'' Neville said, stepping forward, ''you and Ms. Baranova have a plane waiting, Gus. Mariah, I hope you don't mind our tracking you down like this, but Tanya was hoping to see you again and I thought you'd like to know that she's safe now.''

''It's the best news I've had in a very long time,'' Mariah said. ''Tanya, I worried about you after you disappeared. I hope nothing bad ever happens to you again. Mr. Neville has my address and phone number. Call me as soon as you're settled and we'll have a good, long talk and see about that visit.''

''I will, Mariah. And give Lindsay my love, please.''

Mariah nodded as Tanya and the two men climbed into the car and drove off. When she turned again toward Paul, he was frowning after the limo. "Do you think McCord's really going to retire?" she asked as they headed back toward the skating rink.

"I think he meant it when he said it just now," Chaney replied. "The question is, will he still mean it tomorrow? Guys like McCord don't retire till they're dead. He's already done everything there is to do in the areas of business and charity work. I'm not sure he could resist the temptation of running a one-man government if the opportunity arose."

"The scuttlebutt at Langley says that Neville's getting ready to announce his retirement."

"Has someone stumbled onto what he and McCord and Pflanz were up to?"

Mariah shrugged. "Not that I know of. Even Frank Tucker wasn't in on all the details. He'd been working with them on the plan to get hold of those weapons Tanya told us about, but knew nothing about the illegal arms dealing. Neville had played that card very close to his chest. Of course," Mariah added, "Neville knows *you* know and he'll never be certain you won't break the story. My guess is that those guys wanted for you, even more than me, to see Tanya—to drive home the message that their motives were pure, even if their method was dubious."

"I'm not going to break this story."

She looked up at him. "I know, and I know why. To protect Lindsay and me."

Chaney nodded. "The ironic thing, of course, is that it really has nothing to do with you. Neville's scheme probably would have gone undetected if Stephen Tucker hadn't muddied the waters with his desire for personal revenge."

"No wonder Neville seemed so confused about what was going on when I confronted him at Frank's Christmas party. He must have been completely panicked at the way things were unraveling, without having a clue why it was happening. Now it's all over, and Neville will probably follow a long line of ex-covert ops guys making a fortune as security consultants."

"We know one corporation that's looking for a new security chief, don't we?" Chaney said grimly.

Mariah nodded.

Lindsay and Jack were waiting at the edge of the rink when they arrived back. "Where did you guys go, Mom?"

"I ran into an old friend I hadn't seen in a while," Mariah said. "We were just catching up on each other's news. I'll tell you about it later."

"How are you two doing?" Paul asked. "Had enough?"

"No way!" Jack said.

"Yeah, no way!" Lindsay agreed. "Come on, Mom, you promised you were going to give this a try."

"Aw, Lins, you're not going to hold me to that, are you? I like my water sports in liquid form—not this frozen stuff."

"You could do it, if you'd only try. Come on! It's easy, and you've got my old skates."

"I can't believe I'm old enough to have a kid with bigger feet than mine," Mariah grumbled.

Paul grinned. "You're not going to escape. You know that, don't you?"

"Yeah!" Jack said. "No escape! You both gotta get out here!"

"All right, all right! Give me a few minutes to get these ruddy things on."

"Five minutes," Lindsay warned, "and then we come back and drag you guys out on the ice in your stocking feet if we have to. Right, Jack?"

"Right!"

"You're tyrants, you know that?" Mariah called as they skated away, giggling. She watched them for a moment, head shaking. Then she sat on a bench, kicked off her boots and began tugging on Lindsay's old blades. "I can't believe I agreed to this."

Chaney had one of his skates already laced and was expertly doing up the second, a frown of concentration creasing his forehead. "Mariah?"

"What?"

"I know this isn't the time or place, but despite what I said earlier about not pressuring, could you tell me one thing?"

"What's that?"

He sat up. "Well, I'm a very patient man—positively dogged when I need to be—and I know when something's worth waiting for. I think there's something very special between you and me that's definitely worth the wait. But tell me, am I crazy to be getting my hopes up like this?"

Mariah focused intently on her laces, weaving them slowly through the eyelets on the boots. Finally, she straightened, staring straight ahead, and exhaled deeply. "I thought a lot of nasty things about you when we were in Vienna, Paul, things I mostly regret now. But you know what?" she said, looking over at him. "I never thought you were crazy."

His nervous frown collapsed. "Okay," he said, nodding. "That's all I need to know." He finished lacing his skates and knelt down to tighten hers. Then he stood and pulled her to her feet. "Ready?"

"Paul, you understand that I need to go *very* slowly?"

"Are we talking skating here?"

"That, too."

"Gotcha. But I intend to stick close by you, Mariah, and I won't let you get hurt."

"*Now* are we talking skating?" she asked, smiling.

"That, too."

"You can't make that guarantee, Paul. Getting hurt is the risk we take when we choose to participate in life. But the alternative is to sit it out on the sidelines, and I *know* there's no joy in that."

He nodded. "So, you're ready to give this a try?"

Mariah gave her wobbly ankles a rueful glance, then linked her arm through his. "Damn the torpedoes," she said, pushing off.

DOUBLE ENTENDRE
Heather Graham Pozzessere

Reporter Bret McAllistair was after a fortune in diamonds that had been missing for forty years—a secret that had already led to the death of at least one man. He'd always been driven to get the story, but this time there was so much more at stake.

Bret's remaining time as a married man could be counted in weeks, but he refused to give up on his wife as adamantly as he refused to give up on the jewels.

Colleen was as involved in the search as he was, but she was unaware that this time Bret's real aim was to rekindle a marriage where the love had never died.

"A writer of incredible talent!"
Affaire de Coeur (USA)

MIRA

ENAMOURED
Diana Palmer

Diego Laremos was a dangerous man to know—
friend to few, mistrustful of many—yet the
passion he felt for Melissa Sterling was instant
and powerful. But the slim bonds of trust between
them crumbled with her betrayal.

Diego had put Melissa out of his life forever. Until
a fateful phone call informed him that his wife—
and a mysterious little boy—desperately needed
his help.

*"Nobody tops Diana Palmer... I love her
stories."*

bestselling author Jayne Ann Krentz

MIRA

RED
Erica Spindler

Becky Lynn was a nobody. Everybody told her so—the women who snubbed her at Opal's Cut 'n' Curl, the boys who hurt and used her, the family who didn't want her. But Becky Lynn had dreams—and fled to a world where she could make those dreams come true.

Jack Gallagher wanted to be a somebody. He wanted to be bigger than the father who'd denied him, better than the half–brother who'd claimed all their father's love. And he was getting there—fast. As a top fashion photographer, he was hot, he was sexy—and he was damn good.

Now, in a world where beauty and illusion are intertwined, Becky Lynn and Jack command the spotlight. But is the cost of fame too high? Beneath the glittering facade of their world lurk secrets that threaten to destroy all they've fought to achieve.

MIRA

A DAY IN APRIL
Mary Lynn Baxter

A YOUNG GIRL'S SHAME...
Shawnee, Louisiana, was steaming—the very air
thick with passion—the day Beth Melbourne's life
was shattered. She was seventeen, on the brink of
womanhood, when anticipation had turned to
ashes. Tainted and ashamed, she fled—leaving
behind all she'd ever known of happiness.

A WOMAN'S DREAMS...
Years later, no hint of that girl remained in the
assured, successful woman she'd become. Only
she knew the dreams still hiding in her heart. Only
she knew the love she still harboured for the boy
she once had worshipped. But the boy was a man
now—a man with a child he adored and all the
happiness Beth herself had denied him.

But there was a secret connecting them. A secret
as powerful as time and as inescapable as the love
that neither one of them could deny.

*"A tender and touching story that strikes
every chord within the female spirit."*

Sandra Brown

MIRA

CARDINAL RULES
Barbara Delinsky

RULE 1: NEVER GET INVOLVED
Determined not to repeat the mistakes of
her irresponsible parents, Corinne Fremont
had never dropped her guard in her
professional or personal life. She was all
business—all the time.

RULE 2: NEVER RESIST TEMPTATION
Maverick businessman Corey Haraden
conducted his love life in much the same
way he did business—with flair and
enthusiasm. Corinne was not his type, but
she intrigued him. That's why he offered
her a job she couldn't refuse—just to tempt
her.

*RULE 3: RULES ARE MEANT TO BE
BROKEN*

*"One of this generation's
most gifted writers of
contemporary women's
fiction"*
Romantic Times (USA)

MIRA

CHAIN LIGHTNING
Elizabeth Lowell

Damon Sutter had set out to explore the
Great Barrier Reef. His dreams of adventure
took an unexpected twist with Mandy
Blythe's arrival. Their relationship was to
be strictly business—she was too smart and
too independent to suit him. But avoiding
her was difficult—and watching her had
become his favourite pastime.

Though she had been tricked into going to
Australia, Mandy had never been fooled by
Sutter. A womaniser who'd left a string of
broken hearts behind him, he was the last
man she expected to fall for. But the tropics
created a different world and threatened to
melt her resolve completely.

> *"For smouldering sensuality and
> exceptional storytelling Elizabeth
> Lowell is incomparable!"*
> Romantic Times (USA)

THE DEVIL'S OWN
Sandra Brown

HE WAS THE DEVIL—BUT SHE BARGAINED WITH HIM ANYWAY

HER PLAN WAS DANGEROUS

But it was the only way to save nine children and she was determined to try.

HE HADN'T STAYED ALIVE BY BEING MR. NICE GUY

HE was the most disreputable and dangerous-looking man in the bar. That's why she wanted him.

THEY WERE UNDER FIRE

Together they fought the odds—and the searing passion that made the steamy days and nights even more dangerous.

"One of fiction's brightest stars!"

Dallas Morning News

CHANCE OF A LIFETIME
Jayne Ann Krentz

There was nothing subtle about security
agent Abraham Chance. He didn't like
whiners and he didn't like weaklings.
Rachel Wilder was neither—it took guts to
plot against the formidable Mr. Chance.

After he'd wrongly implicated her sister in
an embezzlement scam, Rachel decided to
do her own sleuthing, posing as his
housekeeper. Bad move. Not only was
Chance onto her deception, he was firing a
passion in her even more consuming than
revenge...

*"A master of the genre... nobody does it
better!"*

Romantic Times (USA)

MIRA